"You know, Harold, the people of the world want peace so badly that governments are just going to have to get out of the way and let them have it."

—President Dwight D. Eisenhower in conversation with Prime Minister Harold Macmillan, BBC, 1959.

TRESILIAN

A novel

by

DAVID BASSETT

1968

CANADIAN BRITISH PUBLISHING
Westmount, Montreal 6, P. Q., Canada

AUTHOR'S NOTE

This is a fictitious work. Apart from actual public figures, all characters in the book are imaginary and any resemblance to real persons, living or dead, is purely coincidental.

Printed in Canada - Metropole Lithographing Inc. - Ville D'Anjou, Montreal, Canada.

To *Pia*

BOOK I

CHAPTER 1

Montreal. April 30th, 1967. Glyn Tresilian was on the air. Expo
'67 was two days old. But already the joy and enthusiasm of the
first hours were being broken by the daily irritations of life in a
great city.
"So you don't send Christmas cards eh?".
"No, Madam."
"Well you're a dirty stinking mean bastard."
Tresilian depressed the red delete button on the studio console and waited for the reassuring light to come on. Nothing
happened. The seconds were running out. Panic. Here was the
nightmare — that obscenities and slanders might get through
on the air.
Tresilian jabbed the talk back switch to the control room.
"Relax John," he called to the operator on the other side of
the double glass partition, "there's bugger all we can do now."
And there wasn't. In a moment or so, hundreds of thousands of
listeners in Montreal, in outlying areas of the Province of Que-
bec, and all over the world via the shortwave simulcast, would
hear Tresilian called a bastard.
"O.K. caller, you're on the air — go ahead please."
"Mr. Tresilian?"
"Yes — go ahead."
"How awful."
"Awful indeed Madam — I take it you're talking about the
crowds at Expo?"
"No I'm not and you know it. I'm talking about people who
get on the air and use foul language."
"Oh well," Tresilian sighed, "c'est la vie — even in the best
regulated stations . . ."
"Well I don't agree with what you've said often enough that
the sending of Christmas cards is a form of social blackmail,"
the caller went on, "but I don't have to insult you to say so."

Tresilian thanked the caller and, mercifully, it was 11 a.m. He signed off, picked up his notes, cigarettes, commercial log-book, and emptied the dregs of a coffee vacuum flask into the large garbage can in the corner.

During the five minute newscast, he cleared the studio for the announcer to follow. Tresilian was an untidy worker at the microphone. Nervous too. In the heat of quarrel he moved too much. Many had said that he'd be speechless with his arms cut off. Several ashtrays and cups had been victims of his flailing hands.

"Boy, that was a hot one Glyn. Caught it in the car just as I was parking in the lot," Don Stanfield said as he prepared to assuage the ruffled tempers of CRAK's listeners for the next four hours with Andy Williams music interspersed with low-keyed, inoffensive comment.

Tresilian shrugged. "I suppose there's all hell on out front?"

"Yup — 'fraid so. The Drom's getting and giving all kinds of rockets. But he'll come out smelling of centennials — he always does."

"See you Don."

"Take care, Glyn."

He knew that there would be the inevitable enquiries about the delay system. Why hadn't it worked? Didn't people realise you could lose a station's license for less? And there'd be the buck passing, played by the all time champions — Programming versus Engineering. An All-Star event. And this one promised to be one of the best ever.

On his way out of the studio, Tresilian stuck his head in the control-room. Busy at his board, working Stanfield's show, was the morning operator who would finish at noon. Tresilian and John McFadden had worked together regularly for the three years that 'Crakkerjack Line' had been on the air. They'd established a fine rapport.

So he had been called a bastard. The mean and stinking and dirty were fine. The bastard was not.

"Now don't worry John. I'll sort it out", Tresilian shouted above the sound of loudspeakers, "What happened anyway?"

"Oh, I've told them in maintenance a thousand times about the relay mechanism. There might be a chance that we'll get the damn thing fixed — now that something's happened."

Tresilian left the studio area, went to the news room, put his things in the steel locker provided for the personnel and readied for the drama. He lit a cigarette, his twentieth of the day so far, and went into the General Manager's office. The door was open so that all in the vicinity could hear the "Drom's" powerful braying voice. He'd had a rough morning — with listeners, and with senior staff members of the cosmetics manufacturing company that owned radio station CRAK in Montreal.

The switch board had been inundated with calls from listeners. Tresilian slipped out of the Drom's office, while the Manager was on the phone, to speak with the two telephone girls.

From them he learned that opinion seemed to be equally divided about Glyn's legitimacy. He returned to Brewster who by now was having a noisy altercation with the Chief Engineer. He slammed the receiver in its cradle and bellowed down the hall.

"No more calls to me about Tresilian. For God's sake. What the hell do people think I am? Tell them to write to the Pope. Tell them anything — just keep them off my back."

Before Glyn could sit down, the Manager said,

"Come on — get your coat. Let's get out of this cow pasture quick."

Physically, Burt Brewster was a big man. He'd come to Montreal via a manse in Saskatoon where his father had been a Presbyterian Minister. Rejecting the Ministry as a career he began his working life as an operator and then announcer on the 'Bush League Circuit', gaining experience from small radio stations in Ontario and on the Prairies. This was, and is, the apprenticeship for most Canadian radio and TV broadcasters on the way to the top in Montreal, Toronto or New York.

Despite the 'bigness' of his voice, Brewster realised several years previously that because of a confined personality, attributable in large part to a repressed childhood, he'd never excel as an "on air" performer. And so he graduated through a time sales stint to general management. There was, in his make-up, a perplexing bluster — a feeling of inferiority more commonly found in small sized men, that Tresilian and others found hard to fathom. This bullying manner had once moved an announcer to say that he rode roughshod over people — like a dromedary. And the 'Drom' was born.

They settled at their usual corner table in the tavern.

"Four beers, s'il vous plait, Jean Guy", Tresilian ordered and held up the necessary fingers for confirmation.

"Four up. OK, Glyn. Right away. The wife says you were called a bastard this morning. Mind you I've heard her call you that many times myself," the waiter said, attempting humour.

'Studio 4' was quiet because it was not yet noon. By a minute after twelve the place would ring with thirsty shouts, glasses and plates. The Drom and Glyn drank.

"Aahh, that's better", Brewster sighed as he pulled on the ice cold draught ale and belched resonantly in the bass register. You know Glyn, at times I get so fed up with that bloody shop, I could chuck the whole goddam thing tomorrow. So, alright — some niggly broad calls you a bastard on the air. Big deal. What the hell can I do about it ugh?" He lit a cigar and looked furtively around the tavern. Then he corkscrewed his left eye into what was meant to be a conspiratorial wink and lowered his voice to an unfamiliar dulcet.

"That was great, Glyn; just what we wanted — when we needed it. Have a cigar."

"What do you mean?"

"That bit this morning. You know goddam well what I mean for crissake. Great stuff Glyn baby. The whole town's talking. Great, great, great. Jean-Guy — four more. We're celebrating."

"What are we celebrating?"

"The ballots of course. You know we were expecting the spring rating to be taken in May? Great. Well, we just heard from Smiley in Toronto that they're on right now. Began on Monday. "So," and Brewster patted his belly, "we're celebrating. Believe me Glyn, you can't beat a bit like this morning for the good old audience measurement time."

Of course. Tresilian got the point. Brewster was pleased with him. He had exercised good judgment in letting foul language get on the air during rating week. Great. Just great for business. They ordered more beer. Ratings. The game had no other name. Get them. Get them at any price. But stop short of losing your license.

"Now don't get me wrong, Glyn," Brewster went on, "I've already been on to Dick Ponting. 'Ponting,' I said, 'you play those high powered clowns at the perfume plant. You, not I, screwed up the image they get so excited about. You're responsible for all that donkey equipment. And if I were you I'd tell them to get off their asses and remind 'em they own a radio and television outfit as well a sweet odour factory." The Drom warmed to his theme and went on.

"I told him they pour fortunes into that goddam scent empire — and for what? To keep a lot of crappy women thinking they look and smell sexy."

Glyn knew exactly how much complaining Chief Engineer Ponting would do. Ponting would write reams of high sounding technological jargon, and he would not get more money for maintenance. By the time General Cosmetics Controller Robert Westall had read his report, the heat would be off.

They stayed in the tavern for several more beers. Glyn didn't much like mid-day drinking. It left him with a clothy tongue. A bibulous uncle had once advised him: 'Stay away from middle day drinking, my boy. It ruins you for the evening.'

By the time they got back to the station, Brewster was in obvious good form. Tresilian's morning show and the ratings news filled him with pleasure. The beer hadn't been bad either.

At the front door, Glyn left the Drom and walked round to the parking lot and past the guards on constant watch. CRAK'S central location received the vigil of a sovereign lying in state. In the lot was parked his own ten-year old Armstrong-Siddeley. He'd bought it five years before from a McGill lecturer. He started the 'Black Panther', let her warm a little and inspected the body work. He didn't enjoy looking at the wounds inflicted by ten yearly coatings of calcium and salt. He'd put off for two years the body job that he knew the car needed and deserved. It would have to wait until the fall.

It took a five-minute drive to get up to his comfortable apartment just off Cote des Neiges, north of Sherbrooke street. He lived as a bachelor; and had several times thought that his accommodation was more than he really required. But then, why not a little indulgence? He could well afford his present way of life. As a free lance broadcaster he was well paid for his daily 'Crakkerjack Line'. Too, there were television programs, speaking engagements, some selective commercial work. He could dine as often as he wished at any of Montreal's gastronomic Shangri-Las, and he could get over to Britain every year to see

Michael.

He parked the car and went up in the garage elevator to the lobby. He had a corner unit on the seventh floor. In his cubby-hole Armand observed the traffic flow of Cote des Neiges Tower's tenants. The concierge listened regularly to Glyn's show.

"Bonjour, Armand."

"Bonjour, bonjour M'sieu Tresilian. Mon dieu, c'était un programme formidable aujourd'hui."

"C'est ça Armand. C'est la vie."

CHAPTER 2.

Glyn Tresilian was 37 years old. Born in Calcutta, he'd spent his childhood and school years in India. His mother was born in Madras and his father, after army service in the First World War, had qualified as a chartered accountant and subsequently joined the Indian Civil Service. He received a junior appointment in Calcutta and after two years met and married the younger daughter of a fellow Indian Civil Servant. In the caste systems of the day and place, Indian and Sahib alike were carefully graded; and the Tresilians were placed among the lower middle drawers of the British community. This middling social position allowed Glyn more reach up and down than would have been the case otherwise.

He had loved India. The monsoon seasons were fun. He and his mother journeyed then from the stifling Hooghli or Madras, according to his father's auditing assignments, to the hills at Amritsar or Dalhousie by motor car and train. In the trains there would be oblong blocks of ice, primitive air conditioning perhaps, but wonderful for sliding and cooling little hands. The flowers, made up in leis, soon wilted on the ice — fighting a losing battle with the all-consuming heat and impossible humidity.

He remembered the bearers and their fans. Four of them to the coach to circulate the clinging dank air for the Memsahib and Chotasahib.

For a British boy who had spent the first years of his life in India, Glyn Tresilian was an enigmatic youth. While hardly a rebel, the unevenness of life disturbed him. Even his parents sported six servants. And from his earliest memories, he remembered how servant strength became an important symbol of status and station in life. War time changed nothing, and perhaps because Glyn knew he would never win the servant numbers game, he grew to resent the system which created it. At school in Ballygunge, headmastered by an old Etonian — turned socialist, Arthur Peake-Smythe, he tasted radicalism for the first time. He grew to like political history, and in this he was encouraged by Peake-Smythe, to whom India as a serfdom had been abhorrent since Oxford and his reading of Keir Hardie.

For Tresilian, the Headmaster supplied an endless stream of Bertrand Russell, Bernard Shaw and Ghandi. His parents noted, but were not concerned with his still naively stated guilt that six human beings should wait hand and foot on three other human beings.

"Look at it this way, Glyn", his orderly-minded father told him one night at table, "our servants are very happy. We give them a livelihood don't we? They are not forced to work for us. If we weren't treating them properly they would leave. They're not slaves after all."

"I was talking to Mr. Peake-Smythe about that at school today Dad, and he said that . . ."

"Ah, that red Headmaster of yours. Is Bradford in your form? Yes? I was talking to his father in the club yesterday. He's not at all happy about Mr. Peake-Smythe. Seemed surprised that I wasn't concerned too. Says he's an Old Etonian communist and that he's using his school to brainwash you youngsters. According to Mr. Bradford you'll then be able to help him get the Kremlin take-over under way. Personally I think all that's a bit far fetched. But I interrupted you Glyn. Sorry son — what was he telling you?"

"Well, we were talking about the possibilities of partition after the war and all that, and then we got on to a discussion on the 'Privileges of Imperialism' — it was a pamphlet he read to us.

The point it tried to make was that slavery never was abolished. And then we started talking about the servants and he said that there was a perfect example of what he meant."

"What did he mean?"

"You know, Dad. What you said just now. You said that our servants aren't like slaves — but he says that every servant in India is a slave — even though they don't have chains on their ankles."

"Hmmm. Did he? I think I'll have to talk to Mr. Bradford again. How long have you been doing this stuff at school?"

"Oh only since the beginning of this term — when I moved up into IV A. It's a new subject he started and he takes it himself from IV A to the Sixth. It's called 'Current Events and Public Affairs.' I'm enjoying it very much. But then I like political history too."

"Political history? Oh, yes I seem to remember you did well at it from your last report. But why political history? In my day we learned history."

"Mr. Peake-Smythe says it's useless trying to understand history unless you also know about the political situations of the time. He says politics makes history and both things must be understood as a totality of events", and Glyn felt pleased that he could repeat the words perfectly as they'd been spoken that afternoon.

"Yes, alright, my dear", and his father pulled back his mother's chair. "I agree; coffee on the verandah will be very pleasant. Glyn, I think your Mr. Peake-Smythe talks a lot of bunk if that's the kind of thing he's trying to shove down your throats. And that's absolute rot about servants and slavery. Surely you don't follow all that tripe do you ? If I thought so for one moment, I'd take you out of there. Your mother and I would much prefer to try and find the money to send you to St. Paul's in Darjeeling."

Glyn, who now had no ambition to go to the well known boarding school in the foot-hills of the Himalayas, assured his father that during the weekly Current Events and Public Affairs class he would keep his mind open, but shut to propanganda influences. Geoffrey Tresilian told his son that he would go into the matter again with Bradford at the club.

Shortly after his 15th birthday, Glyn and John Withers, a friend from the middle upper drawer, fist-fought to a blood bath. Glyn and Withers had jointly won the Junior Clive Cup at the annual Gymkhana Club Horse Races. They were quite firm form mates at school but hadn't visited each other socially until the Wither's invitation to dinner following the late afternoon sport. John too, was an only child, but due to his father's higher rank, lived in a bigger house in a better part of Calcutta. They had 12 servants. This, added to the military way they were ordered about, filled Glyn with sudden bitterness. He spoiled for the argument he hoped to have with John that day.

After the meal, they walked off across the spacious lawn

ringed with orange trees. In the stable, one man was grooming John's horse while another slept on a bundle of straw in the corner. A short distance away a three sided metal latrine reeked and buzzed with flies as a procession of servants came and went. Glyn admired the horse and the two boys went outside.

"What do you honestly think, John? I mean is it right? Here you are a schoolboy like me — you have a horse and two men whose only purpose in life is to look after it — and they also live in the stable. I also have a horse — but I do all the work myself. Now don't get me wrong — I'd like servants too — I'm not that fond of manual labour in this climate, but is it right?"

"What on earth are you talking about?"

"Well, I suppose you could call it the "Privileges of Imperialism" — you remember the thing we did in class with Peaky......"

"Oh, come off it Tresilian. Don't tell me that you're paying any attention to that rot. My father says that friend Peaky'd better change his tune otherwise he won't have anybody left to teach. All the parents at the Club are furious."

"Why?"

"What's the matter with you, Tresilian? Are you dense? They're annoyed because he's trying to stir up trouble, that's why. And he's charging the earth in fees while he's doing it. Look, you ought to know by now that in this country having servants is a way of life — like a glass of water. There's nothing wrong with it.

"And the servants are very happy. We give them employment and they're well paid. If they weren't happy they'd leave wouldn't they?"

"I'm not so sure about that, Withers. What would they do?"

"Oh, look; this is foolish. That's their business. I don't know and I don't care what the........."

"Exactly. That's the trouble. Nobody does care. And when nobody cares about ignorance and poverty, revolutions start and countries are taken over by the communists. History proves it's nearly always left too late. One of these days someone's going to tell these people that it's wrong for a family like yours to have 12 servants bowing and scraping round the clock. And why 12? Because the man who washes your motor car doesn't know how to drive it. The man who waters the grass doesn't know how to cut it. And the person who makes the beds doesn't know how to lay the table. But it doesn't worry anybody. The servants are glad to get some scraps of food now and again and the overall cost comes to very little. You see the........."

"Tresilian, that's enough. Drop the subject. People like our fathers have done so much for India and they deserve a few comforts and privileges. It's part of being out here. And if you don't like it, I suggest you take the train to Moscow and tell Joe that you want to help him defend Stalingrad or . . ."

"I'd rather you didn't talk like that Withers", Glyn said heatedly and felt himself losing control.

"Well, it's your own fault. You asked for it. We had a good race and invited you here for dinner but I'm not interested in any of Peake-Smythe's ideas — and if you share them I'm not interested in you. I suggest you leave"

"Withers, I find you a typically prig headed, arrogant, conceited ass and unless....."

John hit him in the mouth. Five minutes later, their riding breeches and shirts were covered in blood. They fought inside the small circle of servants who had gathered. But no one intervened. They were finally separated by John's father assisted by the burly Mali Wallah.

Two weeks later, the Tresilians were transfered for an indefinite period to Madras and Glyn completed his formal education at another private day school on the outskirts of the city. Soon after his 17th birthday, his parents retired in Madras and Glyn went to England for the first time to begin shore based pre-sea training prior to a career in the British Merchant Service.

His years at sea had taken him to most of the world's great ports. He served his time with the Hungor Line as an apprentice. It was recommended by the hardy Principal of the Navigation School as being a fine training ground. Here was a tramp ship company of the old sort with stories of Chief Stewards being fired if famished seagulls trailed the ship.

He had begun his first voyage in Middlesborough when, dressed in a new brass bound doeskin uniform, he reported aboard the rusty, dirty bluff bowed tramp. Enormous toothy grabs suspended on shore cranes clawed at the cargo of North African iron ore in her lower holds. Dust and filth were everywhere. The sour stench of rotting refuse by the galley quickened his step as he looked for the midships officers' accommodation.

He knocked on a door marked "Chief Officer".

"Come in", a Tyneside voice ordered.

"Good afternoon, sir. My name's Tresilian — they told me . . ."

"Right, you'll be the new apprentice", the man said and got out of the worn leather chair in his berth. The First Mate was a large man with sandy balding hair and square ox like shoulders. He was wearing a once white polo sweater, soiled and torn blue serge trousers and sea-boots turned down below the knee. He switched off the radio set on the desk. "My name's Petrie, son. I'm the Mate. Glad to see you — you can give the riggers a hand. There'll be no crew till a week tomorrow. Have a cup of tea in the pantry and turn to. Where's your gear?"

"On the dock sir".

"Come on — let's get it aboard. The sooner you get out of that rig the better. Brought lots of working gear I hope?"

"Three boiler suits sir. At Navigation School they said . . . ."

"Yes, I know. That's just about what I'd expect them to say at Navigation School. No good at all. Engineers wear boiler suits — but they're no use for deck work. You'll find out soon enough. Dungaree jacket and trousers — that's what you want. Hey, foreman, give us a hand to get the lad's gear aboard eh?"

The rigger and Glyn lugged his trunk, sea-bag and suitcase to a door in the Engine-Room accommodation where Petrie swore at a bunch of keys. Nothing would open the door until the Mate prised open the brass ventilator plate and put his arm through the hole. Reaching the lock latch he opened the door and showed Glyn into a space that the youngster judged to measure twelve feet by nine feet. He looked around apprehensively at bolts of old canvas, chipping hammers and scrapers, bundles of oily cotton waste and, on the bulkheads, a dozen calendars sporting nude women — presented with the compliments of various ship chandlers from all around the world. The Chief Officer grunted and kicked a roll of coconut matting off a lower bunk.

"Excuse me sir — but, er, is this where I leave my luggage?"

"This son", and his arm swept the room, "is where four of you eat, sleep and study. Let me see you in ten minutes by the galley pump on the starboard side. Oh — dressed for work of course", and he was gone. Disillusioned and sweating, Glyn quickly pulled a boiler suit from the neat packing that his landlady in Bristol had done.

"Now son", the Chief Officer explained to Tresilian, forlorn and self-conscious in an immaculate but ill fitting brown boiler suit. "See this pump? It's yours. All yours. That's the junior apprentice's privilege. It's called a semi-rotary fresh water pump and you have to push it 453 times each way to fill up that tank there on the bridge. There — see it? That's for the midships bridge accommodation. There's an overflow pipe at the side there and you'll pump until you see the water running out. Then stop immediately.

"One of your jobs will be to pump it up three times every day. After breakfast, dinner and tea. Anytime you're slack during the day, run a tap in the wash-house and make sure there's water. If it's ever empty you'll get the blame. And son — there's just one more thing. When I give you an order, I don't expect you to walk. I don't expect you to run. I expect you to fly."

Tresilian fell to the pump handle with a will. In three minutes his hands were painfully blistered and he went back to the cabin to find the pair of working gloves he knew were in his seabag. He tried the door. It was locked and the Mate had replaced the ventilator plate. He knocked on Petrie's door.

"Yes — what's wrong son? Tank full already?"

"No sir. I don't think so. Not yet anyway sir. But I went to the cabin to get some gloves and the door....."

"I can't find the key for it. Alright, I'll open it again through the vent — but for now, until Chippy gets back from leave, you'll just have to leave it open. What do you want gloves for anyway? They just get in the way and they're bloody dangerous — especially when you're clearing wire. I've seen more than one hand snagged in and crushed on a winch drum."

"Yes, sir. It was just that my hands....."

"Oh, that's nothing. A few blisters. Might as well get 'em toughened up straightaway. You don't want your mates making fun of you eh?"

When he wasn't filling the fresh water tank, Tresilian worked under the foreman rigger. He spent most of that week sweeping great mounds of iron ore dust away from accommodation accesses and ladders.

The ship sailed, bound for Finland and a cargo of pit-props for the coal mines of North-East England.

"Go with the bosun, son." "You'd better turn in — you'll be

on deck at four in the morning — Kiel Canal." "Jump to it son — take your finger out".

"I beg your pardon Sir?"

"Take your bloody finger out — MOVE"

The days were a round of breakfast; turn-to; dinner; turn-to; Smoko! Turn-to; tea; turn-to; 'Clean the deep-tanks.' 'Get a bailer and scraper' 'Number two bilges — start on the port side for'ard' 'DON'T DUMP THAT RUBBISH TO WIND'ARD'.

"Alright son, see if you can keep her steady. Ever steered a ship before?"

"Only a trawler sir; one weekend in the Channel when I was at Navigation School."

"Eh, you really like that Navigation School, don't you son? Well, if you've steered a trawler you should be able to handle this bitch. There she is. Keep her on 217 — she's carrying a quarter turn of port helm."

"217, sir. Thank you sir."

The first mate went out onto the wing of the bridge. In seconds he was back in the wheelhouse. "Let me have her — quick. God, we'll either be ashore at this rate or the bastard'll blow up. What's wrong"? He shouted as he spun the wheel over and back, "Don't you know our degaussing gear's buggered and we're still in mined water? And it's a bloody narrow channel. There — she's alright now. Never mind son. It was my fault. You can start again when we get to open water." Petrie steadied her back on course in the Baltic Sea and blew his referee's whistle. The helmsman took a few more pulls at his cigarette and, disappointed, ambled back to the bridge.

"Collins — you'd better have her again. The lad's not ready for small water yet. 217 — wheel's amidships."

Downcast, Tresilian was on his way down the bridge ladder prepared to face the derision of fellow apprentices and foc'sle crew.

"Tresilian — just a minute son", Petrie called to him.

"I'm sorry sir."

"Never be sorry, son. It doesn't pay. Look, I don't mind you writing your name with the ship's wake but it wastes time and coal when you go back to dot the i's and cross the t's, doesn't it?"

Tresilian who was to hear this and many other incisive admonitions in the years to come, winced. He waited for more.

But the Mate smiled.

"You'll get some hell from the others for this. It's just the beginning, son. Get used to it. There'll be times soon when you'll wish you hadn't been born. Stick it out. Did you learn any Latin at school?"

"Not very much, sir".

"Well, I didn't learn any. I wasn't at the kind of place where they taught it. But I do know one good quotation —· Nil carborundum illegitimi. Know what it means?"

"No, I'm afraid not sir."

"Don't let the bastards grind you down."

Tresilian sailed with Petrie on three different ships. Despite the difference in rank, age and background they got on well. The South Shields Tynesider had made his way to a Master's Foreign Going Certificate of Competency through the 'Hawse Pipe'. He had graduated to command qualification through the foc'sles of trampships as a deck-boy, ordinary seaman, ablebodied seaman. Then, because he had set out to 'improve himself', took advantage of the sea time that he'd served to sit the examination for Second Mate. He subsequently got his 'Tickets' for First Mate and Master.

Petrie looked forward to his prize — command of a Hungor Liner. He was an efficient and popular officer liked by both fellow Mates and crew. Unlike some who had risen from the lower deck, Petrie did not resent the comparatively privileged environment of the average youngster who 'served his time' training for a navigation officer's career. Instead, he openly appreciated the democracy of a profession where a man's progress had nothing to do with background or accent. Where there were no Selection Boards to stamp approval on address, sophistry and speech. Where ability to do a job and take responsibility were tallied only in the Examination Room. He loved to talk about South and North Shields and the pubs there. And which fish and chip shops stayed open after midnight on Fridays.

Glyn would never forget the night with Petrie in Calcutta. The ship Petrie and he were then sailing on had lifted a full cargo of Australian wheat for Madras and the Hooghli river port. He gave Tresilian special shore leaves in Madras so that the apprentice could spend as much time as possible with his parents. And then, in Calcutta Petrie took Glyn ashore. They took a gharry from the ship in Kidderpore Dock and went as far as Chowringee — the Broadway of Bengal. Stepping between dead and dying bodies on the side walks, they went from one bar to another. Quite soon, Glyn was drunk; and so, much later, was Petrie.

"You're not a bad fel, fella, Tresillon. I like you. And tonight we're going to have some fu, fu, fun. Ith all part of your education and training. Leave it all to good old Petrie. You say you were born here but I, I, wath here before you were — ha, ha, ha. I know thith town. Know it better'n I know Showth Sield even. C'mon boy. Come with your old uncle."

They took a taxi. As the Seikh driver pulled the ancient Buick away from the curb, Glyn asked Petrie, "Where, where are we going, sir?"

"Never mind the thir for tonight, Trethillon. The name's Alec. Alexander Petrie. Named after my Grandfather. The old bastard. He wath a blown away Scotsman. Did I ever tell you that Trethillon?"

"No, sir. I don't think you did. I mean Alec." Tresilian felt the danger signs coming as the road and the traffic started to heave around in front of his eyes. He remembered the time he'd been sick in Melbourne — and the waiter's expression as he looked down at his soiled shirt front. He felt it coming and tapped the Seikh on the shoulder. The taxi stopped and he emptied himself at the door. He felt better at once.

"Thath the stuff Tresillon. Get rid of it if it's bothering you. Then you can thart again. We're going to have a very fine thwa, thwa, thwaray to-night."

"But, er, Alec, where are we going?"

"We're going to blow our tubes. Ith about time they had a clean out."

Glyn felt a momentary panic. He'd heard the Engineers use the expression. And at 19 he still hadn't had a woman. He'd often looked forward to the first experience but had always been repulsed by the idea of purchasing it like a leg of lamb. He felt suddenly sober.

"Are we going to a whorehouse then, Alec?"

"Don't use nameth like that Tresillon. You'll see where when we get there. You're going to a very nice thelect house of entertainment."

Twenty minutes later, the taxi drew up outside a dark and dingy building. Petrie paid and tipped the driver generously and stumbled to the door. He knocked on it loudly and waited.

"To-night Tresillon, everythingth on me. Everythings on me."

A panel in the rickety door slid open and they were let inside. The woman after a searching look at Petrie, remembered, and welcomed him warmly.

They sat down in a small room lit only by the flicker of an oil lamp in one corner. The madam brought in tea. They ignored it. She went out and returned with six well-proportioned girls dressed in saris. Petrie and Glyn stood up and swayed. Tresilian's throat was dry as he took in their loveliness. Even though there was hardly enough light to see the colours of their silks — there was sufficient for Glyn to see their charms.

"How are you then, my darlings?" Petrie greeted them, "remember old Petrie? I've got a thpecial friend with me. Young Tresillon. He's brand new. First time. It'll be a hot time on the old town to-night, eh girls? Tresillan — did I ever tell you I always get thith bloody lisp when I'm thozzled? No? It doesn't matter."

The girls' eyes lit up as Petrie announced the news of Glyn's virginity. They looked at the bronzed auburn haired youngster and smiled with pleasure. This didn't happen often, and they all hoped they'd be chosen.

"What say you draw lots for him eh girlth? Thath the only fair way after all," Petrie suggested.

The girls looked at each other and the madam. The madam nodded and the girls giggled. Businesslike, the older woman spoke.

"Mr. Petrie, is this for short time or all night?"

"All night of course, Madam. Ol'Petrie doesn't do things by half eh girls? Hahaha", and he smacked one of them playfully on her rump, "and my young friendth a good fella, madam. A really good fella. And he'th my guest. I'm responsible, see I didn't lithp then, I'm responsible for him. His education, everything. All part of hith training, madam."

"I see. You have to be back at the ship early?"

"Oh, yeth. Seven o'clock."

"Then I'd better have your taxi waiting at five?"

"OK, my darling — anything for a quiet life. Come on. I'm

getting tired."

The girls left the room and the two men lit cigarettes. Tresilian threw his away. His pulse was throbbing and his mouth was parched. When two of the girls came back, the younger one smiled at Glyn and took him by the hand. She led him along the airless ground floor corridor to a tiny corner room at the end. She turned up the oil lamp wick and for the first time he saw her properly. Her black hair fell in a tantalizing tress behind her small neck, and her childish face reminded him of his Ayah's daughter — as a small boy, the girl had intrigued and disturbed him. And he often wondered what she'd look like with her clothes off. But he could only see her as she was — saried, remote and untouchable.

Now it was about to happen. The sari would come off and he would touch her. She adjusted the light to a glimmer and unfastened a pin below her left shoulder. He sat on the narrow tarnished brass framed bed and watched the girl's flowing movements as she unwound the seven yards of shimmering cloth.

.   .   .   .

At seven the next morning Tresilian was secure in his bowsed-in Bosun's chair chipping and painting the for'ard draught marks on the ship's stem. He was hungover, depressed and remorseful. He'd never drink again. Oh, it had been good, very good. And he thought the girl had been happy with him. She'd seemed really anxious to have him back, hadn't she? But why a whore for the first time? Well, at least he hadn't paid her; and you could always theorize like that.

Two mornings later it was worse. Petrie and he had gone ashore together again. And this time, as he tried to forget the noise of his own and several other chipping hammers de-rusting the foredeck, the fleeting agony returned. He remembered the first few seconds of the pain — and then oblivion. Now, with a mouth that tasted like a vulture's crutch, with eyes and head aflame, and his stomach in a turmoil of nausea, he wished he were dead. He looked at it. On his right forearm. A mess of red, black and blue, oozing, here and there, small drops of blood. There was a circle resembling a withered wreath and inside, the words — 'Death before Dishonour'.

He could bank on one thing. He'd never see his parents again. His father's words came rushing back as he had left for

Bombay and the steamer to England — 'You'll do well, Glyn; I know you will. The only advice I have is; don't get tattooed — ever. You're almost sure to be stuck with it for life. And make absolutely certain that you never get venereal disease. Why ruin your life stupidly?'

He'd achieved the first, he thought to himself dejectedly, and could very well be a candidate for the second. He'd heard so much about clap, 'syph' and shankers that the prospect of a 'dose' was unthinkably terrifying. And to make things even worse, after discharging the grain cargo in Calcutta, they were going to the States in ballast. Hampton Roads for orders. Petrie thought it would be Baltimore for grain to Egypt. But, and Glyn shuddered, the port didn't matter. If it was anywhere in the United States it meant the 'short arm' inspection. God, what if he did have a dose? He'd speak to Petrie about it when they got to sea again.

.   .   .   .

When the ship was in the open water off the Bay of Bengal, Glyn found an excuse to visit Petrie during the First Mate's bridge watch.

"Here's that ship construction work you told me to do sir."

"Aye. Leave it in my room, son. I can't look at it up here. We'll be altering course in a minute."

"Sir, may I speak to you privately when you come off watch? I won't keep you long".

"Aye. Be in my cabin at quarter past eight. And have some tea brewed while you're at it."

Later, they sat drinking tea out of enormous 'Seven Bell' mugs.

"What it it Tresilian?"

"Sir, I hate to bring this up but, er, you remember that night in . . ."

"Oh, my God. Don't tell me you've got a dose. The old Man'll go beserk if you have."

"No, sir. At least I hope not. But I wanted to ask you. How can you tell?"

"Oh, if you've got one, you'll know about it alright. You'll feel as if you're passing razor blades instead of water. Let me know at once if you see any signs. We've got some M & B's and penicillin in the medicine chest. But by God, for both our sakes, I

— 19 —

hope you're all clear, son."

"Sir, you know these 'short arm' inspections in the States? Well, officers are exempt aren't they?"

"Aye, but in this case you lads aren't classed as officers I'm afraid. I know we had an argument about it last time I was there. As soon as you can though, get ashore and get a blood test taken. The Agent'll fix it all up."

Everything seemed normal and as far as he could tell, Glyn had not contracted any disease. The ship arrived in Baltimore after a long and tedious voyage. In the anchorage, the crew went through United States Immigration, Health and Customs inspections. The arrival 'processing' in those days of McCarthyism and the Walter-McCarran Act was a rigid and humiliating experience for visiting alien ship crew members. One item on the immigration questionnaire shouted an insult, Glyn felt, to universal intelligence: "Do you intend to engage in any attempts to over-throw the government of the United States?"

Glyn took his place in the line-up outside the saloon where the inspections were taking place. He shuffled along behind old Mac McBride, an able seaman from the Hebrides. Mac was a sailor to every last callous on his roughened hands. He was the only man aboard who had served in sail, and forty-five years earlier had made his first voyage at the age of thirteen aboard a full rigged ship bound for Savannah.

Wiping his hands, the old sailor approached the 'short arm' inspection table in the officers' dining-room.

"OK Pop. Let's see it."

"See what?", he asked in the quiet voice of his islands.

"Your penis — come on. Don't fool. Take it out."

"Why?"

"Because we want to see if you've got clap — that's why?"

"And if I have?"

"You'll be isolated ashore in the medical centre", and the doctor went on chewing his gum, "or if you don't want medical help, you won't be allowed ashore. You'll just have to stay confined to the ship."

"Ah now surr, what's the wurrst that can happen if I refuse to show you my genitals?"

"Same thing. You can't go ashore."

"That's guid surr, very guid. Let's leave it like that", and old

MacBride put on his beret and walked past the customs and immigration officials to the open deck and a smoke.

"Been to the United States before Tresilian?"

"No."

"O.K. Show. Fine. Next."

CHAPTER 3

He served a total of three years as an apprentice with the Hungor Line. A prize of 'tramping' was the greater variety of ports of call. Apart from South America, Tresilian's ships took him to all the continents, all the major sea-ports, the ship canals, all the seas, oceans, weathers and seasons. He served most of his 'time' on the utility type of wartime vessel — American and Canadian built. These were the 'Sam', 'Fort', and Empire class ships. They were slow, wide-gutted, unlovely. Driven by triple expansion engines, coal or oil burning, they were minimally equipped in every way. There was the boredom of interminable Pacific passages, excruciating Red Sea heat, airless humid hells in West African up-river ports, typhoons in the South China Sea, hurricanes in the North Atlantic. Fights on deck and brawls ashore. Pimps and waterside saloons. Happy ships. Miserable ships. Wardrobe drinking Masters. Dry-dock discomfort with no running water aboard. Christmases and New Years at sea. The tropics and boiling greasy food flavoured with dripping sweat from shirtless chests.

.   .   .   .

When he was twenty, he sailed as a junior officer with ships of other companies. The myopia came upon him gradually. For some time he'd realised that when coasting, and looking for headlands, buoys and lights, his eyes became increasingly sore and tired. The binocular setting he used gave him more magnification than was required by the normal vision of others. During his next leave he decided on a check up. Accordingly, he consulted two Harley street specialists who both agreed on the amount of his near-sightedness. With this news he knew his sea-going career was over.

The Merchant Shipping Act stipulated that the minimum eyesight standards for Certificates of Competency examinations must be met without the aid of glasses. While this rule was common to most Commonwealth merchant navies, it was not an international obligation — and especially not among the Merchant fleets of 'Convenience Flag' countries.

When the prognosis was made, and it came as no surprise to him, Tresilian was serving with an old established company whose vessels were manned by Lascar crews. To one who had served his time in tramp ships, the unaccustomed elegance of life on these craft was all the more appreciated. However, as far as advancement in his chosen occupation was concerned, Glyn knew that he was living on borrowed time — and there wasn't much left.

He had a meeting in Liverpool with the Marine Superintendent.

"Sorry to hear about your eyesight Tresilian. Too bad. But nothing in life's ever wasted you know — chalk it up to experience. It'll come in handy some day. Any plans?"

"Nothing very definite sir. I'm not qualified for the obvious jobs — stevedoring, pilotage. So there's no sense in going after them. Oh, I'll probably end up as a sales trainee or something. There seem to be lots of those jobs being advertised."

"Well, look", and the ex-Shipmaster reached over for a file on his desk, "I can probably help to tide things over for you. Give you some time to get sorted out. Let's see now — yes. As I thought. We're pretty short of stand-by people at the moment. And you're perfectly alright for that. New tonnage and survey work. But it'd mean continental stuff too. Quite a bit of short notice travelling around. You're not married eh, Tresilian?"

"No, sir"

"Then that shouldn't bother you too much. Interested?"

"Yes, sir — very. Thank you."

"Could you get over to Hamburg tomorrow? We should have relieved the chap for leave a week ago."

"Er, yes; I think so sir. Why not?"

"Good. Then I'll get my girl to make the arrangements. You'll travel first class of course. I know you don't have the rank — but you're helping us out of a jam."

The 'tiding over' lasted for nearly three years. Tresilian 'stood-by' the company's ships under construction or survey in West Germany, Holland, the Tyne, the Tees, the Mersey, the Thames, the Clyde, South Wales ports, Belfast, Hull and South-hampton. He enjoyed the work and was pleasantly surprised to find how interesting were the many phases of ship design and repair. At times he felt that his responsibility, as liaison between shipyard and the company, was more than he would have enjoyed as a junior officer at sea.

Soon, he knew and became friendly with ship managers in British and continental yards. He got on well with executive and unskilled labourer alike. In particular, perhaps because he was single and unencumbered, he enjoyed the instant mobility of it all. In shipping, things and people change quickly. It was common for him to be sent overnight at a few hours notice from Bremen to Cardiff, Leith to Rotterdam. He always travelled light — a white boiler suit, uniform, a few civilian clothes. Typical would be a fast dash to the station, an overnight journey on the glamorous Scandinavian Express to the Hook of Holland, the day crossing to Harwich aboard a Dutch cross-channel steamer; breakfast on the train to Liverpool Street station, a taxi across London to Paddington and the train to South Wales. Most often it rained in the Bristol Channel ports of Swansea, Barry and Cardiff. There were the ghostly spectres of unemployed ships, silhouetted against cranes and gantries, sulking in dry-dock.

At times, Glyn considered these, the "stand-by" years, the happiest of all. The Super seemed pleased with his work. But, as Tresilian himself knew, it wasn't that important. Without him, the ships would still have been built and re-fitted. But they were good days. Moreover, every now and again he could join a new ship for her trials. The trials were fun — and he noticed the good humour of people who, like himself, went on them, without a care, without specific responsibilities.

During trials, there was an air of celebration. This was the prize — the time of completion when another fine ship was sent down the ways to her element. In the curving wake of her speed turn was the labour of thousands. Men had worked with steel, welding torch, riveting hammer, wire, chain, slide rule and caliper. They had worked with thew and brain. They had created and launched a good thing. A graceful example was the then new intermediate cargo liner, "Angeliana."

Tresilian had been with her for the final three months of her building in Birkenhead. Ever since he'd been aboard, he'd liked the "feel" of her. She was new, good looking, efficient and fast.

He joined her for her test. It was perfect late summer weather in September. Tugs, gulls, trains and cranes clattered across the still morning air as the "Angeliana" was eased out of her berth at Wooffendens' yards. Glyn stood on the boatdeck and looked up river to the Liver Buildings and the twin birds blue-green against the dusty sky. Ferries cried their way across to New Brighton and the Pier Head. He could hear the salty voices of pilots and dock masters easing a big ship through the small apertures of lock and dock gates.

"Heave away quietly, Mr. Mate. Check her gently with your spring sir — don't break it now."

The "Angeliana" gently slid down river, past the Bar Lightship, and headed for the measured mile waters off the Isle of Arran. She teemed with marine superintendents, engineer superintendents, foremen, fitters, carpenters, radio and navigational equipment personnel, fuel oil chemists, radar experts, steering gear technicians. Every part of her was attended by a specialist. A brass plate gleamed on the fore part of the bridge. 'Built and engined by Wooffendens. Birkenhead 1954.'

As a Wooffenden ship, the "Angeliana" would be recognized all over the world as a model of fine naval architecture. The yard's name was famous and respected. The present Chairman of the Board, Sir Timothy Woofenden, Bt., was the third generation head of a company which had been started in the days of sail by his grandfather, an enterprising ship-wright. From schooners and barquentines, Wooffendens had, for a very long time, provided tough competition for the great yards on the Clyde. Since 1950, Wooffendens had won lucrative defence orders for naval tonnage as well as for two super-liners.

The Chairman, his wife and daughter were aboard the Angeliana for her sea trials. He liked to do this now and again. It was a respite from his office and a tonic for them all. Peta, especially, he thought, could do with a bracing dose of fresh sea air. She must be tired and jaded, poor girl, after B.A. Finals at Cambridge and the London Season. The Wooffendens lived the typical life of a family of vast fortune. There was an estate — Wooffenden Hall — within handy Rolls-Royce commuting distance of the yard in Birkenhead. A town house in Chester Square, London. A villa at Cap Ferrat. A steam yacht, other cars and plenty of loyal servants.

Tresilian, dressed in sports jacket and flannels, was on the boat-deck. He watched the Wooffendens arrive at the lee rail just as the pilot cutter pulled away from the ship's side. The wood-stepped rope ladder was whisked aboard, "Angeliana's" engines were put to 'Full Ahead' and the maiden girl picked up her skirts and ran.

"Lovely weather for it?"

"Yes, sir," Glyn had often seen Sir Timothy around the yard (in fact he had once been present at a briefing chaired by Sir Timothy), but had seen only pictures of his wife and daughter in the pages of the popular press which doted on the rich, especially on the daughters of the rich.

"Our name is Wooffenden. How do you do. My wife and daughter Peta."

"How do you do Sir Timothy. Lady Wooffenden. Miss Wooffenden. My name is Tresilian. Glyn Tresilian."

"You're with the ship's people?"

"Yes, sir. I've been standing by her for several months in Birkenhead — and inveigled myself aboard."

"Ah — then you've been keeping an eye on us, what?"

"I'd hardly put it quite like that, but I suppose that's part of the general idea."

"Like her?"

"Very much. She's a fine ship."

A Steward brought beef tea. Tresilian spent the rest of the morning with them walking on the boat-deck and around the ship. At noon a white coated steward came on deck and rang the luncheon bell.

"Well, well," Sir Timothy enthused and rubbed his hands together, "I'd no idea it was time for luncheon. Can't say I mind though, eh my dear? Peta? These salt breezes certainly tone up the appetite, what? I wonder if we have time? Mr. Tresilian — what about a drink before table? Or are you busy?"

"Not at all sir. I'd like that very much. Thank you."

With so much technical brass aboard the ship, Glyn found it pleasingly odd that he should be drinking pin gin with the Wooffenden family. After drinks, they shared the same table in the dining saloon. The talk was light and pleasant — and mainly about the sea. Tresilian was surprised at the interest Peta showed when he described some of his own Hungor Line experiences.

A few deck and engineer officers came in and ate hurriedly — to return as soon as possible to the bridge and engine-room. There was great rush everywhere — as if this was the final performance of an award winning attraction and seats were scarce.

Peta Wooffenden was a celebrated and lovely girl. If due only to Wooffenden employee shop talk, Tresilian had known a fair bit about her for some time. Privileged, self-assured, well educated and charming, she might have been one of the few, and the very few, described by Disraeli. Hers was the world of County, Guards Officers, Cambridge, Ascot, Henley, Biarritz and Cannes.

After an afternoon snooze and dinner, Glyn showed Peta the "Monkey Island" compass platform above the wheelhouse. He wasn't sure, but he felt that she was thoroughly bored by the whole thing and had only come along to please her father. Having had the chance to take all of her in at close range, he thought her physically quite stunning. No wonder the tabloids and popular week-end papers liked running photographs of her at balls and the like, usually showing her in some sort of revealing dress which when caught at the right camera angle, showed georgeous hard full breasts. A far cry from most of the flat-chested, horsey bunch. And, in at least some of the photos, there'd been not one but two highly eligible bachelors.

Even now, although her face was a little distant, it projected a kind of mischievous happiness, probably Glyn thought, because of the unfamiliarity of the scene. It was well proportioned, nothing terribly distinctive such as deep-set eyes or full lips, but with a light tan complexion and some freckles, pinpointing a small straight nose. Glyn wasn't ignorant, and although he had never 'gone out' much in a permanent boy-meets-girl relationship, this Peta Wooffenden was doing something to him.

As he was thinking, and both of them were looking out to sea, the ship altered course and the wind suddenly caught her loosely tied head square, carrying it up and overboard. Glyn lurched after it but missed. He caught the scent of her fresh clean silken hair.

In the fading light he looked at her again. The high firm breast line inside a just right fitting sweater. The narrow waist flared to two well measured thighs, rounding to a flawless cruiser stern. A first class Wooffenden design. And her legs. They were marvellous. He'd seen them in the daylight, but now she'd covered them with well-tailored slacks. She shivered slightly.

"Feeling cold, Miss Wooffenden?"

"A little", she spoke in the voice of the upper crust English but without the annoying stridency that made the sound so suspect when heard out of its own milieu. A slight nasality gave her speech a delicate sensuality. They went down the ladder to the boat-deck accommodation entrance.

"Well, it was nice spending the day with you all. I expect your parents must be looking for you."

"No, I don't think so. Daddy said he was going to get every minute of sleep he could — he looks on this as a rest cure. I expect they're in bed by now."

Although he was more than a little apprehensive, he made up his mind. He wanted her, and suspected she wanted him. She seemed so easily bored, and Glyn was obviously offering her some diversion. He'd ask her for a drink. Sailors, after long voyages and short turn rounds in port, had little or no time for preliminaries or the subtle approach. And come to think of it, this too would be a short turn 'round. He'd vowed after that night in Calcutta that he'd never pay for it again. And he hadn't. It had come from the most unlikely quarters . . . the Evangelist girl from Swansea, for example. What a hot number she'd been . . . They'd been good for each other during the two weeks before she had to go back to America for further study.

"Tell you what, Miss Wooffenden. I've got some Scotch. What about it?"

"That's very kind of you — why not? But need we be so formal? Call me Peta."

"And I'm Glyn. Where's your cabin?"

"Over there. Next to Mummy and Daddy."

"Fine. I'll get the bottle."

He went for the whisky and returned with it to her stateroom.

"I suppose we can't get any ice, at this hour can we?" she asked.

"Possibly. But everything's usually topsy-turvy during trials and the stewards have most likely knocked off by now. I'll hunt round and see what I can do."

"Oh no — in that case don't bother. Here you are; I'm afraid they look like tooth glasses."

He poured large measures and added water from the adjoining bathroom tap. He held up his beaker.

"Happy days."

"And to you. Tell me Glyn, what are you going to do? I mean, this shipyard work must be a bit of a bore?"

"No, I don't find it so. Not having any responsibilities, I quite enjoy it. I like the travelling as much as anything. I never know where I'll be from one week to the next. And a moving target's always harder to hit."

"What do you do that makes you a target?"

"Ah, you'd be surprised", and he laughed. She smiled and sipped at her Scotch. There wasn't much water, and she grimaced.

"But never mind about me", he went on, "you're much more interesting. What's it like being a member of the Princess Margaret set?"

"Oh, a bore sometimes. And I hope I don't have to tell you not to believe everything you read in those ghastly gossip columns. Some of the things they say are really quite awful."

"But I suppose Her Royal Highness does provoke some of it herself. And presumably she knows and doesn't mind. I think it was yesterday — did you see it? That picture taken in Pitts'?"

"Well what about it? Surely there's nothing wrong with being fashionable is there? And if you have the figure, which she has, why not wear a low decolletage? I love them myself."

"Really?"

"Yes. Of course."

Tresilian remembered all right. Stupid gaff on his part to feign ignorance.

On her part, Peta wasn't going to allow this display of real or intended innocence to go by. Maybe shipping so absorbs him that... well, anyway, he had triggered something. "Mr. Tresilian," she said officiously, "you've been around ships too long. Far too long. I suppose you think feminine beauty outside the marriage bed is naughtiness, or are you one of those sailors who appreciates beauty in foreign ports but expects chastity belt purity from his women back home?

"The old codes may have been all right for Queen Victoria and my parents, but they're not good enough for me, or my friends. We've been trapped for too long by the old taboos on dress and other things."

Getting no reply from a momentarily stunned Glyn, Peta continued.

"Perhaps you're part of that great middle class which despises people who want to take some fun out of life, and which yearns to take us back to the Puritans? Really, Glyn! Any more of that and I'll have to send you home."

She had hurt him. But it was true; he was middle class.... middle middle class for that matter. Glyn stood there, his mind racing. He'd have to move now, or lose the chase. He side-swiped the frontal attack, with a hopefully acceptable rejoinder. "Well, if you want to send me home tonight that's not very far, unless you want me to swim for it?"

"That will depend entirely on you," she said, and Glyn wondered what she meant. Was there something here or not? There was no way of knowing. Damn it, he was way out of his depth. He wanted her more than ever if only to make up for his lack. He'd try another tack.

"You asked about my plans, I've none to speak about. What are yours? Here, don't answer. Let me give you the other half first." He took her glass and filled it with more Scotch and water.

"Well?"

"I'd really like to be a hospital almoner I think. I've had a marvellous four-year fling — thanks to Daddy and these ships he builds. But enough's enough, or so Mother says. Maybe I ought to try and do something useful now and again, don't you think?"

"What?", he was surprised, "Oh, yes. Yes, of course. That's really worthwhile work. You have your degree now?"

"Yes, just scraped through."

"You're beautiful, brainy and rich. It surely won't be long before you're spliced."

"Spliced? I don't . . ."

"Married."

"Oh, I thought you meant tight or something. The way you're pouring these enormous drinks, I don't think that'll be long."

An hour and a half later the bottle was almost empty and Peta was flushed.

"I'm quite surprised. Most of the people I know would have started after the second drink. And here you are with the bottle practically finished and not a move. I've never felt safer in my life."

"Do you like feeling safe?"

"Well, that all depends doesn't it?"

He went to the door. "Watch now. If I do this", and he fingered the inside locking bolt, "would you feel safe — or in great danger?"

She didn't answer. Instead she got up and walked over to him. Gently she put her hand on his and pushed the bolt noiselessly into place. Then pulling his head down to hers, she whispered, "It's about time isn't it?"

For Tresilian, Peta Wooffenden was an entirely new experience. Not only in the way she looked, or talked, but in her manner of doing things. He'd been brought up to think in terms of male initiative in these matters. But she couldn't wait for Glyn to play the male role. She turned to him, saw just the slightest hesitation on his face, and said, "Here, let me do that," and her fingers moved to his necktie. She had his shirt half off when he joined the fray, furiously unzipping her slacks. She stepped out of them revealing for him strong, curvy and well-tanned thighs and legs. She was faster than he. While she had already unclothed him, Glyn, still toying with her bra, felt her expert tongue on his face and shoulders. His perspiration ran fast. He disconnected the clip and now Peta too was ready. She took her mouth away and stepped back for him to admire her. Her flesh, suntanned without a trace of bathing suit, was soft and warm. Her breasts stood out straight and bold. They merely confirmed his passion. In his element now, he lifted Peta onto the bunk and took her for the first time. The short pulsating minute was instinctive and gloriously satisfying.

"Cmon" and he pulled her to the shower. He turned the tap full on in the narrow cubicle where there was barely room for both. They soaped each other and Glyn, filled with sudden and renewed desire as he looked at the peach tan of her lather flecked body, entered her again as standing they shook and slithered on the slippery tile floor.

"That was lovely" she said appreciatively while she toweled him down. "I've never done that before. Let's do it in the morning too."

Out of the shower, Peta stood at attention for Glyn to admire, miming her Guards Officer friends performing their duties out-side Buckingham Palace. Facing her model breasts he remem-bered again the point that had crossed his mind before.

"Magnificent, Peta, simply magnificent. But with such perfect breasts, why a bra at all?"

She was gratified to hear the question. It was a good thing that she was a bosom-conscious woman, Glyn, no mean breast watcher himself since many voyages back, thought as he watch-ed her lovely mounds gently rise and fall.

Her voice was warm and coaxing. "That, my darling innocent M-i-s-t-e-r Tresilian," she said, deliberating on each letter and at the same time sitting down on the bunk, motioning Glyn beside her, "again shows that you've been on ships too long." With their loins touching, she demonstrated the logistics of the problem as with one hand on her left breast and the other hold-ing her copious pair of cups, she studiously explained.

"This Glyn, you idiot, is one of my sweater bras. I put it on simply to appear decent in public. Can you imagine me strutting on the ship's deck in a sweater without one?"

At her suggestion they had another shower and between their mutual petting and squeals she furthered, in answer to his naive, infatuated questions, Tresilian's education by in-forming him that she tried whenever possible to free her breasts when wearing party gowns. Tresilian found this particularly funny and as they laughed and gasped for breath she said "They're too restrictive and I've got my pride."

"You certainly have" he thought and they went on giggling uncontrollably.

They fell asleep together in the single stateroom bunk. Once in the early hours after she had drawn him into her, the ship turned hard-a-port at speed. The "Angeliana" heeled over and they were thrown down thudding on the cabin deck. Without parting they rolled and settled with him above her. He gently pushed himself up.

"No, no", she breathed urgently, "keep going. Let's finish like this", and she bit and clawed his neck and back.

At dawn they showered together again and then he went back to his cabin for sleep. He looked in the glass and saw the love wounds. Wearily he decided that they had been worth it and there would be more tonight. He'd take his fun where he found it. What an incredible, privileged, wild young animal she was. There was just no telling where you'd find it... He wondered how many there must have been before him — after champagne and strawberries, 'coming out', 'Eights Week', the Eton and Harrow match. She'd have worn polka dot summer dresses and ridiculously wide brimmed hats and long white shimmering gowns. And young bucks, well bred, horselike and toothy would have danced attendance and charm — and in her case more than the usual amount.

Without either of them realizing it, they each thought of the other as a 'discovery'. Exhausted by the night's events, Peta lay down in the now calm bunk and stretched contentedly. Tresilian was different.... in all ways, she reflected happily. He was like no one she'd known. How could they normally have met? With their worlds running forever parallel and never meeting? She supposed that he had always done what he had wanted to and could with women in Rio or Singapore but watched out carefully for the girls at home. Particularly one like herself. If he only knew! Certainly he could lose any of the others in a contest. Why were they always so drearily polite and apologetic about it? They wore out so quickly. Interesting. Perhaps they were too young. Could be. Carleton-Winfield for example — tight as a coot and useless after two glasses of bubbly. Aahh, never mind. Roll on tonight.

At breakfast, Sir Timothy and Lady Diana were in a talkative mood.

"Some excellent shut-eye, I must say", the shipbuilder said and ordered ham and eggs. "Apart from something falling heavily during the night we slept very well."

"Didn't it wake you up, Peta?"

"What, Mummy? Oh, scrambled eggs and bacon please. The same for you, Mr. Tresilian? Didn't what wake me up?"

"That dreadful noise. You must have heard it. It sounded nearer to your cabin than ours."

"No, but I'm glad I sleep soundly. Was it an accident or collision or something?"

"Did you hear it, Mr. Tresilian?"

"Oh, I may have done, Lady Wooffenden. But I'm used to it. New ships and noises go to-gether I'm afraid. Could have been anything. A bolt of canvas falling — dunnage or what have you."

"Well it sounded very loud and woke us both up. You look tired Mr. Tresilian."

"Oh, perhaps. They asked me to give them a hand on the bridge while they were calibrating the D/F in the middle watch."

"Really? How interesting", and Lady Diana began the delicate surgery on her kipper.

Tresilian was glad, when after two more taxing nights, the "Angeliana" finished trials and tied up at the yard of final work before her maiden voyage. He was convinced that Lady Diana's feminine intuition had been characteristically infallible.

"Good-bye, Mr. Tresilian", she said at the gangway, "I hope you've enjoyed being shipmates as much as we have. Perhaps we'll be able to meet again soon."

"I've liked sailing with you very much Lady Wooffenden. The trials have done you good. You look well and quite rested."

"Thank you. But we've had nothing to do. Good-bye. Come on Peta. Where's your luggage?"

Glyn went on a week's leave and recuperated in a small Lake District country pub. Then he went to Schiedam to stand-by a ship undergoing extensive bow re-building after a bad fog collision in the English Channel. He knew it would be a long job but didn't mind as he liked the Maas ports and knew a girl in Rotterdam. He'd pretty well forgotten about Peta, except for moments of carnal recollection. After a month and a half in Schiedam, and a week before he was due at another job in Southampton, the Marine Superintendent telephoned him from Liverpool.

"My word, Tresilian — this stand-by work must be doing you good. Do you know who called me just now from London?"

"No, sir."

"Peta Wooffenden. They were aboard the "Angeliana" for trials with you, weren't they?"

"Yes, that's right, sir."

"Well you must have done something right because she's looking for you. Got a pencil? Here's her number — CHELsea 8124. She wants you to call her right away and reverse the charges. Oh, and Tresilian, you won't forget we ordinary people when you're running Wooffendens eh?"

Peta could have had an abortion, Glyn thought as the preparations were going forward. But, who knows, maybe she had planned it that way. Even now, she could have had the pick of any number of very eligible young men ready to take her the way she was....carrying another man's child. It wouldn't be difficult for any man to build up sufficient gallantry in Peta's case.

Fortunately, Glyn didn't have much time to think about it. It was a fashionable wedding at St. George's, Hanover Square.

The 'Super' was flattered that Glyn had asked him to act as best man. The columnists were disappointed at the quality of the groom — a coalminer, or barman, or duke would have been better — but delighted with the 'little dicky bird told me' scope of the hasty arrangements.

Sir Timothy and Lady Diana reacted predictably, as their British lips kept up and stiff. To Glyn they were correct and charming. And Tresilian knew how sorry they were that their only daughter and he had met in the first place. Due to recurring bouts of malaria, the senior Tresilians were unable to leave Madras and except for a few shipmates, Glyn was unrepresented at the wedding.

But the show went on and was up to standard. Sir Timothy saw to that; and despite the hints that changed to rumour, and then to certainty, the Ministers of Defence and Transport were in attendance, thank God. Pictures of both pecking Peta's cheeks were in all the Sunday papers. They honeymooned in the Channel Islands and returned to Wooffenden Hall. Glyn objected and insisted that they settle somewhere on their own. He was insistant too that they would live on his means, which in her case meant untried poverty.

But she surprised him. A genuine happiness grew as she made a home out of the flat they rented in an attractive old converted house near Hoylake on the Wirral. He could just about afford this. With an increase in Glyn's salary they bought a new mini car. More than ever now, he was determined to hold on to his job as long as he could. Twice now, Sir Timothy had tried to persuade him to fill the special niche he'd created for his son-in-law, noblesse oblige. Both times Glyn had enjoyed turning it down.

"Obviously, Sir Timothy", he'd said in the Chairman's great wood-panelled office, "I can't and never will be able to support Peta in the way you've accustomed her. But then, very few could. I'll do my damndest though to make her happy. And that's the only thing that really counts, isn't it? Naturally I can do that more easily if I know I'm paddling my own canoe, however small. And on courses that I set myself. No, Sir Timothy, I appreciate your kindness, but the offer is not for me."

"I understand you perfectly, Glyn."

The baby was born exactly six months after the wedding day in London. It was an eight pound boy, healthy and perfect. He was christened Michael Timothy Glyn. With the Wooffendens, the young couple worked out a good 'arms length' system whereby the grandchild visited, but did not stay at the Hall. Occasionally in the afternoons, especially when Glyn was away, her chauffeur would drive Lady Wooffenden in the Bentley to Hoylake.

Whether it was through the kindly Super's machinations or not Glyn couldn't say, but he found himself being assigned to more and more ships on the Mersey and by the time Michael was a year old, he hardly did any travelling at all. This meant that he could get home to Hoylake practically every evening to a contented wife and child. He and Peta were very happy together and they lived a tranquil life within his means. Michael was flourishing and apart from a woman to 'do the rough' Peta cheerfully looked after everything herself. Glyn was surprised, as was everybody else, at how well things had worked out.

Peta's friends wondered how long it would last. They didn't have long to wait, but the shock was the cruelest blow of Glyn's life. Just before Michael's second birthday in 1956, Peta was killed in the Mersey tunnel. She had driven Michael to spend the day with his Grandmother at the Hall, and was going to see a married girl friend in Blundellsands. For Tresilian, the day would forever remain a jagged haze. He was at Huskisson Dock at the time. An urgent call to the dock office phone. The funeral. Weeping. Black clothes. Comfort and kindness. Compassionate leave spent with Michael at the Hall. A mental vacuum close to amnesia. Days and nights of sitting and staring. Mechanical pecking at food. A breakdown.

Slowly he came back. Like a dense barely moving fog at sea, seared at last by a strong sun, the mental obscurity loosened and went away. It had taken three months.

He decided to break completely from all the life he'd known. The 'Super' was sympathetic and understood. He and his parents-in-law agreed that for the present, Michael would live with them. That was a consolation, he realised. The child would have nurses and nannies. But he'd also be with the Wooffendens who unabashedly loved their grandson. Already, Glyn sometimes thought, Sir Timothy was measuring the boy for a Board Room chair.

Once Michael was settled under the care of a genteel Mrs. Southcombe at the Hall, carefully screened and selected for the position, Tresilian took a round voyage cruise for a fortnight down to the Canary Islands on a comfortable but small Norwegian liner. He enjoyed the ship very much. There was good eating and drinking, resting and talking. He played and partied a lot. And thought a great deal too. He also made a decision about his future. He would emigrate to Canada. And said so at dinner on his return.

"Yes, there's no doubt that it's a young man's country, Glyn. No doubt about that at all. No none at all." Sir Timothy took a long pull on his after dinner cigar and passed the port again. Tresilian had made his announcement as the footman cleared the table. The one concession that the Wooffendens made to social non-conformity was that however large or small the dinner party, the ladies did not retire.

"When we need them most, why should we lose them?", was the way Sir Timothy liked to put it.

"I'm sure you would do very well there Glyn," Lady Wooffenden said, "but aren't the winters dreadful?"

"Far less dreadful than ours, Lady Wooffenden. At least people are dressed and prepared for them. No, I don't think the weather would be a consideration one way or the other. In my case it's simply a matter of qualification and challenge. There's nothing I can do about the first, so, automatically, it would seem, it's pretty hard to face the second."

"Ah, well, that all depends", Sir Timothy interjected, "on what you mean by qualification, as old Joad would say. If you mean the sea, then obviously you face a difficulty. You can't go to sea any more —— and you yourself have said that however much you liked it, the stand-by work was still much of a dead-end. A stop gap I think you called it.

"However, and I know we've been over this before Glyn, you've obviously gained a great deal of knowledge about ship construction. More than you would have got as a sea-going officer, and in the process you've learned an enormous amount about human relations or man management — as I prefer to call it. These qualities that you have are scarce. And I'd like to bring them into the firm. Now," and the Baronet held up his hand to restrain Tresilian, "I know all about your views on nepotism and all the rest of it. But how can you rationalize my proposition that way when I'm coming to you with the offer — and not the other way round?"

Sir Timothy sipped more port and sat back. Tresilian looked at the middle aged, greying patrician couple. He wondered what they really thought of him. Maybe, because he'd given them a grandson and Wooffenden heir, he might have gone up a notch or two. But would one ever know?

"I recognize that, Sir Timothy", and he put his glass down for a refill, "but we have to realise that you wouldn't have created this job, er, Ship Liaison Officer, if it hadn't been for Peta. On the other hand, let's assume that you did, genuinely, have such a vacancy.

"There'd have been an open competition and you would have advertised for people to apply. And you'd have been flooded with applications from candidates far more qualified and experienced in every way than I. I know you would. It's the sort of job chaps would stampede to get. I've sailed with dozens of young newly married blokes who'd do anything to get it and be home and ashore with their wives and children.

"And, Sir Timothy," Glyn continued, "you know and I know that all other things being equal, I wouldn't have got it. That's one point. Another is that you, as Chairman of the Board most certainly wouldn't have had anything to do with the selection, even if you ever met the successful candidate."

Sir Timothy made no reply and the talk turned back to Canada. Lady Wooffenden stirred some brown sugar in her coffee.

"And Michael, Glyn — he will stay here with us?"

"If you've no objection."

"Objection? I should think not. We'd be thrilled, wouldn't we Timothy?"

"Of course, my dear. I think it's the only sensible plan. Things at first will be hard enough as it is for you Glyn. Do you have any specific aims? Perhaps I can help. I've got some direc-

torships in Halifax and Vancouver if that would be of any . . ."
His voice trailed off. He seemed to know already that 'that
wouldn't be of any . . .'

"No, Sir Timothy, nothing hard and fast. I think I'll just get
over there and see what's what. I always liked Montreal and I
know a few people there from past voyages. But they're mainly
in the shipping business, and I could probably get something
in that line. But I'd rather not. I'd like to begin afresh in a
completely different field."

"Yes, I see", Sir Timothy murmured disinterestedly and carried on with his cigar and port. Suddenly, he brightened up, and
turned on his great charm. "Well, I have no fears for you, Glyn.
You're a resourceful fellow, with the priceless gift of a damned
pleasant personality. What was it I heard someone say on the
television the other night? Ah, yes. I think it went like this: 'Be
witty if you will, be clever if you must, but be pleasant if it
kills you'. There's a lot in that."

"Of course you'll be able to get over now and again to
see us — and Michael, won't you Glyn?", Lady Wooffenden
stated rather than asked.

"I hope things won't be so bad", he laughed, "that I can't get
back. And regularly if possible. Maybe once a year. We'll see
how things go. But then, I might return very soon. It's one
thing to like and enjoy a place as a sailor on shore leave. Quite
another to settle and live. But I think it'll be alright. I always
got on well with the people in Montreal. French and English
speaking. I enjoyed trying the remnants of my shaky school
French when I was there before. That's always useful in
Montreal."

He arranged everything quickly. He could produce evidence
of sufficient solvency to make his immigration processing brief.
However the officer was obliged to enter some sort of employment category on the papers — even though he knew that
Tresilian intended to find work on arrival in Canada. When the
forms reached another official, they caused some surprise.

Approximate date of arrival in Canada: Mid January 1957.

Type of intended occupation: Stevedoring.

"Stevedoring, Mr. Tresilian?"

"Yes."

"Hmm. Longshoreman's work eh — you're going to Montreal?"

"Yes, that's right."

"In that case I'd advise you to go to the coast — Halifax or Saint John. Even Vancouver if you prefer. Or maybe better still why not wait until spring when the St. Lawrence thaws? I'm from Montreal. I know. There's no ship action till mid April at the earliest. But you must know that?"

"Yes, sir, I do...." and he explained. When he had finished, the official's confusion was cleared up. Somehow the migrant didn't seem to fit the role of waterfront worker with a cargo hook and fur lined parka.

"Ah, now I understand Mr. Tresilian. No, no. That doesn't matter at all. We have to put down something — but as you can support yourself financially for the necessary time, we'll let it go. And good luck in Canada. And by the way, don't forget that our office on Bleury 'll give you advice and help. Here — here's the address and phone number. Take is easy. All the best now."

The official shook his hand and watched him leave. How about that? There was an unusual one alright. Right now Ottawa was screaming for carpenters, plumbers, teachers, doctors. Anyone with trades or skills — and he'd just cleared a myopic ex-sailor who only knew how to navigate ships — and couldn't even do that any more.

Phew! Just as well he had a few bucks under his belt. With nothing to offer, man, he'd need them. Ah, but then he'd likely make out somehow. Seemed a decent enough guy. He'd probably con himself into something or other. But that name, Tresilian? Where had he heard it? Why did it ring a bell? Ah, yes, the newspapers. That's right. He was the guy who'd married the shipbuilding heiress, and she'd been killed. Car crash or something. Jeez, with all that dough at his fingertips, he was emigrating? With fifteen hundred bucks? To Montreal? In January? A limey in the middle of Duplessis' Quebec? Crazy. The Immigration Officer shook his head and went on with his work.

Tresilian said goodbye at Wooffenden Hall and went to London for a few days before the flight to Montreal. He indulged himself with a first class train compartment to Euston and enjoyed, as he always had, the rythm of the wheels rolling on the tracks. He had a good fling in London and stayed in a hotel near Lancaster Gate. Luckily, several friends and shipmates were in town on examination leave and Glyn joined them on pub crawls, beginning each day of his 'vacation' with a hangover.

He hadn't thought until he met them, that his contemporaries regarded him as a minor, albeit fleeting, celebrity. They made several ribald allusions but stopped short when they could see him beginning to boil. But none of them could understand his deliberate rejection of the life long security that would have gone with Wooffenden's offer.

"Seven pints please. You know Glyn, you must be a bloody fool. Spitting on all that lovely lolly. Wish to hell I had a chance like that. Never mind going to Canada, you ought to write a book: 'How to marry a shipbuilder's daughter without really trying, hahahaha!' And they all joined in the loud laughter. He was thoroughly drunk when his friends poured him on the bus at Victoria Air Terminal. Unshaven, shaking and nervous, he arrived in Montreal the following afternoon.

Tresilian worked at a variety of jobs in Canada. These took him from Halifax to Nanaimo. He took work where and when he could. In his case it was often difficult. Frequently he was passed over for unskilled construction work in favour of more likely plaid shirted, lumber jacketed applicants. He saw little point in lying to employers and gang bosses he met along the way. The truth, however, as he told it, was invariably too strong for most. After a while, he could see the minds turning over.

'Something wrong here. Probably on the run. Doesn't add up. Why take the risk?'

"No, fella. Don't think this job and you were exactly made for each other. Sorry. Next . . ."

After a year in Canada, he wanted to get back to the U.K. Things were bad. Once, because a small town store owner knew his story, he almost settled into a permanent job, but balked when he realised that the businessman was promoting him as a 'come on' exhibit. Just a week before, in a desperate moment he had tried encyclopedia selling for a firm calling istelf "Academpedia".

In the late fifties, Canadian unemployment was uncomfortably high, especially in the west. Sometimes, even in the larger cities, the Help Wanted columns didn't run to half a page. Tresilian would usually go after the more honest looking unskilled jobs that paid around $1.05 an hour. This kind of casual work was enough to stem the tide; to keep him in reasonable dress, cigarettes, a drink or two and bus fares from place to place.

He stayed in cheap rooms and went everywhere by bus. He could think well on long distance bus rides and there was no better way to see and get around the country.

In his mail he told the Wooffendens about making plans. And the value of travel in a vast country. And of surveying opportunities everywhere. If not completely honest, it was easier. He knew that they'd only worry otherwise and try to help by urging him back to work for the firm. They might even put on some gentle pressure; after all, Michael must be missing him. He was over three now. Right now though (without a change in the actual sound of his voice he was slipping easily into some North Americanisms) he could use the price of a return plane ticket to the U.K. While he didn't have any debts, he couldn't find much cash either. Five or six hundred bucks would do it. He wouldn't have to spend much, as he'd be staying at the Hall. He only wanted to get back to see Michael. He was positive that eventually he and Canada could get on. He'd like to spend three weeks in England.

A few weeks after the "Academpedia" adventure, when he was feeling particularly low, Tresilian was having beer and steak for lunch in a tavern on St. Catherine Street. It was crowded and he began a conversation at the same table with a man who said he worked for the International Service of the Canadian Broadcasting Corporation in Montreal. From their talk, Glyn was encouraged to try his hand at writing a few scripts about his experiences at sea. Knowing himself to be no Joseph Conrad, he nevertheless rented a portable typewriter for a week and went to work in the rooming house.

He wrote about experiences in Japan, Communist China, the Mediterranean and Baltic. The International Service man, Fred Runton, gave them a sympathetic reading and told Glyn that while the raw material was promising, it would have to be written in active rather than passive tenses. After sweating over the re-writes and editing, the talks were finally ready for recording. He did this at the Dorchester Boulevard studios after which the tapes were transmitted on short wave.

Tresilian was intrigued and fascinated by radio. Especially when, after a couple of weeks, he was shown copies of favour-

able letters from listeners in different parts of the world. He
began to think about broadcasting as a career. But he knew it
was tough and damnably hard to break into. Forgetting all
about Michael, he called Fred Runton and asked him to have
lunch in the tavern.

"Tell you what I'll do Glyn", Runton said between bites of
sirloin, "I know one of the talks and public affairs national organizers in Toronto. You never know — maybe they could use
some, or even all the stuff you've done for me. But on network.
That'd give you good exposure. Something like Trans-Canada
Matinée for example. You've got a bad drawback. Not your
fault, of course, but it's there."

"Oh?"

"Yep. 'Fraid so. That English accent. Too limey. There's no
easy way of saying it. Personally, I like it. Why, some of my
best friends . . . no, no, I'm kidding. But the CBC has to be so
damn careful. They react to listeners' complaints as if they were
guided missiles. Can't blame them I suppose. Public corporation,
public money, public airwaves. And all Canadian. People seem
to explode when they hear too much limey on the air."

Tresilian was puzzled. He knew he had such an accent
but so far it had hadn't set him back anywhere. "Do people
really react like that?", he asked, "I'm surprised. I'd've thought
they'd be more concerned with what you think or stand for.
Not the way you sound — which after all is something you can't
help. Or is that too naive? Unless a person sounds affected I
can't see . . ."

"Ah, stop right there, Glyn. Now you've got it," Runton
interrupted him, "that's the unfortunate part. I know, that in
your case there's no affectation. And there isn't with the majority
of Englishmen who come here. But that voice — the kind you've
got — definitely gets to people in this country. It kind of, well,
irritates Canadians. Of course you'd never get anyone publicly
to admit to prejudice, but it's there and you'd better believe it."

Glyn considered this. He could say truthfully that up until
now, he wasn't even aware that such a problem existed. "Honestly, Fred — I had no idea," he said and had he but known it, his
own voice had levelled off almost to a neutral mid-Atlantic.
But to Runton he was, and would remain, an Englishman.

"OK, Glyn. I've got to go. Back to the grind. I'll let you know about that network thing from Toronto. Meanwhile if you get any more ideas for features just shoot 'em in. You're safe on the International Service. About the only Canadians who seem to hear it are CUSO people in West Africa. Still in that rooming-house? Yes? Great, Glyn, see you. Thanks for the lunch."

The National Organizers in Toronto liked the talks that he had done for the International Service. They used them on the coast-to-coast network with the proviso that the amount of broadcasting Tresilian did would be governed by the amount and type of listener reaction.

The response on the whole to his early work was good. There were the inevitable letters, usually unsigned, which castigated the Corporation for letting yet another 'goddam limey' on the air. But his work and voice sufficed to start him on a broadcasting course. Freelance and sporadic perhaps, but at least a point of departure. After six months, the assignments were coming in at an encouraging rate. And the money he earned, from radio talks and some television interviewing, saw him on his way for that England trip. He was half a year late, but he could now report some progress made when he'd see the Wooffendens. Freelance broadcaster didn't sound too bad. And with every program he did, Tresilian became more and more sure that he would succeed. Somehow, he had to keep his end up. For Michael and the Wooffendens. He must make some sort of mark. And he'd do it.

He found, as recognition came in slow spurts, that he had to bear down heavily on an enlarging ego. It all seemed to happen in direct ratio to the increased confidence and sureness that he now began to enjoy. He'd had some very good critical reviews. One had referred to the 'new dimension' he brought to local TV, and that he was 'an interesting blend of Gilbert Harding, Lord Boothby and Eamonn Andrews'. He was flattered and much impressed. Were not these people the high priests of British broadcasting? But he also knew that he was plying a dangerous trade, — one that had to court the fickle hand of public taste.

With mind and heart lighter than they'd been in a long time, Tresilian boarded Air Canada's night flight to London. He was in a good mood and felt well. In a few hours, he'd see Michael and his in-laws again. And he had lots of work lined up for his return in three weeks. He was full of good dinner and euphoria. Everything was wonderful.

It was misty in the very early morning as the aeroplane touched down at London Airport. The public address system crackled.

"Your attention please. Calling Mr. Glyn Tresilian, passenger on Air Canada. Will passenger Tresilian please report to the Air Canada desk in the main hall?" Waiting for him was a uniformed driver.

"Mr. Tresilian?", he asked deferentially.

"Yes?"

"Good morning, sir. I am Oates, Sir Timothy's chauffeur. I've only recently joined his employ. I have the car outside. If you will give me your luggage tickets sir, I will claim the suitcases".

This was very good of the old boy, Glyn thought. A drive north would be a fine prelude if the mist cleared up. And possibly there'd be a stop at a country pub along the way.

A brand new Bentley too. Ah, but it was grand to drive through England again. He relaxed in the back, cut off from Oates by a glass partition and watched as the deep rich greens of the countryside shimmered and danced in the strengthening morning sun.

Glyn spent three days in London and the rest of the time at the Hall. At first Michael didn't know his father, but slowly they got through to each other. He and the boy spent a lot of time walking around the lovely Cheshire countryside and there were trips to see ships at the yard and fun at New Brighton. Michael was barely old enough for this kind of diversion but the attachment was strong and by the end of the visit, Glyn dreaded the parting.

Michael was now four and a half and Glyn was very pleased with the way he was developing. But he felt guilty that he'd had nothing to do with his progress. He was a normal, happy pleasingly mischievous little boy. But then why shouldn't he be healthy and well fed? He was a privileged child — more so than Royal children. He didn't have to play in a gold fish bowl. Peta would be happy.

Tresilian returned to Montreal and hurled himself into broadcasting. He accepted any and all assignments. He wanted to make haste at this adopted career and he found that the mentally exhausting work that went with it deadened the pangs of longing he knew he'd now continue to feel for Michael until they were to-gether again. He wished he knew how or when that would be. He didn't feel settled or equipped enough to bring the boy over now. But God, how he missed him. And to bring the hurt on even more, he was getting frequent spasms of remorse. The kind that he'd suffered during his seagoing days when crippled by headache and nausea, he'd vomit the debauch and leachery of the night before in some hot foreign port, oceans away from the stern, unforgiving eye of witness. Neither could he conceal to himself the ill camouflaged attitudes of Lady Diana and Mrs. Southcombe. He was philosophical enough to accept this. There was nothing to be done.

But in Canada, things were going well. And he felt very much at home. This had to be home. To hell with Sir Timothy's sinecure. And the hell with trying out some mediocre, soul rotting job in England. He was damn sure that no broadcasting doors would ever have opened there, even with the old boy's influence. The only good and sensible course then was to get rooted as firmly as possible in Canada and bring Michael over. He'd think this plan to himself and would feel better. For a little while — and then the gnaw would hurt again.

CHAPTER 4

For a few more years Tresilian consolidated his broadcasting position in Canada. He'd become quite well known in Montreal as an interviewer, commentator, and moderator to that small, limited audience who faithfully watched and listened to the CBC.

Generally speaking, this was an aware audience not frightened away by the large doses of austerity programming which formed a large part of the publicly-owned system's day. Comparatively free of competition in the commercial sense, there was little in the CBC's broadcast schedule to excite the mind that craved cacophony and sensation. It followed therefore that the Corporation's listening and viewing faithful were fanatically loyal, but relatively small in numbers.

There were enough of them however to make it possible for Tresilian to get back to Wooffenden Hall every year. And each time the return to Montreal was easier. In growing up, Michael understood that his father would be there again. He had just started at an expensive prep school near Wallasey to which he commuted as a day boy from the Hall. Glyn dreamed of the day when he could repay every penny that Michael's upbringing and education would cost.

Now the prep school — and then Eton, like his Grandfather. Tresilian wondered whether, if he did go there, the boy would turn out like Peake-Smythe.

But by 1963 Michael was in his ninth year and his father in a rut. He had a stable audience, but too stable in an industry where change was the rule. Even at the CBC. His five years had been fine but after the champagne of mild recognition had worn off, staring at him was the truth that he'd gone about as far as he could go in Montreal on the unavoidably restrictive programming of the CBC. He felt an unrelieved frustration. Such talent and experience that he had were acknowledged so far as they went, but his reach was limited to local exposure. Try as he might, he could make no headway on the national CBC radio or television networks.

. . . .

Mrs. Janet O'Leary chose her moment carefully that morning. A tall thin-faced woman, she was quite a contrast in that respect to the run of Montreal housekeepers. She had known Glyn Tresilian ever since he had been working at the CBC, ever since he had moved into her 'homy' and comfortable lodging house. She knew him to have travelled widely, but had not heard or seen him on the CBC more than a few times, and then for only long enough to confirm that it was her boarder, before turning to something she understood.

Glyn Tresilian was the serious young Englishman who stayed in his room a lot, who when he did go out onto the porch on Saturday afternoons talked about the weather, asked about her son in the Yukon and told her about his.

But this morning she was going to corner him, and ask him about that new man at CRUX and what he had said about, "those pompous eggheads at the CBC who play the culture song all year long, but when a once-in-a-year sports event like Grey Cup football comes along, then they outbid the private stations with public money. They use your money to hog the whole show, whether it's a Royal Visit or the Grey Cup!" the man had shout-ed. Mrs. O'Leary was a great sports fan, who especially loved hockey, and although a Montrealer for 33 years that summer, she had always thought of the Toronto Maple Leafs as her team. She had come from a small home on Toronto's Monteith Street. By contrast, Montreal's 'Les Canadiens' were French (never mind the brewery which owned them), and Mrs. O'Leary was herself a living example of the gulf which separated English and French, Catholic and Catholic in Canada.

Now she collared Glyn on his way to work, and told him all about it . . . adding for good measure that she agreed with Denny Trample 100%. And that's how Glyn Tresilian first heard of Denny Trample.

Out of breath by the time she had related her story, Mrs. O'Leary failed to mention the final sentence of Trample's deri-sive assault on the CBC: "Stick to your lily-white programming for the educated and the few on Westmount hill and at McGill, but leave the popular interest programs to the private stations who know and understand the needs and wants of Mr. and Mrs. Average Montreal. In fact, just stick it!" The outburst resulted in Trample's well-publicized suspension from the air for two weeks on the order of the Board of Broadcast Governors in Ottawa, which had jurisdiction over both the CBC and all private stations at the time.

But the suspension came later, two or three days later when the Board had had time to go over the tapes. It had been the CBC which protested, and it was felt the giant public octopus wouldn't have heard about the commotion at all unless Trample had attacked it directly.

For a month now, "Did you hear Denny Trample yesterday when . . ." was a question that thousands were asking each other. The fact that Tresilian hadn't heard of him was typical of the public broadcasters' indifference to the private stations. Tresilian himself had only recently heard of the phenomenon called 'open line programming'.

Denny Trample was an American import by way of Windsor, Ontario. He was a remarkable catalyst. Now infuriating, now soothing, now dramatising, always spell-binding. "Trample's a genius at manipulating housewives particularly and blue collar families generally," a psychiatrist declared in print.

The secret of Trample's technique was his ability to keep an audience off balance for hours on end. Would he be rude? Would he put down — or be bested himself in argument? Would he verbally lacerate an infirm grandmother who had questioned his judgment? The need to know and listen was rocketing Trample and CRUX to the top in private radio.

Born in a Brooklyn slum section where he'd had to fight and kick for survival, Trample's early life had been a run of hunger, rags and gang brawling. As he never failed to remind his audience, as soon as he could reason, he hated his environment and vowed to shake himself free. He graduated in public libraries and became a walking encyclopaedia on any number of subjects. Predictably, because of his erratic character, his appetite for learning and self-improvement was not understood by his friends.

At 16, he had witnessed a brutal knife fight resulting in the death of a friend a block away from the walk-up where he lived with five brothers and seven sisters. He ran to a public pay phone and called a New York radio station. He reported the scene live on the telephone and impressed the news director so much that he was hired as a copy boy the next day. He worked hard and developed the arresting metallic quality in his voice which, many years later, led to the messianic throne he was just beginning to fill at CRUX.

He'd been in Windsor only two years, but in that time had pushed the station to the top and had digested the Canadian scene to the point where, in that fiercely nationalistic Canadian border city, he was more Canadian than the Canadians. In Windsor a long-time smouldering management dispute between an "Old-line" owner (one who was sour on gimmicks and the like) and a ratings-conscious General Manager was climaxed in the dismissal of both Trample and the General Manager.

Already using a modified version of the "open line" format by inviting 'experts' to come in and answer listeners' questions, CRUX brought Trample in to sew up the market. The key to Trample's success had been established in Windsor. Added to his own frantic and combative air of showmanship was Trample's love of the underdog and a disdain for 'they' and 'them'. 'They' wer the doctors, lawyers, dentists, businessmen and local municipal politicians.

The structure of all North American society was order-made for Trample, but especially Montreal society. He grilled 'them' all, and became a kind of unofficial ombudsman for the masses — for the 'little guy'. He and Cyril Carter, the General Manager, rumour had it, had taken a $150,000.00 per year four-year contract at CRUX. After their month in Montreal, and as a result of fast surveys, they were considered a shoo-in for all that CRUX had asked — the highest recognized rating in the market.

Managements of other Montreal radio stations admitted they were 'plenty worried'. However the advertising agencies thought 'panic stricken' a better word choice. They had to counter-attack. Montreal was Canada's biggest market. It was big business and the ratings book was the measuring stick. Lose that ball game too often and . . . The answer was to fight it out with CRUX in a series of head-on collisions with Trample.

.   .   .   .

At the time, Glyn's own knowledge of private radio and television was limited to their call letters, billboard advertisements and some of the broadcasters he had met at the Media Club. The radio and TV men were mostly news types, who were nice enough, but hardly the kind, Glyn thought, who drove radio and TV stations to market success. The struggle, as Glyn was to find out, raged at the level of the station managers and 'personalities', the disc jockeys and 'open line' moderators.

CRUX had come in with hurricane force, copying in their total programming the frenzied formats of stations already enjoying huge audience ratings in the U.S. The formula worked, and advertising time contracts flowed in, allowing the stations at the same time to raise their commercial time rates. The business of private radio and TV is business, as Fred Runton (who hated the private stations "lack of quality and money obsession," with a hate now shared only by the older pre 1935 era CBC veterans) explained to a confused Tresilian at one of their early meetings in the public broadcasting system's cafeteria. "It starts and stops with ratings. That — all the time. That — and nothing else," Runton had said.

When CRUX delivered for the first time in Montreal the purest possible form of the 'open line', it produced a prodigy first conceived in the U.S. Exactly where, is not known. For years, North American radio had wrestled and failed to grapple with the steam roller competition of television. As TV began to dominate air time all day as well as prime evening time, many radio stations were forced to the wall.

Then someone, somewhere, 'out there in radioland', as the old-line stations loved to say, struck gold. It cost nothing. Perhaps it was simply listeners phoning in requests to disc jockeys, with the D-Jays engaging in added friendly conversation. In any case, radio had discovered a way to compete — when a simple truth came home — that the greatest show on earth is people, and the involvement of people in everyday problems, and through controversy, real or synthetic. Like most inventions, it was so obvious that it had been overlooked by a generation of broadcasters.

When CRUX began its 'open line' shows for several hours at a time, at first with local announcers and 'experts' turned 'open liners,' and then spaced all over the day and night, it placed an extension of the radio station in every dwelling where there was a phone within its transmitter's range. It worked like magic. Even in prime television time people were pulled as by a magnet to CRUX. They listened in their hundreds of thousands.

At CRAK Radio, General Cosmetics and CRAK executives had huddled for a solution to their ratings dilemma long before Trample actually arrived on the scene. An old-fashioned programming policy dropped 'old CRAK' to fourth place in English Montreal. The first decision was to return the then General Manager and Program Director to the 'plant' as VP-Public Relations. The second, was to hire a new General Manager. While the moves added up to a decision to get back into the market, there was no clear-cut directive on what the weaponry ought to be: disc jockeys, 'open line', or more of the same, hopefully better.

After discussions with a firm of broadcast consultants, Burt Brewster was brought in to raise the ratings. More than anyone else, he realized that his maximum period of grace was to be one year.

CRAK had been a member of what it called 'the Montreal Community', and nothing could better suggest the old image, for almost 30 years. Its economic fortunes had varied, although it had scored several outstanding news beats to earn the greatest number of news awards of any radio station in North America. A reason was the legendary Chuck Dorman — at one point a 'roving ambassador' news broadcaster who in the mid-thirties and war years had gained a succession of news-worthy interviews from Mussolini, Hitler, Laval, Chamberlain and, later, Churchill. He always seemed to be on the spot when news was breaking, allowing CRAK listeners to get the feel of crisis in Europe whether it was snipers firing in Vienna as Hitler arrived in the city, or the sound of German bombs at Dunkirk as the Allied troops waded to the small boats. The broadcasts were naturally repeated across Canada and the States, giving CRAK a fantastic news reputation.

The station and its new television subsidiary CRAK-TV, had been purchased five years earlier by General Cosmetics Corporation, headquartered in Montreal. They were the largest of their kind in the country. General Cosmetics had moved into broadcasting as a result of a Board decision to have a ready-made advertising vehicle in it's flagship market.

While the station had been in difficulties prior to the General Cosmetics purchase because of its old-fashioned 'community service' format against the 'with it' trend of the newer, 'swinging' stations, the more pertinent financial reason was that more private stations had been granted licences to operate in Montreal. Altogether, there were now 12 stations in the total market, compared to six in slightly smaller Toronto. Six of the stations were French-language, two were multi-lingual or bi-lingual, leaving four stations, including the CBC's radio entry, to fight it out.

When Brewster took over, CRAK was firmly bedded down in fourth spot. He began by changing the music policy from a middle-of-the-road 'smile on knees' type of sound to what was also known in the trade as the 'Chicken Forty' format, whereby a station would only play the first forty tunes sold that week in record stores. It didn't work. Mainly because CRUX had over a year's start, and when they weren't 'Trampling Town', as they now put it, they rocked the station. They knew how to 'dig' 'Chicken Forty'. It was their 'bag'. All their announcers were 'Rock Jocks' of the highest calibre. Each one did his 'thing' and did it very well.

CRAK's air personnel on the other hand were sepulchral by comparison, no matter how much they strained for the, to them, elusive sound of frenetic honey — a vital accompaniment for the wailing guitars and screaming simpers of the Fleshpots, Muckrakers, Cockroaches, Mossgatherers and other well known vocal groups of the day.

The trade had called the next rating "CRAK's Calamity." It showed that the few loyal listeners CRAK had before the programming change had now switched over to another middle-of-the-road station, or even to the CBC. The young adults, Glyn never did find out the difference between them and teenagers, were deliriously happy with CRUX, who programmed Rock'n' Roll to fit in with school and holiday time.

CRAK, all its life, had avoided controversy. If the station had an 'image' before Brewster's rock and roll, it was that of a staid and slightly severe old lady. A good newsroom with a better tradition. Little excitement. But words to watch now were merchandising, marketing, packaging, campaigns, promotions, contests. Get people listening to you. Somehow. If necessary, buy the bastards. If you understood these words and knew what to do about them, you had arrived.

The months raced by and Brewster's year was nearly over. The station was losing more and more. A high level conference was called in the General Cosmetics Boardroom to "clarify and assess the situation at CRAK Radio." Brewster would be in the dock facing a potentially hostile jury.

General Cosmetics Corporation had first been a chemical firm founded in the 1840's by Daniel Horton who was the great-grandfather of the present Chairman of the Board, President and Chief Executive Officer, Jonathan Horton. Although the firm name had been Horton and Son Chemicals Ltd., the decision to change the name was taken deliberately many years before when a chance cosmetics formula worked out in the chemical labs had resulted in cosmetics becoming the firm's major business. Since no Horton wished to have "Put on a beautiful Horton Face" thrown at customers in magazines or drugstores, the decision was made to call the firm General Cosmetics Corporation with "Arctic Mist" as the major brand name.

So General Cosmetics was a very, very conservative firm. Old Montreal English money. The Hortons were typical of the "old" families British immigrants encountered when first coming to the city. More British than the British, Jonathan Horton actually resented titled Englishmen who had come to Canada after the war for not being as British, as disparaging of the French-Canadians, as formal and as "loyal" as he thought they ought to be. Except for several French-Canadian regional product sales managers, Horton was proud of the fact that he had kept management in the hands of the "right" people as far as the cosmetics firm was concerned. On the other hand, sticking to his own rule that the individual management of the subsidiaries should be left in the hands of professional managers, he had never interfered with the employment practices of CRAK Radio and TV, or any of the other subsidiaries, some of them — especially the ones purchased in recent years — having a very distant relationship to the cosmetics business at best.

As far as the broadcasting subsidiary was concerned, Horton's title of President meant President for the purpose of fiscal responsibility only. Today, however, was such an occasion.

Horton was now concluding his careful financial review. He said by way of summation: "We must start therefore by working on a diagnosis, and having found the trouble, prescribe the right formula, as we would for any of our products that might be in trouble. Mr. Brewster, as you are in charge of CRAK on a day-to-day basis, would you begin?"

"Mr. Chairman," Brewster began formally, "CRAK right now's a bit like a sick child. As one who knows quite a bit about babies, and er, radio babes as well, ha ha, I'm reminded of the old saying that 'A baby is God's reason why the world should go on'".

Brewster's attempted show-business beginning fell flat. Horton remained expressionless, and the other members, following Horton's lead, simply stared ahead.

Brewster had started badly and he knew it. He realised now that he was to be the sole scapegoat. Instantly his mood changed from nervousness and fright to rage. Why the hell didn't they leave radio to people who knew it? Why the hell were they sitting there so smugly when they had to pull one of their own miracle working Vice-Presidents out of CRAK a year ago and put him where he belonged—drooling over lipstick? And why in hell's name didn't they at least titter at his joke? To Brewster they were a bunch of gutless, lifeless, corporation morons. What was this anyway? A goddam tribunal? Yeah, that's what it was. And he was in the dock. Fine. Well, he'd fight the unctuous looking bastards. He'd show 'em who was conducting his own defence. It had taken but a second or two for him to go from launch pad to orbit in the weightless void of extreme anger. He shook with suppressed fury and his hand trembled as he lit a cigarette.

"Now. Let's get the language straight for a start. I don't know about perfume and cosmetics. That's your business. But radio is my business. I've been in it all my working life." The Board's stiffening face muscles flicked sternly into place. Brewster knew it couldn't last long, but he'd enjoy it while he could. He soared on.

"The trouble with CRAK is mainly your fault. When I proposed an image breaking change, I meant exactly that. To fracture your precious 'Arctic Mist' optic completely. Because, and how I wish you'd get this between the ears, the image that sells perfume won't win the ratings battle for us. It might've up until very recently but not now. No sir. The ball game's changed. Listen to CRUX. What kind of goddam, excuse me Ma'am, what kind of image do you think they've got, eh? I'll tell you. Gutter radio. That's about their image. Now pay attention. What kind of ratings do they have? How much national business do they have? What does their P & L sheet show? Those are the questions — and now I'll give you the answers.

"Tops. Sold out. A big, big profit. How do we shape up against that lot — in every category? Alright, let's drop that one right where it is. Now then, when I made my deal at CRAK, some, but not all of you, were parties to the agreement. And for me the best part was the absolutely free hand you said I could have. But you haven't kept your word. You've broken your promise. Perhaps it was my fault. Maybe I should have just gone ahead and done it anyway. But then I guess you'd've stymied me with the bucks the same way you did with programming. You didn't give me half the scope I wanted."

There was no question that his Boardroom audience was transfixed. By shock.

"OK, now. When I talk about image breaking, I'm not speaking about any half measures. I mean total severance." He liked that. 'Total severance'. Good line. Right off the top too. "But we've only gone part of the way. And in radio that can be worse than not going any way at all. People don't know what we are any more. All we've done is to substitute rock' n'roll music for the bland middle of the road garbage you had on before. That's no good. Not on its own. You've got to dress the whole thing up. Package it. Put ribbons on. And by that I mean, in case you can't understand my language, you've got to get the talent to go with the format. How do you get the kind of people you want? Easy. With money. That's how. And you haven't given me a free hand with money. And if you won't give me the budget I want and won't even talk about it, then," and he lost control, "what the hell do you think I can do about it? Eh?

"Having those nice old company retainers playing 'Chicken Forty' is like asking Rembrandt to design an 'Arctic Mist' carton. But it isn't just the music. The biggest competition we and the others are facing is Trample. The guy, let's face it, is setting the market on its ear. He and that enterpreneur of his earn, or let's say make, with fees and commercial action — where they're sold out — over a hundred and fifty G's a year. And they've got sponsors fighting to get on. And when they do get on, they're just delighted to pay the hefty premium if he personalizes the stuff for them.

"Eighty-five bucks a throw, Ma'am, gentlemen. Now get that. Eighty-five green backs per. And you, you prefer not to have controversy? I don't have to tell you what our raté card looks like. Exactly like it should look. Cheap. Again, I suggest to you that I should have gone ahead. I should have spent your money. I should have gone way over budget. I'd have done you a favour. But in the meantime you'd've fired me just as you're intending to do right now I'll bet. But, and I'll tell you this for nothing, if you would've stuck with the shopping I could've done, you'd've been screaming for me to come back.

"Now, this talk show and controversy thing. There's nothing to beat it. It's skyrocketing all over the States and Canada. I'd love to get in on it. That, plus some hotshot rockjocks, plenty of money for contests, giveaways and promotions and man, would we go. You'd see it in six months. It's no good trying to play it any other way. I know. I've lived, eaten and slept the demography of this market ever since I came to Montreal. Ask the wife. Ask the kids." He decided it was now time to try a little sentiment. Ah, but that 'demography' had really got 'em. That's it — blind the bastards with science. He'd got it from an agency man the day before who said it was the current rage on Madison Avenue. 'Get the demography of the market first — then plan.' Demography.

"Do you people know", Brewster said heavily and nearly in a whisper, "do you know that I've only had supper at home with my family on Sundays in the time we've been in this market? Why? Because I've put everything I've got into the job. And I've risked alienating my family. And I'll tell you something else. They're up to here with it," and he saluted at his forehead, "they're fed up with the crazy hours I work. With the frustrations and the pressures. With my irritability. Touch wood, as far as I know, I haven't started an ulcer. Yet. I'm too scared to get checked and find out. I've put my all into this operation — for you. Question. How much have you helped me?"

It was strong and Brewster knew that he had delivered it

well. He lit another cigarette and watched as all eyes turned to the leader. No one but a fool would speak first now. At times like these the prudent kept quiet, kept watch and waited by the weather vane.

The Chairman had decided, some minutes earlier, that this was new. Very new. In forty years he'd heard nothing like it in the Boardroom. He'd noticed with his practiced eye that a few board members had come perilously close to losing their composures while Brewster was fulminating. That was something you learned never to do. With shareholders, directors, executives, staff. Composure, control, omnidirectional ears, eyes in the back of your head. That was the tool-kit. Out of his formidable earshot, General Cosmeticians called Horton 'The Silver Eminence'. He took command.

"We have heard a very direct and I may say, impassioned, account of Mr. Brewster's thinking in connection with CRAK. Personally I regret the er, somewhat inconsiderate tone that crept in now and then, but I haven't the slightest doubt that these indiscretions can be charged against the er, cut and thrust of debate — ha, ha." The Chairman cleared his throat as the laughter murmured round the table. Horton smiled paternally at Brewster.

"I don't really know what you're talking about, Mr. Chairman. I meant every word I said — and some I haven't said, begging the lady's pardon." An accomplished swearer with a huge repertoire, Brewster was annoyed that the woman had confined him, by her presence, to a very good, rather than brilliant performance. If only he could have tapped his rich arsenal of words . . . "In any case I haven't noticed any cut and thrust of debate. So far I've done all the talking. I'll tell you when it hurts."

Ah, now this was too much. The line had been reached.

"It would pain me Mr. Brewster," the Chairman said coldly, "if in this Boardroom we were to lose the opportunity for constructive discussion in favour of premature adjournment brought about by an urgent need to take a refresher course in elementary good manners." The table alerted. Bulleseye. This was it. Here was the rallying point.

"I propose now that we find ways and means of finding solutions. Mrs. Goggs?"

An oldish, sharp featured, beaky woman spoke from the

other end.

"Yes, well of course I don't really get much chance to tune into CRAK or any radio for that matter. Far too busy. With my social work and charities. But it does seem to me, it seems to me as a woman, that we should have a kind of woman's program — cooking, needlework, gardening, that sort of thing. After all, it is the women who listen surely."

"Thank you Mrs. Goggs. Yes. Mr. Snaith?" Here was the Vice-President in charge of purchasing.

"I think, Mr. Chairman, that we should hear the call letters CRAK far more. Maybe they could be sung. What do you call those things? Yes — that's it — jingles. Let's have some of those."

"Mr. Westall?"

"Yes, sir". Robert (Bob to his friends) Westall was the Controller, and a senior stanchion of the local Rotary.

"I must say that Mrs. Westall finds our present diet of, ah, pressure cooked music a little indigestible, but of course as one who keeps a finely tuned ear to the finances of the corporation, I know we must eschew personal tastes in favour of ah, the most popular, ah, menus."

Brewster stared up the table at him. That's it, you bloody fool, he shouted to himself. Now you've got it. Well done. But why the hell don't you just come out and say so? Because you'd be scared of filling up your pants — that's why. All you yesmanning bastards want out of this meeting is to make sure you come out of it smelling like an 'Arctic Mist' export line. Let the crap fly around my ears. He looked at Westall. A man with the highest qualifications and experience but obviously no guts. With a few of those he'd do well anywhere. But no, Brewster deducted, like so many others he preferred to shelter in the lee of a well kissed ass. He tuned back to the Board. The talk continued for half an hour. No decisions were made. Horton began to sum up.

"I think I can safely say that we are all cognizant of CRAK's major difficulties as er, outlined by Mr. Brewster. If he is correct, then clearly we have not the means to buy the tools. Mr. Westall and I have conferred thoroughly about the station's budget. We cannot afford to implement the General Manager's proposals. We must do the best we can with what we have."

"Mr. Chairman," Brewster interjected, "can you afford not

to buy my suggestions?"

"I see no point in going over old ground. Thank you Mrs. Goggs, Gentlemen, for attending." The Chairman left the Board-room and the others shuffled out of their seats.

.   .   .   .

Brewster drove back to the station. Although nothing had been said or even hinted, the Drom doubted very much that he was still employed. You just didn't perform like that in Board-rooms. The truth was unforgivable at the best of times, but when you showbizzed it up as he had done . . . man, oh, man.

He found a message on his desk. 'Call Mr. Westall at the plant immediately. Urgent.'

Hmm. Urgent eh? He must have gone over bigger than he realised. But then, why would Westall have to be the hatchet man? Surely this was work for either Patrick Holt, the Public Relations Vice-President, or Jonathan Horton himself. Well, they'd have to live with him a little longer. He'd go for coffee first. Ten minutes later he dialled the number.

"Mr. Westall? Brewster here. You called me."

"Yes, I did Burt. You don't mind if I call you that? Fine. Then make it Bob with me. I've been waiting for your call. Now listen. Can you and I have dinner to-night?"

Brewster was puzzled. Was it that painful? "Now, look er, Bob. You don't have to do that. I'm expecting it. Just say it — that's all. Do you want me to stay on for the month, or shall I take off now? No sweat either way. You call it."

The Controller's manner had changed. Less obsequious than he'd been at the meeting. Stronger and more definite. Brewster wondered what game he was playing. "Honestly Burt. You'd do me a great favour if you could. Sorry about the short notice, but you'll understand why. I won't say anymore on the phone. I took a chance and called my wife. She's expecting you. OK?"

"OK. Where and when?"

"Seven o'clock." And he gave an address in Hampstead.

At home, the Westalls were gracious and kind. Mrs. West-all had prepared a pleasant meal and after it, and some brief small talk, Westall took Brewster for cognac in his finished basement 'den'.

"Now, Burt. Everything I'm going to say to-night is by way of being off the record. The fact is that without causing any crises, we might just be able to do something. I read you loud and clear this afternoon. All I ask of you now is that you don't ask me why I didn't say what I felt at the meeting. In a nutshell you told us that in the face of intense competition from CRUX we'll simply go on losing unless we give the people what they want better than CRUX can give it to them. Right?"

"Absolutely."

"Essentially that means not just 'Top Forty' music but the presentation and frills to surround it. And controversy or talk show programming. Now here I must take you completely into my confidence — otherwise I'd be fired at once. You remember the Old Man saying this afternoon that he and I'd had all kinds of brain storming sessions about your budget? Well, that's stretching it a bit to say the least. Actually, he doesn't even know what your budget is. Let's assume that we can juggle some money around for you — but not enough to do everything you want. What would you suggest as a priority? I mean if we can't get the rock-jocks, as you call them, and the talk program as well, but only one of these things, how would you choose?"

"Hold it, Bob," Brewster was mellowing with the liqueur and beginning to like the man, "aren't you being a bit premature with a question like that? How can you be sure I haven't already been fired?"

"How can you be sure that you have?"

"You were there this afternoon weren't you?"

"Yes — so what?"

"Well you could hardly call my performance the kind that keeps jobs", Brewster said emphatically, and Westall smiled.

"Let's just say that you haven't been fired, Burt."

"In that case I'll answer your question. If we had budget for either proper Top Forty format or talk — I'd settle for talk."

"Do you have anyone in mind?" Westall asked him.

"Yes. Right here. In Montreal. Had him in mind some time ago."

"Who?"

"Tresilian."

"Sorry. Who?"

"Tresilian. Glyn Tresilian." Recognition slowly dawned on Westall's face. It fell noticeably.

"Oh, yes, Tresilian," Westall echoed and looked in his glass, "yes. You mean that fellow who's on the CBC sometimes? The English guy? Surely he wouldn't give Trample much trouble would he? I don't want to be negative now, but..."

"No. Right now, if I put him in the booth, he wouldn't give anyone trouble except himself. But he's got it. The talent. I just know goddam well he has. The raw material's there. The big question is whether he can take direction. If he can, I'll do the rest. I know what's wanted alright. We can take Trample."

"Do you know him? Have you met?"

"Who, Trample?"

"No, Tresilian."

"No, I've never met him. But I've seen his TV work a few times, and I've caught him now and again in the car radio. But here, believe me, I can tell. Damn it, that's my job. Judging potential talent. He needs milking — and that's one thing the CBC 'll never do."

"What about his voice? That accent? I suppose the CBC can get away with it because they don't have P & L sheets to worry about in the way we have — but Burt, wouldn't he bomb out — to use your words?"

"O.K. let's say, he did bomb. How far's he got to fall?"

"Yes, well there, I must say you've got me. You're saying we have nothing to lose anyway. Hmmm. Give me your glass," and he poured another drink.

"Frankly, Burt," Westall went on, "I can't see it. But then I'm not the expert. You are. Not that I've got anything against Englishmen personally. I was over there. During the war."

"Now, there you go. Bringing your own likes and dislikes into it. But I'll be more honest than you, though. I don't like limeys — never have. They come over here — I've seen the bastards — and in two minutes they think they own the place. But the very first goddam lesson you've got to learn in radio Bob is to forget you've got personal tastes of your own. If your individual preferences don't fit in with mass taste, and they hardly ever do, man.... you're dead."

"Ah, ah. But surely you're not saying that Tresilian's stuff is mass taste are you?"

"Of course I'm not. Not as he is at the CBC. In no way does he have anything but a very small limited appeal. But the point I'm trying to make is that he could skyrocket — if he could be trained for this kind of talk show. And I'm convinced of his possibilities."

"But why does it have to be English, ah, British raw material?"

"I'll tell you. Two reasons. No one's tried such a voice before. That should be enough. But the second's more important. He's got some depth and obvious intelligence. He's been all over the place. Sailor, I think. I heard him doing a talk on that the other day. And goddam interesting it was too. Also, if I'm any judge, I'd say his politics were quite a bit left of centre — which doesn't do any harm at all when you're going after the lunch pail guy's wife. Never mind the brief case set. You'll never get them to fill ratings ballots in. Grass roots radio, Bob. That's the only name the game's got." Brewster finished his glass.

Westall stroked his chin, and then asked, "Left wing you say. Wouldn't that come across as some sort of intellectualism? Now I think about it, I don't follow your other reasoning either. You're talking about the lunch pail trade. Tresilian, whenever I've seen him, sounded pretty professorial to me. Sorry, Burt — I don't get it."

"Goddam it Bob. How many times do I have to spell it out?" Brewster exploded, "all this stuff you're giving me is right, absobloodylutely right. But for God's sake understand what I'm saying. I'm simply telling you that I can mould one hell of a mass appealer out of the guy. And as he's not established in that sense, I can't see that he'd be too difficult over the money bit. I don't even know that he'd want to do it. This I don't know. Maybe he and I'd hate each other's guts on sight. Maybe a hell of a lot — but there's only one way to find out what's maybe and what's what. Right?"

The next day, Tresilian finished on the live CBC afternoon program he appeared on occasionally. The interview had been with a drug addict. He picked up the message sheets, noted a good deal of listener reaction, and dialled the 'Please Call' marked urgent.

"Hello, my name's Tresilian, you called me...."

"Oh, good. Look Glyn we haven't met. But I've watched and listened to you a lot. My name's Brewster. Burt Brewster. I'm General Manager at CRAK Radio. I'd like it very much if we could meet. How about lunch or dinner sometime soon? I think you might be interested in an idea I have. What about it?"

"Yes, I see." Glyn tried sounding blasé. "That's very thoughtful of you Mr. Brewster. I..."

"Call me Burt."

"Don't see why not."

"Great. What about to-night? If you're free. A drink or three and a mess of dinner." Tresilian thought for several moments. Certainly he had no engagements, but one wasn't really supposed to be available at this short notice. But he'd never liked the game very much and had practically stopped trying to play it. He now broke an important rule.

"Yes, I'm perfectly free this evening and I'd like to meet, Mr. Brew, er, Burt."

"Great Glyn, just great. Let's make it for cocktails first at five thirty. 'Auberge du Ciel'. I know what you look like. I'll find you. Don't worry. Till this evening then. Bye."

He'd only been in the 'Auberge du Ciel' once. And that had been when the Wooffendens had come over with Michael for a visit. Sir Timothy had paid the bill. It was fictitiously expensive. Like other restaurants at the summit of Montreal's skyscrapers, the view at night was beautiful with the mountain on one side and the broad St. Lawrence on the other...between the lights of the financial district high-rise buildings to the south-east and the competing office towers close by on all sides. About the only people, it seemed, who could afford to buy it were the expense-account-padded advertising agency executives. Glyn had heard somewhere that the prices had become so disturbing that several of the big Toronto companies, their accountants often handled tabs of $150 meals for two, had ordered their sales personnel to clear special permission before entertaining clients there. Needless to say, Tresilian was impressed by Brewster's choice.

He greeted him heartily at the bar.

"Boy, it's good to meet you finally face-to-face, Glyn. I've admired you for a long time. Come on — let's get with the sauce".

They managed to get a corner table from where Montreal, in evening sparkle, looked its very best — just as Glyn had remembered it the last time. A waiter brought two large powerful Manhattans. 'Auberge du Ciel' was filling to capacity.

"Now look, Glyn," Brewster began, "I'm not one for small

talk and I don't think you go much for that stuff either. OK. First, I'm damn glad to be speaking to you. I won't tell you what led up to it. But I've just come through one hell raiser of a time with my principals. You know them eh? You married? Oh, well then maybe you're not familiar with "Artic Mist". General Cosmetics Corporation. Didn't you know they own CRAK Radio and TV?"

"I'm afraid not, Burt. But I'll tell you this and I hope you won't be offended — of all the television commercials I've seen I think "Artic Mist's" the most horrible in a pretty bloody awful league. Ghastly, insulting crap." Tresilian said with considerable satisfaction. He liked this colossal man. He talked like a sailor. No horse-trough about him. And what magnificent drinks he ordered.

Brewster beamed at him.

"Put it there old buddy,"and he swallowed Tresilian's hand with his own, "you're so goddam right. Same again please, waiter. OK, Glyn. You must've heard of Denny Trample. Yes? Fine. I want to talk to you to-night about the possibility of you going on against him. Oh, I don't mean minute for minute — that'd be crazy. But a morning slot. That's where he's strongest and we're weakest. I'm talking the nine to eleven spot. Think you could do it?"

They both drank. Glyn grinned. He'd listened to Trample a lot recently — ever since Mrs. O'Leary had rebuked him for working at the CBC. He was fascinated not so much by the Trample touch as by the limitlessness of the idea. Potentially, after hearing Trample's show for a while, he saw such programs as being the ultimate in communication between people. It was that simple.

"Well now Burt," with the second punchy Manhattan well on its way he was contentedly relaxed, "there are times when I think I can do anything. And then again there are times when I don't think that. Certainly at this rate of double Manhattans, I know damn well I can do it. Did you ever think I couldn't?"

"Now you got me boy. OK, let's agree right now that you'll come to the station to-morrow. Ten o'clock and we'll talk for real. That's if we don't get too loaded to-night. Anyway, that's all I wanted to get out of you this time around. Fine Glyn. Great. Now let's call it fun time."

Many, many king sized Manhattans later, and after the cooks had left 'Auberge du Ciel' for earth, the Drom decided it was time for a 'mess of dinner'. They floated down to street level and ate enormous tender steaks on St. Catherine street.

"Coffee? Hell no, Miss. We're in the middle of starting — not finishing. Let's have a couple of beers. That was great steak by the way. Tell the Chef will you honey? You know Glyn, you're a good guy. You're a goddam limey — but you're a good guy. I can tell that. I normally don't like you limey bastards. My old Dad, he was a clergyman you know. He used to tan my ass for saying that. But you're OK. You're a good fella. What's the time?"

"About 1.30."

"Good. Should be starting about now. Let's go and see those broads. No no. Don't get me wrong. I don't screw around. But I like to see the sexy little bastards. Nice place too. New craze called 'Topless.' How're you feeling?"

"Fine, Burt. Just fine. Having a hell of a time. I love to tie one on now and again. You must work for good people Burt. Paying for an evening like this. I can almost forgive them for those rotten commercials."

They left the restaurant.

"What time did you say it was?"

"About 1.30 now."

"OK, tell you what. There's lots of time for that Topless bit. We'll go to Foch's first," and the Drom led the way to one of the city's best supper clubs. Foch's was one of the few remaining night spots in Montreal capable of booking the big names. They were in time for Jean Hogan's last show. Boy, she can really belt them out, Glyn said to himself. But he wasn't much of a popular music fan. The fact that he'd taken part in several CBC serious programs was no accident. Funny thing, he loved beer and hardly cared what he ate or drank, but asked for the world's best in music.

They had three more drinks apiece. Then they took a cab to the 'Heaven'n'Hell'. This was Brewster's place for Topless Go-Go dancing. The Drom certainly had a sense of style. The place reeked of being 'in'. There was an expensive look to match the club name, and furniture of the same genre. The patrons looked very much a part of the costly scene.

Nice to be a radio station general manager and have to keep

up with the latest entertainment trends, Glyn reflected, wondering whether he ought to be impressed or not. The heavy-set, dignified Maitre'D led them to a table near the stage, and for the first time Glyn saw the young, tanned and shapely girls, some of whom were said to be 'putting themselves through college,' their nipples covered with minute and near transparent pasties, all the while contorting to the earsplitting barrage of rock and roll. Tresilian couldn't take his eyes off their bouncing breasts and spilled his drink on the table.

"You clumsy bastard, Glyn — what the hell..."

"Sorry, Burt. Wasn't looking what I was doing. Why should I? Those tits must be some of the best. Burt — I'm loaded, old son. What a bloody fine evening it's been. Here's to General Mists or whatever they're called. Very generous people. I think..."

"Aw, cut that crap out, Glyn. You might be seeing general mists, but I see plenty of General Cosmetics — right here. Look — see that bald guy with the blond broad? Yeah, by the cage over there. He's big at the plant. That's Ted Bowen, Vice President in charge of Export Sales. And that hard faced job's not his wife."

"Really?"

"Really."

"See that table over there? By the wall? All highly respected members of our community", and he chuckled. "There's a charity chairman, Fitzhenry Hughes; that's his wife by the way. He phones Horton to get his group free time on the radio and TV station. And the guy next to him's Jacques Lafleche, a big realtor and also a City Councillor. Guess he's with that haughty looking broad. She comes from a loaded old establishment Montreal family. Looks cold eh? Think her married name was McHenry. They tell me she's a tigress in the sack. Good tits I'd say. Show's em too. Goes to every goddam ball there is. Anyway, If Lafleche's out with her, it shows there's hope for a French-English partnership yet, eh Glyn?"

They stayed in the 'Heaven 'n Hell' until dawn. Then they had breakfast in all night restaurant downtown. It was clear to both men that regardless of anything else they were born drinking companions. At sea, Glyn had found that a night's revelry in port was an infallible way of judging a shipmate's qualities. Tonight Brewster had passed the test. Tresilian admired his capacity and control.

By the time they got taxis home in the early morning sunlight, Glyn felt that he knew a great deal about CRAK, 'Arctic Mist', the Silver Eminence, Bob Westall, ratings, budgets, 'chicken forty' formats, pacing, buying the bastards, grabbing the donkeys, mesmerising the broads.

He flopped in his bed, and waited for the room to stay still. Then he passed out and had a frightening dream in which he was being pushed off a lofty building. Terrified and sweating, he woke up just in time. His heart was pounding and he knew he'd sleep no more.

He shocked himself with a dead cold shower, dressed and walked up Cote des Neiges to the Look-Out. It was half past seven when he got there and looked down on the city below. All over the island, the streets began to fill and clog with cars.

The Drom was in better shape than Glyn. More likely to be in training for this sort of thing, he thought.

"Hi Glyn. How are you boy?"

"Terrible. I can hardly stand up."

"Just stick it out for an hour or so — then we'll go and lick a wound. That'll put you right." The Drom motioned to a chair. His desk was cluttered with hillocks of paper.

"I won't be too long Glyn. Just have to go through these goddam grief sheets." It sounded funereal.

"Grief sheets?"

"Yeah. Holy evidence of why operators think announcers should be fired and vice versa. Look at this crap. Here read it." Glyn ran his bloodshot eyes over the barely legible scrawl, obviously written under angry pressure. 'Announcer failed for seventh time to wait for end cue to cartridge commercial 109'. '11 p.m. newscast 40 secs. late'. 'Announcer missed three station I.D.'s as logged at 9.15, 10.30 & 11.45 p.m.' 'No weather report for sign off news'.

"I don't mind people playing politics with bits of paper. You've got to expect it in any operation. But this stuff. It's petty. Real small. So what I do with this garbage", and he went on writing furiously with a ball point pen, "is to give the whole damn lot of them a rocket. Announcers, operators, supervisors. The whole rotten mishmash."

Relieved, his massive face took on an expression that was

almost beatific. He glanced at some letters, scribbled notes on them, put these in his secretary's tray and said, "OK, let's go. I'll show you round the sweat shop."

Brewster introduced Glyn to a lot of people. Then Tresilian met Studio 4 for the first time. Here was where they'd lick a wound and talk turkey. Solemnly Glyn was introduced to all waiters, kitchen staff and M. Hurtubuise, the licensee.

"Take a good look at him guys. You'll be seeing a lot of him. How about four to start eh?"

After a pull at his first beer, Glyn felt much better. Then they began to talk about money.

"You see Glyn, let's face it. I've got my neck stuck out with you as it is. It's one hell of a risk, this business of you doing a talk show for us. But at least I can get you on the air. Now at first you'll be bloody awful. Nervous, inexperienced, pressured. All these things'll get hold of you and you'll sound bad. Very bad. No question about it. Now the thing that bugs me is how much pressure I'll get from that goddam cosmetics factory. And whether I can fight 'em off until you settle down to the good job I just know you'll be able to do after about ten weeks. That's the bit. Whether I can hold the bastards off for the time you need — and I need."

He shook his head. "That's going to be a tough one. I know damn well my phone'll be ringing off the hook after you've done a couple of shows. They're not used to radio at all; they're in scent and powder. And then there'll be the curves that'll come once we open those phones. You won't know what to do about them. But they'll come. They'll come for sure. I'll help you all I can. But when you're on the air you're on your own." The Drom looked gloomily into his beer. Then he set about it with a will.

Glyn wondered. Was this a prelude to reasons why he would be asked to start with payments per show far less than he was getting at the CBC? He'd soon find out.

"So you see Glyn, I just can't start talking fancy figures. Not now anyway. Now, if you do the job — pull the miracle — then it'll be Riviera time and champagne. But for the present, it's tavern and draught beer. Sure you'll take a cut. I know that. But you've got to look ahead. Do you have that much to lose where you are now anyway? I don't think so. You've pretty well blocked yourself out it seems to me."

Here of course Tresilian knew that Brewster was right. No one knew this better than he did.

"Alright Burt — anything you say. I don't feel like haggling today. With the head I've got, just breathing's a hell of job. I'll give it a whirl. What do you want me to do?" They agreed on a per show amount that was far below his CBC stipends and on the proviso that there was no guarantee of anything more than day to day employment. Glyn appreciated the Drom's honesty here: that he mightn't be able to resist the principals' pressures for a minimum ten weeks probation.

"What this means Glyn is that you don't have a grace period. I might have to pull you off just like that. God, I hope not. But we might as well face up to the possibility. Now if that happens how would you stand with your CBC work?"

"Oh, I don't know Burt. They've always treated me very fairly; let's cross that bridge when we come to it."

"Fine. Now I can't pay you for this but try to get around as much as you can in the next two weeks. You know — hospitals, courts, police stations and all that jazz. Hell it'll be in your own interest. I'd like you to start with the opening show on — let's see," and he fished for a pocket diary, "oh yes, here it is, the first Monday next month. That's in just over a fortnight. Feel all right about it?"

"As well as I can feel."

"Great. Now when we finish our beer, we'll go back and I'll put you on to the studio supervisor. I'll tell him to expect you at any time and any number of times in the next couple of weeks and you can bug the hell out of him getting familiar with all those buttons, and gismos, and rinkydinks and all that technical crap like relay and delay systems. Actually it's easy, the mechanical stuff that is, but be damn sure you know it before you go on the air. You'll have enough on your plate without worrying about what button or switch you've got to hit. Find out the operator you'll be working with. Get to know him. Kiss his ass. Buy him a drink. Because those guys can screw you so fast or get you out of trouble so fast it isn't even funny. That's the most important thing of all. Make damn sure he likes you. Four beers here please." The Drom tore out a sheet of paper from an envelope and started making notes. "We've got to find a name for this donkey show. Got any ideas?"

"How about 'Crakkerjack Line'?"

"How do you spell it?"

"Two k's."

Brewster belched.

"O.K. you've got yourself a name. Can't beat that. Great. Let's think now. Promotion. Next week you'd better come in and cut one or two tapes in your own voice. You know — 'This is Glyn Tresilian. Join me on Monday for a brand new audience participation program — CRAK's Crakkerjack line, where if you have a telephone, you have a radio station.' That kind of thing. Work out something yourself. I suppose we'd better get something in the papers as well. But I don't want to break it too soon. We'll have a hard enough job as it is warding off the 'too late copy cat' bit."

"Is all the physical equipment in good working order — these relays and so on that you were talking about just now?"

"Yeah, but thanks for reminding me," and the Drom wrote away, "check telephone company re conference line. I'll explain that. Let's say you're into an argument about, oh hell, the goddam pill for example, and some broad calls and says she used to use it but stopped when a friend of hers got ulcers. And she believes that it's an ulcer cause. Here's what you do. Call somebody; an expert. You'll get the run around but finally you'll probably end up with a doctor who's prepared to say something. While you're working at getting him, put the broad on hold. Then after you've got him, hit the 'conference' button and that automatically connects the woman on your regular phone line and the doctor or whoever it is you've got on the conference hot line. They can hear each other and speak between themselves and with you and the whole shebang goes on the air.

"That way, you get the informed opinion you want — but even more important — you're using the most vital thing of all — participation. Now you'd better get used to that word, Glyn. Because I'll be hitting you with it every day until you don't think a newscast is any damn good unless a listener's reading part of it. Dig?'

"Dig."

"I hope so. Because if you don't dig that you're dead. You see with this talk show thing you've either got a winner or a complete bomb. It isn't just the fact of opening the 'phones to the public. That alone isn't going to do it. It's the way you broker the talk.

"Look at Trample. I'm surprised you didn't bring this up. He doesn't use all that much participation. But then he's unique enough in himself. He only needs the phones for a cue — doesn't matter what the subject is. Then he takes off and the caller's had the course. Don't get me wrong now but I've got to say it straight. He's brilliant and experienced. You're not. Yet. That's the point. Not yet. Finish your beer. Let's go."

On the short walk back to the station, the enormity of the job suddenly filled Glyn with terror. Apart from the dangers of program content, there were all those other hurdles. Microphone technique, pacing, timing, balance; to say nothing of the mechanical and technical co-ordinations that the Drom had dismissed so airily. Near the door, Brewster stopped.

"From here on in Glyn, I want you to promise me one thing. Don't listen any more to Trample or any other open line shows — from the States or anywhere else. You'll be tempted to, but don't. For obvious reasons. There's no disc jockey way of doing this kind of thing. Basically you stand or fall on your own personal style. You're dead if you try to copy someone else's. Come to my office now and I'll dictate a memo to you confirming everything we've agreed."

CHAPTER 5

In spite of everything operator John McFadden tried to do to help him, Tresilian's first program 'bombed' so badly that it surpassed by far even the Drom's most pessimistic estimates. Fumbling and dithering, by 11 o'clock Tresilian was soaked in what he later knew to be 'flop sweat'. The first call — about bad ventilation in the Montreal Transport Commission buses seemed to be as big a problem as the Metro was later. He dealt with it fatuously.

"Perhaps you could open the windows?"

"That's the whole point you idiot — there aren't enough windows. What do you think I'm talking about?" And so on until the complete ruination.

"What did you say your name was?"

"Tresilian. Glyn Tresilian."

"Tre what?"

"silian."

"Well you sound like a silly bumbling fool to me. Now listen, what's happened to that station CRAK? Have they been sold or something?"

"Er, yes there has been a change of er, er,", hell what was the word, blast he couldn't find it; "er, yes a change of management." No use.

"Management or ownership?"

"Er, yes sorry sir. I meant to say ownership."

"Well that's completely different isn't it — or don't you know the difference?"

Terror had taken up all his mind space and so there was no room for the curative blast of rage that he needed as a life-line. Instead, there was a pause for several seconds of dead air as no sound came from the studio end of the line.

In the control room, McFadden was waving his arms in all directions — at the same time going through the motion of cutting his throat. In a spasm of clarity Glyn thought he might take that advice. Unfortunately this was a signal that Tresilian didn't know. And what McFadden was saying through his urgent mime was that Glyn should 'cut' off the caller on the line and then let the operator take control so that he could get a commercial on the air giving the fiasco respite for sixty seconds.

McFadden acted instantly. A veteran, who knew disaster when it came, he flew out of the control room into the studio, switched off Glyn's microphone, cut off the phone call, dashed back to his console board and turn tables, reached for the first record he could find, cued it in and filled CRAK's air with music. He hit the talk back button and spoke to Tresilian.

"Phew. OK, Glyn — relax. This'll go for over two minutes. Give us a chance to get sorted out a bit. Now it's none of my damn business and sure as hell I'm no producer but if I were you, until you settle down, just cut these curves off. Right off. Don't give 'em a chance. Hit that 'off' button. I'll try to screen as much as I can but the bastards'll still get through. I was bleeding for you just now. Try to keep your cool — and don't let these clowns rattle you. Remember — you've got control. Not them. I'll cue you any time you're ready — or we'll let the music finish. Whatever you say. I'll just check these calls on the line. It'll work out fine. You'll see."

"Thanks, John. Might as well get back into it sooner than later — so any time you like."

McFadden spoke briefly to the callers, asked them to wait, faded down the music with the pot on the console face making the necessary five second allowance for the delay system, raised his right hand and pointed to Tresilian for his cue.

"Crakkerjack line, can I help you?"

"Yes — take off and go back where you came from, ha, ha, ha."

The juvenile hung up and Glyn didn't know what to do about the dialling tone. It was loud and continuous and sounded like a stuck car horn. McFadden to the rescue again. More music. More reassurance from the other side of the glass.

"Crakkerjack line, can I help you?" he tried again.

"Yes?" bawled a strident female, "do you mind telling me whether this is an open line program or a music show?" The faint light of a little inspiration. "Certainly madam. We've had a few technical problems and had to play some music while the necessary adjustments were being made."

"Is that so? Do you call that garbage music? What's happened to the good music we used to hear? Like Frank Sinatra, Andy Williams, Dean Martin and those guys? The way you CRAK people are going you won't have any listeners left at all. And I'm one you won't be having after I hang up —which is right now." This time at least Glyn knew what to do about the dialling tone and was actually able to take another call without the catastrophe of a musical bridge. But like everything that day it was negative.

Brewster, who hadn't slept the night before, drove aimlessly around the Lakeshore road. He had deliberately got himself 'lost' until after Tresilian had finished. And man had he finished. He listened to his car radio in agony for the first half hour after which he could stand it no longer. He drove into a clearing on the lake front, parked, and switched off both car and Tresilian. Then he hung his head in his hands and cried like an elephantine baby.

Luckily the spot was secluded so there were no passersby to witness the grotesque spectacle of an enormous man shaking and sobbing with grief. To make it worse, in his tiredness and pre-occupied worry, the Drom had forgotten handkerchiefs on this ill fated morning and was obliged to use an oily rag to wipe the rivers of tears from face, hands, and dash-board. And then suddenly the blubbing turned to laughter. Loud, uncontrollable, maniacal, hysterical. It came in torrents.

"Oh, God," he gasped, "what I wouldn't give to see Horton right now. He must be going through all the colours to purple. 'Watch it carefully now, Mr. Chairman, sir'."

Brewster fell helplessly to the floor on the passenger side wedging himself between the seat and facia. Convulsed, he shook for several minutes and gradually regained control. He felt wonderful. Timing it accurately, he reached his office at precisely 11.05 a.m.

Nothing mattered now. He'd be very happy to take Horton's call. After which it would be a pleasure to call the mover. One thing — they hadn't been in town long enough to feel any unsettling when they'd go to that job in Winnipeg he could have any time.

"Morning Nellie" he greeted his secretary cheerfully.

"Good morning Mr. Brewster. I've put the mail on your desk. Nothing very pressing."

"Thanks. Chairman call yet?"

"No. At least I didn't get any message. Shall I check the switchboard?"

"Yup. You'd better."

"You were expecting him to call sir?"

Brewster leafed through some letters. He looked up at the pleasant, mildly attractive girl.

"What do you think, Nellie?"

She smiled sympathetically and went out. For all his bluster, noise and roughness, something she could never equate with a manse background, Nellie Porter liked her boss. And boy did he ever have problems right now. She came back with coffee in a plastic cup. She wished they had somewhere to make it properly instead of having to rely on that machine.

"No, Mr. Brewster, they've heard nothing from the Chairman or any one at the plant this morning. Shall I . . .?"

"No, Nellie, you shall not. File this junk will you? And on these — the answer's 'no'. Get some copies made of this Engineer's report — usual distribution. Oh, nip out to the board again and get me a phone sheet on this morning."

"You mean on Mr. Tres . . ."

"Yes — that's exactly what I mean". Hmm. Funny that Horton or Westall hadn't called already. Probably taking longer than expected to get over it. But just wait. Another hour or so. At the most. And then some dung would hit some fans. He wondered whether he and Bob Westall could share the same mover. Cut costs a little that way.

"Right, Nellie. How bad?" Brewster asked without looking up from the paper work on his desk.

"Quite bad I'm afraid. A great many calls and all complaints. They said they were either switching over to CRUX or that they just wouldn't listen to radio any more.

"How many?"

"117 up to now."

"OK, Nellie. Thanks. Find Tresilian for me will you? Ask him to come here right away." 117 eh? He didn't think that number would have been tuned in. Surprising. Oh well, it didn't matter. They'd obviously lost the whole goddam lot now anyway.

Ten minutes passed. Then quarter of an hour. No action at all. Where the hell was everybody? Where had Nellie disappeared? And Tresilian? No calls. Nothing.

Finally, his secretary returned. She'd obviously been running.

"Mr. Brewster, sorry I've been so long" and she caught her breath, "but I've looked everywhere for Mr. Tresilian. It seems he's left. I checked with John McFadden but he doesn't know where he is. He drives an old black car doesn't he?"

"I dunno. Haven't seen it."

"Well I'm sure I saw him getting out of it last week. Anyway I checked in the parking lot and it wasn't there."

Brewster's phone rang. Ah, here it was now. Horton or Westall or both maybe. He might as well be brusque.

"Yes, hello. Brewster speaking."

"Burt?"

"Ah, there you are Glyn," he waved Nellie away, "Where the hell have you been? We sent search parties out for you."

"Sorry, Burt. I've just got back. I honestly couldn't get away soon enough. It hurts like hell to say this — but I'm obviously not your man. I didn't realise until I got on the air what it was all about. I wouldn't get the hang of it in a million years. It just isn't for me. I don't care too much about that. But I feel terrible about the fool I must have made of you today."

"Well, I tell you Glyn. I don't know how much of a fool you made of me because I only heard a quarter of it. Couldn't take any more. Switched off at 9.30. Hang on a minute. Be right back." Brewster left the phone to answer a knock at the door. It was a man from one of the advertising agencies still using CRAK. Glyn could easily hear the conversation.

"Oh, hi Don. Come on in."

"Hi, Burt. Here's that Stephenson copy. Can you get a tape out for me today? Good. Then I'll try and get it approved by the end of the week. Hey, what was that God awful mess you had on this morning eh?"

Tresilian heard the squeegy sound of the Drom's palm on the mouth piece. A few seconds later, Brewster spoke into the phone again.

"Fine sir, I'll attend to that at once. But leave your number so that I can reach you if there's any change. Yup. OK. Got it.

Bye."

Glyn knew things were bad — but so bad that they had to use code? He brewed some coffee on his apartment kitchen stove.

The trouble was, he thought to himself, two fold. He couldn't, so soon after burning them, try to reconstruct his CBC bridges. Secondly, having made a complete mess of it on radio, he'd suffer the extra embarrassment of being recognized through his TV exposure. Word of the debacle would very soon become a joke — especially in the trade.

.   .   .   .

As he brooded with his coffee, and waited for the call, he'd never been closer to the notion that maybe after all it was time to swallow hard and accept Sir Timothy's job offer. Michael was still his complete responsibility; and the way things were going he doubted that he'd get out of the Wooffenden's debt. He re-read the boy's letter he'd received last Saturday. He was reading and writing quite well now. And doubtless, Tresilian thought, talking better than his father too.

> Wooffenden Hall, Nr. Chester,
> Cheshire,
> England.

Dear Daddy,

Grandmama and Mrs. Southcombe both say that spring and summer will soon be here and then I can go swimming. We have three days holiday for Easter. Grandpapa and I played badminton last Saturday. I beat him easily. He says I'm much too fast for him. I think I am too. When you come here again soon you and I will play. I don't expect I can beat you though Daddy.

Have you been to that smashing restaurant at the top of the building again? I thought it was super the way we seemed to be flying with the aeroplanes high up in the sky. Gosh, I'd hate to fall down all that way, wouldn't you?

I'm getting on quite well at school although I hate arithmetic. Did you like arithmetic? Have you been on the television today? I tell the chaps at school about you being on the radio and TV. One of the chaps in my form is called "Mr. Know-all." He thinks he knows everything and says of course he's seen you on TV and heard you on the radio because it all bounces off the telstar and satellites. I told him it's too far from Canada and anyway what was your name? He said Tresilian and I said what Tresilian and then he blushed and guessed and said Michael Tresilian of course. And then I jolly well knew he was a liar. I like Canada Daddy. Any chance I can go there and be with you? I hope so very much. Please tell me as soon as you can. Saunderson, who is the same age as me went all the way to Singapore last summer hols on his own. So I am old enough to come to Montreal. Is it true that everybody speaks French there? I can't really remember. Grandpapa says Canada is a young country but I don't know how young. You must know so please tell me. When will you come in the plane again? Soon I hope.

Mrs. Southcombe says I have to say my prayers and go to bed now. We had chicken and blancmange for supper. I will write another letter quickly. Yours should come any day now. I would like to get one every day and told the postman so. He is a nice man and laughed and said if you don't write every day, he would. But I think he was joking. Good-night Daddy. I hope everything is alright for you.

Your loving son,
Michael

He tore up the envelope and put the letter with all the others he'd had from his son — in a special binder. Little did Michael realise at that moment, Glyn thought, how close his father was to phoning for an air line reservation there and then. One way.

But then, that, however you looked at it, would definitely be a form of running away. And when he woke up that morning he had no such intentions. He knew a bit about setbacks—but did they have to be so publicly embarrassing? Perhaps Brewster just wouldn't bother to call at all. Couldn't blame him really. Probably thought it was kinder this way. He wanted to drive down to the waterfront, park on a wharf near Jacques Cartier bridge and take that walk he liked so much to Victoria Pier and back. But he'd better not. Just in case Brewster called. An hour later the telephone rang.

"Hi, Glyn, Burt here. Look, sorry about all that gobbledygook just now but I had to deal with an agency guy. God knows he's about the only one we've got left so I didn't want to blow it."

"That's OK. Burt, it doesn't matter."

"How're you feeling boy? A bit down eh?"

"Yes, I guess you could say that."

"Well it's easy to say this I know, but no amount of sweating by you, me or anyone else is going to undo what's done. This morning's history — and you can't rewrite it. It's happened. It's flown. Gone. For ever. Can't bring it back. So the hell with it. That's all."

Glyn smiled. He envied the Drom's powerful direct turns of phrase.

"Yes, I suppose you're right."

"Yeah, now listen. This is what's fazing me. So far there's been no sound from anyone at the plant. Can't figure it out at all. I thought Westall at least would have yelled by now. Or someone. Maybe you put the whole lot of 'em in hospital."

Glyn, who neither needed nor understood the humour at this particular time, replied testily, "Why not call a few emergency departments? Then at least you'd know what's keeping them. I only hope Blue Cross'll take care of the bills — because I won't be able to."

"Ha, ha, ha," and Brewster was roaring with laughter, "that's good Glyn. Really good. But," and he went into paroxysms again, "but why the hell couldn't you do it on the air this morning?" The lunatic side of the whole thing suddenly caught Tresilian too and he became infected by the Drom's merriment. They both choked and spluttered for a minute, after which Brewster described his morning in the car. This reduced Glyn to gibberish. It took some time for a return to normal.

"Look Glyn, if I don't hear anything by mid afternoon, let's assume it's safe to go again tomorrow. Will you be in? Yes? OK. Let's leave it like that. But if they don't call it'll be as big a miracle as the reason why Hitler didn't invade after Dunkirk. One thing we've got going for us. You've got the worst show of your life behind you. It just wouldn't be humanly possible to bomb like that again. We'll play it by ear. Bye."

Five o'clock came and went and still no one from General Cosmetics had called Brewster about Tresilian's appalling debut. The Drom swore that to his dying day he'd never know the reason.

.   .   .   .

Tresilian tried again the next day. After a week, he had

graduated from the impossibly bad to the very bad. And there was still no word from CRAK's principals. During the second week the Drom joined him in the studio giving encouragement and guidance by visual hand signs and hurriedly scribbled notes. Especially hurtful were the negative comparisons to Trample that listeners enjoyed airing on the show. While Glyn tried valiantly to raise interest in municipal reform, library facilities and so on, Trample would blast away all day at a specific item of local graft, uncovered by a listener, cajoling mayors and police chiefs on the phone for hours.

A month passed and a first ray of hope dawned. But after Tresilian had been on the air for two months an important rating survey showed CRAK's position to be so low that at ten o'clock in the morning on a Monday through Friday average, the midway point of 'Crakkerjack line', a sickening horizontal stroke indicated that Glyn's listeners were so few as to be unaccountable. And this in prime time. Such returns would be permissible late at night on a small country station perhaps — but not in Canada's biggest market during the rich mid-morning hours.

Even though the two had nothing in common by way of background, views of life and tastes, except in beer, Brewster and Tresilian were becoming close friends. In many ways this rating news was worse than the disaster of the first show. There really seemed to be some promise showing at last. There was something now — something to lose. They went to studio 4 for beer.

"I dunno, Glyn. I just don't know. I've been on the canvas for a few nine counts in my time — but I think it has to be ten and out now."

"What about Trample's figures?"

"Up. Right up."

"Everywhere?"

"Yup."

They drank lugubriously. There wasn't much conversation. And none of the life saving hysterical laughter that had given so much balm before.

"Look Burt. Let me save you one job anyway. Obviously I can't go on. I've been going for three months now and . . ."

"Two months."

"Three, what . . ."

"Two — when the rating was taken."

"Well I don't think it makes any difference. It's got to be a nose dive situation all the way so . . ."

"Hold it. OK. I know what you're going to say but don't bother your ass about it one little bit. I'm too old and ugly for all that stuff. I wouldn't give it a second thought. I'd fire you like that. Would have done it long ago but for the fact that I still think — and you can believe it or not — that you can do the goddam job. So however crazy it looks, I'm still not going to move until they do — at the plant. But we'd better not kid ourselves. This time they have to. Come on — drink up. Let's get back. A spy told me Westall and Horton've been huddled over their copy of the book all morning."

Nellie met them at the door to Brewster's office.

"Ah, there you are sir — hello, Mr. Tresilian. I have a message for you Mr. Brewster. The Chairman and Mr. Westall would like you to call them as soon as you can. In the Chairman's office. They want to have a three way conference. Shall I get them for you?"

"Yup, go ahead Nellie. Sit down Glyn. Pick up that other phone but for God's sake don't cough or make a racket. Might as well relax and enjoy it. Here's a pad. If you think of something jot it down and pass it over. Just as well to have two heads at our end too."

Glyn was on the point of asking the Drom whether this was cricket. But he brought up sharply when he remembered that what was de rigeur at Lords would be thrown out at Yankee Stadium — and vice versa. Different games altogether.

"Pick it up now — before she gets them on the line. Otherwise they'll hear the click." There was a short tinkle and then Nellie.

"There you are gentlemen, you're through now."

"You can say that again Nellie," the Drom tried to mutter to himself.

"What was that Mr. Brewster?"

"Nothing Mr. Horton. Just saying something to my secretary. Good afternoon to you and to you Mr. Westall." An exchange of greetings and small weather talk. Then it came — the Chairman spoke.

"Well the score doesn't look too good does it Mr. Brewster?"

"No sir. Afraid not."

"You couldn't have predicted such a bad result."

"No, of course not. But the man who can predict anything for sure in this business hasn't been born. And never will be."

"Yes, I seem to remember going over general points like that before. Ahem. Mr. Westall?"

"The thing that bothers us mostly, Mr. Brewster," the Controller said, reverting to the formal approach for Horton's ear, "is that not only do we lose whatever audience we might have had before Tresilian's time, but having gone before his program starts, they never come back. With due respect to Mr. Tresilian, he does seem to be rather like a Pied Piper leading a very small group — er, over a precipice."

"Well put, Mr. Westall. I think that illustrates the point very well. Don't you Mr. Brewster?"

The Drom looked at Glyn. Poor bastard, he thought, having to listen to all this. Maybe he shouldn't've got him in on it. Too painful. He clenched his massive right fist, giving the handset a series of imaginary short jabs to the mouth-piece, rolled his eyes up in exasperation until only the whites were showing, and inhaled deeply.

"Gentlemen, it doesn't matter what I think. And you know it. What do you want me to do? If anything. Apart from getting the hell out of here." In the Chairman's office they both spoke at once.

"Oh, Mr., come, Brewster, now we . . ."

"Well?"

"Mr. Brewster," the Chairman said, "at the risk of making a possibly wrong observation, I must confess that I find your instant and unprovoked hostilities a little trying. Surely we can discuss our mutual difficulties more amicably?

"I get the impression that you feel every conference between us is arranged for the express purpose of either humiliating you or dismissing you. I ask you to believe that such a notion, if true, would be ridiculous. We have every confidence in you. And we're trying to manifest that confidence in every possible way. Principally, by offering help — I hesitate to use the word advice in your case — whenever it would be intelligent to do so. You must agree that the time for such assistance is now. Is what

I've said, in your opinion, unreasonable?"

"The way you put it, no. But specifically just what kind of assistance do you have in mind?"

"Ah," Westall broke in, "that's the point. However it may surprise you Mr. Brewster, the fact is that our opinion on the telephone talk show concept has changed. Radically. Whereas before we were negative to the idea, we now agree with your thinking about its huge potential. We are convinced of that.

"We also realize that the size of return from on air talent is in direct ratio to the price of that talent. Which in Tresilian's case isn't very much. Either on the debit side of the ledger or measured by the slide rule of performance. We think it was a valiant idea on your part to try him but it's simply not working. Therefore we have some very real help available.

"We're prepared to increase your budget so that you can take some time to travel, go anywhere you want — but find the right man. We'll give you the money for him. Now what do you say?"

The Drom looked at Glyn doodling with a pencil in his free hand on the note pad.

"Fine, gentlemen. Thanks. Give me a few days to get sorted out. I'm pretty busy with other things right now but give me a little time and then I suggest we meet in your office and we'll go into the thing properly."

"Very well Mr. Brewster, but we do suggest that you don't take too long. We're all ready — we'll look forward to seeing you as soon as possible. Then we can discuss figures and limits, which we assure you, to achieve our aims, won't be too far from the sky, ha ha. Goodbye now."

"Goodbye and thank you, Mr. Brewster."

"Goodbye gentlemen."

They hung up the phones. Neither said anything for several seconds. Then Tresilian spoke.

"Quite an experience. Worth listening to."

"Glad you think so."

"Well there's one thing Burt; you can't beat hearing something first hand."

Glyn went on doodling. In his swivel chair the Drom lounged his big frame back and put his feet on the desk. Putting his hands behind the back of his head, Brewster alternated his gaze from the ceiling light fixture to Glyn and then back again.

There was no talk. Running through the Drom's thoughts were three choices.

One: take Tresilian off the air immediately and go back to music tomorrow. Two: let him go until shopping for the new man had been done — thereby at least giving continuity to the concept. Or three: and if he selected this course — and failed — CRAK without question would be in the market for another General Manager. Choice number three meant sticking with Tresilian. Subjecting him to all the 'crash' training it was possible to give. To spend every available minute with him — in the studio and off the air. When all his waking hours would become an endless talk show. When their conversation would consist only of the Drom playing the parts of callers — and Glyn, himself. If they had the time and this was doubtful, Brewster would know that the shock treatment was working if he saw unmistakable signs of anger and irritability. It was the last card in the pack. Win some. Lose some. Well they'd done a hell of a lot of losing recently. He made up his mind. He'd pull that one armed bandit one more time.

Brewster jerked out of his chair, and paced the office floor.

"Listen now. And listen hard. We've got two weeks. Max. Absolute max. If we last that long. You got any beer in your place?"

Puzzled, Tresilian answered quizzically,

"The better part of a case I think but wh . . ."

"Never mind the goddam questions. Get your coat. Come on. Go. GO."

Glyn looked back on the next fortnight as a hellish memory. After 48 hours, far from just hating the Drom's guts, he could have quite easily strangled the big coarse oaf. From a benign rough diamond, Brewster had become in Tresilian's mind, a crude bully, resorting now and again even to shoving and pushing him into chairs and cabs with unnecessary force. At the end of the second week they'd almost come to blows.

"Look — I wish you wouldn't shove like that. I can see the bloody door too. I know where it is. If you're so damned anxious to go in — go ahead — I'll gladly step aside. But," and his temper was white hot now, "just STOP THAT BLOODY SHOVING."

"Who do you think you're talking to?" Brewster shouted.

"I don't have to think about that. It so happens I KNOW

VERY WELL. That's a bloody stupid question. But typical. Just what I'd expect." Let the big bastard swing. He probably wouldn't feel it much. With his weight and power, the Drom could do it in one.

Brewster put his hands on his hips.

"I've got a problem," and he caught hold of Tresilian's lapels with his left hand, "because I don't know whether to smash your head in first — or put your teeth behind that loud mouth of yours. Trouble is I can only do one. Because there'll be nothing left any way." Then Glyn did something he'd never done before. He steadily went berserk.

"You bloody apology for a human being. Make your big decision. Go ahead and act like the orang utang you are. But if I live, I'll get you for everything you've got, and if I don't — at least you'll swing with all the grace of . . ." Here speech left him and with blazing madness in his eyes he drew back his right arm. As if grabbing a straw in a light breeze the Drom plucked it out of the air and locked it in his outsize hand like a vice.

The Drom released his grip. And then grinned.

"OK, old buddy. That's it. All over. Well done. I think you've made it." Bewildered, Glyn said,

"Made it? Made what?"

"The course. You can do it now. For instance, how've you been feeling about the shows recently?"

"Terrible. You've made me so furious — no livid, that I've taken it out on the few poor devils who've at least been calling up. Been giving them nothing but a pack of rudeness and short temper and . . ."

Stopping in mid sentence, Glyn smiled as comprehension came. Ah, yes of course. This had been the Drom's plan all along. Make me mad on and off the air and the subsequent ill humor would automatically induce that confidence and "control" that he was always emphasising so much. Come to think of it, how bloody naive he'd been not to recognize the stratagem.

"You dog, Burt. You bloody dirty dog."

"I couldn't think of any other way to do it Glyn. And I've got a little bit of news for you. The plant don't quite know what to do right now. They're beginning to dislike you intensely. Which is excellent. And believe it or not, so are quite a few other people too. All to the good. Do you realize that Westall hasn't called me for two days? This means we could, I repeat, we could be on our way. If I can just stave off that shopping expedition for your replacement another two or three weeks I think we might get out of the bog.

"But by God — I'm in the doghouse. At home. My wife suggested I take a room somewhere as I obviously don't need the house. And with the other guys at the station. The program supervisor was telling me yesterday that they're all fed up. With me. Nor do they care for you much. They're saying I must be on your private payroll. Certainly I'm not doing anything for them. No help. No interest. And they're the ones who're keeping the station going. And you're just bombing out all the time, and I'm helping you." He yawned. "Can't say I blame them really. It makes sense. I'd feel the same way myself. So would anybody."

The gamble and the 'treatment' paid off. Tresilian settled down to a good, individualistic style of expertly blended moderation and wrath. Small sample ratings a few weeks later showed that CRAK was beginning to hold its own, and perhaps a little more. After several years, an atmosphere of hesitant confidence but confidence nonetheless was returning to the station.

Brewster's aggressive handling of Tresilian to the exclusion of practically all other interests in the station had not endeared Glyn to the other members of the staff, as the Drom had himself suggested. But with extreme tension decreasing, Glyn made a few friends in both the radio and television sides of the tightly-run CRAK organization. Although CRAK radio and TV were segregated on the 14th and 15th floors respectively of a relatively small Montreal downtown building, communication wasn't difficult at the programming level. He had made tentative overtures to participate on some of the public affairs programs on CRAK-TV and was assured of a date as soon as possible. The advantage was simple: Tresilian was in the building, he was available and any appearance would help to promote both the radio and TV stations.

Other than programming, CRAK radio and TV were worlds apart. The two stations were separate profit centres as far as General Cosmetics was concerned, with quite different operating staffs. Horton and Westall officially headed both operations, even though TV was technically a subsidiary of CRAK Radio.

Brewster couldn't have cared less — he lived and loved the immediacy of radio. "Hell, do you suppose we could break into a "TiddlyWinks" children's hour on TV on a weekday morning with a second San Francisco earthquake? Sure they'd put a 'flash' on, but we'd be covering from 'Frisco for eight hours before they'd finally 'cover' on the 7.00 pm TV news, probably carrying our 'voice'. Unless they've set something up days in advance, they're licked."

. . . .

As the weeks and months rolled on, Tresilian worked hard to improve his show. He discovered his imagination was more fertile than he'd thought, and he also found a hidden flair for recognizing good debate material in human interest news stories. He read voraciously to keep abreast of current events. From the beginning, as the Drom had suggested, he made a business of keeping a sharp eye on City Hall, the Law Courts and the hospitals.

On his own he took a keen interest for the first time since his school days in India in politics and world affairs, reading widely from current history books, the local Montreal newspapers, and magazines, from the New York Times to the Manchester Guardian, from 'The Nation' to 'The New Statesman'. Gradually he gained recognition for being well informed, thought out and read.

As time went on he introduced his listeners to the weightier issues on the international scene. Where Trample would deal with de Gaulle's 'anti-English' bias vis-a-vis the Common Market, Glyn would call both the French and U.K. representatives in Ottawa for comment, presenting his own analysis of the problem both in direct statements and in the questions he posed. After the initial exchange with Tresilian, listeners would then raise whatever points they wished.

His listeners tended to like him or ignore him. Unlike Trample, he would never become their personal focal point of attention. The reasons were obvious. Every issue raised on Trample's show became a personal crusade. Vendettas were not uncommon. Glyn depended more on ideas and the personalities he phoned. Most fascinating to Glyn was the feeling of competition that now began to consume the atmosphere. Since all the other private stations fighting 'open line' with 'open line' were in fact fighting Trample, they kept their eye on 'No. 1'. There were informal weekly conferences with Brewster, Tresilian and the sales staff reviewing 'Trample's Week', what he was saying, how he was saying it, and how to combat it.

Most important, some people at any rate were switching over to him from Trample. They said as much on the air. He developed something Trample either wouldn't or couldn't give. Some laughter and humour. Even though innocuous household problems dominated air time, he tried, on an average of two occasions per week, to arrange a 'spectacular' on the conference 'hot line'. He called crowned heads and presidents, international politicians, show business personalities, interesting people in the news — anywhere in the world. Listeners were as fascinated by the ramifications of the calls that failed — to Mao, Kruschev and de Gaulle — as the ones that actually got through. Through these calls he grew to acknowledge the vast possibilities of radio and telephone as a unit.

More and more Glyn heard himself being discussed. In bus line-ups, on the streets, in greasy spoons and gourmet restaurants. This was a good sign. It meant interest by both the overall and mink trades. In the industry his performance was often discussed in comparison with Trample. The word leaked out from CRUX that some of the top dogs were getting worried. A little. Oh, they didn't have to do anything of course, but Tresilian would bear watching.

The calls from the plant to the Drom almost dried up, and stopped altogether after the publication of a rating survey that had been taken some three months after Glyn had really begun to settle down and feel his feet. CRAK's news was good — if not spectacular. CRUX still easily outrated them three to one. In the advertising agency research departments it was suggested that 'a slight trend might have been established'. The most promising thing about this rating looked to be the 'spill over' factor, which showed an increase in audience before Tresilian's on air time of 9 a.m. Recognizing this, Brewster ordered a sustained editing and dubbing routine whereby sizeable portions of his morning program would be replayed at other times of the day and night. He instructed, through memos to all announcers, that these 'inserts' should receive saturation 'ad lib' mentions. Thus, listeners tuned to CRAK were never more than a few minutes away from hearing either the sound of 'Crakkerjack line', or an announcer talking about it. This 'cross promotion' strained CRAK's already over-worked recording facilities and staff to the limit, but was well worth the burden. It got Tresilian talked about that much more and helped nourish the upward trend of CRAK's figures for the next survey.

The gap between CRAK and CRUX narrowed. The excitement continued to mount, and as it did, more and more local advertisers wanted Tresilian to endorse personally their products and services.

Tresilian's problem now was simple. He didn't appreciate the currency or 'third party approval' value of his name. But he did all the commercials that came his way on a personalized, live basis. The extra talent fees came in handy, especially as he was still receiving the same stipend. So far the Drom had not initiated a review. But Brewster was a good and fair guy. He'd leave it to him.

As Glyn's listeners increased, so did the number of the products and services he advertised. Adverse 'feedback' soon became a major embarrassment. Many personalized endorsements were questionable. Worse, prices and promises were not honoured. He first heard about these things on the air. It was a horrible sensation. At least Denny Trample had these things thoroughly checked out.

At first, Glyn was able to soothe listeners by intervening directly with the advertisers concerned. But all hell broke loose on the Monday after the show's heaviest-ever spate of 'weekend special' commercials. Tresilian saw Brewster right after the program for a showdown.

"Yeah, but that's the ball game, Glyn. They're our bread and butter. Don't knock'em. Anyway you're getting the talent on it aren't you?"

"I know — but what's the point of talent fees if the main thing — the audience — leaves you? After you've had to sweat your guts out to get to every one of them?"

At first the Drom — enjoying increased revenues for the first time — had been writing off Glyn's objections to an emerging prima donna-like attitude. If so, it was an encouraging development for a radio personality. But he didn't think so. But damn it, anyway. He wanted those local sponsors. On the other hand, they wanted Tresilian. He decided to apply a little pressure test.

"What're you saying, Glyn? Exactly?"

"I'm saying this. As a result of breaking faith with these commercials, I'm convinced we're losing audience. And everybody loses. As sure as hell I do. The little I've built up. The listeners get screwed when they buy and find it all a hoax or a come on'. And the honest sponsors come off badly by association with this negative word-of-mouth stuff. You know better than I do how quickly that news travels. Putting all these people on my show indiscriminately, with my personal endorsement, without proper integrity inspection, is dangerous. And false economy besides. God knows, I realise how bad things have been. You don't have to tell me that 'commercials' is the name of the game. The question now is — can we afford to take them when they insist on the personalizing bit as a condition of sale? In my view, the problem is that once the listeners don't trust me I've had it. The answer must be 'no'!"

For a few seconds, there was silence. The Drom stared straight ahead. Glyn broke in. "Look at this way, Burt. If they listen now it's because what I say in argument and discussion is believed to be the product of my own thinking — free of commercial pressures. Besides, we've been able to develop the show dramatically enough to the point where nobody, including me, knows what I or the listeners will do next. Excitement of the unknown, if you like. With that formula we'll get the good ones."

A change had come over the man, the Drom thought. Confident and sure. In complete control of himself now.

"OK, Glyn. I think the first thing to do is call the sales boys to a meet. I'll try to do it this afternoon. Don't worry about it. Leave it with me. We'll work something out. Let's get to-gether tomorrow after your show. By the way that was a beauty this morning. Heard it all. You handled that de Gaulle bit really well. See you old buddy. Bye."

It was agreed that the only sponsors who would be allowed on Glyn's show, with their commercials delivered and personally endorsed by him, would be those who were prepared to 'bond' themselves by signing a contract addendum. This would hold the advertiser responsible for any misrepresentations and dishonesty.

It worked like a truth serum. In the next year and a half "Crakkerjack Line" was firmly established in the Montreal market. Trample's lead was pulled back. On matters of religion and morals and a sense of purpose in life, confused and solace-seeking listeners found refreshment in Tresilian's eclectic views. Denny Trample's menu of entertainingly hypnotic atheism was beginning to pall.

For two hectic years the battle raged on. Trample held the spotlight all the while. Out-of-town broadcasters and politicians had all heard of the treatment he could dish out. Many experienced it.

Trample's greatest moments were the great events. Because of a series of federal and provincial elections, Trample's rating shot up suddenly, then fell back again when the contest was over. To a remarkable degree Trample became the star attraction. Businessmen and lawyer candidates who might only vaguely have heard of him, assuming their wives were tuned to the CBC or the one other station that hadn't gone in for the 'open line', testified to his power as soon as they began knocking on working class homes. Trample's views on election issues were taken as gospel by housewives. Especially the older housewives, many of them widowed.

Broad policies were of little concern to him. When talking to a politician, he'd bore in on the man's 'capacity' to represent 'the people'. Speaking on behalf of his audience, 'my broads in the kitchen,' he'd pounce, his voice jabbing into the vitals of the victim, asking the 'have you stopped beating your wife yet?' type of question. Such as having the candidate explain voting himself a salary increase in Parliament. After the fellow had mumbled incoherently for a moment or two, Trample would grill him for 'voting yourselves a 25% salary increase when unemployment goes up 2.7%!' then turn the microphones over to 'You vampires out there for questions . . . eat him alive.' His listeners saw Trample as their hero, their 'very own' knocking the pretentious politicos around. The result was that few politicians dared go on the air with him. That didn't bother him either, as the next charge was cowardice — true as far as it went. Also he'd put new twists into the old technique of debating against an empty chair.

Nor did he spare his own audience. A poor housewife who may have complained about being over-charged for legal service in a divorce proceeding would be told: "How often must I tell you broads, don't trust them, don't ever trust lawyers and politicians, or any professional. Lincoln knew the word for lawyers — 'liars'. Now you stupid dame, give the name of your lawyer to our operator and I'll call him. And he better be there," growling out the words as he prepared to battle the legal profession.

His listeners loved every minute of the Trample circus. They loved being brow beaten, and they loved it when he stood for Mrs. Average and called the 'Big Shot Lawyer.' Once, when after a third Board of Broadcast Governors lay-off, and with CRUX indicating they might have to let him go, he took his case to the listeners and they organized a 'Keep Denny Trample in Montreal' rally. Some 30,000 screaming women jammed the arena to hear him. After that there was no question as to who was top dog at CRUX.

Trample's greatest continuing battle was with the Separatists. During the worst of the crisis, when home-made bombs threatened to terrorize the city, Trample reached new heights as the hero of the mass of English-speaking citizens, worried about their jobs and their future in a separated Quebec. His talent for stirring the latent emotions of people was such that riots broke out in one of the poorer bilingual suburbs of the city, pitting English against French.

Trample put it this way: "When are we going to fight back? When will we stop following our so called 'English business leaders' who will protect only their cushy jobs in a separated or special status Quebec, and allow the rest of us to drift? When? I know the average French-Canadian wants to stay and fight for Canada. Now, when are we going to give him some help? You, who are of English stock, remember, Wolfe won! You who are Scots, Polish, Ukrainian, Greek, Jewish, remember we have a right to our language here — and no Pierre Bourgault or René Lévesque is going to stay 'out'!"

While the broad meaning of Trample's message (the defence of English-language rights and the rights of all the other minorities) deserved a spokesman, the tone of the message was taken to be anti-French by both Trample sympathizers and French-

Canadians alike. 'Boy, Denny Trample sure gave it to the damn Frenchmen today, eh?' was a constant theme. On the French side, Trample's audience was fantastic even though the reasons were incomprehensible. French-Canadians who considered themselves more Canadian than French were among his most faithful listeners, as were Separatists 'trying to read the Anglo-Saxon mind.' The broadcasts could not go unanswered, with the result that gangs of separatist hoodlums attacked the CRUX studios, seeking revenge.

This was Tresilian's competition. It wasn't easy, but fortunately for Glyn, election battles and separatist bombs weren't a daily occurrence. Glyn concentrated on the more solid fare. He worked hard at relieving problems. He'd bring political antagonists together in an attempt to rationalize the debate on policy rather than personal grounds. It worked too. Several times he was able to resolve a husband-wife conflict, holding the man's wife on one line while the operator got the husband on another. Sometimes he'd have lawyers advising on a third outside line. Immigration cases became a specialty, having been an immigrant himself. With the assistance of the Canada Department of Immigration he became a go-between to new immigrants; with the immigrant on the line he'd get a friend in the Immigration Department on the air and most often a problem would be solved. In this way Glyn attempted to achieve drama in radio, whether it was a husband and wife situation, white-negro riots in the U.S., the French-English at home, or the French-English conflict across the English Channel. He could be tough and he could shout too. He had learned to feel when the right moment had arrived for the push to a decision. The Drom called it 'reconciliation radio'.

On the international scene, which more and more absorbed Glyn's thinking, the reconciliation idea intrigued him to the point where he put it to work several times, as in the case of the Watts riots.

A year after the 'open line' war began, the ratings showed Tresilian fast beginning to close the gap. He also felt strong enough to begin taking his audience with him. Although less naive, he was still very much the idealist. The Vietnam war began to obsess him. He put Vietnam correspondents on the air when they returned to their home cities, U.S. draft dodgers settling in Montreal, and even discharged American soldiers. While the ideas expressed were varied and many, the theme of a dirty, unwanted war established itself.

The other side had its innings too, and hardly a day passed without Tresilian being called a Communist, a phoney, even a 'misguided Trotskyite' from a listener who identified himself as a Communist of the card carrying type. Glyn's worst day came when he put all his naivety and idealism into an attack on a U.S. Catholic Bishop who had been quoted in Saigon as backing the U.S. action in Vietnam to the effect that it met the 'approval of Providence.' The statement had been reduced to headline form to mean 'Kill one for Jesus.' Glyn lit into it, condemning the Bishop as a madman and one unworthy to carry the mantle of Christ; and one who should listen to his Pope more than his President. The statement resulted in 10,000 letters flooding the station, most of them in bitter, outraged protest, culminating in a week of anti-Tresilian harangues. The Drom was hard put to let Glyn stay on the air.

Trample waded in obliquely on 'misguided young men who would tell the clergy what to do.' Glyn's confidence was shaken, and he was sure the incident proved he'd never beat Trample. The fascinating contradiction of the man Trample, he thought, showed itself in the episode: Trample, the avowed Atheist, was the most popular broadcaster in the poorest Catholic Parishes, while Tresilian, a believer in a Supreme Being, was supposed to be the Communist sympathizer.

To reassure himself, the Drom called a fast rating on Glyn in the Spring of '65 and confirmed what he'd suspected. The 'Bishop Incident' had boosted Tresilian to within a few points of Trample. For the worst possible reasons Glyn was 'in' again as far as the Drom was concerned. Confidence was restored. His regular audience, which liked his probing, reconciling programming was joined by thousands more who relished the 'spectaculars' and the occasional intemperate outbursts. It was now only a matter of waiting.

CHAPTER 6

Late November, 1965. The crucial Fall rating survey had been taken. Crucial because a large portion of the next year's buying was based on it, particularly the buying of the national sponsors through their advertising agencies. As this was a big 'greater' metropolitan area measurement, the findings had taken six, instead of four weeks to compute, publish and distribute. Glyn would never forget that Friday morning. When he reached the office hallway, after completing his show, he saw signs of an orgy. Glyn was set upon by young and not so young women who fought to hug and embrace him. Standing in the thick of it all, and enjoying every moment was the Drom, grinning like an ape. Glyn saw that he was brandishing a newspaper.

"Hey Glyn. Com'ere, he yelled. Get a load of this." Glyn took the 'newspaper', which turned out to be one of those 'make-your-own headline' things.

TRESILIAN WINS RATINGS BATTLE
Tramples on Market

Brewster had received a call the night before from an associate in Toronto who'd been able to sneak a look at the figures before they were to be mailed at the beginning of the next week. He had telephoned the Drom at home—giving him the news that Tresilian's 'Crakkerjack line' was now the Number 1 show in its time slot. And by a good margin. The Drom had several copies of the 'paper' printed and circulated them before Glyn got out of the studio.

Glyn stared at the printing for a long time, oblivious to the happiness around him. He was just barely aware of hearty slaps on the back and a stream of congratulations. He had done it. He had beaten the great Denny Trample. Slowly he returned to the company of the station personnel, thanking them for their plaudits and their help. He was touched that they, for the most part, stenographers, clerks, accountants, continuity writers, newsmen and switchboard operators should care that much about his triumph. He had helped put CRAK back on its feet.

The Drom's voice carried all over the building through the deliberately open door of his office. He was now bellowing lyrically into the phone as Westall and Horton held their handsets away at the other end of the line.

"How about that Gentlemen, eh? How about that eh? Didn't I tell you? You just stick with the old Drom and you won't go far wrong. A goddam dromedary they call me." The senior men winced in unison. "They say I ride rough shod over the bastards. That's what they say, but I'll bet you're damned pleased about it now eh? Didn't I just tell you?"

"Yes. we're delighted with you, Mr. Brewster." Horton chimed in. "Please remember that we have always had complete confidence in you — which has now been conclusively justified. I join with Mr. Westall in an expression of thanks and congratulations."

"Good, thanks," replied the Drom, a little quieter now, "but just do something for me will you? Pen a little note of appreciation and send it to Tresilian. He'd like that and you've no idea how much good this kind of thing does. Remember that it's not just his show we're talking about. Because with all that cross promotion of his tapes, we're well up in other time areas too. There's no doubt, and you'll understand this when you get the figures, that we're enjoying considerable 'backlash' and 'spill over' in the shows adjacent to 'Crakkerjack line'."

There was a short pause. Then Horton spoke again. "What you suggest would not really be customary, Mr. Brewster. As you know General Cosmetics Corporation is very large. Perhaps regrettably big. We find it altogether more desirable to channel our gratitude to individuals for work well done via the standard routes of Divisional and Department Heads — which of course means you in the case of CRAK. We have found in the past that a departure from this policy creates localised frictions and jealousies."

You pompous silver tongued bastard, were the Drom's unspoken words. "I read you loud and clear, Mr. Horton but I think Tresilian's production is more than just a case of work well done, isn't it? Let's face it, he's carried the whole operation on his back. What else is there, until we get some hot shot rock jocks, that makes people tune in and talk about us? Hell, you stop a 100 English speaking people on the street and ask them who Glyn Tresilian is — and I have a hundred bucks that 95 of them will know. Ask them to name two other guys on CRAK — and the same money says all hundred of them couldn't tell you. Look. I'm not asking you for a controlling share in General Cosmetics. All I want is for you to write a few lines under your signature to a guy in one of your operations who's slugged his guts out under impossible pressures and who's made it — not so much for himself yet, if we're talking money — but for you.

"You're the one's who're tasting the cream. He's not. Do you realize that we haven't raised that original payment by a nickel yet? Don't worry; we'll have to now. Do you mean to say that the guy's not worth three or four lines in a letter from you, Mr. Horton?"

"I'm sorry, Brewster. But I have explained our thoughts and policy on matters of this kind. May I take it that all is clear and understood? Then good day and again congratulations from us all."

For another year things continued to go well for CRAK and Tresilian. Through the acquisition of two 'Hypo' type 'rock jocks', the juvenile audience also fell CRAK's way. The station was now Top Dog in all time areas of the English speaking radio market in Montreal. With the departure of Denny Trample for Los Angeles a few weeks after Tresilian's win, Glyn had the field to himself. If he had a problem, it was his old bête noir of the personalised commercials. Making hay while the rating sun shone, the salesmen had gone all out with their campaigns and had secured dubloons for the station and themselves. Big chunks of the revenue came from 'Crakkerjack line' and with the commercial harvest booming, some of the earlier disciplines drawn up to ensure integrity had loosened and dubious advertisers were again receiving the stamp of Tresilian's approval. He was hating the process more and more.

.   .   .   .   .   .

Darkness had fallen on Montreal, and in falling brought on the city's fairyland shimmer of light. From the double-windowed balcony of his apartment, Glyn looked at the city, his city, as it came to sparkling night. He loved the place, like no other, even the India of his early boyhood before the war. It was the only metropolis in the world where a love-hate relationship was constant rapture.

The telephone rang as he was leaving for Expo.

"Yes, hello?"

"Ah Glyn. Jean Fournier here." It was one of the bilingual salesmen at the radio station.

"Say, Glyn can you come with me to see Mathieson tomorrow right after your show?"

"Mathieson?"

"You know — the developer. Pastoral Suburbs. Anyway, he's putting up a new apartment block in the Montreal West — Côte St. Luc area and he wants to start an advance rental campaign right away."

"Well, fine Jean. I wish him luck."

"Yes, yes."

"O.K. then Jean."

"Glyn?"

"Yes?"

"He wants you to do the commercials."

Tresilian had known this from the moment Fournier had called. The position was simple and clear. CRAK Radio had given Glyn maximum editorial freedom. Unhampered by station and corporate politics, Tresilian had so far been able to conduct what he thought to be a truthful open-line radio show. Although not always approving, CRAK's management had the commercial good sense to realise that free rein was the only way for Tresilian to attract the very large audience which the show now enjoyed. Local advertisers saw this too. After all, they reasoned, if the public believes that he speaks honestly on contentious issues — all fair grist for his program — then it follows that as long as he personally endorses and guarantees the commercial announcement, listeners will take as gospels what he says about a sponsor's products and services.

Recently, Glyn had been badly hurt more and more by a handful of clients whose commercials were grossly misleading. It was a sordid affair and hundreds of customers had been cheated. The lawyers letters came in bundles to CRAK with copies for Tresilian.

All of this had been bad enough, but the big blow came when

he overheard himself being discussed in public places. "You know, I always listened to that guy. Mind you, I hardly ever agreed with a damn thing he said — but I never suspected his integrity. Now, after that last con job he pulled — took my wife in too — I'll never believe another word he says."

That was real the trouble. General Cosmetics' legal retainers could easily handle the court cases — but how to regain personal trust once it's gone? He knew that if he lost listener confidence in his own views about the French-English business in Canada and Quebec, on the Viet-Nam war, on Rhodesia, L.S.D., South Africa, breast feeding, driver education, the Monarchy, the Pill, Neo-Nazism, the CBC, the racial problem in the States — then, then there was nothing left.

If he had a major dislike about his work, this was it. Although he exercised his freelancer's privilege of declining to do any more 'personalized' commercials, the pressures still came on. Often, in the past, Tresilian's endorsement was a condition of sale. And the insisting clients were big spenders.

There had been an ugly confrontation with Mathieson in the New Year. CRAK lost a $25,000 order when the exasperated businessman told Fournier, "No Tresilian, no personalization, no twenty-five thousand dollar order." And that was that.

Through channels, and through no fault of Fournier, the problem grew, reaching the president of General Cosmetics Corporation. Horton, accustomed to running a firm with sales of over $100 million annually, was nonetheless annoyed to hear that CRAK had needlessly lost a $25,000 order. In the Mathieson affair, the Chairman's word came down. A phone call or meeting with Glyn were eschewed in favour of a curt one-sentence memorandum to Brewster: "Make sure that Tresilian fully understands that the only difference between him and us is that we own a radio and television operation and he doesn't."

That was all. And now Fournier was on the phone. And they'd have to go through the whole mess again. Same condition. Same client. Same problem multiplied by two. Now Mathieson was ready with a $50,000 check and happy to pay in advance.

"Oh, hell, Jean."

"I know, Glyn. But what can I do. Mathieson's big potatoes and this game's tough enough as it is. And I don't have to tell you what it'll do for my own quota. I'll tell you something though — the Drom wants this one badly. He called a meeting when he came back from lunch — by the way were you and he drinking it? Anyhow, he was bubbling away about the ratings, you being called a bastard on the air, sales figures and the whole bit. What do you say."

"I'd rather not say anything, Jean. I don't like the way it's shaping up at all. How long ago were we in trouble with this lot before?"

"Four months."

"How long can we stall?"

"We can't stall at all. Mathieson wants to start this Friday — to get the week-end drivers out to the site. And then on Monday he'll saturate. I've got the schedule here — and I can't see how anyone else can even get on the air. Mathieson's got all the availabilities, ha ha!" Fournier laughed hopefully.

Tresilian was fed up. Short of asking him to pitch a tent outside his apartment construction, Mathieson would consider Tresilian an exclusive rental unit for the period of the contract. And with $50,000 worth of advertising, even on a saturation basis, that would be a long time. Too bloody long.

"Look Glyn, I've got to take off. I'll pick you up outside the studio at eleven and we'll go to his office in my car. He's reserved a table for lunch at his club — you know, the Metropolitan. Twelve thirty. Oh, by the way Glyn, he told me to say that in return for the great job he knows you'll do for him, you'll find him very loose when it comes to your talent fees. OK then, Glyn. See you to-morrow when you get off the air", and the salesman hung up the phone.

Tresilian didn't like Mathieson. Oh, he and his kind were legally defensible — naturally. They spent a lot of money making damn sure they were. Pillars of local communities. But still bad news. Very bad news. However there was no point in worrying about it now. To-morrow would tell. And at this point he didn't care what it told. Could anyone work in a crazier set up than one where the word 'freelance' had no meaning at all? When one couldn't exercise the right of making a choice of working or not working without bringing on crisis conditions? Depressed, he decided against the Expo visit and turned in early.

A few minutes later the telephone shrilled again.

"Hi, Glyn. It's the old Dromedary here. How you doing boy?"

"Fine thanks Burt."

"Listen, Fournier called you huh?"

"Yes."

"Yea, well we can't afford to miss this one Glyn. We just gotta go with it. It's all set. Mathieson's giving you and Fournier lunch tomorrow eh? Great. Then you'll all come back to the station afterwards. I'll make goddam sure I'm free. And we'll all have fun at ball-point-pen time. Ha ha ha! Nothing like getting the good old signature on the beautiful line that is dotted, eh Glyn?", and Brewster chortled on.

"Hey Glyn?"

"Yes, Burt?"

"You're with me eh? No problems?"

"Everything in life can be a problem Burt. I . . . ."

"Now, you see; there you go again. More philosophical crap. Goddam it Glyn. How many times do I have to tell you to cut it out? On and off the air. Eh? All I want to know is whether you've got any problems with Mathieson's goddam commercials. All $50,000 worth of the green bastards. And what do you do to me? Eh? You give me the start of a crappy lecture on life. Why, I don't even know why I have you on our air."

"Good point there, Burt. I've often wondered myself."

"Ha ha", Brewster laughed.

Glyn held the phone away from his ear. The noise was almost deafening.

"OK, Glyn baby. Very good. See you tomorrow. What're you doing tonight anyway?"

"Thinking, mainly, Burt — I know. Don't say it. Don't tell me not to think in case I strain myself."

It all happened precisely as he had predicted. They went to the brink. Eyeball to eyeball. General Cosmetics, CRAK and Pastoral Suburbs on one side, and Glyn on the other. Tresilian insisted that the amount of money Mathieson was to spend in advertising was irrelevant to the principle of the policy that CRAK had laid down in the matter of Glyn's personally endorsed commercial deliveries — that all clients must sign the contract addendum as proof of good faith and honourable intent.

When Glyn brought this up, Mathieson blanched, then fumed. There was considerable unpleasantness all round. That afternoon orders came down from Horton himself that Tresilian must waive his insistence on the addendum in the case of Pastoral Suburbs — or face dismissal.

.   .   .   .

The next morning thousands of 'Crakkerjackliners' tuned in at the usual time and heard bland music on the air. With no notice of change in programming, they'd been caught completely unaware. To the last moment Brewster had hoped to see Tresilian bounce into the studio, counting on Glyn's new desire to break fresh broadcasting ground with his audience. But there was no Tresilian. To find out what had happened after 9:00 a.m. his listeners paralysed the switchboard so badly that the station could not get any normal business done for several hours.

Local newspaper columnists, traditionally hostile to competing media, sniffed a good story and enthusiastically reported on the fast circulating rumours. From CRAK only the terse comment: "Mr. Glyn Tresilian is no longer with us."

From Glyn: "Unfortunately CRAK and I could not come to mutually agreeable terms on a matter of commercial policy."

"Specifically, Glyn?"

"No comment — sorry."

Denny Trample was hastily recalled from Los Angeles by CRUX. Glyn for his part was tracked down by several radio stations in Canada and the western U.S. He remained noncommital, and didn't really know what to do next. Fortunately, there was no hurry. Of one thing he was sure — he'd been bitten by the broadcasting bug, and there was no antidote. This, in one form or another was his new life and calling. He'd never be very far away from it.

For several weeks he explored Expo and the tucked-away delights of the Laurentians and the Eastern Townships. Manoeuvering the 'Black Panther' on and off near-forgotten mountain roads and through dozens of story-book Township hamlets which in a century had subtly, but never completely, changed from that of the typically picturesque New England town setting to that of the French-Canadian village, Glyn had much thinking time and an opportunity to listen to radio with a completely different ear. He was surprised how it really sounded.

He also wondered if he should use this hiatus to go back for another visit to Michael and the Wooffendens. He hadn't told them yet about his break with CRAK. No, he'd get sorted out on his next course, make it a condition that before starting at whatever it was, he must take three weeks, go over, and then tell them. That was the best way.

Among the offers he'd received, he liked the one from a Toronto radio station best. Their approach had pleased him, and despite his declared wish to stay in Montreal permanently, particularly during Expo year, they sustained their interest and gently pressed him to accept their invitation to visit. Finally he decided to fly and see them. He telephoned.

"Good Morning. CORK Radio Toronto. We have 62 degrees at 10:17. May I help?"

"Yes please. I'd like to speak to Mr. Greenway. Dan Greenway."

"May I say who's calling?"

"Tresilian. Glyn Tresilian — from Montreal."

"Oh, with pleasure Mr. Tresilian. There you are sir."

"Dan?, Glyn Tresilian here, I . . ."

"Great Glyn. Very glad you called. If you didn't reverse the charges, we'll make this a collect call — as I said before. Now, when can we meet you?"

"How does the middle of next week suit?"

"Good Glyn. Let's make it Wednesday. Come early. I'll clear the whole day and Thursday — that'll give us lots of time; and we'll make overnight reservations for you. Just call me as soon as you've booked your flight. Oh, and make it first class."

Tresilian was impressed. He knew that CORK was suffering. The station had been started by a group of professional men — lawyers, stockbrokers, doctors, even a high school principal — each of them long on the future of responsible broadcasting, but short on cash. In the trade they were considered too stupid to give up. In any case, the Board of Broadcast Governors had been sold on the need of just such owners and had gambled on giving them a license. Despite hours of commercial-free broadcasting they refused to change their non-dramatic approach to the news, nor did they yield to frenzied music, gimmicks and sensationalism.

Dan Greenway was a good man. He'd long since given up trying to persuade his principals that integrity and basic beliefs needn't be dirtied by healthy profits. He had, however, persuaded them to agree on Glyn, but only because of, in Greenway's soft sell, 'Tresilian's unsullied, thinking man's dedication to the medium.'

When Glyn heard about that from Greenway, he smiled, then paled, wondering how long he would have stayed in contention with Trample using that formula. Greenway obviously hadn't heard of Tresilian's target market — B.O.V.H.: Broads on Van Horne, a reference to a typical Montreal residential street. No one ever accused Brewster and Tresilian of running a philanthropy at CRAK. While Glyn had aimed at responsible programming, he'd also worked at getting the biggest audience to justify the formula. In the world of commercial radio and television the public was always right. In any case, Glyn thought, CORK would have to learn to adjust to the market.

Tresilian and Greenway discussed all the implications of the 'open line' format, including the B.O.V.H. market, and Dan in turn discussed them with his leading principals in three fast paced telephone conversations. The upshot was that CORK made Glyn a very attractive proposition, promising editorial freedom of the kind that he'd enjoyed with CRAK. More than anything else though, it was the prospect of associating with windmill tilters that pleased Glyn most. Here were real life Don Quixotes who, 'regardless of their doom', still tried to play their game. Perhaps he could do something to help save them from going under.

Greenway drove Glyn to the airport for Air Canada's 'Dinner Flight' back to Montreal. He promised to give CORK an answer in a fortnight.

The sea, as an element, was Glyn's first love. But he liked aeroplanes and flying — particularly night flights to the UK. There was a glamour and excitement about it all.

He hadn't felt so well in weeks as he settled in the Vanguard's after compartment. Soon they were airborne and the stewardesses went around gathering pre-dinner drink orders. There was limited time on this flight and cocktails were brought with the meal tray. The stewardess was very pretty.

"There you are sir. Gin and tonic. I hope you enjoy your dinner."

"Thank you."

In 40 minutes the food debris was cleared away and the aeroplane began the descent to Montreal. Soon the signs went on and the Vanguard came to a stop alongside an arrival entrance at Dorval. He was, of course, glad to be back in Montreal even after a short absence but he was in no hurry to leave his seat. Tresilian really liked the look of her. He had flown a lot and found this girl to be unusually attractive to be serving on an airline in the sixties. He thought that there had been a definite decline in the number of beautiful airborne hostesses in the last few years — probably the glamour of the job had long since worn off. But this girl was different. He'd been watching her all through the flight.

He'd wait until the other passengers had left and then offer to drive her home. He saw her at the gangway smiling and saying good night. The sky blue uniform set her off well. She had close and tidy blondish hair, and by her accent, Tresilian guessed at a Scandinavian origin. She reminded him of a well known American movie actress he'd recently met at a press reception, but couldn't place. Her face and arms were lightly tanned; her eyes hazel and clear. He'd glimpsed her moving up and down the aisle and inside her white blouse he'd admired her, high, well held breasts. Not what he'd consider magnificent (his memory of Peta was still very clear on this point), but well-rounded nonetheless. Slim waist, good legs. Nor did she seem to have to wear a corset. He estimated that she was about 5'7" and 125 lbs. She looked about twenty-two or three. Her nose was small and straight. With all this, she had a clean, dainty and feminine presence. Glyn saw her voice, soft and calm, and spiced with a touch of European, as a topping to a very natural sex appeal. She'd excited him since he saw her at Malton.

"Goodnight sir. Goodnight madam. Goodnight sir — thank you. Goodnight sir — yes? I hope you'll fly with us again soon."

He picked up his flight bag and went to the door. He was the last one to leave by the first class entrance and he'd already pondered the way he'd put the question.

"Goodnight sir. Excuse me — but are you Glyn Tresilian?"

My God, he said to himself, this couldn't be better.

"Yes — as a matter of fact I am," not wanting to appear too eager. "How did you guess?"

She ignored the question.

"What are you doing now Mr. Tresilian? I used to listen to

you whenever I could."

"Oh, so you live in Montreal?"

"Yes — NDG."

"It was very nice of you to recognize me. But do you really want to know what I'm doing now?"

"Of course — I wouldn't have asked otherwise," and she blushed very slightly.

"I'll tell you then. Right now, at this very instant, I'm trying to find enough courage to offer a lift to the nicest looking Airline Stewardess I've ever seen. I'm parked outside and NDG's right on the way — not that it matters."

"You're quite a fast worker," she said and looked embarrassed. He noticed the reddening flush on her light rose cheeks. "It's very kind of you to offer but we usually go downtown together in the limousine."

"We?"

"Yes, the other girls and I."

"Would I be right in saying that that lovely voice has some remains of Swedish or Norwegian or Danish?"

"Wrong. Dutch."

"Dutch? Oh, in that case you must let me drive you. We have so much to talk about. I'll tell you about the experiences I had in Rotterdam and Schiedam and . . ."

"What about Amsterdam?"

"No, not guilty."

"OK. I'll tell you about Amsterdam then," she said.

"Good. I'll be in front of the arrivals entrance in ten minutes. That alright? No? Twenty? Fine — Miss, er . . ."

"de Vries. Juliana. But as you can imagine it never gets past Julie. I know yours."

"What is it?"

"Why, Tresilian of course."

"No, it's not."

"Oh, I see. You mean it's Glyn?"

"Now you've got it."

Tresilian left the airplane as the other girls were finishing their cabin duties and walked slowly to the parking lot. He started the car and let her idle as he waited. He caught the news on CRAK and then switched off the radio. He was quite pleased with himself. Fast, efficient, no wastage. He doubted that he'd get very far with her though. Girl like that — with all she had going for her — bound to be hooked somewhere along the line. He'd find out soon enough.

He drove up 20 minutes later but there was no sign of her. He went round the airport concourse twice and decided to make the third circuit the last one. If she didn't show, what the hell? There were always plenty of others. Not up to her standard perhaps, but adequate. Like Jenny and Marielle and Angela at CRAK. They were alright now and again. Now that he'd left the station, he supposed they'd be easier than ever — and not being in the building himself would make it simpler to take them one at a time. There'd been more than a few close calls . . .

Then she was there. Slightly out of breath and apologetic, but there.

"I'm so sorry," she said gasping a little as he held open the door for her, "I couldn't get in touch. We got caught up in the office — they wanted to hold a short briefing. Thank you. Yes, that's all. One good thing about this job — you can always travel light. It was nice of you to wait. I really thought you'd have gone."

"Oh, no. I knew you must have been delayed. I was going to wait. I don't think you'd ever let anyone down deliberately." He took the car round the airport again and out on to Côte de Liesse for Decarie. The highway was crowded and slow with Expo visitors driving in from Toronto and the U.S. middle west. He was glad for all the traffic as it would give him more time with her.

"Where in NDG?" he asked.

"Near West Broadway — I'll show you when we get there. Sure it's not out of your way?"

"Surer now than I ever was. OK. Amsterdam. You were going to tell me."

"Oh, yes. Well, nothing to tell. I was born there, and went to a school on the outskirts until I was fifteen. Then we came to Canada. And as you noticed I've never been able to lose my accent completely."

"Don't — it's delightful. Tell me more."

"There isn't much more to tell. My parents and I settled in Montreal when my father came ashore and . . ."

"Don't tell me he was a sailor?"

"Yes, he was. Ocean going tugs. You've heard of Holland's Glory of course?"

"You bet I have. Was he in command?"

"Oh, yes for years. Then they made him Operations Director for Canada."

"And then?"

"Well, I finished high school here, graduated in nursing and joined Air Canada."

"Did you do any nursing?"

"For about a year. And I'm going back to it after I've got the travel bug out of my system. And that's about all the news of me. Now I did ask you on the plane, remember? What are you going to do?"

"I'm going to ask you to have dinner with me tomorrow night. But I know you won't. Even if you wanted to, you'd be flying off somewhere I suppose."

"You're very direct aren't you?" she looked at him and blushed again.

"Anything wrong with that?"

"No, I guess there isn't. You certainly let people know where you stand don't you, Mr. Tresilian? Sorry — it slipped out."

"What about the invitation. Impossible?"

"Not really. As a matter of fact, I'm starting ten days leave. It'll be a great chance to see some of Expo before the huge crowds arrive."

"They're pretty big now. Been down there much?"

"Just a couple of quick trips. Well now — about your kind invitation. The only problem is that I promised my parents that I'd go with them to some reception or other at the Dutch pavilion. My father's involved with the marine side of it and I think they'd be disappointed if I didn't go. We don't see a lot of each other as it is and . . ."

"Of course. I understand that perfectly well. How about the night after — or anytime before you fly off and out of my life for ever?" He looked ahead and concentrated on his driving. The traffic was dense now and moved in starts. Julie laughed cheerfully.

That sounds terribly melodramatic — but I'm sure we can fix something up. Aren't you very busy though?"

"Never been more idle in my life. Unemployed now.

Remember?"

"It's hard to think of you being out of work. The average listener probably thinks of you leading a hectic and glamourous life, going from one exciting event to the next."

"And that's where the average listener is wrong on yet another count. I'll tell you what Julie. Why don't you write down your phone number, then I can call you sometime tomorrow to set a definite time and place. Maybe we'll go down to one of those pavilion restaurants at Expo. But the trouble is they're so damned crowded all the time. And the better places in town 've lost all their best people to the site."

She took a notebook out of her regulation purse and wrote down LAurence 9-2370.

"What's a good time to call?" he asked.

"Oh, any time after ten. Here — where shall I put this?"

"I can't take my hands off the wheel. Put it in my shirt pocket, could you? I usually keep cards and notes in there. Safest place."

She leaned across from the bucket seat. He thrilled as he felt the light touch of her longish fingers on the shirt above his heart. He was pleased that the man in the store where he bought them had sold him three with button pockets. He couldn't be positive, but he had a notion that she wasn't hurrying as she opened and closed it. She put the slip of paper in and saw that it was empty. He inhaled the bouquet from her hair as it touched his right shoulder. She took her hand away and lit a cigarette.

"Oh, sorry. Would you like one? Yes? Then I'd better give you this. Hope you don't mind. After all you can't take your hands off the wheel can you?" She put the end of the filter tip between his lips. He left it in his mouth savouring the sweet moisture from hers. Then she brought out a small gold banded holder and lit her own.

"By the way I hope you haven't lost any important papers. There aren't any in your shirt pocket. Perhaps it's not a very safe place after all."

He left the elevated Metropolitan Boulevard at Decarie circle and headed south. The expressway traffic was moving comparatively well. Soon they reached Sherbrooke street and turned west. She directed him to a snug looking cottage with Elizabethan-leaded windows. He made a "U" turn at the end of the cul-de-sac and pulled up at the sloping driveway.

"Hang on. I'll come round," and he let her out of the car and carried her small case to the door.

"Mummy and Daddy are probably at the Pavilion. They spend a lot of time there of course. I'm sure they're not in yet," and she opened the front door with a latch-key. The house was empty. He put her bag inside the porch. The car was still running and he hadn't closed the passenger door.

"Would you like to come in? The least I can do for you now is to make a cup of coffee. It was so nice of you to drive me."

"No, I don't think so, Julie. I'd better not. But I'll call you tomorrow?"

"OK, Glyn, I'll be waiting."

He waved goodbye and shut the door. He'd liked the sound of her voice. It looked promising.

.   .   .   .   .   .

He called her at one in the afternoon.

Julie took the lead. "Listen, Glyn, here's an idea. I was telling my father and mother about you last night. How you'd very kindly driven me home and invited me to dinner. Mummy's thrilled. Apparently she used to listen to you all the time and feels she knows you personally. She says she'd love to meet you. So Daddy suggested that I invite you to join us at the Pavilion this evening and then he'll take us all out to dinner after the reception. How does that sound?"

"Almost perfect. But I'd like to have you to myself."

"I do have ten days you know. Or have you forgotten?"

"I hope I'll never have reason to forget it. That's wonderful though, Julie. Just fine. Why don't I pick you up? I have a press pass and that allows parking in the lot behind the Autostade. It's just a short walk to Place D'Accueil."

"That's nice. We have to be there at five thirty or so. How about four forty five? That alright Mummy?" he heard her ask, "Yes?"

"Excellent Julie. I'll be there."

.   .   .   .   .   .

With Mrs. Wilhelmina de Vries in the back seat of the Armstrong-Siddeley, Tresilian drove down University Street and on to the new Bonaventure Expressway turning off for the Autostade parking lot past the Administration entrance. Julie's mother was a charming middle aged Dutchwoman and spoke good grammatical English with an immovably thick accent.

"Offen, I haf vanted to hit you over the head vith en very big stick, Mr. Treseelian — but after your kindness to Juliana last night I vill refrain van doing it."

Julie swivelled round.

"Mummy, how could you say such a thing?" she asked with mock reproach.

"Ach, he knows it's true. I think many vomen vill haf vanted to do the same thing — eh Mr. Treseelian?"

"You're quite right, Mrs. de Vries. But I've always managed to duck out of the way just in time. Oh — please call me Glyn. Julie does."

She looked at her daughter.

"Juliana alvays found it easy vith people. But ven you get older, especially if you come van Europe, you are inclined to hang on to the old vays. But if it vill make you happier I'll do it. Now, Glyn. Vhot are your plans? And vhy didn't the radio station tell us vhot had happened? Some people say you vere fired — and others inzist that you fired them. Vhot is the true story?"

"Oh, somewhere in between I'd say. But it doesn't matter. I don't know what I'm going to do right now. Although I must say I'm enjoying the rest. It's wonderful just to have that morning pressure off. I may do something in Toronto. I spent a couple of days there with some people. They came up with a pretty attractive deal. But I still hate the idea of leaving Montreal. Especially this year."

"Oh, vell. Zomething good and proper vill turn up as your Micawber vould say. You are a resourceful man, Glyn. Jan, my husband, is looking forward to meeting you. He alzo used to listen. He offen said you talked good common sense — as a zailor should. He doesn't like shore people very much — even zo he hasn't zailed for all these years."

"He only talks like that Mummy. I'll bet he wouldn't want to go back to sea again though," Julie said.

"I don't propose to let him find out vhether he'd vont to go back or not." Mrs. de Vries laughed heartily.

"Your first name's Wilhelmina, Mrs. de Vries?"

"Yes, vhy?"

"You must be a very patriotic family to have two queens. Wilhelmina and Juliana."

"Yes, ve are, Glyn. Very patriotic as a family and as a country. And ve are proud of our Royal family. Not ashamed of it. There is nothing better than countries vith monarchies. I haf no time for the Republic idea. And Canadians shouldn't have either. This talk makes me so sick. They don't realize vhat they haf. En vonderfol country vith everything in it. And en good Royal family. And they want to spoil it. For vhot?"

Tresilian wasn't in the mood for politics and was glad that they had arrived in the parking lot. He locked the car and they began the walk to Place D'Accueil. It was an unseasonably warm afternoon for May and Julie and her mother had dressed in light summery cocktail dresses.

In mufti she looked even better. And he revelled, as they strolled along and through the hurrying crowds, at the modest decolletage of her bustline. Just the right amount, he decided. Correct, but not demure. They passed through the turn-stiles and went down to the crowded waiting Expo-Express for the ride to Place des Nations. For once, Glyn appreciated a packed public place. They stood in the compartment and he felt the warmth and tingle of her limbs against him as the train lurched on its way. He was glad that Mrs. de Vries was a prolific talker. It saved him work, which this afternoon he didn't want to do. It was enough for him to be with Julie — to hear and see her. Her mother was obviously pleased at the looks of recognition they were getting in the train and on the walk along Lac des Cygnes. Soon they were in the receiving line at the Netherlands Pavilion shaking hands with the greeting dignitaries in attendance. Julie introduced her father to Glyn. His English was almost accentless.

"A pleasure to meet you, Mr. Tresilian. Welcome to the Dutch pavilion. What will you have? Gin? Good. A sailor's drink. Then let us drink Bols to-gether. Your first time here?"

"Yes, I'm afraid so, Captain."

"Nothing to apologise about. The Exibition's only been open a short time. I can't understand these people who expect to see everything in a couple of days. And if you haven't seen it yet, you save me the trouble of asking you for an opinion."

"Thank you, Captain. Fair winds." They drank the rich oily

gin of Holland. It went to work at once.

"What reactions are you getting about the Pavilion, Captain?"

"They seem to like the view from that side," de Vries laughed and waved to the panorama of the mountain and downtown Montreal seen to perfection from the river side of the scaffolding-cradled Low Country building.

"But seriously," he continued, "we're quite satisfied. A few people are saying that there's too much water emphasis, but as you know that's the story of life in Holland. Floating on it or stopping it. Julie tells me you'll be able to join us for dinner. That is good. I always like talking to sailors. Thank you for your kindness to her yesterday — she was grateful for the lift."

Glyn shrugged in the Gallic fashion.

"But it was nothing, Captain, nothing. I mean no trouble for me. She's a lovely girl and she did me the favour."

"Yes, she's a good girl. We're very pleased with her. I'd better mingle a bit now. Ah, there's Julie — with her mother. Do you like L'Auberge du Ciel?"

"I do, but . . ."

"Never mind, never mind. That's where we go to-night."

Tresilian was glad when they left shortly before eight. He'd been trying to talk to Julie alone but it was impossible. And he, a veteran of the press conference, reception, and general free-load circuit should have known better than to try. He met, inevitably, a lot of media colleagues and drank far more Bols than went with safe driving. He wished he hadn't brought the car. Apart from that, he was feeling exuberant and looking forward to dinner in the sky. He hoped with all his heart that an understanding government in the Hague would be picking up the tab.

The de Vries were all in good form as they started walking to Place des Nations station. Before they'd gone far, Tresilian stopped.

"You know, I think we ought to walk to the Metro on Ile Ste. Helene. I'd rather leave my car where it is for the night if you don't mind."

"Ah, very wise, Glyn. Very wise. Must be sober on the bridge eh? Ha ha haha, haha! There you are Moeder — leave it to a sailor to do things properly," Captain de Vries roared and shook Tresilian's hand vigorously.

At L'Auberge du Ciel, Glyn told them about the times he'd been there with the Wooffendens and Brewster. They all seemed keenly interested in his story. Like his wife and daughter, the Captain asked him his plans.

"I get asked that a lot these days, Captain. But I honestly don't know. I just got back from Toronto yesterday — with Julie incidentally! I might go there and do the same kind of show. I like the people at the station, but I'm not keen to leave Montreal. Mrs. de Vries and Julie and a lot of others have already heard this, so it must sound a bit boring by now."

"They've offered you the job?" de Vries asked.

"Oh, yes" Glyn replied to a man who liked to be clear about such things.

"That's quite a life you haf had Glyn. Although we who used to listen to you felt we knew you perzonally, I now realise how very little people would know about you. Your zon, now. He is happy with your late wife's rich parentz?"

"He should be, Moeder," the Captain interjected. "His Grandfather owns one of the finest shipyards in the world. I know because I've taken three tows there — and I've seen the jobs when they were done."

"Yes, I think Michael's very happy with them. But I think I can say we're missing each other now. But it wouldn't be fair to bring him over the way I'm set. Even if I could afford it, a housekeeper's not really the answer. He's nearly thirteen already."

"Then I will tell you vhot. You must marry again and give him another Moeder — mother."

"Yes, Mrs. de Vries — that would be the best solution wouldn't it? I must start my thinking in that direction."

Tresilian never did find out what the celebration was for — if anything, or what the size of the bill was. They hailed a cab and Glyn got off at Sherbrooke Street and Cote des Neiges.

"He is en good man. I like him — now I haf met him faze to faze", Mrs. de Vries said in the manner of a Chairman casting a vote after Glyn had left the car.

"Of course, Moeder. He's a sailor."

"But Mummy I thought you liked him before. You said you always listened . . ."

"Ach, yes, but that vos on the radio. I disagreed with a lot of vhot he said but I like him as a radio perzon becos he made people think. Now I like him as a private perzon. That vos good — the vay he left hiz car behind. I do not approve of anyone getting dronk — but I hate people who drive when they are dronk. He shows a good zenze of rezponzibility. Vhot do you think of him Juliana?"

"Oh, I like him too. I always thought he was a nice person even when he didn't sound it on the radio. But socially I only know him half an hour better than you do. Of course he's quite a bit older than . . ." she caught herself, stopped and looked out of the window. The Captain was nodding up against his wife's shoulder and began a few soft snores.

"Stop it Jan. You had too much Bols too. How old is he Juliana?"

"Oh, Mummy", and she turned her head at right angles, "how should I know?"

"Wait. I think heard him zay once on the radio that he was fifteen when the war in Europe stopped. Letz zee. That makes him thirty-zeven minuz nearly twenty four comes to thirteen. Your father is eleven year older than I am. Not too old for you at all."

"Mummy, please stop it," the girl said without enthusiasm. "You know very well we've only just met and he drove me home. That's all. Don't start jumping to conclusions as you did with that intern and that co-pilot. So I'm nearly twenty-four. Attractive, or so they say — and no wedding bells in sight. Now what's that supposed to make me? A freak or something? Right now, I like life just the way it is, thank you."

"Ach, your Moeder has a hunch about these thingz Juliana. I haf en intuition about him — you vill see. It vill be quick. I never did haf this feeling about all the many other boy friendz you haf had. Before long you vill not know vhot has hit you. I know I don't haf to tell you to be carefol, my good darling little girl."

Tresilian slept late, showered and had a leisurely breakfast. He was looking forward to four o'clock and having her alone with him for a few hours. He'd try to talk her out of Expo if he could — too many people and too much activity. Perhaps she'd go along with a run out to Knowlton for dinner at a place he knew. He'd play it off the cuff.

The weather was fine and he had lots of time so he lit a pipe and walked down to the autostade parking lot to retrieve his car.

He drove back, parked and went up to his apartment for a short snooze. He had just got his head down on the pillow when the phone rang.

"Yes, hello, Tresilian here."

"Mr. Glyn Tresilian?"

"Yes, speaking"

"Thank you. Long distance calling. Go ahead sir."

"Hello, Glyn we haven't met — although I've seen and heard your work often when I've been in Montreal. I'm Doug Binnings, producer of Public . . ."

"Yes, of course, Doug. And may I say how much I've admired the fine shows you've done . . ." Binnings was at the helm of Canada's top rated and best public affairs show, the CBC National Network's 'Public Affairs One'. 'PA 1' consistently justified its arrogant choice of name by presenting weekly programs of the highest calibre in the primest time. As an hour of television depth, style, importance and digestibility it was a peerless model of its kind. Binnings was its heart and soul. A man who deserved having his work called brilliant.

"Thanks very much, Glyn. I hear you've left CRAK. What happened?"

"Oh, problems with a commercial I was supposed to do. Big account and they wouldn't sign the integrity addendum on the contract. So that was that."

"They let you out?"

"Yes."

"Hmmm. Must've been big. They tell me you were leading the market. Oh, well. OK — just so you won't get any wrong ideas, I'd better tell you why I called. We're not planning to stir your case, although from what you've just said I think it could make a hell of a story. I'll think about it as a future project perhaps. Nor do I have a job for you. But I'd like you to come on the show early next month for a punchy panel job. Could you come here to Toronto?"

"Sure I could. What's it all about?"

"Well, I really got the idea from you the other day. I was in Montreal for the Expo opening and I heard you one morning in the hotel. That was some great stuff you had about getting governments out of peace-making. Was that showbiz — or do you honestly believe what you were saying?"

"Every word of it."

"Good. Then we'll do it. It'll be live — and we'll pay all your expenses of course. You'll get a confirming letter with tickets and arrangements. I'm going to use half the show for it and I want thirty very lively and meaty minutes. I'm calling it the 'Way to Peace' and there'll be three others on with you. I'm not sure who they'll be yet. But probably a clergyman, a print journalist, and a scholar — something like that. But I'll be relying on you to goose the thing. You'll be the voice of the people — frustrated by governments in their individual quest for peace, exactly the way you put it. If you give as I heard you the other day it'll be dandy. OK Glyn and thanks. Looking forward to seeing you soon. Bye"

.   .   .   .   .   .

He picked up Julie in time to get across the Champlain Bridge and on the Eastern Townships autoroute before the rush hour began. Not that there was much difference in traffic congestion at any time of day or night surrounding the Montreal area in the spring, summer and early fall of 1967.

"Do you drive, Julie?", he asked her as the car hummed along to the first toll gate.

"No. I wouldn't have the foggiest with all those gears and things that you have on your car. Oh, I steered one a bit sometime ago. But I've never been all that keen to learn."

"Whose car did you steer?"

"Oh, I've forgotten. Someone I went out with I suppose."

"I bet you go out a lot?"

"Not so much now of course. Flying's not too good for social life. But yes, I went around a fair bit before. Especially after I'd graduated from nursing."

"Lots of boy friends?"

"Yes, quite a few."

"You like playing the field?"

"I think it's better than getting stuck before you know what you're looking for, don't you? Although Mummy thinks I've been on the shelf too long. But you must've done the same as a sailor before you got married?"

"Oh, yes I imagine I did. But tell me more. No, wait. Do you have any quarters? Surely they must have paid for this road by now. Same damn thing with the Laurentian autoroute. You need to be a millionaire to drive on these highways."

She took some change from her purse. He loved the touch of her hand as she put the coins in his. He flung two quarters in the basket and set the car off for the next interception a few miles further on.

"Now. What's this about you being on the shelf?"

"Oh, that became a family joke a long time ago. When I was training at the hospital I used to go out with a lot of interns. Mummy wanted to meet them all. It was quite funny the way she used to size them up. 'Ach, Julie,' she'd say, 'it vill be good for you to marry en doctor. You vill have en good life vith zecurity' — you know how she talks. Daddy thought it was quite funny too. And then since I've been flying they've met one or two co-pilots as well."

"Hmm. Doctors and flyers. That's some contrast. How do they stack up?"

"Oh, about the same I'd say. Most of them only want you for you know what. You do like to ask questions don't you?"

"That's about the only way I know how to earn a living."

"Well, I must say I do feel a bit as if you've been interviewing me. Now let's turn the table. Mummy was getting you married off again last night wasn't she? What did you think about that?"

"Much as you do, I'd say. Sure I'd like to get spliced. But when you've already been married once, it's even harder to know what you want a second time. Say, do you mind if we catch the news a minute? There may be something more on the de Gaulle visit. They've started fencing already in Ottawa and Quebec City."

He switched on the radio and they listened to the network newscast. It looked like trouble, mainly over the protocol of whether the Federal or Quebec Government should welcome the French President as he stepped off his cruiser at Quebec City. He turned off the set and they chatted again.

"I agree with Mummy," Julie said, "Why don't they stop all this nonsense about separatism? There's so much for everyone. And as to who should be the first to shake hands with President de Gaulle — of course it should be the Governor-General. He'll be arriving in Canada, won't he?"

"Yes, but you try telling Danny Boy that. Or better still — some of the people in his cabinet. I'm convinced they're the one's who're really hurting. Anyway, enough of that. I don't want politics to spoil the evening. Tell me Julie — have I jumped the queue?"

"What does that mean?" and now she was looking at him all the time with her chin resting on the hand that she'd put across the back of the seat.

"Well, right off the top of your vacation, I've been lucky enough to see you two days in a row. I've not pre-empted anyone have I?"

"Oh, that's what they say on the television when they cancel a program for something else. No. I don't think there's anyone moping at home considering suicide just because I'm with you tonight. A couple of fellows know I'm home and said they'd give me a call to go to Expo — but that's about all."

"Did they call yet?"

"Not that I know of."

"Who are they?"

"My, you talk like a jealous lover or something. One's just finished interning, and the other's a flight engineer I flew with once."

"Then perhaps there's a chance that I could see you again before you go back to work?"

"I'll answer that when you ask me."

"Then here it comes. I'm asking you now."

She turned her head and looked at the road for a few seconds. And then at him again.

"Alright. But I do want to see Expo as much as possible."

He sighed, and smiled as he glanced at her for a moment.

"Then let me be your guide, Julie. Oh, and I've got a pass too. Frankly I hate using the thing unless it's for a legitimate reason but you're a wonderful reason and . . ."

"What do you do with it then?"

"Well, it allows you to go in pretty well anywhere ahead of the lineups. They've issued thousands of them to press from all over the world. The idea is that you can get in for filming or whatever without having to wait in line. But most of us are just using it for our own personal benefit I think. God, I felt awful the other day. There was a hell of a line outside the Western Provinces pavilion and I wanted to see it quickly. 1 walked up to the head of the queue and showed the guy my pass. He recognized me anyway and so did a lot of the local people who'd been waiting a long time to get in. I wish I hadn't heard some of their remarks."

"That I can believe," she agreed and nodded her head. The setting sunlight glinted the smooth shine of her hair. "But then — you must have grown a pretty thick skin by now. I'm surprised that things like that would worry you."

"Oh, they certainly do. Skin's much too thin for comfort with the crazy work I've been doing."

"Why do it then?"

"Because I love it. And whether you believe it or not, the fact is I believe in it too. Used properly, and by that I don't mean the way we use it on commercial radio stations, it could be one hell of a force for good. I've always thought that — that the open line idea was the most conclusive form of communication between people. I was convinced of it when I first heard Denny Trample and having done a show myself I know it's right. But it's useless when you use it just for audience-getting bait. Anyway, we're almost there and I don't want to bore you with my ideas. We'll have a fine steak and some wine. You like filet mign . . ."

"No, please carry on. I find this kind of talk very interesting. I want to hear more. Remember I only know about sutures and safety belts."

"You asked for it," he said. "First chance we get for some serious talk. But not tonight eh?"

It was nearly ten o'clock by the time they had lingered over and finished dinner. They were both mellow and in good spirits as he started the car for the drive home. They set off on the narrow winding road bound for the autoroute entrance. After a mile or so, he slowed the Armstrong-Siddeley.

"Tell you what. We're almost at Brome Lake. How about a romantic moonlight stroll? It's such a fine night and I know a great little spot just down there and neither of us have to......."

"Well, at least it's more original than running out of gas. Shouldn't we be getting back though?"

"Why? Do you have to work in the morning? I don't". "The stroll, yes. Anything else, no," she said firmly.

He stopped the car at a small sandy bay on the lake off the road. He held her hand as they picked their way down the stony slope to the water's edge.

"What a fine place," she said and looked up and down at the few yards of beach, "we can walk for miles and miles. Across the lake perhaps."

"Ah, now you're being unkind, Julie. Now your mean streak's coming out," he said jokingly. "So we can't walk anywhere. Let's sit down then and have a smoke."

They sat down on some drift wood. Tresilian lit her cigarette and held on to her hand. After a moment or two he threw both burning filter tips into the water, and cautiously put his arms around her to protect her from the oncoming cold. She yielded as he kissed her lips and ears. He opened her mouth with his tongue. She warmed to him, and as she pulled him to her they rolled off the planks, lying side by side on the rocky ground.

"You're beautiful", he breathed and kissed her on her chest above her dress, "and I don't care what you say, but I think I'm falling in love with you."

She didn't answer and went on playing with his hair and caressed his ear. Slowly and gently he eased down the zipper at the back of her dress and undid the clasps on her white brassiere. Delicately, he slid his hand behind and around and then put his fingers between the loose cup and her breast. Then suddenly, she moved.

"No, Glyn, no. We mustn't. That's enough. I don't want to get so far I can't stop. Come on, I think we'd better be going."
Reluctantly, he brushed off his coat and his temples stopped throbbing. Neither of them spoke until they came to the auto-route.

"All the people who take you out make passes?"

"Look, Glyn, I'm always being told I've got a sexy body and face and all that so l don't blame you. I'm not a prude, and I hope it won't turn your head if I tell you I was enjoying it too. But I'll tell you something now — and I hope you won't think I'm some kind of oddity. I'm still intact — I'm a virgin. And I'm going to stay that way until I can really relax and enjoy losing it."

"Julie, I'm sorry I......"

Oh, for heaven's sake." she laughed. "Men can carry on for hours worrying about nothing. I didn't stop you from the beginning, did I?"

"Did you hear what I said when we were down there?"

"Yes, I heard you. Now let's change the subject completely. When do you . . ."

"Ask me anything except what I'm going to be doing."

"That's exactly what I was going to ask. Surely you must be worried about the uncertainty?"

"I am. Damned worried about the uncertainty — of your feeling for me. Because I'm getting more and more certain of mine for you."

"Now, Glyn, I don't want to talk about that any more tonight When do you think you'll be going to Toronto?"

"I'll be there again next month. Oh, I forget to tell you. They want me to do something on PA-I."

"Oh, how exciting. You mean for one show or are you . . ."

"No, no. A one shot deal. Panelist on a discussion about the ways to peace. They want me to be vox populi."

"Your radio show should qualify you very well for that part. When will it be on?"

"The eleventh, I think he said."

"I'll try very hard to watch it, Glyn. Wherever I am. And that'll probably be in the air I expect", she said and laughed sadly.

"What will you actually have to do?"

"Oh, stir the pot, I suppose. Doug Binnings, the producer heard me running off at the mouth the other day about peace and Viet-Nam and all the rest of it. He seemed to like the concept of ordinary people creating this vast demand for peace, and governments not supplying it. You know the basic business tenet? 'Find a need and fill it'? Well the need's there — that's for damn sure, but no one looks like filling it. The other three'll doubtless be experts in their own field — I think he said a clergyman, print journalist and a scholar or politician or maybe both — and me. And I'll do the outraged average-man-in-street bit."

"Do you have any ideas?"

"Plenty. But not the kind you approve of. No, sorry. What sort of ideas?"

"Well, about this program. You'll have to come up with something won't you? I suppose they'll be full of learning and theory which you as the average man aren't supposed to understand."

"Oh, yes. I see. Well, that's very simple, Julie. I agree with Buckminister Fuller. I heard him say once that if people want peace to come and hunger to go, they should put every single politician in orbit around the sun for a million years — and the world would be populated by well fed peaceful people. I don't know whether he was joking or not. But that's one point I'll raise on the show. And you know what?"

"What?" she asked.

"One of them — the clergyman probably — is bound to come out and condemn that scheme as being impracticable! But I just don't see any way to world peace or a solution in Viet-Nam until you can actually put people in touch with each other. And that's an impossibility. For all kinds of reasons. But you only need the main one — language. I've beaten this subject to death for a long time. On and off the air. We've had politicians, diplomats, experts of all kinds. It doesn't matter where you talk and question, the problem's the same. Governments and nationalism go to-gether. But people want to go in peace and they're not allowed to. I used those very words on the air the day before I left CRAK. But I thought we weren't going to let politics spoil the evening."

"Spoiling it? Certainly not. I love this sort of conversation. It's very seldom I hear any of it. Listen — I've just thought of something."

"Yes?"

"Yes. But I doubt that it would do you any good. I might as well tell you though. If, as you say, you really believe in radio open line programs being a good way for people to communicate with each other, why not suggest it on a world wide scale?"

Tresilian dipped his headlights. He didn't reply for a few seconds.

"Very good theory Julie — and that's all."

"Well, that's what I thought, but if you're going to be talking about getting rid of all the politicians, why not bring that up too? I don't think it's any crazier is it?"

"No, that's just the trouble. It's not really crazy at all — and that's why no one would ever take it seriously. But, now you mention it, no one's going to take anything I say seriously anyway — so why not? Thanks for the thought. I'll work on it and throw it in. Do you want to make an early start tomorrow?"

"Yes. I want to see as much as possible. I don't know if I'll get another chance."

"OK — I'll call for you at nine. How about doing the theme pavilions first?"

"You said you'd be my guide didn't you?", and she leaned over and kissed him on the cheek.

.　　.　　.　　.　　.　　.　　.　　.

He parked in the basement garage and went up to his apartment. He was tired and happy and he couldn't get Julie out of his mind. Gone completely were his first thoughts as he'd watched her in the airplane aisle. Never again, he swore, would he see her as a glorious roll in bed for a night or two. Sure, he told himself, he'd been in love with Peta. But with her it came after Michael was born.

He showered and got into bed and thought about her. He forced himself to think about the CORK offer. If he was going anywhere with Julie, he'd better make up his mind soon. He liked the possibilities of Greenway's offer — but not the idea of settling in Toronto. However, now he thought about it, he felt sure he could do for CORK what he had done for CRAK — and probably in less time too. He'd gone through the pains of experience — and Toronto wasn't a split-personality and two-language market.

He slept and woke up to a fine looking early morning. He went to the balcony and did his usual breathing exercises with a thin stick held behind his back. He did this primarily as an aid to voice conditioning. He'd learnt the simple but effective measure a year before from Dame Gwynneth Rhondda-Llandaff then on a promotion tour for her London Opera Company. Dame Gwynneth, the aging high priestess of the aria, had spent a week in Montreal. In her day after World War I she had been the favourite of the old aristocracy, as well as the rising new class of industrial princes.

After a few months at CRAK, Tresilian had found that he didn't really like meeting celebrities, particularly when they came from the stage and screen. Too often they were disappointingly empty, anxious and confused. But then he usually met them under the trying and tiring conditions of publicising a film, or a book, or a new series of programs. Dame Gwynneth was an exception. He was awed at the prospect of meeting this woman whose name shone with the fame of a Tetrazini or Melba. As the time of the broadcast neared, he suffered badly from an uncharacteristic touch of nerves.

Gwynneth Jones had been born the fourth child of a miner in the Rhondda valley coal fields of South Wales. As she grew up and sang with her playmates at school and in concerts, it soon became apparent to the local adjudicators that in the natural range and beauty of her voice they had found a diamond in the coal face of the valley. The news spread through the towns and villages of the Rhondda. The people of Llandaff started and sustained a fund for the little girl to which thousands of music loving South Welsh families contributed. Soon there was enough money to send Gwynneth to London for training. She made her debut at the Royal Opera House Covent Garden when at 22 she sang the lead part in Puccini's 'Madam Butterfly'. She received a tumultuous ovation helped along by a full trainload of Welsh miners, many of whom had seen their Principality triumph that afternoon at Twickenham. The atmosphere, as she took bow after bow, was wet with the sad happiness of Wales.

As a mark of appreciation for the people who had paid for her training, the soprano took Rhondda-Llandaff as her professional name. Her agent was very pleased. Compared to Jones, he thought the name Rhondda-Llandaff sheer majesty.

As Tresilian had waited for Dame Gwynneth in the lobby at CRAK, he realized how unqualified he was to interview her -- which he would have to do briefly before opening his 'Crakkerjack line' to the listeners. Here was no politician, or showbusiness 'personality', or television star. In a few minutes he'd meet a real artist for the first time in his life.

A chauffeur helped her to the main door. Frail and leaning on a stick, her eyes still sparkled and she bore herself well. Glyn knew that she was in her early seventies.

"Mr. Glyn Tresilian?"

"Yes, Dame Gwynneth. A privilege to meet you. As you're so punctual, we have time for a little tea or coffee before going on the air. Will you come with me?"

"How very kind of you. I think you're very generous in giving me all this time to talk about the opera. But we're hoping that this experiment of taking a road company out will work well. And so naturally we're deeply indebted to you people of the radio and television for all the wonderful help you're giving us. Thank you — one spoonful of sugar please."

She drank her tea and smiled at him. Now, never at a loss for long, Glyn dried up.

"I've heard quite a lot about you since I arrived in Montreal Mr. Tresilian. You'll be pleased to know it's all been good," and she laughed — almost as he'd heard on one of her records.

"And what a splendid sounding name. Tresilian. Like the tinkle of a silver bell. Cornish of course?"

"Er, yes, Dame Gwynneth."

"Ah, then we shall do well together. You Cornish and we Welsh are almost kinfolk. Now they tell me that you have one of these 'open line' programs that people talk about so much nowadays — and they wanted me to talk to the listeners or something? How do you do this? Will I have to wear those dreadful earphones that crackle and make such a noise?"

"No Ma'am. It's very easy. We'll have a short opening interview — in your case it will be very brief as you're so well known. Then we'll open the telephones. The idea, when we have a guest, is to put the people in direct touch with each other and the guest. True communication you might say." And he hoped it didn't sound too corny.

"Do you really think they're interested enough in Grand Opera to ask questions about it for two hours?"

"I've found Dame Gwynneth, in this work, that you can never be sure of anything when it comes to public taste. I've been wrong so often in trying to predict successes and failures with topics. For example; once I was persuaded against my better commercial judgment to have a lady archaeologist as a studio guest. Now you'd think, when dealing with grass roots audiences that the subject of archaeology would be anathema. Especially so when you find at the last minute that your guest wants only to talk about some exciting new finds of Etruscan pottery.

"It was one of the best and liveliest shows we've ever done. But only because the lady was an unintentional 'character' in her own right and fascinated everyone by bringing the whole thing to life. She dramatised the 'digs' and painted in the picture of intention and hope and near failure and cost — and then the final triumph. I think radio is at its very best when it does this kind of thing.

"On the other hand, soon after the Etruscan pottery smash, please forgive me for that, we failed miserably when a much married, internationally famous Hollywood bombshell turned up in the studio. But only on the condition that she would not be obliged to talk about her marriages. This of course was about the only thing the public wanted from her. Cut that off and you had nothing left. So really she had nothing to say of interest about anything and the response fell away to zero.

"But I suppose she still helped the local movie house box office where her latest picture was playing. And that was really the only object of the exercise."

He felt much better now and at complete ease with her. The broadcast was a honey. The audience and Dame Gwynneth got on famously. So much so that the show was extended by another hour. And it was noon before they finished. The great lady was delighted.

After warmly complimenting Glyn for an unusually nice speaking voice she added. "But would I be right in saying that it has never been coached or trained — and moreover that no one has ever told you about breathing and the diaphragm?"

"Right on both counts."

"I thought not. I noticed, during the broadcast, that you find it necessary to force your voice — especially at the end of a sentence. This is because you have a tendency to slouch — which rounds your shoulders and brings them forward at the same time. Now because you work with this slovenly posture, you don't get enough breath in your lungs to see you through. It's rather like a car having to refuel an unnecessary number of times. In other words, fill your tank to the brim." Then in front of her car Dame Gwynneth demonstrated the exercise for Tresilian which he had done without fail each morning ever since.

To meet and spend a few hours with the Dame Gwynneths of this world were the real prizes of life. As he filled his lungs and exercised, he hoped that Dame Gwynneth would recover well from all illness that had recently laid her low. She was in England — in a London hospital and today before calling for Julie, he would write to her, wishing her all the best and asking if he might call on her when next in the U.K. He felt sure she'd remember him. He showered and changed, and boiled himself an egg. Afterwards, he wrote and mailed his letter.

CHAPTER 7

The weather was summery and perfect without much humidity. They went around a few pavilions on Ile Notre Dame and took a ride at La Ronde. Then they rested by a lagoon — one of several oases for the feet at Expo. Julie took off her shoes and sat upright with her arms clasped in front of her legs. Tresilian lit a cigarette. Apropos of nothing he said.

"Dame Gwynneth would be pleased with you."

"Dame who?" and she looked at him quizzically.

"Dame Gwynneth".

"Sounds like a fortune teller — is she?"

He told her about the great soprano and his admiration for the old lady.

"Oh, yes — of course I've heard of her, Glyn. Who hasn't? But why do you say she'd be pleased with me?"

"Posture. Yours is good. Upright and straight. I'm all twisted and curved. Never mind. How about the Japanese for dinner? If it's not too crowded. I wish they hadn't gone quite so modern though. I've heard the girls are all wearing European dress," he said and got up off the grass.

"What's wrong with that?"

"Kimonos are better. I know. I've been there. And they can remember their roles more easily when they wear them."

"What roles?"

"To be completely subservient to men of course. You don't go for that? No, I didn't think you would. OK. Let's go and see if we can hit the sake and saki-yuki."

He took her to Expo every day during her vacation. When her intern and pilot friends had called, she asked them for rainchecks. She was due to report for duty at the airport on Sunday evening. They spent the Saturday night roistering in the excellent beer garden. They sang happily and lifted their steins in merry toasts. Tresilian joyfully flung small change into the voracious jaws of the sousaphone as it came round with yet another roopy 'Ein Prosit' and heavy servings of 'Gemutlichkeit'.

"Oh, this is fun, Glyn. I've never drunk so much beer in my life," Julie said happily, "but I think I might as well stay in the bathroom all the time. Ah, there's a bit of a lull in the line-up I think. Better go while I can. Won't be long."

They left when the beer garden closed with much hand-shaking, singing and beery goodwill. Tresilian predicted that he'd have a hangover in the morning. In the cab going back to her parents' house in NDG, he asked her.

"Julie, What time did you say you wanted to go to Church to-morrow?" and he put his arm around her waist.

"Eleven o'clock, I think. I'd rather like to get to High Mass if I could. Sometimes I never make it at all when we're flying on Sundays."

"But you don't have to confess that. It's not your fault if . . ."

"No, of course it isn't. If you can't go. But if you can go and deliberately miss — well that's another matter."

"Have you ever purposely missed going?"

"No, never. I'm glad to say."

"What's it like being a Roman Catholic, Julie? I must say I could never go for the confession bit." He put his head on her shoulder and held both her hands.

"That's a funny question. What's it like? I don't know. It's just like being normal as far as I know. I've never known what's it like being anything else. But I don't think anyone who's not a Catholic can understand the confession bit, as you call it. All I know is that I feel a lot better once I've got rid of something that's been bothering me. It's like someone carrying a heavy suitcase for you when you're in a hurry and you're late and you're tired. It gives you a kind of fast, fast relief as they say in the commercials. But this is a funny subject to get on to after the evening we've had isn't it?"

"No, I like it," he murmured and kissed her. The cabdriver glanced in his mirror. "Would you like me to come with you again tomorrow?"

"To Mass?"

"Yes."

"You know, I would."

After church, they went back to join Captain and Mrs. de

Vries for lunch. Julie spent the afternoon writing letters and sorting out odds and ends.

"With you rushing me off my feet, I havent done anything at all that I'd planned," she said and sealed another envelope.

"Sorry, Julie."

"Oh, come on now, don't sound so sad. You know I've loved it. I don't know when I've had such a good time. And we've seen nearly everything at Expo. I'm sure I'll have a chance to see Labrynthe before it closes."

He was lounging on her bed while she worked at the small desk in the corner.

"Would that be with me that you'll be seeing Labrynthe?"

"That depends on you, doesn't it? But I hope so. And now you really must keep quiet or I'll never get finished."

He kicked off his shoes, fluffed up her pillow and slept for an hour. He woke up and heard crockery rattling. Mrs. de Vries put a tray of cups and coffee on the night table.

"Vhot next, Glyn," she said, "sleeping on my daughter's bed. Disguzting behaviour. You vere tired eh? Kom, haf en cop of coffee. You vill feel better. Juliana, at vhat time do you haf to be at the airport?"

"Seven thirty, Mummy."

"Glyn vill be driving you I suppose? And vhat about zupper?"

"Oh, not to worry Mrs. de Vries. I'll get her there in lots of time and we can have a bite in the restaurant. I don't think we'll need much in any case — after that good lunch you gave us."

When they were ready to leave, Tresilian thanked her mother and father and waited for her in the car. Julie kissed her parents in the hallway.

"Vhen do we see you again, Juliana?"

"In a couple of weeks. I'll be on the Toronto - Vancouver route for a few days now."

"Now, I don't vant you to laugh, my little one. But zurely this time you must . . ."

"Alright Mummy, alright," and she winked at her father, "I know what's coming next. Yes, I like him very much. More than anyone else I've been out with. But don't go jumping to any conclusions. It's been a very short time. He's quite a bit older than I am, and by to-morrow he might forget all about me. Goodbye — see you both again soon. And, Mummy — don't worry."

She got in the car and the de Vries waved from the front door as they set out for the airport.

"Julie, I'm going to miss you. Do you think you'll feel the same?" he said as they left the cul-de-sac.

"I think I will. But let's just wait and see shall we? I think absence is a good way of finding out about things. I really hope you'll do well on that show, Glyn. I'll see if I can't wangle it so that I can watch. I'm positive about the schedule — but I'll manage to catch it somehow. If it'll help — just feel sure I'm watching," she said and looked at him — a tender expression softening her lovely young face.

"I'll do my best. Especially if I know that. But then I suppose if you pose as a pro you should do your best all the time. I heard a good bit on that the other day. 'A professional is someone who can perform well when he doesn't feel like it — and an amateur can't when he does'. But that idea of yours — about some sort of world-wide open line radio show is good."

"Have you thought any more about it?"

"How could I have thought about anything but you in the last week or so? No, don't answer that. But, honestly Julie — I can't see how much more thinking one could do on the subject. It's an idea. Unworkably idealistic, they'll say. And that's about it. But it'll be good stuff to throw in. Might even get me marks for another bit of useless originality."

They drove on in silence and he parked in the big space in front of the terminal building at Dorval. As she was in uniform, Julie decided that it would be better if they didn't go into the licensed bar. So instead they had coffee and a sandwich at the horseshoe counter in the snack bar. For the first time, she felt self-conscious in her uniform as the stares at Glyn came their way. She was glad when he picked up the check and they left.

"I guess this is it for now, Julie. But I'll see you again in a couple of weeks?"

"Yes, promise. No, Glyn — we'd better not. Not here. Not in uniform. Be good. I'll be thinking about you. And thanks for everything." She lowered her voice to a whisper. "Consider yourself kissed. Bye." She turned, and walked pertly down the concourse. He watched her turn the corner.

He was miserable and depressed. He spent the next week

lounging around his apartment. He thought about her constantly and longed to hold her in his arms again. At the end of the week there was a letter from Dame Gwynneth in hospital.

Dear Mr. Tresilian,

You really are most kind to think of me and write. Thank you for your good wishes. I don't believe half the things the experts say — as far as I'm concerned, it's just been a mild case of the 'collywobbles'.

I was surprised to hear the news that you have left the radio station. I will always remember it fondly and the hours I spent with you. They were great fun. It surprises me not at all though that you may go elsewhere. At a guess I would say that you've received many propositions. Particularly now that you have your breathing, lungs and resonance all functioning properly with the diaphragm!

I didn't know about your son and in-laws in Cheshire. I do like it there; the countryside, especially the Wirral, is quite delightful.

Do please let me know when you intend coming over. I should be most put out if you didn't at least try to get in touch. I shall be leaving here in another day or so, and will go down to my cottage in Sussex where a friend is coming to stay — and she will be good company and a lot of help. The address is on the card attached.

Then I must be busy with plans for the Autumn Tour of the Company. You'll be glad to know that the 'experiment' was such a success in Canada and the U.S. that talks began about doing it again this year before we were half way through our itinerary. I'm so pleased about it all. And you can be sure that wherever you are I'll be calling on you for help!

Somehow I know that things will work well for you. Try not to be anxious. My intuition, usually reliable, tells me that life has not always given you what you wanted. All will be made good. You'll see. Be happy and remember your breathing!

With affection,

Gwynneth Rhondda-Llandaff

P.S. I hear very good reports about the Expo. Do wish I could see it — but I think it will be over by the time we arrive. Pity.

G. R-L.

He read the letter several times and felt better. Apart from talking and stalling with Dan Greenway who called him from CORK in Toronto, he'd stayed home since Julie left. He found it hard to concentrate on anything for very long and his days were an endless journey between the kitchen, bookshelf and record player. But the days were passing and that was the main thing. She'd soon be back and he'd see her again. Oh, my God, there was that 'PA 1' show in a couple of days. He hadn't done anything about it. But he'd better do well. She'd be watching alright. Might as well get off the butt and bone up a bit.

He went to the Atwater Public Library and dug for some background to augment his own radically unacceptable views on world peace. He looked, but found nothing to confirm his belief that the world could have peace if there weren't any governments. He took out Trygve Lie's 'In the cause of peace', and read a lot of it that evening. He found particularly interesting the 20 year peace plan that the first UN Secretary-General had drawn up and circulated. By now, had it been used properly, he thought, there would be peace and co-existence.

．　　．　　　．　　　．　　　．　　　．　　　．　　　．

"Hello, Glyn. Good to see you. Thanks for being punctual. I can see you're not a politician! Be right with you. That telecine problem solved now Carol? Good." Doug Binnings was busy. It was two hours before air time for 'Public Affairs One' when Tresilian reported to the producer in the studio.

There was ceaseless activity on the big studio floor as technical producers, floor managers, script assistants, lighting men, sound men, cameramen, set designers, graphic artists and stagehands all made their special contributions to the organized chaos that sets in before a major television program. The size of preshow confusion varies in direct ratio to the size of the production. 'Public Affairs One' was the biggest in Canada.

Tresilian sat on one of the audience bleachers and watched the frenzy mount as the busy crew members matched cameras, adjusted lighting, moved and painted sets. Two script assistants checked long, wide, yellow giantsize rolls of paper for copy accuracy. These would be attached to the teleprompter stands above the camera lenses for the hosts to read.

The Floor Manager came over to Glyn.

"Mr. Tresilian? Mr. Binnings would like you to join him and

the other panelists in the Conference Room. Just down the hallway there, second door on the right."

"Come right in, Glyn. I think we're all here now. Glyn Tresilian. Frank Fogarty — he'll be moderating you. Now meet your fellow panelists — professor Archibald Whiting; the Reverend George Glendower; and Tom Pelluet. Just let me get through with my bit first and then you can chat among yourselves. Sit down anywhere. I don't have much time I'm afraid. We've had problems with the telecine chain and we're late for camera rehearsal." Binnings took out a pipe and rested against the edge of the table. He was a tall grey man in his middle fifties, and knew more about television than anyone in the country.

"I'm glad you could all come. You three Toronto people are possibly wondering what Glyn Tresilian's doing here. Well, I'll tell you. To needle you. Oh, I know we've got lots of them here — but he's a new face. And the other reason is that I liked what he was saying about the subject on his radio show a while back in Montreal when I was there."

From a professional point of view, the others on the panel were experts in comparison. Glyn thought he'd be out-classed if he attempted any sophisticated expertise. He'd better play the 'innocent-man-in-the-street' role to the hilt. Professor Whiting was introduced to Glyn by Binnings as "a career diplomat for years with External Affairs — now has a History Chair in Toronto. Mr. Glendower's an Anglican Minister with special experience on Human Rights Committees and other work at the UN. And Tom Pelluet, as you probably know wields a mean pen as the Toronto Tribune's international specialist. You're the grass-roots expert. Altogether, on paper, it looks like a great panel. Just make sure it works that way. Frank, don't give any of 'em an inch," he smiled at 'PA1's' well known co-host. "Sail in and whip 'em right back to the point if they get even a centimetre off it.

"I don't want any theology, George — or any vague theorising, Professor Whiting. Tom — resist, on tonight's show, your over bearing cynicism. Glyn, I want you to blow your cork.

"We'll open off the top with a two minute film animation showing 'Man and his Wars' from the cavemen to Hiroshima. An instant history of mankind, if you like. That's if they can get the damned telecine working in time. None of you will see the film until air. When you get your cue Frank, before anything else, ask each one to give about 20 seconds of comment on it. Then go. OK gents? Good. Have fun."

Tresilian had not met any of his fellow panelists before, but knew them all well by reputation. They were clever, experienced and respected in their fields. Each of them had broadcast many times in the past, and as he sized up his partners again, he longed for the ordinary and non-academic world of his 'Crakkerjack line' . . . How much easier that would be. Tom Pelluet was the first to speak.

"Why don't we try and find some coffee?"

"Good idea, Tom. I'll go if you like. There must be some machines or a coffee shop handy," Tresilian offered.

They went off and filled in the time at a table in the cafeteria. In spite of the closeness of their interests, it took half an hour for them to put their diviners away and feel comfortable. A script girl came down and took them to make up. Not long after they'd had their faces powdered, they sat down at the desk table on the set. 'Voice checks' over, they were ready. The show was on the air.

"Good evening, Canada. I'm Frank Fogarty. Welcome to 'Public Affairs One'. The way to peace — is there one? You may not think so after you watch this", and he pressed a cue button on his desk, "short piece of animated film." By the time he had reached his last word the film was on the air and the panelists watched it on one of the big studio colour monitors.

There was neither narration nor music. Several dozen pictures in frenetic succession traced man's history from primitive clubmanship through improving mechanized warfare to the atom. The picture held still for a few seconds and then the words 'The Last War' were boldly superimposed on it. The image moved to Fogarty and the floor manager dropped his arm from the horizontal.

"To discuss The Way to Peace, if there is one, we have a distinguished and articulate panel. The moderator introduced them in turn. "Gentlemen, to begin with, I'd like you to comment for a few seconds on the film which you and our viewing audience have just seen for the first time. Glyn Tresilian."

"I thought it was an admirable compression of the story of man. If 'The Last War' at the end of it was meant to be a definitive statement in the past tense, I would disagree. The historical record we've seen is true. Unless every individual is prepared to take the responsibility of changing his own attitude by himself, 'The Last War' is the next war. And it may come at any time."

"Mr. Glendower?"

"Yes, well, our friend Tresilian here reacts in a gloomy way and I find his remarks depressing. He should . . ."

"No doubt, Mr. Glendower and you'll have ample time to express yourself on that point later on. But first we want your own brief comments on the film."

"Good boy Frank", Binnings said in the control room as he watched the live picture and three others on the bank of monitor screens. "Take three. Move in camera one. Right in. Give me a really hard close up on him. That's nice. Take one. Camera four — move round to a cover shot. Camera two — see if you can set Pelluet up over Frank's shoulder. Ready one."

Nearly five million coast to coast viewers watched as the zoom lens on camera 1 held Glendower's eyes, nose, mouth and chins it its stare. It panned imperceptibly to the bulbous carbuncle on the left side of his middle chin and pitilessly X-rayed the inflamed bunion.

"My opinion of the film? Certainly. Superficial, obvious and insignificant."

"Thank you. Professor Whiting?"

"I agree with Glyn Tresilian that it was a good precis but I don't share his prediction."

"Good. Gentlemen — the floor is yours."

The discussion began like this:

Glendower   "Of course there is a way to peace. In these nuclear times, there must be a way to peace, otherwise . . ."

Tresilian   "Otherwise what, Mr. Glendower?"

Glendower   "Otherwise I'd appreciate being allowed to finish the flow of my observations before being interrupted. Obviously if we do not find the way to peace — it could be the end of mankind."

Tresilian   "Then we agree. That's precisely the point I made after we saw the film. I concede that my remarks must sound gloomy and depressing — but there's every reason for that. What is there to cause us joy?"

Glendower "I find your reactions gloomy and depressing because you seem to rule out all hope that man will find the way. I don't share that pessimism. I merely said solutions to world problems must be found and I am sure that they will be found. The alternative is so unthinkable that we mustn't even envision it."

Whiting "It's difficult, at this early stage in our discussion to understand what precise ways to peace Glendower has in mind. It would appear that Mr. Tresilian has long since resigned himself to the near arrival of Armageddon. I believe that the way to peace or to the solution of any problem is along the road that leads to negotiation."

Pelluet "I'll be less philosophical. In 1945, when the UN was founded at San Francisco, I had hoped it would have been the first step on a ladder to world government. In my opinion there is no other formula if you want the kind of peace that will last. I gave up hoping that the UN would become a catalyst for world government when I realised that, more important than anything else to the Great Powers was their work for a reduction of the Secretary-General's powers and authority."

This provoked a general discussion on the United Nations, its few successes and many failures. Tresilian remained quiet, satisfied that the argument was going in the direction he wanted — to an analysis of nationalism. He waited for the opening and it came. He waded in:

Tresilian "By talking about the reasons why the United Nations can't work, I think we've finally reached the nub. I have a very simple equation, and please remember that it has to be simple in my case — representing as I do, the average man-on-the-street. It goes like this: 'Politicians plus goverment plus nationalism equals war'. No. Wait, please. I'm convinced Eisenhower knew this in 1959 when, as President of the United States he visited Britain and appeared on television with Prime Minister Harold MacMillan. I remember his words — I saw the show. He said, 'You know Harold, people in the world want peace so badly that governments are just going to have to get out of the way and let them have it.' The equation tells me that there is a way to peace — and one way only. And that's for people to act individually. People, not governments, should be put in touch with each other. And that means communication......"

Glendower   "Now really. Is this supposed to be a serious television program or a circus? I mean this is ridiculous, Mr. Fogarty.

Whiting   "On the surface — yes, I agree. But I'm sure that Mr. Tresilian is quite sincere when he presents an attractive but highly oversimplified proposition. He is modest enough to refer to himself as the spokesman for Mr. Average to-night. But one of Mr. Average's great problems is that he cannot, why should he be expected to, grasp the intricate and complex machinery of issues beneath the surface and behind the scenes. I agree with him that one cannot be a party to government without also being a party to the political process — and I further agree that politics can be a very bad business. But Mr. Tresilian, I leave you at the point where you think there is a substitute for government. There is an alternative of course — anarchy."

Pelluet   "Personally I'd like Tresilian to finish. You were saying something about communications I think."

Tresilian   "Yes. Now let's get one thing straight before we go any further......"

Glendower   "If we get one thing straight it will be a great achievement."

Tresilian   "Until quite recently, I moderated a daily open

line radio show in Montreal. And as far as I'm concerned there's no greater communications medium anywhere. I know the good it can do — and the harm it can do. If these programs are used solely to attract the largest possible number of listeners for the sake of advertising revenue — then, as is the case in North America, they generally hurt more people than they help. The reason is obvious. People will respond to and talk about the negative, salacious and smutty aspects of life. So the programs are built up mainly on that formula. And I'm not without guilt. I have dozens of examples from the three years I handled an open line show to convince me that nothing can bring people together or divide them more effectively than broadcasting of this kind."

Glendower   "Without wishing to impugn your motives in any way Mr. Tresilian, I get the impression that you are taking advantage of this program to salve your own conscience in public and that you're telling us that in this respect you are not like other men in the way you handled a radio program. But I'm puzzled as to what it has to do with the pursuit of a vital question on the national television network."

Tresilian   "Mr. Glendower, you're an Anglican Minister. You've married, christened and buried more people than you could count, I expect. Tell me now, Mr. Glendower — how many estranged married couples have you personally reconciliated?"

Glendower   "This is becoming absurd."

Tresilian   "No, it's not absurd at all. I want to know. How many?"

Glendower   "Mr. Fogarty, I regard the question as being irrelevant and impertinent."

Tresilian   "It certainly is......"

Fogarty   "Glyn Tresilian — you've had your moment. Now . . ."

Tresilian	"Mr. Moderator, please! I was asked to come on this program to put a case. I will not press Mr. Glendower. I can say however that 'Crakkerjack line' in Montreal tracked down and reunited sixteen couples in less than three years. If anyone in this visual age should doubt what radio can do -- let them remember its power. The way Goebbels used it in Nazi Germany. The way Churchill rallied the English speaking world with it during the war. The way in which Orson Welles, unintentionally, terrified a continent with his 'War of the Worlds'. Roosevelt and his....."
Whiting	"Yes, yes, of course. These proofs are quite acceptable and sufficient for me, Tresilian. You've made your point well — I suggest we move on to the next one."
Pelluet	"I think Mr. Tresilian is telling us that a way to peace is through a greater use of radio? Do you mean more and better dissemination of news and editorial comment — and discussion? That kind of thing? Because if you do, you're suggesting something that's been going on for years. There's Voice of America, Radio Moscow, Radio Peking, our own International Service, the BBC's Overseas Service. Dozens of powerful transmissions going everywhere. What are these radio programs doing for peace?"
Tresilian	"Nothing — absolutely nothing. And if I may say so Mr. Pelluet, you miss the point completely. My premise is that the world will not get peace through governments. Only through people. These shortwave broadcasts you mentioned — Voice of America, Radio Moscow and so on are propaganda agencies of their respective governments. So how can they possibly do anything to promote peace? They can't."
Fogarty	"Mr. Tresilian, we'll have to move on. Mr. Glendower."

Pelluet	"Actually, I'm wondering what our 'Open Liner' has in mind." — Tresilian didn't wait to be asked.
Tresilian	"Now the other day I was discussing to-night's show and my part in it with someone in Montreal. This person knew my views and my disenchantment with governments and therefore the UN, and suggested a kind of open line program to the world through which people could hear each other and talk to each other — understand — talk to each other. I hear you gentlemen, and at least four and half million viewers at this very moment say 'Ah, very nice. But romantic, idealist garbage.' I'd probably feel the same way if I knew nothing about the medium and heard such a scheme proposed for the first time. Obviously I don't expect to be taken seriously. But if science can do so many other things for us nowadays — why can't it put us all in touch with each other — so that we can settle our differences between ourselves as people if our governments won't settle them as nations?"

As Tresilian finished speaking, the floor manager nipped smartly out of the camera angle trained on Fogarty. He had just relayed a message from Binnings to the moderator. Fogarty must rope them all in and force the rest of the panel to discuss Tresilian's point. 'Nuts' thought Fogarty, but he was paid to follow instructions.

Fogarty	"Gentlemen, however improbable it sounds, the fact is that Glyn Tresilian's method is at least original. I too thought he was referring to shortwave transmissions put out by countries. An open line to the world? I'd like you all to concentrate on it for a few minutes. Could it ever be done technically for instance?"
Glendower	"Mr. Fogarty. I really think this is a futile pursuit — so with your permission, I will withdraw from the discussion."
Pelluet	"Surely it's inconceivable to think it couldn't be

	done technically? Expecially when you measure it against other recent communications achievements."
Whiting	"Yes, it should be simple enough. You're referring to two comparatively elementary items — radio and the telephone. But without wishing to drop out of the debate, I also reject the notion as being fanciful. While we may not always like what governments do, there is no other way. Consultation, diplomacy and negotiation — that is the formula."
Tresilian	"How long can we wait for it to work?"
Whiting	"If you're talking about a nuclear war you don't have to wait at all. There just won't be one. Governments everywhere long ago learned the lessons of deterrent power."
Tresilian	"Again, as the average man, I can't share your much more qualified optimism, Professor Whiting. On that point I simply state my conviction that escalation to a nuclear outbreak in some part or other of South-East Asia is only a matter of time..."
Whiting	"Oh, come off it, Mr. Tresilian, you . . ."
Tresilian	"But leaving atomic conflict aside for a moment. By training and experience, you have confidence in governments. I don't. Perhaps you'd care to make a prediction on the future of biological and chemical warfare?"
Whiting	"Many people were asked that same question at the time of the Kaiser and Hitler wars on the use of gas. It was not resorted to on either occasion by either side. Does that answer your question?"
Tresilian	"No, Professor it does not, and for this reason. It is possible now for any country to conduct a war of attrition against another power without the subject or object powers even being aware that a state of war exists. The means of . . ."
Whiting	"I'm surprised that you haven't been retained by one of the major powers as a broadcasting advisor

Emeritus to . . ."

Tresilian	"The means of delivery can be as simple as a tourist carrying a harmless medicine kit or a make-up bag. And as I am sure you realise, the object of this type of deadly aggression is the destruction of the enemy's food, livestock and people through the spreading of inexplicable viruses and bacteria."
Glendower	"Mr. Fogarty. I have better things to do with my time than listen to empty phantasies. With your permission I would like to leave." — The floor manager nodded vigorously at the moderator.
Fogarty	"That is your privilege of course Mr. Glendower. Glyn Tresilian — you were talking about governments and wars of wheat rust and rice rust I think?"
Tresilian	"Yes — and the frightning thing to me is that the scientists know all about it and appear to have agreed to go along with their governments on the worst possible agreement of all. And that's a conspiracy of silence. People are completely unaware of all this. Scientists have been given their heads and without wanting to stress the obvious, no opportunity should be missed to speak out on it. I very definitely feel that people everywhere should be alerted and alarmed. Because this sort of chemical horror can assume monstrously large proportions. Unless people force their governments to make public what's going on . . ."
Pelluet	"That's all very well. And as you yourself intimated, Mr. Tresilian, pleasantly idealistic. But things just don't happen that way. What do you mean — 'force their governments?' When countries force governments — they force them right out. Through insurrection and revolt. And usually the replacement is either mob rule or a dictatorship. Now surely any form of government — incompetent or nationalistic — is better than either of those alternatives?"
Tresilian	"I agree entirely. And again you miss my point. The last thing I would want on the way to peace —

which is what we're discussing — is a call to world wide revolution and violence. But I would like to see some mobilisation of world wide opinion whereby governments wouldn't be overthrown — but could be persuaded by their people to drop those dangerous nationalistic and warlike attitudes that will probably destroy the human race either through a global nuclear war or invisible chemical attacks. Now, what's wrong with that? And why the hell should this man-in-the-street's view be airily dismissed as amiable garbage?"

Whiting "Frankly, I think this kind of thing does far more harm than good. Mr. Tresilian, these things you're saying tonight — are they your own genuine conclusions? Or, are they, as I suspect, all in the cause of what one might call attention-getting showbiz? Because, if that is the case I feel that . . ."

Tresilian "No, Professor Whiting, I assure you that most certainly is not the case. In self defense, let me restate my terms of reference for being on this program. I am convinced that ordinary people everywhere have lost confidence in governments to provide peace and to ensure the security of our civilization. Now if that's an oversimplification there's nothing the average person can do about it. Except to have his opinion aroused. And he must be reminded that he, and he alone, multiplied millions of times has the key to supreme power."

Pelluet "Supposing it were technically possible to do this by a kind of open line radio to the world — what country could be trusted to take the initiative?"

Tresilian "I don't follow you. Trusted by whom?"

Pelluet "Well, everybody. Any government starting such a scheme would be vulnerable to all kinds of charges about propaganda and brainwashing."

Tresilian "Oh, I know that. And the problems would be enormous. But the encouraging thing to me right now is that at least we've been ready to discuss it for a few minutes. That alone is quite a stride."

'The way to peace — is there one?' ran for its allotted thirty minutes and then 'Public Affairs One' took up the remaining half hour with filmed reports on three other items. The panel members stayed in the studio until the show was over. Then they were told about the reaction.

When Glendower had walked off the set, Canadians from St. Johns to Victoria, had angrily left their chairs and telephoned the local CBC stations. Reports coming into Binnings long before the show ended told of an overwhelming interest in Tresilian's ideas. As for Glendower's departure, Glendower and Tresilian were both accused of haughtiness, while Glyn alone was accused by many of "insolence", and "arrogance" for pushing the minister to the wall.

Binnings was very pleased.

"Now that's what I call a panel show," he enthused. "Switchboards are lighting up like Christmas trees all over the country. Nice job Frank — well handled. I'll have to buy Glendower a box of cigars. That was the turning point of course. Let's face it 'The way to peace', doesn't sound like the most exciting subject, eh? Great, Glyn. Oh, thanks," he said to a girl who gave him a sheaf of messages. He shuffled through them.

"My God, Glyn — look at these. Nearly all for you. Do you want to speak to any of them? You'd be on the phone all night."

"I don't mind. Let me take a few anyway."

Tresilian spent the next hour on the phone talking to people from all parts of Canada who had seen the program. Several offered to start fund raising campaigns to get the necessary money for the project. Others wanted to donate directly to him. He was surprised and elated at the response. People appeared to be more interested in peace than he thought. Along with well wishers came the crank minority. One of them asked Tresilian when he thought a nuclear war would break out — or whether the chemical battles would do the job first. But then he hung up.

A particularly articulate Montreal caller called Tresilian a "Low down scaremongering glory seeker. I know all about you. You were fired off the air in Montreal because you're a goddammed pinko — and now you're trying to horn in with Binnings with your peace and godlessness. He and that crowd of his are all a bunch of reds. But now they've gone too far. There'll be questions in Ottawa about this."

It was well after one o'clock in the morning before Glyn reached his hotel room. He was exhausted but couldn't sleep. He flung himself restlessly around the bed as he fought to drive the program and the phone calls from his mind. But they wouldn't go and all that night he stayed awake. The room lightened with dawn and he got up and bathed. Then, after an early breakfast he took a limousine to the airport and the first flight for Montreal.

He was amazed to find that papers in Toronto and Montreal carried stories of the show on their front pages.

'Peace idea enrages clergyman.' 'Storms out of TV show,' said one. Another, "Open-Liner insults clergyman on national TV".

The press had excellent sport. Glyn realised that they were concentrating more on Glendower's walk-out than on the substance of his argument. For a week the incident sustained itself as the number one topic of conversation on every open line radio show in the land. Tresilian was tracked down in his apartment by program hosts from Newfoundland to B.C. He spent hours on the telephone talking and arguing with listeners on the 'add-on' conference lines.

Then the subject, like a violent storm, blew itself out, was dropped, and forgotten. But he'd been glad of it. And in twelve more hours Julie would be home again for a long weekend.

CHAPTER 8

He met her at the airport.

"My, my, we must be quite the celebrity now," Julie said when they were settled in the car. "How does it feel?" He took his time.

"I couldn't get much out of you on the phone when you called. What did you really think of it?"

"I told you. Very good indeed. But somehow you seemed so different."

"Oh? In what way?"

"Well, I was expecting you to blow your top at any moment — as you would have done on radio I'm sure. Especially if people had been as condescending as that Reverend Glendower and the others were."

"Different ball-game altogether. Check with Marshall Mc-luhan. Radio's a 'hot' medium. TV's 'cool' — so you mustn't lose yours on it. I think he's right. Any way there was a hell of a lot of feed-back. I wouldn't have thought it possible. Can't get over it."

"I know. Nor can I. I heard people talking about it everywhere. Especially in Winnipeg and Edmonton for some reason. But for the record don't you think you were a bit rude to the clergyman, even if he was an Anglican?"

"That's how I learned to play, and it works with pompous . . . OK let's drop it. Great to see you again." "Same here," she said warmly, "I was talking to Mummy this morning from Toronto — she wants you to have dinner with us to-morrow. She says there'll be lots of Bols and Dutch cooking. Want to come?"

"Is the Pope Catholic?"

"What's that got to do with it?", surprised, she turned to him.

"Nothing — just my way of cutting out any confusion about the answer."

Glyn couldn't remember, the next evening, when a dinner

party had given him so much pleasure. The food, drink and talk were all excellent. "Now, Glyn," Julie's mother had said when he arrived, "I vont you to have en really good Dutch evening vith us. Jan, for en start, pour him zome Bols."

"We saw the program of course, Glyn. I thought you were very good — but I disagree with your views," the Captain stated and handed him a glass.

"Oh?"

"As far as nuclear war is concerned that professor was right. I believe that if we were going to have it — we'd have had it by now. It's well over 20 years since Hiroshima, you know. No, for once I think the politicians are correct when they talk about the deterrent qualities of bombs. As long as both sides have a good supply and all the delivery systems are as safe as they're suppose to be, I don't think there's any danger."

"I hope to God you're right Captain. What did you think of the show on the whole?" Glyn asked him.

"That clergyman shouldn't have walked out. I expect he'll get a lot of trouble from his church about that."

"Did anyone hear Trample this week on the subject?" Glyn asked with a note of impatience.

"Once or twice driving in the car. I don't know about Wilhelmina. Wilhelmina," he called his wife in the kitchen.

"Yes — vot iz it, Jan?"

"Did you hear Trample talking about that show Glyn was on?"

"Chust vait en minute. I am komming in. I do not like converzing in shoutz," she replied loudly and Julie laughed.

"Oh, that's good — very good coming from Mummy."

"Did I hear vhot did you say?"

"Trample."

"Yes — I tuned in ezpecially. But he didn't seem all that keen to talk about it. Maybe he vos jealouz that he did not suggezt it on the programm. Did you not hear him Glyn?"

"Only for a few seconds at a time, I'm afraid. For the rest I was on the air by phone all week long. The stations were calling me from all over."

"This morning I was talking to a girl I used to fly with," Julie said, "and she's a great Trample fan. But according to her, he's been concentrating on the Arab-Israel war."

"Oh? what side was he taking?" Glyn enquired.

"Oh, heavily pro-Israel, I think. And I must say I agree," the girl replied, "it's terrible the way those Arabs have been carrying on."

"Well, you may have something there, Julie," Glyn said, "but I'd still like to have the trouble sensibly explained from the Arab point of view. Maybe someone'll write something sane and sober on the whole middle east mess soon."

"Did you see this in the paper?" and Julie passed him the evening edition. "Look at those children — and women." There was a picture of Arab refugees. A dozen out of a million and a half.

"Oh, thank you Captain. That really is first class gin," and he accepted more Bols from his host. "Of course, we're not Arabs, and therefore don't know what it's like to be joined by a kind of European community in a native desert do we?"

"By that do you mean that the Jews shouldn't be in Israel?"

"No, of course I don't mean that sir and you know very well I don't. Their historical right to the country can't be argued. But the fact is that during their long absence the area grew to be anything but European in its outlook and culture. Whether you like it or not, the Israelis have definitely introduced European colonization methods to the middle east. Rather like Rhodes in Rhodesia."

"Well what's wrong with that if it means building up and developing a country in the desert?", Julie asked.

"Nothing at all — providing that you can get on with your desert neighbours. And that I think is the crux of the whole trouble. The Israelis have performed industrial and commercial miracles out there. The Arabs see all this and compare the way their own countries have been standing still for centuries and then they react. They worry and immediately assume that expansionist ambitions are bound to follow all this drive and technological capability. And so they feel threatened and become hostile. My only point is this — what has Israel done to reassure them?"

"Really, Glyn. I'm surprised at you," Julie countered. "How can you reassure anyone when they're sniping at you and terrorising your borders?"

Before he could comment, Mrs. de Vries called them to the dinner table. She had prepared a delicious meal of bean soup and a generous roast of beef. He looked at Julie's beautiful features glowing in the candle light across the table. Their eyes met and she winked at him mischievously. He smiled and watched her as she daintily took her starched napkin from its ring.

"Now, Glyn. Help yourzelf en haf en good time. You zertainly caused en furore vith that programm eh?" Mrs. de Vries chuckled and set to her dinner.

"I suppose so. But I don't think there'd have been reaction like that if old Glendower hadn't taken off. That was too good to be missed. That a clergyman would walk out of any discussion where peace was the topic. I doubt that anyone would have taken much notice of it but for that. You'll notice that there wasn't much mention of the idea was there?"

"But I thought you said the viewers were very interested and even offered . . ."

"Ah, yes," he interrupted, "the viewers. But not the press. The story was Glendower's leaving — not the essence of what I was saying. But that all comes back to something you can't change. It's easier to sell the negative. Commercially there's no point in trying to accentuate the positive. Look at what I had to do on my own show."

"Yes, I can understand that," de Vries said. "I heard somewhere the other day that wherever they have race riots in the States the open line show ratings immediately go up."

"They do — and for the wrong reason. I've heard some of them at night. I sometimes wonder if the riots weren't started by these shows in the first place. I think they ought to be banned during riots — or else conducted by people who realize that they could help to stop them. It's as easy to use one approach as the other. But obviously you're going to attract more listeners to your show if you set one lot against the other. The sad thing is that bringing people together isn't much good for business. It's far better to let them rant and rave at each other. Then, as long as you've got the good old disassociation tag on the end of the show, everybody's happy — or the sponsors are, and that's the main thing."

"Vhot dizazzociation tagz?"

"Oh, you know — those announcements at the beginning and end of any open line show. I had them on 'Crakkerjack line'.

'The opinions expressed on Crakkerjack line' are not necessarily those of this station, its management or any of the sponsors'."

"You're completely sold on the power of these programs, aren't you Glyn? You definitely put that across on the TV show I thought," de Vries said, ladling more soup.

"I think you can put anything across if you believe in it yourself, Captain."

They chatted about the de Gaulle Expo visit to come later in the summer and about the way the different Montreal open line shows would probably handle it. Trample, they thought, would more than likely sail into the French President. He seemed to be spoiling for it even now — weeks before the visit. It seemed to Tresilian that everything they talked about during the meal was weighed against the treatment the visit would receive from the tongues of the various open line moderators in Canada.

"But by now you must be convinced yourselves," Glyn said while they were having coffee. "All evening we've virtually talked about nothing else but open line shows. I'll admit that's because I'm here. But it's the same wherever I go. People want to know. They're fascinated by the sheer amount of human involvement. I don't think there's any greater sharing process in the world than this kind of show."

"Why don't you do something about it then?" Julie asked him reproachfully.

"About what?"

"Well, this open line to the world business that you thought of. You've already suggested it in front of millions of people and you know how they responded."

"Captain and Mrs. de Vries, do you know that you have a unique daughter? She has all the talents — including the rare one of tact".

Mrs. de Vries enjoyed this.

"Ve are not zoppozed to be en tactful people, ve Dutch."

"Oh, Mummy whoever told you that? What a pack of lies."

"I'm sure Julie's right. But no. This idea that I threw out on that show came from Julie in the first place. She brought it up — not me. One day as we were walking around Expo."

"Did I? Well it doesn't matter who thought of it. But serious- ly why not work on it Glyn? You don't seem very keen to go to that station in Toronto do you?"

"No, but I just don't see how any individual could ever begin to 'work on it'. And money's not the only thing. With money you could build the studios and transmitters and all that stuff but unless you could get people on the air by phone all over the world there's no point. It'd have to be an all-people to all-people thing. And there's not enough money anywhere to put in telephone systems all around the earth. In any case, since you'd be using wave lengths illegally, what country would let you operate on its soil?"

"Oh, come on now, Glyn. And you a sailor?" Captain de Vries said and looked at him with mock incredulity.

"What's that got to do with it Captain? The fact that I was a sail . . . oh, yes, yes, yes," he said slowly. "Stupid and dense of me. That'd be the only way wouldn't it? A ship. Of course. Keeping out of territorial waters. Just like those commercial radio pirate ships off the British and Dutch coasts."

"Yes," Julie joined in "and then perhaps you could send small boats ashore with portable telephones or something."

"Or helicopters ashore with — oh, thank you again Captain," he said and lit a cheroot, "as I was saying you could send helicopters ashore with portable telephones or something. But now we're really dreaming aren't we?"

"Yes, I should zay you vere, Glyn. If you can take time out van zaving the vorld, vhot about zome more coffee?"

. . . .

The next day, a Saturday, Julie went downtown with a girl friend to do some shopping and then arrived on her own at Tresilian's apartment where she prepared a light lunch from the meagre supplies in his kitchen. They now took it for granted that they would be spending just about the entire weekend together.

"What would you like to do this evening Julie?"

"I'm easy to please. Anything you say," and she put the kettle on for coffee.

"How about a walk up to the Look-Out? Get some exercise."

"Are you sure that's all you want to get?"

"No, the view's not bad either. You know I've been thinking a lot about that ship idea we were talking about last night. I know it's crazy, but the thing is I have no doubt whatever in my mind that if it could be done it would work. Honestly, I mean it. You probably think I'm nuts but there it is. I am off my trolley aren't I? Even thinking about it? Tell me to forget it and never to talk about it again."

"Why should I do that?"

"You don't mean that I should consider it even slightly seriously do you?"

"Yes, I think you should. As far as I'm concerned, with your background of the sea and broadcasting I can't think of a more natural thing for you to try. And especially as you've got these very strong views about governments and people and all that kind of thing. No, don't laugh — you asked me and I've told you. Oh, I know it must sound like a fairy story right now. But if you were able to do it — I'd say go ahead. I don't know what you'd do about money of course. But they say lots of people didn't know that either when they started out to do something they wanted to do very badly. You were telling Daddy last night, and I've heard you say before, how much you miss the sea. What a marvelous way to get back to it."

"Oh, Julie, you're a good girl. But nuts — quite nuts. Just like me. Money. God knows where you'd get it."

"Yes, He probably does," she said quietly and poured them both coffee. He watched her and knew that he was in love. Tonight, he hoped that they'd find a quiet spot near the summit of Mount Royal and with the distant glitter of Expo and the city below, he'd propose to her.

He did not have a profound faith in the religious sense but a belief nevertheless in a Supreme and benevolent Being to whom all things would be accountable in the end. This woolly appreciation of a deity was the closest he could ever get to a God and often regretted his non-membership at any church. And now, as she made that remark, he was envious of Julie's simple, uncomplicated belief. How he wished that he could share it with her. If she accepted him, would there be any difficulty with the church? He knew that in a 'mixed marriage', a term he detested, there were certain obligations that the non-Roman Catholic partner was required to discharge. He could only hope that he'd be finding out about them soon.

They went down to the Expo site in the afternoon and circled round the film at the Canadian pavilion. They watched the Coast Guard ice breaker demonstration nearby and then had dinner in the Ontario restaurant. They left early and he parked the car in the basement garage of his apartment building. They walked up Côte des Neiges.

"You seem very keen to scale mountains all of a sudden," she said and exaggerated her breathlessness as they went up an incline. He didn't reply. They sat down on a bench near Beaver Lake and then strolled to the Look Out.

"Oh, that's just beautiful, Glyn. It's funny but it doesn't matter how many times you come up here. Especially on such a clear night. The view always looks as if you're seeing it for the very first time." She was wondering about him now. She was sure that his long silences and unfamiliar reticence to touch and kiss her augured a proposal. Almost from the beginning she'd realised how serious he was. If he asked her, she wouldn't feign surprise. They leaned on the parapet for several minutes without saying a word to each other. Tresilian was the first to break the quiet.

"Yes, it's a great sight. Julie?"

"Yes, Glyn?"

"Let's change the subject. I love you," and he took her in his arms and kissed her.

"That's nice," she breathed and he revelled in her warm breath as it floated around his mouth.

"I said I love you," he whispered in her ear.

"I know. I heard you," and she nibbled his cheek.

"Julie, will you marry me sweetheart?" he closed his eyes and his pulse pounded as he waited for her words. None came. Instead she kissed him on the lips and their tongues touched. He felt the drop of her warm tears on his face.

"Oh, God Julie, I didn't want to make you cry. It's not that bad my darling. I can take it."

She went on sobbing for several more moments and he held her close and tried to comfort her.

"You don't understand, Glyn dear. You made me cry — but I'm glad you did. You see, you see — I love you as well. And you asked me to, to marry you and I cried because I was happy. I never knew how it would be, you see. But I love you so much that I can't speak properly and . . ."

"Don't try. Just say 'yes'."

"Yes", she whispered. And they walked off down the mountain.

.　　.　　.　　.　　.　　.　　.

He went to Sunday Mass with her the next morning and lunched again at the de Vries home. He spoke to her father privately. Her parents were very pleased. He drove Julie to the airport in the late afternoon.

"Well, I suppose we'd better get used to the idea of living in Toronto," Tresilian said gloomily.

"I don't see why we should unless we really want to go there. I don't think you should make any decision yet. Let's set the date and get married as soon as possible. In the meantime, why don't you see what you can do to sort yourself out with another job here?"

"Such as?" he asked unenthusiastically.

"I don't know. What about CRAK again?" she suggested.

"Oh, God, no. That was a boat burning operation if I ever saw one. And now that Trample's back at CRUX, I can't see any action there either. Much as we'd like to stay here in Montreal, the job bit's going to be tough. Can't see any way out of not going to CORK I'm afraid," he sighed and kept his eyes on the fast moving Côte de Liesse airport traffic.

"Everything'll be alright, Glyn — you'll see. But as I said before, I'd definitely like to stop working as soon as possible now. Otherwise I know what'll happen. We'll go on salting it away until we've got enough for a down payment on a house or something and it'll just drag on." She cuddled into him and stroked the back of his neck.

.　　.　　.　　.　　.　　.　　.

He spent most of that week and the next, driving around and off the island of Montreal. He kept out of his apartment as much as possible mainly not to be there when Dan Greenway called every day for his answer to the CORK offer. Even when the phone bell sounded he let it ring itself off. Without Julie now, he felt depressed and suffered from a bad sense of let down. What sort of life could he give her? Would she and Michael get on? How would the Wooffendens react to the news of his engagement? Oh, God he hadn't even written to anyone over there yet. He'd better get his finger out. Pronto. What about the ring — and could he even afford to buy her a decent one. What would he do? Where would they live?

Money was going to be a bloody awful problem. He'd earned nothing for some time now and had been spending as if he were on a drunken shore leave. Money, or the lack of it didn't seem to bother her too much, thank God. What a doll. No money grubbing hard boiled bitch. Ah, but that was her parents' doing, obviously. What damn fine people they were.

And when he wasn't thinking about problems of money and future employment, he daydreamed himself out of trouble. As he used to on open sea bridge watches when there was nothing to do but enjoy a tour with the mind.

In those days he thought about women, and the kind he might marry some day and the children they would have. And he saw himself on the bridge of a fine great ship. As Master of her and king of a floating realm. He'd embellish all this with visions of docking and undocking her in impossible weather conditions during tug and pilot strikes. And he'd work out the manoeuvres and give the orders. And wind and tide would work for him in the narrow spaces of an ocean pier. And the risks would make news and he'd be called a brilliant seaman.

But now, as the aimless days passed by, thoughts of the peace-ship idea started to haunt him. He was on the bridge again. The more he considered it and dreamed of what the scheme could do, the more it became reality.

He saw a wartime Liberty class ship converted to an immense radio capability. She would sail around the world and people everywhere on the planet would be able to talk to each other through her. Technically, only God would know how — but somehow a way must be found.

He put on the brakes and the tires screeched frantically.

"Look where you're going, you stupid bastard. What's the matter — are you asleep or daydreaming for crissake?"

"Sorry, sir — I didn't see you when . . ."

"Well, keep your goddam eyes open when you're driving."

He drove to his apartment and parked the car. Then he wrote letters to England.

Dear Sir Timothy and Lady Wooffenden,

I do hope you're both well and thank you very much for your last letter. I'm writing to Michael as well by this mail.

I think it better for me to get right to the point — which I fear may surprise you. But I trust, pleasantly; even though you've had no indication of my news up until now.

The fact is I'm getting married. I find myself irretrievably in love with a Dutch girl — but Canadian by citizenship. She is a Roman Catholic and her parents both live in Montreal. Their name is de Vries, and until he took up a supervisory position ashore in Canada, Captain de Vries for many years commanded a Dutch ocean going salvage tug. That reminds me that he more than once brought salvage for repair to the Wooffenden yards. Her mother is charming and kind.

At any rate we haven't set a date for the wedding yet as things are predictably a little unsettled with my own affairs being in a state of mild flux, and with Juliana, I call her Julie, working for Air Canada as an air hostess. But be sure that we'd like it to be soon — and if you possibly can, we'd love to see you both over here for the event. I don't think it'll be a big affair — what with the bulk of both families being in Europe.

Obviously we must think about Michael. With a mother, albeit not a blood relative, and a proper home, of course he'll come over and live with us. I hope it wouldn't be too long before he was joined by a half brother or sister. I realise fully that education is the key — and at the moment it doesn't look as if he'll go to Eton. But I think that the early prep school grounding he's had, and the general preparation that you've given him so well, will be a good platform for a high school in Montreal. The standards are pretty good here. But that is life and however hard we try — we cannot tailor it all to our precise liking.

As soon as we have more news we'll give it you immediately. In the meantime, as always, my heartfelt thanks for everything you have done and are doing.

Aye,

Glyn.

He kept the letter deliberately vague — and a little on the aggressive side. Good people though they were, he knew he'd be in for some trouble when it came to uprooting Michael. He insisted that Michael would come home — to him and to his stepmother. Too, his in-laws knew nothing about his leaving

CRAK — and he hoped that his affairs being 'in a state of mild flux' would suffice as a good enough cushion for the time being.

To Michael, he wrote:

My dear Michael,

Thank you very much for your last two letters. Please forgive me for answering them both at the same time. I find your letters extremely well written — and I would say that you have a fine flair for words. Keep this up and work hard at your English composition.

I have some news that I expect and hope will please you. It is good for us both. Shortly, you will have a new mother. Yes, Michael; I am in love again — just as I was with your real mother. Her name is Julie and I feel sure that the three of us will get on very well.

Now by the same mail, I've written to Grandmama and Grandpapa telling them about it all and although we don't know just when we will get married, I hope very much that all of you will be able to come over.

After that of course you will live in Canada with us even though it may not be in Montreal — but possibly Toronto which as you know is another big bustling city. I'm sure you'll like it. It looks then as if you won't after all be going to Eton as planned — I'm sorry about this, because I know how much you were looking forward to it — particularly the rugger and cricket. I realise full well that you're beginning to excel at both these games but as you seem to be a 'natural' you'll take easily to ice hockey and Canadian football. If you get a chance right now you could even practice some skating. See Mrs. Southcombe and the grandparents about this.

I know you will understand that this is the right thing to do. That with a proper home and someone to look after us, we should all live together. We haven't been able to do this since Mummy died — and we will never forget everything that Grandmama and Grandpapa have done for us both. But I know how much you enjoyed being in Canada before when you visited and now that you're older you'll like it even more.

There's just a chance that Julie and I will come over before we get married so that we can all meet. But I'm not sure about any plans at this very moment. However as we make the arrangements I'll let you know. In any event, whether it's over here or in Cheshire we'll be seeing each other soon. I'm very pleased with you Michael. And all I want is for you to share my own happiness that we can be to-gether — and a family again in the proper way. Do let me hear from you soon. In the meantime, just go on being the very good young man I know you to be.

With best love,

Daddy.

P.S. I know how much you like airplanes and flying. Julie is an air hostess with Air Canada. We met while I was coming back from a trip to Toronto. D.

Tresilian spent the next week thinking more about what he now called the Plan. He spent hours in the Westmount Public Library combing works of reference for any clue to the background of a rich man that might lead him to such a person — who might at least give the peace-ship idea a hearing. It had become an obsession in his mind and even knowing the Mitty like quality of it all, he had expunged all traces of laughability — at least to himself. Even though he could forecast to the last hoot of derisive laughter the reactions that would come from others.

But after research, his work yielded nothing. Oh, there were masses of living Midas's who'd endowed hospitals, universities, human and research foundations. There were plenty who had the funds, but none with the real spirit for such an adventure.

He wondered candidly to himself if he had enough funds to get married at the present time — the ring alone would cost a packet; and although presumably the de Vries would pay the shot for the wedding there'd be the honeymoon and all kinds of expenditures. There always were when you got involved. Hell, he hadn't even thought about the cost of settling Michael. There would be new and different clothes to buy and sports gear and . . ." But then the phone bell rang and it was Julie from the airport at Edmonton. After a few words she detected some depression in his voice.

"You don't sound too cheerful — what's wrong?"

"Oh, nothing really. Just thinking about money — or rather the lack of it," he said mournfully.

"That's all?" she said. Good, I thought it might have been something serious."

"Well isn't it?"

"Not as far as I'm concerned. You mean for you and me? We'll make out — that's the last thing I worry about. Have you heard from Michael or the Wooffendens yet?" she asked, changing the subject. God he was lucky. He told her how the Plan was taking hold of him.

"An idea," she said brightly, "got it a minute ago. Listen — you know the old saying that sometimes you can't see the wood for the trees? Yes? Well with all your research on millionaires, have you thought about the Wooffendens? I think you said once that he was a multi-millionaire in his own right many times over — and that you admire him as a man of considerable principle. Why not approach him?"

"My God, Julie — you may have something there. Hadn't thought of it. Not only does he have the loot but we could do the conversion and re-fit right there — in the Wooffenden yards. Brilliant. One thing then we can settle immediately. We'll go over to see them and Michael before we get married. That way we can all meet before the wedding — whether they could come over for it or not — and I can pitch him personally and at leisure. Let's see now. Snags.

"There's the money bit. I'm broke pretty well right now. And even if you could get some concession on the air fare for yourself — it'd still cost a pretty penny. And I wouldn't want to get into the Wooffendens for this kind of thing. I've been able to play it my way so far — and I'd really like to keep the record intact. Especially with what I'm going to propose to the old boy when we get there," and he laughed — nervously waiting for her words. It wasn't easy — telling the girl you worshipped, that you were on your uppers.

"As far as that goes," Julie came back on the line, "I've got a little bit you know. That's one thing about this work — you seldom get much of a chance to spend it — particularly when on a vacation you meet and fall in love with someone who spends a small fortune on you. N'est pas cheri?"

He wanted to clasp and kiss her. He loved her so much. And how big and generous a nature she must have to think of the Woffenden approach for the Plan — and then tell him about it. It would be the most understandable thing in the world for her to want to get as far from memories and reminders of his previous marriage as possible. And indeed, from his crazy Plan idea too. But then how good she'd been about Michael when they'd discussed their plans for him. 'But of course he must come and live with us.' She had said, 'what else?'

"No sweetheart," he continued after a few seconds pause, "you just forget about that. We'll work something out. Actually the bank balance may not be as bad as I think. Perhaps I've been unnecessarily pessimistic." He hadn't been — but that would do for now.

"One thing I must say Glyn," Julie went on, "you don't fool around when it comes to decision making do you? I just call up with a thought and the next thing you say is 'fine — we'll do it'. But that's good. Well, if you've decided, for better or worse, we'd better get on with it hadn't we?"

"Yes", he said, "I've just been thinking about that myself. No time like the present. Look. I'll tell you what we'll do. Let's wait until to-morrow for the mail. I think we'll be hearing from them then. We'll see about it after judging their reaction to the news."

He waited a few moments and then went on. "Here's another point though. I know you're over twenty-one but we don't want to upset your parents. Would they take kindly to us both going to England — while we're not married?"

"Oh, I think I could explain that to them."

"Ah," Tresilian laughed, "but do you know if they can trust me?"

"I'm sure they can — and do, my love."

"O.K. Let's leave it like that and we'll talk again to-morrow night. You'll be in Regina I think you said? Fine. Let's hope I'll have some mail to read to you. 'Bye, sweetheart. Happy landings."

As Tresilian had predicted, there was mail for him the next day. A letter and short note in one envelope from Sir Timothy and his wife — and a separate sealing from Michael. His heart pounded a little before he opened them. He decided to read Michael's first.

My dear Daddy,

What super news you sent me. When can I meet Julie? And can I call her that or do I have to call her Mummy? I don't mind which one it is.

Does this mean I'll be having some brothers and sisters? I'd like a brother — because, frankly I find girls a bit of a bore. You don't though Daddy. Ha, haha. That's meant to be a joke.

I'm very glad you enjoy my writing. I hope you'll be pleased with my next report. I think I might become a journalist in that case.

Of course I agree with you Daddy about coming to live in Canada. And I'm sure I'll do well at ice hockey. Mrs. Southcombe is going to get me some ice skates when she goes to Liverpool to-morrow and after I get the feel of them I can practice.

Of course I had rather got used to the idea of going to Eton — but now I'm looking forward to school in Canada. Do you think the Canadians will be able to understand my accent? Or do you think I'll talk like an American?

I'm so excited about your news that I think about it all the time. So far Grandpapa and Grandmama haven't said anything about coming to Canada for the wedding because they say you haven't made any plans yet. But then I showed them my letter where you said you and Julie might come over here first. I'm sure that by the time you get this you will know everything Daddy. I'm longing to see you and to meet Julie. Do you think we'll get on? I'll bet she's very good looking if she's an air hostess. They have to be you know. You didn't say whether she's a blonde or a brunette. It doesn't matter though if you like her. I think I prefer the darker shades personally.

Well Daddy I have to go and do my prep now. Please write immediately and tell me the exact time that we are going to meet. Also please tell me whether it will be here or in Canada. I'll bet you're still very busy on the radio and the television but please write to me at once because I look forward to your letters so much. If it's quicker I don't mind if you dictate the letter to your secretary but I must hear from you at your earliest convenience.

I remain,

Your ever loving son,

Michael.

Tresilian smiled as he folded the letter. Then he opened the Wooffendens' envelope. He took out her ladyship's note first.

My dear Glyn,

As you will see from Timothy's letter, the news, which did indeed come as quite a surprise, makes us very happy for you. We know you too well to doubt the goodness of your choice — and subsequent decision. Michael is delighted — and as you'll probably gather from his letter — is in excellent spirits.

Affectionately as always,
Diana Wooffenden.

And then Sir Timothy's words.

My dear Glyn,

The news of your future marriage came to us as you predicted. Both surprising and pleasant; and Diana and I send you our warmest congratulations. We look forward to hearing about your plans and arrangements with pleasurable anticipation — and if it is at all possible we will certainly come to Montreal for the wedding — and of course will bring Michael with us. More about him later.

How interesting that your intended father-in-law, I suppose we shall share you as a son, should have a sea faring background. And in ocean going salvage at that. Surely one of the most tasking branches of the whole seascape endeavour. From memory I cannot recall any Captain de Vries bringing a crippled ship to us. There again it's possible that we'd have had little or nothing to do with him as Master but rather with his owners or their representatives.

You mention that your affairs are in a state of mild flux. I take the liberty of asking whether this pertains to heart or professional matters! No offence meant my dear Glyn — but if the latter, then I reiterate again my full willingness to help in any way I can. Especially if your business affairs are so unsettled that they may be causing you anxiety.

And now Michael whom we, like you, have grown to love. Like you, I think it much better to come straight to the point. As our only grandchild we are most pleased with the general progress he has made in his young life. I intended broaching this to you on your next visit here — but having regard to your present circumstances and intentions I think it as well to sketch a rough outline for you now. We thought that after Eton he would go on to Cambridge and then come in the firm.

Somehow one's old age would be freer from uneasiness if one knew that although without a son, one's grandson would be groomed and ready to carry on another generation of a family enterprise that has not always been shorn of a certain tradition of excellence.

Selfish, I grant you my dear Glyn. And perhaps not at all close to any ideas you may have about his future. Naturally, discussion will be easier when we meet soon — either, according to Michael, here, or in Montreal for the wedding.

I repeat the standing offer that I made when you and Peta were married. The position I had in mind for you is still vacant — and only because we haven't been able to find a person with the total personal qualities you possess. Some people we've seen have been close — but not sufficiently. Please accept this report of earnest recruiting at least as a contradiction of the nepotism you suspected when I spoke to you about it first. Do think it over so that we may talk about it fully when we meet — a date and place for which I look forward to knowing shortly.

I am happy to say that business has been very good. Only last month we secured orders for two Greek supertankers, three bulk carrying dry cargo ships for India, and one intermediate refrigerated liner for British owners. Although costs are high and profit margins low, we mustn't grumble when such business comes our way with almost no competitive fight. Morale in the yards is high — as well it might be when such good news is told. We are currently negotiating for the biggest order in the history of Wooffendens. A massive American naval contract for both nuclear surface and submarine vessels, which if we get it, will quadruple anything we've ever done before. Because of the volume of work and delivery deadlines, it will also take us into the sub-contracting business which experience has told me to avoid if possible. But it would be hopeless to try to build new ways and yards in the time available — notwithstanding the fact that they may become redundant after the work has been done.

I realise that it's probably immoral to spell it out, but as Chairman of a difficult business at the best of times, it does strike me that war — or at least the threat of war — is very good for business. What a pity that the same industrial enthusiasms cannot be channelled for peaceful purposes — I expect you have a lot to say about these matters on your broadcasts.

The team I have working on the contract with the Americans, tell me that it may be fairly soon now that I have to fly to Washington to enter the final round of talks. From what I can gather, our greatest rivals are the Japanese yards at Osaka.

A strange paradox. That the Japanese should be doing their damndest to add to the American seaborne nuclear arsenal.

But we seem to be getting carried away. Believe me when I say again how very pleased we are to hear the news and we shall be delighted to meet Julie. But those arrangements are yours. And no doubt we'll be hearing from you soon. In the meantime, my dear Glyn, our very best wishes.

Aye,
Timothy Wooffenden.

CHAPTER 9

Tresilian read the letter from his late wife's father several times. He found it matey and confiding. Sir Timothy had not written in this man-to-man vein about the business before. Glyn was surprised that he should mention a big naval nuclear contract for the Americans in such a chatty style. While the bargaining and haggling were probably public knowledge, he found it uncharacteristically loquacious of Sir Timothy to describe it so confidentially. Then he realised that it was possibly Sir Timothy's way of expressing faith and trust in Glyn. An indication that heady responsibilities could be his for the asking.

But Michael was the locking pin. Wooffenden quite definitely must have his heart set on the idea that the boy in his time would be groomed for the Wooffenden leadership.

What, he considered, the accident of birth could do for a person. And what a life awaited Michael — providing it was played the Wooffenden way. And if the Tresilian way — what then? Certainly no assured Board Chairmanship of a multi-million pound and growing shipbuilding empire.

'War or at least threat of war', he read again, 'is very good for business'. Hmmm. This wouldn't help the Plan very much. But then he read on a little. 'Pity . . . couldn't be channelled for peaceful purposes.' Glyn had no means of knowing which one of these would win in conflict with Sir Timothy's conscience. The tycoon was an enigma and Tresilian often wondered whether anyone, including Lady Diana, really understood him. He'd discuss it all with Julie when she called to-night.

At about noon he prepared a brunch of tomato juice and boiled eggs with toast and coffee. He'd never been able to judge that precise consistency of soft hardness that makes all the difference to a boiled egg. But then, soon Julie would be taking care of all this and she'd be so good at it. He looked at his watch and the eggs bubbling and rattling in the pan. Any second now and he'd switch off the burner on the stove. There. This time perhaps he'd got them just right. And then the door bell rang. He wondered who it could be as it wasn't the day for his cleaning lady to come. With money the way it was right now, he'd considered the thought of doing away with this luxury. He walked to the door and opened it. Standing there was a young uniformed messenger from the CN Telegraph office.

"Mr. Glyn Tresilian?"

"Yes?"

"Telegram for you sir. May I just say Mr. Tresilian I used to enjoy your program on CRAK very much. And my mother listened every day. Will you be coming back on?" Glyn was touched by the youth's appreciation but had already begun the icy sweat that a non-greetings cable brought on.

"Er, no. I don't think so — but I'm very grateful for your kind thoughts. Please give my best wishes to your mother and thank you for your trouble." From his pocket he took out fifty cents and gave it to the CN lad. The boy thanked him profusely and left. There was really no need to do this — but his ego had been primped — and that always brought results.

Oh, God what could this be? It had to be something to do with Julie. No — it couldn't be that. He'd caught every newscast this morning and there'd been nothing on the radio. Then maybe she'd thought the whole bizarre business over and decided to call if off. He couldn't really blame her. Their backgrounds were so different — so were their ages and then there was the religious bit. To say nothing of his ludicrous obsession with this idiotic Plan. He could see the contents already — they'd go something along these lines 'Have thought it over Glyn stop Know it wont work. stop. Writing separate mail ends Julie'.

He thought of eating the eggs and toast first to fortify himself but instantly felt that uncontrollable loosening of the gut and bowels.

He tore the envelope open and took in the message with a glance. And he stood like a statue for a minute — the telegram held out at arms length. He looked around the room, put the cable on a coffee table and with a fork from the kitchen door stabbed himself on both arms. The sharp pain told him that he was very much awake and that the wireless message was real.

He set on the eggs and toast. Although they were cold, this time he'd actually got the consistency. And they tasted — this noon time — more lucullan than anything Escoffier in the prime of his noble life could have produced. And the toast. Cold and brittle, but it fell on his palate like ambrosia. Warm elation gushed right through him. The Gods, through a stroke of which only they were capable, had taken the immediate heat off him.

When he'd left the sea some years ago, Tresilian had bought ten pounds worth of Harold Macmillan's premium bonds. On coming to Canada, he'd made arrangements with the Manager of the small Midland branch in Hampshire where he banked, to safeguard the dockets and to claim them — if Dame Fortune chose to smile. The telegram's message was as follows:—

DELIGHTED INFORM YOU ONE OF YOUR PREMIUM BONDS HAS WON FIRST PRIZE SIX THOUSAND POUNDS STERLING STOP. CONGRATULATIONS STOP LETTER FOLLOWS IMMEDIATELY SIGNED MANAGER.

Too excited to stay in the apartment that afternoon, and not caring for the complications of driving through Expo strangled Montreal, Tresilian walked, on this hot jubilant afternoon to the Exhibition. There, basking in the euphoria of the shining news he beamed on all he saw, and chatted where he could. He longed for eight o'clock and the sound of Julie's voice from a prairie city. He'd forgotten which one. Not wanting to be late, he walked back slowly playing out the hour he still had left.

She called punctually and they talked for an hour and a half. At the end of it they made their plans. Julie was to resign as soon as she respectably could from Air Canada — after which they'd take their time and sail to England for the meeting with the Wooffendens and Michael and the presentation of the Plan. Optimistically Julie thought that Sir Timothy's point about 'peaceful purposes' would supercede his desire to land the nuclear naval American contract.

Tresilian wouldn't bet on that, he thought.

.   .   .   .

Three weeks later, they were both unemployed. Julie had left Air Canada, and Tresilian had told Dan Greenway on the telephone, not the details of the Plan, but of his intention to work on a broadcasting scheme with his father-in-law. Naturally the CORK manager jumped to the commercial pirate radio station conclusion.

"OK Glyn I understand; believe me. With the kind of bread you've got in the family — I'd spend my life in Florida. But listen. When you've got that pirate ship blasting away on the air, don't forget your old friend Dan, eh? I don't want any truck with rocking away on some old boat at anchor — but just think how I'd look in the executive suite ashore. If you haven't taken all the room! It is a pirate ship of course eh Glyn? This scheme of yours?"

"Yes, Dan. I guess you could say that," Glyn answered nebulously. They said good-bye on the agreement that Tresilian could come CORK any time he liked.

"I want you to know that Glyn. And be sure that I mean it. Just in case the old guy doesn't want to dig that deep in his pocket. Bye Glyn boy; lot's of luck and just keep in touch, that's all."

The de Vries were more than slightly shocked when he and Julie told them one evening of their serious intention to follow through an attempt to implement the Plan and go over to England to-gether, to meet the Wooffendens and Michael; and to use the occasion to give Sir Timothy first refusal on the peace-ship idea.

But the meeting passed smoothly enough and Glyn and Julie were sure that they had the elder de Vries' blessings. When they discussed it privately later, Julie's parents consoled themselves in the firm belief that they could trust the couple implicity — and that they were at least engaged.

They booked passage on the Cunard Liner "Europia", embarking at Halifax on a special summer sailing of the ship from New York to Liverpool via Cobh. They chose the Cunard Line and the "Europia" because she was going to Liverpool and this would mean minimal travel to Cheshire.

Through correspondence, all was arranged for the Bentley to meet them at the Pier Head Landing Stage, after which they'd proceed directly to Wooffenden Hall where the family would meet them. Lady Wooffenden and Glyn had agreed that this would be a better setting for introductions than among the excitement and over stimulation that the arrival of a great ship generates.

With eighteen thousand dollars falling from heaven, Tresilian determined that they should indulge themselves on this visit to Britain. Life was short and for living — and the future for them both was nothing, if not obscure. Accordingly he made reservations for a fine late night gourmet meal in downtown Montreal to soften the blow of a six a.m. flight arrival in Halifax. They landed at the Nova Scotia airport bleary eyed, sated but happy, having slept fitfully in the first class section of the Air Canada Vanguard.

Tresilian insisted that they travel first class in suites on the "Europia". Julie had protested this extravagance but Glyn was firm. "We'll probably only do this once in our lifetimes, so let's make sure we do it properly. If it hadn't been for that one-in-several-million break, we wouldn't be doing it at all. We've got the time and money right now. Next month — who knows? We'll do this the Omar Khayam way."

After breakfast, and a stroll down Barrington street in Halifax, they collected their baggage from the lockers in the rail road station and got a taxi for the short distance to the ship. They settled in luxurious spacious panelled suites — he to port and she to starboard. They met their bedroom stewards, who with the experience born not of years but generations, made them welcome and at home. The "Europia" sailed at noon, shook off the last traces of the shore and leaned into the vast Atlantic on her great circle way to the Old World.

After they had unpacked casual clothes, Glyn and Julie went for'ard to the "Europia's" boat deck and took in the pure clean Atlantic air. The liner gently rose and fell in rythm with the long swells. The Cunarder's passengers sniffed the scene. Tresilian felt romantic and philosophical. He put his arm around Julie's waist.

"Do you know sweetheart that the man who started all this was born in the port we've just left?" "Started all what dear?"

"Well this — steam navigation across the Atlantic," he explained.

"No. I didn't know that. But tell me anyway."

Tresilian lit a cigarette using her as a lee for the lighter against the breeze.

"This man I'm talking about, a Nova Scotian Haligonian called Samuel Cunard, was regarded in his day as probably a bigger nut when he proposed his scheme, than I will be when

I present mine. They laughed and ridiculed him."

"Why?"

"Because," Tresilian went on, "he came up with an idea that the so called experts of the time dismissed as being fanciful and deranged.

"Although in the eighteen thirties, steam had long since been discovered, Cunard was convinced that the 'new' power could be built into ships on the North Atlantic run thereby ensuring some degree of increased speed and punctuality. So, completely under his own steam, forgive me, he went over to Britain to try and interest the people there to back him. But everyone he met thought he was crazy. A screwball. And one renowned scientist said when he heard of Cunard's madness, 'Man might as well project a voyage to the moon as attempt steam navigation across the stormy Atlantic.' Wonder what the great man would say to-day?"

Julie, her voice rising with the wind, said.

"Well, not everyone could have thought him crazy. We're going on a Cunard ship today aren't we? I must confess I didn't know that the 'Cunard' was a Canadian name. Somehow one always thinks of Britain and Cunard all being the same. Must be something to do with the 'Queen' liners. Nothing could be more British than that."

Arm in arm they did a few circuits of the deck. The deck steward was arranging chairs and blankets and talking to the passengers. Glyn and Julie spoke to him for a little while, then went into the Lounge where the orchestra played light tea music with the afternoon refreshment. It was a cheerful sight and sound. The tinkle of spoons and cups and saucers, and trippy Offenbach.

With the tea, there were thinly sliced cucumber sandwiches and cakes. Between bites, Tresilian said to Julie, "Better not eat too much now. Just wait until you see the dinner menu. Thank God they don't carry any scales. At least that's what I was told. Oh, but I was forgetting." And he picked up some printed matter.

"We were talking about the way Cunard tried to promote his idea of North Atlantic steam navigation. Well, he finally met two people who believed in him. They were Napier and McIver who understood what he was driving at. And with their support, and despite widespread official scepticism, the first Cunard steamship, 'Britannia', was built and made her maiden voyage across the Atlantic in 1840. You know the rest. Here, read it for yourself."

"Glyn," she said, "Glyn, wouldn't it be wonderful if Sir Timothy saw the point of the Plan? I mean the way these two people did. And you didn't have to waste a lot of time trying to convince him. Do you think they'll like me? I get a little nervous at times when I think of that first meeting with them. And Michael?"

He took her hand and they left the tea table for another stroll on deck. Later in the evening, the Lounge would be transformed for cabaret and dancing.

"Don't worry about a thing," Tresilian reassured her. "They'll like you on sight. All of them. Including old aristocrat Southcombe."

The couple enjoyed the voyage. They relaxed and unwound and did exactly as they pleased. Although "Europia" encountered a severe storm two days out of Cape Race, Julie proved herself to be a good sailor. Finding that Tresilian had himself been at sea, their table companions questioned him a lot. They asked about navigation and stabilisers, tonnages, speed and fuel consumption. Although he pointed out that he had long left the sea, they still, in a pleasing and flattering fashion, persisted.

They saw a movie every day and joined in the various deck games and contests. Tresilian especially welcomed the exercise from deck-tennis, ping-pong and shuffleboard. All this and the bracing fresh sea air sharpened them to the gourmet food. Glyn won the ship's fancy Head Dress Parade. Inspired by several lunch time drinks at the bar, he rescued an empty gin bottle about to be cast away. Julie fashioned an Arab head-dress with a holding pouch and he triumphed in the contest as 'Gordon of Khartoum.'

And then came the last night at sea and the Landfall Gala Party and Ball. As the time of her meeting with the Wooffendens approached, Julie became increasingly tense and nervous. She told Glyn how much she hoped that his previous in-laws would like her.

"They will, sweetie — don't worry," he comforted her. "This thing tonight ought to be fun. Let's enjoy it. I can't wait to see you in that new gown you had made before the trip. You'll knock em dead in it."

"Well, I hope I'm still me in it. Thank goodness Mummy didn't see me in it. It has too many daring cut-outs for her." Earlier that day the Captain had predicted she would be the belle of the evening. Dressed for the first time in a long glittering white sheath gown designed especially for her by Rancourt, one of the new and avant-garde Montreal designers, she stunned everybody with her total look of wordly innocence. She was the success of the Gala, and knew it, revelling and glowing in the recognition. Added to this was the effect of the champagne, and she felt her morale soar. She was in heavy demand all evening and more than one tipsy businessman, gazing down at the long slit which exposed a portion of lovely right leg, was to lose his balance.

After dancing and a few cabin party drinks, they went to his stateroom. "No, Glyn, I think we've both had enough dear," she said as he began to pour a nightcap for them both. "I've never had so much champagne in my life."

"Oh, come on, Julie. Let's finish off properly. Here — to us — always." They drank, and he sat beside her on his bed. He put his arm around her shoulder and looked down at two provocative breasts partially revealed by a see-through portion of her gown. Mellow and happy with drink, he longed to take her. She resisted only slightly as he undid her dress at the back and kissed her bosom.

"I love you Glyn, darling — but let's not go too far," she murmured.

"Don't say anything — just enjoy it." He took off his dinner jacket, bolted the cabin door and switched off the light.

.   .   .   .

The morning sun glinted on the Irish sea.

Tresilian woke up when he heard the knocks getting louder on the cabin door. He got up and looked at Julie sleeping peacefully in his bed. Although immobilised by the giant hangover, he was capable enough to appreciate how lovely she was even after the escapade of the night before. He went to the door. It was the Steward Beelson with, as usual, a pot of steaming early morning tea on the dot of eight o'clock.

"Good morning, sir. Lovely weather and we're just off the Irish . . . ."

"Shush, Beelson, please." Tresilian put a finger to his mouth.

"Ah, I understand sir. You will require tea for two?"

"Look, Beelson, I'm afraid . . ." he whispered.

"Perfectly alright sir. I will put the tray here on the floor for a moment. Perhaps we can have a better conversation in the bathroom?"

"I've made an awful mess of things Beelson," he said to the Steward as if her were talking to him through a confessional screen, "and I don't . . . . . . "

"I beg you not to worry sir. Leave it all to me. If I may perhaps have the young lady's name and stateroom number?"

"de Vries. Miss Juliana de Vries."

"Of course, sir. A delightful young lady. She's also in my section. If you'll just be good enough to leave your door open sir, I'll make the necessary arrangements."

The veteran Bedroom Steward was back with another tea tray before Tresilian had finished cleaning his teeth. "There you are sir. Some more tea. When you're ready perhaps you could put the young lady's evening clothes in this linen bag? I took the liberty of placing some outer day attire in it for Miss de Vries. Please leave the bag outside and I'll see that it gets to her cabin. Then, when you're ready to leave for breakfast, please ring the bell for me and I will arrange for the coast to be clear. No trouble, sir. No trouble at all. A pleasure, Mr. Tresilian."

They had a light breakfast and after it Julie freshened up in her cabin. Then they went for a walk on deck and watched the coast passing by. He was worried about her. And wondered what she really thought.

"Sweetheart, there's nothing we can do about it now. It's happened. Do you regret it very much?" he asked her as they stopped midway down the promenade deck.

"Yes, in a way. I mean I just feel guilty — that's all. I just thank God it was with you. You were first and you'll be the only one." And they went on walking hand in hand. As they turned, he stopped her again.

"Julie — I don't want you to feel guilty."

"No, don't be silly. We were both at fault. I guess I secretly suspected what that gown might do to you. And with all that champagne! But let's make a pact if you don't mind, Glyn. No more till we're married — and then — well just you look out."

"OK, honey. I really thought you wanted to all along last night. The gown and all the rest of it. I, I just wasn't sure."

"Nor was I. But I'll tell you this though — I'm looking forward to lots more of the same. Did you hide that towel as I told you? Good — let's throw it overboard as soon as we can. You'll be up for murder or something if you get caught with evidence like that. And now let's forget it. When I can, I'll probably want to get it off my chest though," and they went on with their stroll.

"Oh, that'll be easy enough," he laughed. "Especially in Liverpool. If not, there's always Farm Street and the Jesuits when we get to London."

. . . .

Sir Timothy's chauffeur, Oates, met them in the shed. He was pleased to see Glyn again and with his help the couple soon cleared their baggage through the Pier Head Landing Stage at Liverpool.

They loaded the cases in the Bentley's capacious cargo compartment and Tresilian looked up and waved at the liver birds who kept watch on the Mersey. He had always done this on arrival in Liverpool and every time he thought he saw them reply with an approving wink. They were on their way. Half an hour after leaving the Mersey Tunnel on the Cheshire side, the Rolls swept up the gravel drive stopping outside the portico columns of the mansion. Rhododendrons and summer flowers blazed away everywhere as the clock, high on the central tower of Wooffenden Hall chimed eleven. Michael, flushed and breathless, came running out and hugged his father in the car.

"Oh, Daddy I haven't slept all night. I thought you would never get here — but you're right on time." The boy chatted away nervously never taking his eyes off Glyn. Tresilian decided to give him time. Let him run down a little bit. Then, as the chauffeur and footman busied with the baggage he saw the moment.

"Michael, I want you to meet Miss Juliana de Vries. Yes," and he laughed, "I know that's quite a mouthful but we call her Julie. Julie — meet Michael."

"Hello Michael. It's very nice to meet you at last. I just know that we'll be friends — and you look even more handsome than your photographs."

The boy, now poised and completely confident, said, "Hello Julie. I'm jolly pleased to meet you too. May I really call you that? I suppose it'll be alright until you and Daddy get married anyway?"

Julie laughed. "Of course, Michael." Oh, this at any rate, was much easier than she could have hoped.

As yet, there had been no sign of the Wooffendens. But Mrs. Southcombe met them in the Main Hall — and that introduction passed off smoothly enough. The governess explained the Wooffendens' absence. "Mr. Tresilian, Michael's grandparents had intended to be here when you arrived. But late last night Sir Timothy learned that he was needed urgently in the office early this morning — and Lady Wooffenden was called to an emergency meeting of one of the local charities. They deputed me to welcome you and Miss de Vries. They should both be back by twelve thirty for luncheon. In the meantime may I suggest that you may want to see your rooms? I'm sure Michael will be pleased to show you the way. Miss de Vries has the Wolseley — facing the West Lawn; and of course as usual you'll be in the Henry room, Mr. Tresilian. Lady Wooffenden said that we won't be dressing for dinner tonight. I do hope that you'll both be comfortable. I will call for you at twelve-fifteen for sherry in the morning room. Michael, I'm sure you'll be glad when I tell you that I've cancelled your music lesson this afternoon."

"Yippee", cried the boy unceremoniously and they moved off to the bedrooms. Wooffenden Hall was a large "E" shaped Elizabethan mansion, and in spite of Glyn's descriptions, Julie was overwhelmed by the splendour of it all and a way of life that she'd only seen in print or on the screen.

She was aghast at the wealth. The Wooffendens must be incredibly rich to live like this in England in the nineteen-sixties. She found the 'Wolseley' to be a vast bedroom with separate boudoir, balcony and an attached private bathroom. She thought how meagre and out of place her modest baggage and personal effects looked in the midst of such opulence. She wanted so much not to let Glyn down. And prayed that she wouldn't seem too gauche. Although not of 'the manner born' to such riches, Glyn by now had the necessary wordliness and savoir-faire to see him through any situation, but she now began seriously to doubt her own poise.

This was more, far more than she'd imagined. Too, it wasn't as if she was an ordinary house guest. Betrothed to the father of the House's grandchild, and with nothing in common by way of background, she felt panic as she thought of her close association with the fantastic idea that her fiancé would shortly ask the Lord of the manor to support with millions of dollars. She wondered how and when he would do it.

She understood that these things were better broached in the mellow setting of after dinner brandy talk. She didn't know what Glyn's plans were. The whole thing was double crazy — but in the end she knew, she just knew, that he would do it. She also had a hunch that the Wooffendens had staged their arrival at the Hall in a quaintly kind way.

She didn't really believe Mrs. Southcombe's explanation. Rather she felt that they had been absent on purpose so that the younger couple could have a gentler 'breaking in.' First with the house — and then with the people. If true, it was a beautiful piece of tact.

She certainly appreciated the breathing space. And looked with pleasure on the wide green lawn from the balcony and watched for a minute or so as the gardeners pottered about with shrubs. They must have a very big staff to keep the house and grounds in such impeccable shape.

Just before twelve fifteen there was a soft tap on the heavy oaken door. Mrs. Southcombe was ready to take her to the morning room. They walked along wide corridors hung on both sides with rare paintings and down a sweeping staircase to the huge room on the ground floor where the Wooffendens did their pre-dining room entertaining.

Glyn and Michael were already there. The boy was chatting animatedly to his father. They stood in a small group in the centre of the room as the butler entered, a silver tray in hand. Julie couldn't really believe it yet. She was sure that at any moment someone would come in shouting 'Cut'. But it was real enough; and how far away her parents' compact cottage in NDG seemed now.

She longed to get the introductions over. She was sure that after the first meeting, she'd be alright by just being herself. And then they came in. They greeted Glyn first with obvious affection.

And said hello to Michael and Mrs. Southcombe. And then it was Julie's turn.

"We're delighted to meet and welcome you Miss de Vries," Lady Wooffenden said. "We hope that you and Glyn will stay for as long as you can. Just do as you like. And come and go as you wish. We'll try to make you comfortable."

"Congratulations on your engagement," said Sir Timothy and he lifted his glass. "To both of you."

Until the butler announced luncheon at one, Sir Timothy handled the flow of small talk and kept it going pleasantly. Once Julie scored when talking about her work in the air, in answer to a question from Sir Timothy. She said that the safest place in the world was in an airplane landing or taking off . . . . when tired business men were strapped in their seats. The tycoon roared with laughter.

Then they all went into the large ornate dining room, where places were set at a round table beside the long one with chairs for twenty four. For the meal there was cold consommé, poached brill, cold roast beef and a cheese board. Tresilian and Sir Timothy spoke about shipping and business at Wooffendens, while Julie, Michael and Lady Wooffenden talked at length about Montreal, Expo '67 and Canada. The crisis was over and when they got up from the table they all felt better. They returned to the morning room for coffee.

Sir Timothy took Tresilian aside. "What are your immediate plans Glyn?" he asked.

Tresilian lit a cigarette and stirred the small coffee cup. "I hate to answer your question like this, Sir Timothy, but my immediate plans rather depend on you."

The magnate looked momentarily confused and then his features broke into a pleased smile. "Ah, Glyn. Good. Wonderful," and he shook his head vigorously with approval. "In that case your immediate plans are made. I suggest you and Julie marry as soon as possible — and after that, you can start any time you like. This is good news. I'm so glad you made the decision." Glyn was going to cut in but let his father-in-law finish.

"No, Sir Timothy. That's not it, sir. I loathe to say this, but I've never been further from accepting your kind offer." He walked away from the group to one of the French windows and

Sir Timothy followed — coffee cup in hand.

"The fact is, Sir Timothy, that I do have a proposition to put to you. This was the other reason why we came over. Oh, I must tell you. Sometime ago the radio station I was working with in Montreal — CRAK — and I parted company. In the interim I met Julie and negotiated with a Toronto operation who were particularly keen to have me on their air. But recently, from an idea Julie had, I've become obsessed with a notion. And I mean really obsessed. So much so that I call it 'The Plan' with a capital 'P'! If I may, I would like your undivided attention for an hour or so that I may present a scheme which on first hearing you may wish to laugh out of the room. I know how busy you must be at this particular time — especially with the big American nuclear naval contract — but I'd very much like a chance to talk to you."

Sir Timothy sipped his coffee, hardly able to conceal his disappointment that Glyn hadn't come to discuss his position in the firm as well as to introduce his fiancée. "Hmmm. I don't think for a moment I'd want to laugh at any scheme you have in mind, Glyn. But you're quite right about business. Since my letter to you, it looks as if I'll have to go to Washington at the beginning of the week after next. I have to go back to the office this afternoon — perhaps you'd care to join me and we can talk in the car? No. No, that's not a good idea. Very well then. Tonight. After dinner. We'll have brandy in the library and leave the ladies to their own devices for a while. That suit you?"

"Perfectly Sir Timothy," Glyn replied, "that's very kind of you."

In the afternoon, Glyn and Julie let Michael take them for a walk around some of the boy's favourite haunts in the soft green Cheshire countryside. They stopped for tea in a little village Tea Shoppe where Michael ravished splits and clotted cream. They returned to the Hall by six where they bathed and changed for dinner.

Mrs. Southcombe, who had not joined them at luncheon — disappearing after the drinks, was nevertheless present at the dinner table. During the afternoon walk, Julie had tried to draw out Michael on his feeling about a governess. Somehow the idea jarred on her, and she sensed the same reaction from Michael who, however, was politely noncommittal. Once on the ship Julie had mentioned this to Glyn. After all if the boy was now going to be one of them, they could hardly afford or need Mrs. Southcombe. Tresilian had felt uncomfortable, and had vaguely said something about the Wooffendens being quite capable of sorting it out. But Julie was disturbed — and tonight at dinner with the severe woman in the company, she detected a definite stiffness in the conversation.

But the meal ended and as promised, Lady Wooffenden took the other ladies in tow, Michael said goodnight, and Sir Timothy and Tresilian went to brandy in the library. A footman stoked the fire in the book lined room, and put footstools by the deeply upholstered leather arm chairs. He placed the decanter and cigar box on the table between the chairs, and bowing, took his leave.

"Well now Glyn," said Sir Timothy as they settled, "what is this incredible scheme that you think I will laugh at?"

"Before I begin sir, I would ask one more favour. Early on you will be tempted to smile and probably will have rejected my invitation long before I finish. Please hear me — right out."

Tresilian spoke for some twenty minutes. His thoughts were completely collected and he'd rehearsed this speech in his mind as he would have prepared an important radio or television show. He made all the germaine points. Including the ones about war and peace and commerce. Graphically he described the progress of the peaceship as she would sail to and around the world with the ultimate in radio and telephone equipment — mobilising world opinion through direct dialogue among all peoples. She would voyage, with people talking to each other through her. The futility of the space and nuclear arms race would become self-evident.

By breaking down the barriers of prejudice and intolerance, all would learn the simple lesson that nations, races, colours, religions and languages all have a sacred right to be at peace. His major point was the reaction on 'Public Affairs 1', and he described the program and the week that followed in detail.

Sir Timothy listened in silence, calmly smoking his cigar. Even during the most improbable moments as Glyn warmed to the Plan, he didn't change by so much as a facial flicker the set impassivity of his well bred features. Tresilian wound up his appeal.

"That is the Plan, Sir Timothy. I ask you to back it in the name of humanity."

Glyn sat back, lit a cigar from the box and took a snifter of brandy.

Leaning back, the shipbuilding magnate looked for a moment at the high ceiling above, before replying. "Glyn — did you think of approaching me first because I'm a shipbuilder with yards and facilities to carry out the conversion you speak about — or because you think I am a great humanitarian dedicated to the cause of world peace?"

Not expecting this, Tresilian flushed and stammered. "Er, that is, neither, really Sir Timothy. I wanted er, to approach er . . ." He suddenly realised there was no point in trying to fool this man and collected himself. He intentionally left out any form of address. "I approached you because you are the only rich enough person I know. Let's say I've abused the privilege of our relationship."

"Why?" rebutted Sir Timothy, "why say that?"

Unaccountably, Glyn found himself getting annoyed. He'd known of course that he'd never get anywhere. He could just see Sir Timothy speaking to his Board and Shareholders . . . 'And so Ladies and Gentlemen, I'm sure you'll all be very pleased that we at Wooffendens have added another glorious chapter to our history. I am proud and happy to announce that we have just forfeited the record breaking American nuclear naval contract. Instead, we are working at top priority to complete the conversion of a wartime Liberty ship that will sail around the world on a mission of peace through instant international dialogue made possible by the most sophisticated and powerful radio and telephone equipment in the world today.

'Commanding the ship, and producing all the broadcast talk, will be the husband of my late daughter who sold me on the idea during an after dinner chat. After a bumper share and dividend year, I'm sure you won't mind the loss that this venture is bound to show in next year's balance sheet.' Oh yes, Wooffenden was certain to make such a speech. Tresilian, not caring now and thoroughly disheartened even before the spoken rejection, decided to attack.

With heat he said, "Well, why did you ask the question in the first place then?"

Sir Timothy coloured a little. "I see no point Glyn," the baronet went on, "in asking each other questions. You have presented an idea, which I'm bound to say, is the most extraordinary I've ever heard. But I congratulate you on your originality. As you portrayed what you call your Plan, you expanded on some of the obvious points that one would have raised. But I'm glad that you reiterated the idealism of the scheme.

"You would not wish or expect me to accept or decline your invitation this evening. You are also I know, not naive enough to think that the Board would receive it with any pronounced enthusiasm. I suggest that after we have finished our cigars, we play a game of billiards and then rejoin the ladies. About your Plan I will say this. The decision would have to be mine and mine alone. It is one that as Chairman of the Board and controlling shareholder I could and would take. But — and I repeat this: alone."

Already Glyn was regretting that he had done it. Although their relationship had been hard to define, confused by undercurrents, it could be said that there'd been some small amounts of pleasant warmth between the two men. This now seemed to have gone. Hardly surprising thought Tresilian. What alternatives have I left him with? If he backs the Plan, he spits in the face of colossal industrial gains through loss of the American and other defence contracts. And if he doesn't support the peaceship, then he's saying, in effect, that war's alright — because it's good for business. And then he can reconcile all that by saying that he's applying himself responsibly to ensuring a livelihood for all the thousands of Wooffenden employees who look to his acumen and leadership to feed their families. They stubbed out their cigars and got up to go to the billiards room.

Tresilian decided that he might as well finish the whole thing now. "One more thing, Sir Timothy — before we drop the subject. Suppose, let's suppose that you decide not to back the Plan," and he paused, "and I was able to find another sponsor — would you still accept the conversion contract even though news of this might jeopardise your defence orders?" Tresilian was being unreasonable and he knew it. No not just unreasonable. Bloody ill-mannered under the roof of a man who had done so much for him.

Wooffenden looked quickly at Glyn. He was surprised at

his son-in-law. Whatever else he might think of him — he had never thought of accusing the younger man of boorishness. But there were distinct signs of it now. He spoke coldly. "I suggest that we go at once to the billiard room, leaving the subject at rest until further notice."

Glyn told Julie about the meeting. She knew that he was discouraged and depressed. Without trying to dampen him, she did once broach the thought of forgetting the Plan.

"Of course it's unworkable. When you first hear it. You didn't expect Sir Timothy or anyone else to fall over themselves with it did you? But if you really want to do it you've got to persevere. And be more than ready for disappointment. Right now, you're the only one who takes it seriously."

"That's just the trouble," he said mournfully, scraping the grass with a stick as they sat on a bench in the grounds of the Hall. "I've got so entangled with this whole thing now that it's become a kind of madness. I suppose that's how it must appear to others. And then I feel full of remorse too. I was really damned unpleasant to the old boy last night. But I couldn't help it. I was just worked up for the kind of non-committal reaction I got from him. I honestly believe I'd have been pleased if he'd just come out and thanked me for some crazy but entertaining garbage. Anyway, I can't see things between us being the same any more now." The girl looked sadly at him; then spoke. "Don't feel too badly about it dear," Julie said soothingly, "you tried and there'll be other people you can see. And he hasn't actually said no yet, has he?"

He didn't answer. The new tension between Sir Timothy and Glyn had reached the others. Mealtimes were painful and stilted. Wooffenden had obviously told his wife about Glyn's peculiar conduct and although she tried valiantly, she couldn't conceal her uneasiness. Glyn determined to leave the Hall as soon as they could, go back to Canada, settle down one way or the other and then bring Michael over to live with them. Oh, the hell with it. Maybe it would be better after all to establish himself in Toronto with Greenway and CORK and do the best he could there. God knows there was a lot to do — on the ratings scene anyway.

Two evenings after their meeting in the library, Sir Timothy greeted Tresilian affably as they were having drinks before dinner.

"Please forgive me Glyn. I should have proposed this last evening and can only offer tiredness as an excuse. The matter we were discussing the night before last — what about cigars and brandy in the library again — after dinner?" Glyn thanked him and they went into the dining room.

Michael too, had noticed a definite difference among the adults in his life. Like a diplomat he stepped into the table breach, entertaining his elders with class-room and playing field banter, until another six course meal was over.

Afterwards in the library, Sir Timothy told Glyn with kind candour that for his own reasons he must decline his son-in-law's invitation. He went on to say that this probably came as no surprise — but he hoped, he earnestly hoped, that the decision would in no way adversely affect their relationship. Then, as if he had finished reading a painful balance sheet, Sir Timothy held up his hand and smiled in anticipation of a better year.

The shipbuilder walked up and down the library with his hands folded behind his back. "Ever heard of Barton Mills-Cragley?"

"Vaguely, I think. A Midlands heavy industrialist or something?"

"That's him. Very wealthy man. Now I don't know him all that well, mark you, but I'm pretty sure he'd like to listen to you. He's a member of the 'Wicket' — my club in Town. Confidentially a lot of the members don't care for him very much and I remember there was quite a row when he joined. But someone discovered that he wanted to come in very badly and the committee agreed to put him up when he indicated that as an initiation gesture he'd pay for the Morning Room renovations.

"As far as I know, this was absolutely his own idea. The job needed doing badly and with taxes the way they are these days everyone was very pleased. It cost a packet of course and took a long time. But he seemed to be there all the time checking on progress and inspecting the work. I'd say he was the most conscientious new member we'd ever had. They tell me he's at the club a lot. The only trouble is some of the chaps don't like the way he's trying to convert them. In that sense he's most unusual as a member. Complete teetotaler and non-smoker. Nothing

wrong with that — but he insists on buying everyone cold tomato juice at the bar. And then tells them how his own business
prospered after he decided on the need to change himself. I
don't have to tell you Glyn — that sort of thing isn't done. I'm
telling you all this just so that you'll be prepared if and when
you meet him. The reason I'd like to offer you an introduction
to him is that he's also Chairman of the World Reformation
Society. Heard of it?"

"No, but it sounds like a new evangelical religious group.
That'd be fine. I wouldn't care about the ideology behind it —
just as long as we . . ."

"Candidly, I'm not too sure what's behind it. Oh, once he
tried to buttonhole me — wants the whole club to join of course.
But I'm afraid I left him when he told me four brandies were
too much after dinner and that I should exercise and lose some
weight."

"Oh? And I suppose he's socially out of place too?"

"I'd have hardly put it that bluntly myself — but just let me
say that I admire and envy your adopted Canadian directness.
But that's irrelevant at the moment. I do suggest however that
you and he may have more than a little in common. Whether
you like it or not, it is obvious that you yourself have been
gripped by some sort of reforming zeal. I think there's a chance
that you and he could form a perfect partnership. You with the
idea — and he with the money. You see Glyn, the problem you
have with me is that the only thing I wish to reform or lead
crusades for is the prosperity of those who get their livelihood
from the yards. That alone is more than a lifetime's work for
me." He stopped to sip at the brandy glass.

"Would you like me to write to him?"

"Yes — if you will, Sir Timothy. I can't see any harm being
done. We'll be going on to London anyway."

"Very well. I'll do it tonight, before I retire. I'll ask him to
contact you. Where will you be staying?"

"The London House."

"Capital. Leave it to me."

. . . .

The next day, Glyn and Julie announced their intention of
having Michael live with them in Canada as soon as they were
married. Tresilian conceded that this might appear selfish and

that the Wooffendens might think they were being used to suit the younger couple's convenience. It would be regrettable too, he agreed, that plans for Michael's education and subsequent employment in the firm would not now materialise. But his mind was made up. And he was sure the Wooffendens would understand that Michael was his son — and that this was his and Julie's decision.

They left Wooffenden Hall the next day. Michael was close to tears — tears that as a little boy he would have shed gladly, but which now, at well over twelve, he kept back. The farewells inside the Hall with the Wooffendens and Mrs. Southcombe had been painful enough, and then there was the goodbye to Michael . . . And now Julie was weeping uncontrollably and flooding a second handkerchief. He put his arm around her neck.

"Take your, your," she said between sobs, "take your hand away. Oh, Glyn how can you be so heartless? The poor boy's heartbroken and you just tell him to go on waiting. He was crying inside but was too proud to let you see it. Why don't you forget all this Plan business and settle down? If you're getting married you've got to be responsible. I'm sorry if I hurt you but you won't find anyone to back you in a million years. It's," and she choked over her tears, "it's, it's, what's the word, it's preposterous. And deep down you know it. I know how you feel about the world and things but why should you suddenly decide to save all the people? When you've got governments and the United Nations and Churches and things?" He let her go on — and hoped that Oates, if he noticed her distress on the other side of the sound proof glass panel, would not report on it after he left them at Lime Street Station in Liverpool. She recovered by the time they reached the Mersey Tunnel, and Tresilian thought she looked even lovelier in the afterwash of crying.

She perked up a little. "Sorry, dear. That must've upset you. But when I saw Michael — just longing to be with us — it got to me. Besides you can't exactly say that our visit was a great success. I'm positive Mrs. Southcombe dislikes me intensely. Perhaps you shouldn't've talked about the Plan to Sir Timothy. Although I must say I found them both perfectly charming in the way they welcomed us. Perhaps Michael's right after all. Maybe we should get married — like to-day. I think I'd feel better."

They unloaded the baggage at the station and thanked the chauffeur who went on his way in the Bentley. They had planned to spend a few days in London and see some shows. After which they'd fly back to Montreal.

Julie marvelled at the quietness and speed of the electrified train as it sped at well over a hundred miles an hour to the London Euston station. They enjoyed the countryside and canals flashing by as they took their time over lunch.

"Glyn," Julie, now recovered, said brightly, "I've got an idea. As we're not committed to any rigid schedule and haven't even got our airline tickets yet, why don't we try and see Dame Gwynneth? You have her address don't you?"

"Yes, I do," he replied cheerfully, "and that's a damn good idea. It'd be fun to see her again."

They checked in at the London House, had an after dinner stroll along Park Lane and turned in early. They met at half past nine for breakfast. Moments after they ordered, the waiter brought a message.

"Mr. Glyn Tresilian? I have this for you sir."

He read the folded slip of paper.

'Please telephone Mr. Barton Mills-Cragley at his City Office STErling 8754.'

They finished in the dining room and went up to Glyn's suite. The Greek room-maid went on with her vacuum cleaner and then ran terrified out of the room when Tresilian gave her the universal broadcasters' throat slitting signal to cut the uproar. It took at least two minutes to reassure the hotel detective and housekeeper that the girl was in no danger of being slain by him. However, an Italian girl was summoned and formally introduced as a replacement. With calm restored, he sat on the unmade bed and called Barton Mills-Cragley.

"Looking forward very much indeed to meeting you Tresilian. Got a fine long letter from my old friend Tim Wooffenden. So you're the one who married Peta eh? But I understand you're engaged again. Very good. I'm anxious to hear about the scheme you have in mind. Tim only said that he thought I'd be interested in listening to you. I most certainly will be. What about this evening at the club? Yes. Good. At the Wicket, then. Oh, about six o'clock. I'll meet you at the main entrance

— that's it — on St. James's. Looking forward to it. Goodbye."

Glyn hung up the phone and they went out. Julie wanted to do some shopping and he thought she'd like Knightsbridge. They walked down to Sloane Street. "Well, that was short and sweet I must say. God, he sounded so positive on the phone. But you often find that when you're setting up a meeting. When they know what you really want it's usually another story altogether," he said taking her arm.

"Just take him as he comes Glyn. Let's face it, if you're long on ideas and he's long on money and you both want what the other has, why shouldn't something come of it?"

"We'll see. He didn't mention anything about you dear — I wonder if . . . . "

"Oh, don't worry about that. I think it's much better that you see him on your own. Besides I thought I'd take the opportunity and go along to that Farm Street place — and clear things up. You know."

"Fine."

They spent the day browsing around some Knightsbridge stores and the Science Museum. They went into the Albert Hall and sauntered through Kensington Gardens. Then they took a taxi back to the hotel for tea. She poured for them both and he munched on a water cress sandwich.

"He didn't say anything about dinner, so I might as well get stuck into some of these."

"Here you are — one lump only. That's the way I'll start reforming you, I think. You could afford to miss dinner. You'll find two or three glasses of tomato juice very nourishing."

BOOK II

CHAPTER 1

The Wicket (Stumpers to the Members) was one of London's proudest clubs. It's history went back to the early eighteen-hundreds. Ever since then it had occupied an exclusive corner of London's clubland. Wealth had always been a good companion for membership but more than that even, the members through the citadel of their committee, insisted that applicants be sponsored by no fewer than six other Wicketeers. This gave the club a unique set of rules to which it clung tenaciously, even after the birth of the wretched Welfare State.

The Wicket was also different in another way. Unlike the rest of the fortress of St. James's, a polyglot of callings and interests were represented. There were august old Bishops, and finely bred young aristocrats. Some Generals, Admirals and Air Marshals. Commercial tycoons, like Sir Timothy. There was even a titled actor or two. But the club was not totally resistant to change, and the medical profession, which had once been considered vulgar and not a fit calling for gentlemen, now had its name-plate on the Members List.

But this was as far as the club could reasonably be expected to go. It could never countenance the thought of actual Trade coming in. What Trade was and what it wasn't had never been an issue for definition or discussion. Sir Timothy Wooffenden was not Trade. Barton Mills-Cragley was. On the whole, members preferred to forget that the Morning Room renovations and other repairs had cost nearly a quarter of a million pounds whenever they were invited to tomato juice by the benefactor member who came to the club ill disguised as the only serious lapse of judgment in the Wicket's history.

There were stories galore about the old Stumpers. And they were nearly all rooted in the Members' legendary love for quiet and the things that were done. It was done to drink the Club Port after dinner. It was never done to talk or conduct business on the premises. And tomato juice, if it were to be tolerated at all, might be included with the dreadful Vodka that foreign visitors sometimes drank but that one would never dream of having oneself.

As he drove up Piccadilly in a cab, Tresilian recalled a couple of tales he'd heard about the famous old place from Sir Timothy himself.

Rumour had it that on one occasion a frail and very senior member had complained to the committee when a cat crept across the Reading Room.

'Please see to it', the old man thundered with his pen, 'that you stop this wild animal at once. Make sure in future that all beasts are prohibited.'

Shortly after the war, when the Catering and Wages Act came in, the life of the London club underwent some inconvenient changes when employees were only allowed to work a certain number of hours, and weekend work entailed overtime payments. There was particular hardship during the summer months when club servants took paid leave. So the committees got together and arrangements were made by which during the summer holidays Club Members could use each other's facilities when their own closed down for the fortnight's staff holidays.

The Wicket's first temporary guests came from the Waterloo Club where membership had always been restricted to 'senior rank and battle glory.' Sometimes, the Smoking Room of the Waterloo looked and sounded like a front line trench or the setting for a naval engagement as retired Field Marshals and Admirals lived again their grand exploits of the past.

For the first exchange visit, two senior Wicket men stood guard in the main entrance as their Hall Porter negotiated the bath-chair and sticks of two warriors from the Waterloo.

"Do you think they're from the Waterloo?" one Wicketeer asked of the other.

"I rather think they must be," his companion replied, "they have such brutal faces." Sir Timothy had really liked that one.

Punctually at six, Glyn walked through the heavy revolving doors at the main entrance of the Wicket. The ladies' entrance was down a side street somewhere. Tresilian had also heard that one Wicketeer, a member for over forty years, could not give its precise location when asked for directions once by a member's stranded spouse.

"Ah, there you are — Tresilian?" A florid stocky man with grey hair and green tweeds was waiting for him.

"Yes, sir. Mr. Mills-Cragley?"

"That's right. Very good timing too. You walked from the London House I take it?"

"No, I must confess I didn't. Much too lazy. Took a cab."

"Ah, that's not good Tresilian. Not good for that," and he poked his guest sharply in the stomach. "Nothing like walking to keep you fit. Walk miles every day myself. Flat to office. Office to flat. Now, let's hang up your coat in the cloak-room."

"I'm a teetotaler myself," he said as they sat at a table in the bar, "but I'm not a bigot. Mind you, I don't conceal that I'd like everyone else to be dry as well, but live and let live and all that, eh? Oh? You're a tomato-juice man too?"

Tresilian was anything but a tomato juice man. But he would be one tonight. He disliked the man instinctively. At a guess, Glyn estimated that his host's rubicund face had cost a fortune in best whisky. His use of the word 'dry' did not suggest a life of abstinence. And he was right. Mills-Cragley until years before had been one of the highest living people in the land. He had met the World Reformation Society just in time and wanted the rest of mankind to meet it too.

"Try a little Worcester with it, Tresilian. Gives it a fine perky piquant flavour. Here's a spoon." He spoke of the merits of tomatoes and their juices for the ten minutes it took them to leave their glasses coated with pinkish brown ooze.

"And now let us have some dinner. Come." And in the correct club manner he propelled his guest to the Members' dining room.

"They dine very late here you know, Tresilian. I asked the head waiter to let us have a table for six-thirty. He's a good fellow — walks here every day from Fulham. Ah, good evening, Williams; everything ready for us? Good. Thank you." They went to a corner table in the still, cavernous, deserted room.

"I usually have a little clear soup, one veal cutlet with spinach and then blanc mange. What about you?"

"If I may, I'd like to have exactly the same please sir."

"Excellent, excellent. Williams, the usual for my guest too. And now my boy — it's your turn. Tell me all."

Tresilian cleared his throat and filled a water glass. He had decided on more or less the same approach as he had used with Wooffenden but thought it best to preface it for Mills-Cragley.

"Before I present my scheme in detail, Mr. Mills-Cragley, I should clear up the question of motive. At the moment I'm unemployed but fortunately came into a little capital recently so that I'm not yet on the bread line. I hope therefore that you will not consider the proposal I'm about to put to you as a means of uncovering a job for myself. I don't know how much you know about my background but . . ."

"Quite a bit Tresilian, quite a bit. One heard about you marrying Peta of course and Tim Wooffenden filled in the gaps very well when he wrote to me. Let's start the soup — I won't interrupt you again."

By the time the veal cutlets were brought in, Glyn was well into his stride and a great light of understanding was dawning on his host's face. My God, don't tell me he's buying it, Tresilian thought and plunged on with mounting enthusiasm. Barton Mills-Cragley was nodding his head, gesturing in agreement and generally behaving like a man who was being sold against impossible odds. Oh, Lord, this was magnificent. Look at him beaming with pleasure and approval. Glory be to tomato juice. He'd drink it for ever. He'd walk to Trois-Rivières every day. He'd do Yoga. He'd keep fit. He'd sign the pledge and never touch another drop. God bless you Mills-Cragley and seeing the light and your bloody marvellous World Reformation Society. Oh, you fantastic rich man. Let the other Wicketeers mock and scorn you and say you're Trade. We'll give 'em Trade, won't we Mills-Cragley? If you'll go for this, you've got yourself another yes-man for life.

He finished half way through the blanc mange. And used the same ending.

"You have heard me out sir. And now I ask you, Mr. Barton Mills-Cragley to back the Plan, as I call it, in the name of all mankind." He put down his spoon.

"I have understood you perfectly, Tresilian. And congratulate you on a lucid, moving presentation. I made my decision as soon as I saw the possibilities. And that was before you were half-way through. I will back you." He poured some cold milk in his coffee.

"Milk in your coffee?"

"Sorry, sir. What was that?" Tresilian asked as if a hypnotist had put the words in his mouth.

"Milk — do you take it in your coffee?"

"Milk? Yes — of course. What else?"

"Good for you. Much better than cream with all those fatty elements. Now, I suggest that when we're finished here, we go for a brisk constitutional and get some good air in our lungs. Then we can talk about the scheme at greater length."

They left the Wicket and headed for a bracing walk to and on the Embankment. Tresilian looked at his watch. It was just after seven fifteen. It would be some time before any other members would be in the dining room, he reflected as he realised what he had achieved.

Pubs and discotheques en route to the river were already roaring with business.

"Wish we could do something about these places, Tresilian. Such terrible temptations for our young people inside. Drink, women and drugs. Trouble is we've got nobody in government over here with any backbone. No sense of right and wrong. They're a lot of loose livers themselves and encourage the youth to behave in the same way. I keep on talking about this at the Wicket. Lot of powerful and influential people there. God knows I do my share, but I can't do it alone. That's why I'll get behind your scheme. The problem's not just confined to this country you know — it's world wide. And the result is that communism's sprouting up all over the place. Look at the students everywhere — particularly on your continent."

"I'm not quite sure what you mean sir — what this has to do with the Plan."

"Everything, Tresilian, everything. If you say it can all be done technically without encroaching on anybody's territory then I'm all for it. Look at the control we'll have."

Tresilian slowed down his pace — already formidably quick, set by Mills-Cragley.

"What control sir?"

"Control over people of course. All that broadcasting in all those languages. Ah, don't get me wrong now. When I say control, I don't mean that in a takeover sense. But we'll be able to reach people and change them. Because that's what the world really needs. Change. From the useless hedonistic attitudes to something worthwhile like self-reliance and initiative and belief in the existence of a Higher Power. That's the way to do good in the world. Spread a message that's really worthwhile. I believe that implicitly and that's why I'm Chairman of the WRS. And that's why we'll start you on your way. One of the first targets we'll aim at will be the American troops in Vietnam. We'll tell them how . . ."

"Excuse me sir — I'm a little confused. You refer to 'we' doing this and doing that — who are 'we'?"

"The Society of course. The WRS."

Tresilian's spirits, so high a few minutes ago, dropped sharply. Now he could see it coming.

"But Mr. Mills-Cragley, I thought you said you would back the thing?"

"I did — but as Chairman of the World Reformation Society, not as head of my companies. Oh, I expect I'll be putting up most of the money and some of the other chaps will be giving me a hand of course."

"Then I take it that the WRS would have control of the whole thing?"

"Come, come, Tresilian, I'm surprised at you. Who else? If we're putting up the money?"

"Well then I think we'd better get this clear before we go any further. Specifically what will you want to do?"

"Get people thinking straight for a start. We'll get the physical and mental poisons out of them. We'll tell them about the joys and rewards of good hard individual effort. We'll, we'll," Mills-Cragley was now well on the way to his platform style as he swiped the Thames air, "we'll make them excellent. Through this powerful medium we can change the people of the world by reminding them of their huge individual responsibilities. We can encourage the fighting men in Vietnam and urge them on to even greater efforts. Too often they're bogged down in the brothels and taverns. All this outlaw sex demoralizes the troops. We can inspire them with messages of virtue and hope. We shall fuel them to victory. They will win for us."

Tresilian glanced across at the Battersea power station. The four enormous stacks were smoking well. He might as well finish it now.

"Mr. Mills-Cragley, I'm grateful for your hospitality and for listening to me. But we're not thinking about the same thing at all. As far as control goes, the Plan calls for the people to have it — that's all. The idea is to get the massive weight of international public opinion forcing governments to give up all the nationalistic attitudes that bring on and escalate wars."

The man from Trade stared at him, an amazed look on his features. Tresilian thought at that moment that he even looked a trifle sinister.

"That, my good Tresilian, is ridiculous. How on earth would you do it?"

"With the ship of course. That's the only reason for having a ship — so that it can go to countries and put the means of individual communication into ordinary people's hands. That's the point of the broadcasting I have in mind. Multi-way radio. I don't think you understand that. You have in mind a ship to function with one way propaganda like Radio Moscow or the Voice of America. And that's exactly what I do not have in mind. If the World Reformation Society were going to run the show it'd be suspect before it even began. While perhaps marvelling at the technical achievements, people would react at once and say 'Oh, more brainwashing' or something. Not that I'm saying that your kind of brainwashing isn't highly desirable and far better than the stuff governments push out, but it would still end up by being a divisive thing. And I'm only concerned with stopping all war killing."

"Exactly, Tresilian — almost my very words. I spoke just now about the huge individual responsibilities on every person and . . ."

"I know you did. But then you went on to say that if the American fighting men in Vietnam could reform themselves as individuals they could 'win for us'. That's not it, Mr. Mills-Cragley. That's not it at all."

He lit a cigarette and they walked a few more paces. Then the WRS man stopped again.

"I must say I'm beginning to have my doubts about you Tresilian. You're not, I hope, intimating that you'd like the other side to win?" Glyn interjected wearily, "I don't want any side to win. I just want all sides to stop killing each other before we all commit suicide with nuclear bombs. How I wish somebody could understand that. Is it really all that difficult to grasp, Mr. Mills-Cragley?"

Big Ben sounded the quarter hour as the Midlander was about to respond. He thought better of it and hailed a taxi. He opened the door for Tresilian and they drove in silence to the London House. There had been no conversation. He offered to pay the driver but his host shook his head.

"Again — thank you for your kindness sir. Goodnight."

"Goodnight."

He took the elevator to Julie's floor and tapped on her door. She was back and writing to the de Vries. Cheerful and bright herself, she saw at once that he was down. She kissed him tenderly.

"Well? You don't look too happy. He didn't go for it?"

"Oh, yes he went for it alright. All the way. If you can . . ."

"Glyn, how wonderful. Then why . . ."

"No, let me finish. If you can call wanting to reform the world's character by getting everyone to stop smoking and drinking and walking miles every day and guzzling tomato juice all day long — yes, then he went for it. If you consider an attempt to make every American serviceman in Vietnam see the light and lead a life that will make him 'win for us' — yes, then he went for it. If you ask me whether he understood one single point about the Plan, the answer's no."

"Oh, never mind that now. Just keep on trying. Are you going to call Dame Gwynneth? She'll cheer you up."

"Might as well. How did you get on?"

"Oh, I feel much better. He was so nice about it. Of course I realise you can't understand it — but honestly, if you're genuinely sorry and do your penance truthfully it's just like having a big load taken off your conscience. It must seem a bit strange to you I suppose but . . ."

"Sometimes I wish to hell it didn't seem strange."

"Perhaps one day it won't. Come on now, cheer up. There's the phone. Let's give her a call right now."

Dame Gwynneth, speaking from her cottage in Sussex, was surprised and delighted to hear from him. But of course he and his fiancée must come down. And besides she wanted to check his breathing. Tomorrow for lunch would be wonderful.

Feeling much happier at the prospect of seeing her again,

Glyn looked at his watch and decided that they had time for a show. They went to a revue on Shaftesbury Avenue, returned for a nightcap in the hotel and turned in.

In the morning, they took a train from Victoria and two hours later got off at a small halt near the Sussex coast and boarded an ancient taxi to "Verdi", Dame Gwynneth's snug thatched home.

"How nice to see you both — Miss de Vries, this is such a pleasure. Now come in and make yourselves completely at home."

Inside were all kinds of bric-a-brac and signed photographs in frames from monarchs, buskers and admirers in between. In a corner of the main room there was a baby grand piano and the tables were littered with papers and letters. An appetising smell of roast duck came from the kitchen. Dame Gwynneth introduced her housekeeper who poured sherry for them all.

After a delicious lunch, they sat in the copy-book garden. It was a perfect afternoon and they continued the conversation which had centered mostly around the touring company. Dame Gwynneth had not so far asked Glyn any questions about himself or his future.

"I'm quite ashamed, Mr. Tresilian. So far all we've talked about is me. Now what about you both? Did you have a pleasant stay in Cheshire?" Glyn had wondered about Dame Gwynneth and the Plan. Was there any point? Would she at her age — and with her highly specialised own interests be bored with it all? But he did feel like unburdening himself.

He decided to take the risk. Julie watched him carefully as he replied. "Yes, very pleasant on the whole thank you Dame Gwynneth. It gave the Wooffendens an opportunity to meet Julie too. And of course we saw Michael — my son. But the parting's always hard. However, we hope it won't be too long before we set the date — and after that Michael will join us in Canada."

Dame Gwynneth looked at him intently, and then said. "Now you're really going to think me a nosy old parker — but may I ask this of you? What is the delay?"

Tresilian told her about the Plan. Not carefully as he'd proposed it to Sir Timothy. But — just as his thoughts rushed. Dame Gwynneth listened without interruption — or surprise.

"You're really obsessed with this project?"

"Yes, Dame Gwynneth. I feel that these tools of communication are there for a good and not a negative purpose. And I just can't agree with those who don't admit that the greatest wrong in the world today is a misuse or lack of communication between people everywhere. We've got the equipment. There's nothing in the Plan we can't do. If we can do it — here's the real question — why don't we do it?"

As if wanting to change the subject, Dame Gwynneth asked almost abruptly. "Have either of you heard of . . . oh, you must have heard of him. He's a Canadian after all. Gaston Yerbury?"

"Oh, but of course . . ." they both replied together.

"Yes, I'm not surprised you've heard of him. Of course. It was a silly question. But I want to tell you something now that I will ask you not to divulge." Glyn and Julie murmured their assurances. Surely, Tresilian thought, she's not going to tell us that she and Yerbury had an affair years ago. Although they were about the same age . . .

"Yes," Dame Gwynneth went on. "I must ask you to keep this a secret. The fact is that if it had not been for Mr. Yerbury — I could not possibly have started the touring company. And all the wonderful operas that we can do would not be going around the world to-day bringing so much pleasure to ordinary people everywhere. I will tell you. Mr. Yerbury not only pays all the costs — and I mean all of them, they're too numerous to mention, but he also subsidises the theatres where we perform. He would not do one without the other — as he sees no point in taking an opera on tour so that only comfortably off people can enjoy it."

Tresilian and Julie looked astonished. Suddenly Glyn realised that there must be dozens of stories like this — purposely kept under wraps by the old 'miser'. He said as much to Dame Gwynneth.

"I can't vouch for that of course Mr. Tresilian. But I'd be very surprised if what you're saying weren't true. Would you like to know how we met?

"It all seems so long ago now", she reminisced to the buzz of summer sounds in her garden. "It was, let me see, it was 1925 and I was singing the title role in Bellini's 'Norma', at La Scala, Milan. After a performance one night, they brought round a card to my dressing room from a Mr. Gaston Yerbury of Montreal and Toronto. On the card was a message — not a request to see me. He thanked me for the pleasure my singing had given him that night — and at the Metropolitan in New York. He said that if at any time there was anything he could do for me, I was to get in touch with him.

"Nearly forty years later I took him up on his offer. I went to see him in Toronto and asked him to support the touring company. He agreed instantly — on the condition that I mentioned earlier. He made my favorite dream a reality. And away we went — as Mr. Gleason would say."

Tresilian sat shaking his head in disbelief. This must be costing a packet — certainly in the millions every year. Especially if Yerbury was picking up the slack between commercial prices and the amounts actually charged to the patrons.

"Dame Gwynneth," he asked "do you watch television?"

"Not very much I'm afraid, I'm . . ."

"No, I didn't think so," Tresilian interrupted her and then went on.

"Julie, do you remember ever seeing a series called 'The Millionaire'?"

"Oh, yes," Julie replied, "you mean the one where an anonymous rich man gave a cheque every week to someone he thought needed and deserved it?"

"Yes, that's the one," he smiled at Julie and explained the program to Dame Gwynneth.

"Maybe that's Yerbury's right 'image' after all." Glyn said. "The popular conception about him — in Canada anyway — is that he's a mysterious old hoarder of fortunes. A miser."

"A miser, Mr. Tresilian," Dame Gwynneth said quietly, "is something he certainly is not. That I can guarantee."

"But Dame Gwynneth," Tresilian pressed, "is there any connection, do you think, between him and this fictional T.V. millionaire?"

"Apart from you two and a few trusted associates in the company, no one knows who our benefactor is. That evidently is Mr. Yerbury's way and so I suppose you could say that the anonymity is a connection. But unlike the rich man on television you describe, I don't believe that our patron sends out a search party looking for weekly beneficiaries."

"Hmmmm," sounded Tresilian. "Dame Gwynneth. Do you

think there's any point in me trying to see him about the Plan?"

"Not only do I think you should see him — but I will arrange the introduction. What time is it now in Toronto? I always get mixed up with these tiresome time differences. I have to telephone him quite often, and never know whether they're five hours behind or ahead of us. Which is it?"

Glyn and Julie looked at each other — awe struck. Surely the old girl wasn't going to call him there and then on his behalf? That just couldn't be true. On the other hand she didn't look as if she was about to go off her rocker either. He explained. "There's an easy rule of thumb for that, Dame Gwynneth. Just learn to say Longitude East — Greenwich time least. Longitude West — Greenwich time best. We know that Canada's longitude is west of Greenwich therefore British time is best — or ahead of Toronto. Simple."

"Oh, that's much too complicated for me Mr. Tresilian. I don't know the difference between longitude and latitude. Just tell me what time it is in Toronto." Glyn looked at his watch.

"Well," Tresilian said, "it's half past three right now. Or 15:30. We're ahead of them by five hours so we take five from 15½ and we get ten and a half. Ten thirty in the morning. That's the time in Toronto."

"Good," said Dame Gwynneth getting up from her chair. "Ten-thirty. Mr. Yerbury should be in his office. I want to tell him a few things about the Australian tour anyway, so if you like I'll try to arrange a meeting for you now. I won't of course tell him what you want to see him about — naturally that will be up to you Mr. Tresilian. But I will certainly say that I know you to . . . well never mind what I'll say. But I must know this. When are you going back to Canada?" They looked at each other, and then Glyn said. "To tell you the truth Dame Gwynneth — we don't know. That must sound foolish but we'd planned to spend a few days in London and then fly back to Montreal. But we're flexible. I'd say that if you can set something up with Mr. Yerbury and he agrees to a date — we'll go back to be there in time." The old lady left them in the garden and came out beaming some fifteen minutes later.

"Good news for you," she said, "I only hope you can get aeroplane tickets in time. Mr. Yerbury is expecting to see you a week tomorrow in his office, Mr. Tresilian. That's a Wednesday.

He invites you to lunch with him in his private dining room — it's in his suite — and from personal experience that's a meal I advise you not to miss."

.   .   .   .

They landed at Dorval International Airport, Montreal, the following Monday afternoon, and went straight to the de Vries home in N.D.G. where Julie's parents insisted he stay in the spare bedroom. They were kind, and hospitable and obviously thrilled to see their daughter again. Her mother and father, when told of events, were certain that Yerbury would hear out their future son-in-law in the most gracious way and then treat the invitation as Sir Timothy had done. And that would be an end of it. Glyn would have got it out of his system, and realising the futility, would drop it and return to normal with CORK in Toronto. Then they could get married and all would be well.

Shortly before noon on the appointed Wednesday, Tresilian stepped into the elevator in the tall Toronto skyscraper called Yerbury House. For two days he'd boned up on Yerbury in libraries, going through books and several articles.

The elderly Canadian had become a classic example in his own time of a country's unlimited opportunity. Here was a man who controlled vast corners of the Canadian economy through his personal holdings in oil, ores, timber, transportation and prairie. The youngest of a family of eleven, he was in business for himself at the age of fourteen before he could read and write. His father was an immigrant Roman Catholic English labourer and his mother French Canadian. They settled in the small village near Donnacona where Yerbury senior could get work in a local lumber mill.

Although poor and illiterate and overcrowded, the house was clean and the children nourished. A devout family, they found schooling at Sunday Mass — the classroom sort was meagre. And then through early initiative and luck, young Gaston had gone on in his own way. He had a flair for business and by dint of hard night school work learned to read and write and count.

He came to understand the principles of business and grappled with stocks and shares. By reading financial papers and trade journals he got to know a good buy when he saw it. And from selling discarded lumber by the foot, he went on to become Canada's wealthiest citizen — sitting atop his Toronto skyscraper.

He had an obscure 'image', and no heirs. He granted no interviews and made no public statements. Politically, he had become a vacuum. It was said that no one knew him — or could get close. In his seventies now, he had long been a widower — his wife having died childless of an incurable malaise after only two years of marriage.

He endowed no hospitals, universities, museums, art galleries or research centers. He did nothing remotely resembling the norms for multi billionaires. And as far as was known, he hadn't donated a nickel to charity. The press had long given him up. But the numerous corporations he controlled were all highly successful operations and it was a mark of professional 'arrival' to work in any one of them.

In the Province of Quebec he was disliked intensely by the Nationalistic fringe who thought it very wrong that he, a province reared son, gave nothing of himself or his fortune to the cause of Quebec independence.

Even those who criticized Yerbury for his non-philanthropical role, grudgingly conceded the excellence of his labour relations policies. Ever since the Yerbury Group of Corporations had been founded, it was an indelible mark of tribute to its head that there had not been a breath of labour dispute — and unions collected not a penny from any one of his over 210,000 employees. This alone, in the nineteen sixties was seen as a mark of pure genius on his part by management and labour experts all over the world.

The only way most people could pin down Gaston Yerbury to an 'image' was that of a remote and insular old man gloating over his billions. And because nothing was done to deny it, this was the prevalent thinking about him.

Now it was noon on the dot as he got off at the 37th floor. The magnate's confidential secretary took him into Yerbury's spacious paneled office. Glyn was surprised. Normally the game called for at least a ten minute wait — but here he was — shown in at once.

"Welcome Mr. Tresilian. I have been looking forward to meeting you after Dame Gwynneth's call from England." Yerbury spoke in a quiet average Canadian voice with just a touch of French. He was of medium height and carried his seventy-five years well. Scorning conformity, he dressed in the tradition of an older age. Sitting neatly on his well proportioned frame was a dark grey double breasted suit with high wing collars. A white shirt, plain blue tie, and old fashioned boots completed his dress. A legend in his time. An enigma — and yet an example to the system.

Tresilian did his best to speak calmly, although inwardly he quavered. "I appreciate you seeing me like this Mr. Yerbury," Glyn said, "especially at such short notice. I only hope you won't regard our meeting as a complete waste of time." The tycoon smiled.

"I doubt that very much Mr. Tresilian. I think Dame Gwynneth Rhondda-Llandaff is much too sensible for that. I've no idea what it is you wish to discuss with me — but I accept her recommendation to listen. Come, let us go next door for some refreshment before lunch." And Yerbury led the way to an adjoining reception room where a waiter stood by the small round bar in the corner.

"I believe Mr. Tresilian," Yerbury said chattily, "that as well as having in common the privilege of knowing Dame Gwynneth — we share a liking for pink gin. Of course with your sea-faring background that's understandable. In my own case, conversion came when I was entertained several years ago aboard a British warship in Halifax. I find it a very satisfying aperitif." They had a pink gin — one each — before going into the private dining room for lunch. During the mulligatawny, Tresilian realised that Yerbury knew a lot about him. Casually, he referred to the hot taste of the soup. "While not a curry, I imagine you like hot and highly flavoured soup, Mr. Tresilian?"

Surprised, Glyn looked up in mid-spoonful, "Er, yes. I do Mr. Yerbury."

"And again," Yerbury went on, "as a sailor you must have sampled a great many dishes. I've often thought that sailors should be the best read and most interestingly fed people in the world."

Tresilian laughed easily, replying, "Nicholas Montserrat once said that they should rule the world — but personally I don't think I could qualify on any count."

As the waiter cleared away the soup dishes, Yerbury said,

in a manner suggesting that it was time to get to business, "Now Mr. Tresilian what can I do for you?"

The younger man presented the Plan as he had to Sir Timothy. Yerbury listened without a question through the fish, braised pigeon done in wine — and cheeseboard. Glyn finished just as coffee was brought. His heart beat furiously as he looked up to get some idea of the way Yerbury had taken it. But there was no clue in the rich man's expression as he passed the cream and sugar. "Yes. I see." Yerbury said, and stirred his coffee cup. "I understand that your father-in-law, who might have been in a financial position to support your scheme, declined the invitation. Why, do you think, Mr. Tresilian?"

Glyn coloured. Now the old tycoon was beginning to enjoy himself. And would toy with him before getting up and expressing thanks for some entertaining lunch time conversation. Well, he, Tresilian, would have some sport too.

"I should think for this reason. Sir Timothy Wooffenden is running a very big enterprise. Not nearly so large as yours — but still big. At the moment, in addition to his normal mercantile shipbuilding and ship repair activity, he has a lot of defence contracts — and has almost secured a very big U.S. nuclear naval order. To get involved with the backing of a scheme like mine would certainly ruin his chances for the Pentagon orders. And, I suppose if you think about it in terms of his responsibilities, why should he throw away that volume of business? In shipbuilding there's enough competition as it is."

"Yes. You might say that was true of most business."

"I suppose so," said Tresilian — his manner almost casual and disinterested.

Yerbury looked at his guest for a few seconds and held him with fiercely blue eyes as if making a final inspection on a promising property. "Mr. Tresilian, I am a billionaire — nearly twice over. I deserve to be — I hope you'll agree — because I began in business with nothing — not even the ability to read and write. That much is known about me. I succeeded because I had the priceless gift of decision. Quickly. While others need to sleep on it, ponder and take committee advice — I don't. I make up my mind at once — relying on what is called 'seat of the pants instinct'. Some of my senior men would much rather leave their important decisions to the computer — and in this

I don't interfere. But when I am faced with a choice, I prefer to rely on my own divining fork. Which, I think, can claim a good record.

"In business and life, the great thing is to be able to see the point. And steer clear of cloudy and confusing elements. Oh, now and again some of my team say that I tend to oversimplify too much; and that I must talk the language of progress and so on. And that brings us to another common denominator doesn't it, Mr. Tresilian? Your listeners have charged you with the very same thing on your radio program. Now, I've been quite busy since Dame Gwynneth called, finding out as much about you as possible. That is always necessary, Mr. Tresilian. If for no other reason, it saves time. I'm afraid my personnel and management consultant people would throw your application out of the computer," he said with a twinkle, "if you were ever to ask for an executive position in the group. But then they'd throw mine out too. It seems we're a couple of candidates for the scrap heap."

The old man continued. "Yes. You wouldn't do at all. Background much too varied. Unstable. Impulsive. No record of settlement. Far too nomadic Mr. Tresilian. I have a confession and an apology to make to you. Once I had all the available 'data' I sent it to our personnel specialists asking for their findings — or 'probabilities' as the computer puts it. Naturally I used a fictitious name and took pains to see that the enquiry didn't come from me. Because I wanted their truthful assessment, Mr. Tresilian. And had they reported anything else, I doubt that our conversation would still be in progress. For I have found that true originality comes from those who invariably are rejected by the modern processes of selection." Yerbury cleared his throat and took a sip of coffee.

"It is good to have ideals, Mr. Tresilian. But, if you are to have any chance of doing something about your idealism, you must be a realist too. And that I am. Most of the people I see, who are not of my business, want money. To finance commercial schemes — or for charity. You will know, of course, about my miserly ways; that I give nothing to deserving causes. Realism, Mr. Tresilian. That's what counts. The realist does not believe in temporary patchwork — which most charitable campaigns are — accompanied very often by suspect motives.

"No. It is possible to be an idealist and a realist at the same time. It is a question of selecting ways that are not wasteful — ways that get to the real hearts of issues." Yerbury paused and got up from the table. He walked to the window of his private dining-room. Tresilian held his breath. My God, he thought, don't say he's going to do it. No surely he . . . but before he could think any more, Yerbury swung round and faced him.

"Mr. Tresilian, I see the point of what you call your Plan. For it, I congratulate you. I will give you all the financial support you need on one condition only. My sponsorship must remain anonymous. No, this is not altruism. It is realism. Your Plan is an idealistic project which I have decided can be made to work — and if it does, mankind's benefits will be immeasurable.

"However from a business point of view, I am more vulnerable even than your father-in-law. And like him I do not want to see a recession in my group of corporations that would lead to lay-offs and suffering. I too Mr. Tresilian, am a 'people person' — one of your radio phrases I think. But this is exactly what I mean when I say that one can be both — idealistic and a realist at the same time. A simple premise, but one that's universally indigestible.

"Of course, as your peace ship starts its work, the pressures on you to divulge the support source will be enormous. But my trust in you must be total. And so there will be no companies specially formed; and I will ask for no formal reports or accounting. My previous sentence says it all. 'My trust in you must be total'."

Glyn's head reeled and the room began to swim around him. He'd known this sensation before, when after a heavy night of drinking, nothing could stop the bedroom from its mad rotation. He folded his arms and furiously dug nails into wrists — as he had done since early childhood to apply the test to good news. His eyes started to fill, as they did when extreme pleasure and contentment came — from a view, music, or conversation — or in the settling of a disagreement. He opened his mouth to speak, but Yerbury raised his hand.

"I know what you are going to say Mr. Tresilian. Please don't. We must all do what we can to make man's chances for survival greater. You will have done far more than I. Now I have no idea how you will begin. That's up to you. But your expenses will be considerable. You will leave the building this afternoon with a special account opened in your name. Rest assured that no check will bounce. By the way, what do you intend to call the ship?"

Tresilian gulped. "I don't know yet, Mr. Yerbury. I've thought about it once or twice — but of course that hardly seemed to be the biggest problem."

He tried hard to control the shaking in his voice — and then said with a smile. "Do you have any suggestions, sir?"

Yerbury answered at once. "Yes, as a matter of fact I do. I have always loved the Latin — and frankly was disappointed when they went to the vernacular in the Mass. Latin is as internationally derivative as any language, and as your Plan is all about a peace ship, I suggest the name 'Navis Pacifica'."

"Thank you, Mr. Yerbury. It fits perfectly. That will be her name. 'Navis Pacifica'."

CHAPTER 2

Tresilian returned to Montreal and went to work at once. First, he took out papers for an unincorporated but registered business called 'Navis Pacifica.' He opened an account in this name at a different branch of his Montreal bank. Then he moved his personal effects to Julie's house in NDG and turned his own apartment into an office — buying chairs, desks and filing cabinets. Julie was the receptionist/secretary. They agreed that she should receive $85.00 a week paid out of the premium bond windfall. The de Vries, once they'd got over the initial shock, were now completely won over and enthusiastic. They vowed secrecy.

The essential priorities were.
1. Buy a ship.
2. Convert her — structually and electronically.
3. Recruit sailing and broadcast crews.
4. Do all this in secret. Premature news of intention could ruin the whole venture.

There was only one way to deal with point four. If questioned, he'd let it be known that the ship was being fitted out as a purely commercial satellite broadcasting research station. But it would be difficult to ensure that no one involved would divulge the real purpose.

Because of the Vietnam situation and State Department sensitivity, Tresilian decided to purchase the kind of 'Liberty' ship he wanted from Greek rather than American owners, even though he knew that hundreds of these ships were laid up in Texas river reaches and could probably be had for very little. He didn't want to risk any political ramifications at this stage.

Before leaving for Monte Carlo to negotiate with one of the world's biggest tonnage owners, Julie typed letters for Glyn to Dame Gwynneth and Sir Timothy as follows,

Dear Dame Gwynneth,

I can't express what I feel — so I won't try. I leave for Monte Carlo tonight and will try to buy a ship from Nicholas Archimedes. Then I hope we can get her quickly to Wooffendens for the re-fit — by the same mail I'm writing to Sir Timothy. Our biggest problem will be recruiting and secrecy until all is done and nothing can keep us from our aim. If music really be the food of love — what about some performances by the touring company? On board and live. If it's not too wild a notion, do think about it. By the way, we're going to call her 'Navis Pacifica'.

Aye,

Glyn Tresilian.

P.S. Julie, who typed this so badly, sends best wishes! G.T.

And to Wooffenden.

Dear Sir Timothy,

I am happy and proud to announce that we have found a backer for the Plan. I leave tonight to see Nicholas Archimedes about a ship. I hope he won't be difficult. He shouldn't be — as I understand he's phasing out his dry cargo interests and concentrating on tankers. Be that as it may. I won't be stopping over in the U.K. on this occasion, so please accept this letter as an invitation to do the re-fit. In toto. Structurally and electronically; and within twelve months if possible. I agree usual terms. I look forward to your reply. I think you know what's required in general. At this point, we are as interested in secrecy as you are.

Aye,

Glyn

Tresilian wrote to Michael as well, sketching in the 'Navis Pacifica' as a new and exciting scheme he was working on.

Nicholas Archimedes, in Monte Carlo, thought Tresilian was quite mad. Not because Glyn had told him about the Plan, but that he wanted to buy a Liberty ship. Out of date, slow and commercially redundant. Gladly though, the shipping magnate flew him in his private plane to Bone, Algeria, where one of his few remaining 'Liberties' was loading a last cargo of iron ore before being sold for scrap. So that he could get the feel of her, and study her general performance, Tresilian sailed with the old tramp as far as Gibraltar and then flew back to Montreal. He was satisfied that although dirty, run down and badly commanded and crewed by a cosmopolitan ship's company, she would do. She was bound for Middlesbrough in North East England. He had promised to give Archimedes delivery instructions as soon as possible.

On his return to Montreal and the 'office', Julie had mail waiting for him from both Dame Gwynneth and Sir Timothy. From the former, there was a short delighted note saying that she would indeed think about the touring company doing their bit for international understanding — and from Wooffenden this letter.

My dear Glyn,

Congratulations. Thank you for the order to handle the modifications you require. As soon as you have purchased the ship, please let me know and we'll arrange to berth her immediately pending your further instructions. Without guarantees, we'll do our best to get it done in a year. Presumably the first job will be a Class I Survey? What with news from you and Washington, this has been an eventful week. Yesterday we learned that we won the U.S. naval contract. There was great jubilation everywhere in the yards and offices when this was announced.

Aye,
Timothy Wooffenden

Tresilian called Archimedes immediately in Monte Carlo asking him to leave the ship after discharge with Wooffendens on the Mersey and to pay off the entire crew repatriating them to their widely scattered home ports. They had agreed on an 'as is' price of £655,000 for the ship, and he told the Greek shipowner that a cheque in this amount would be in the mail to him that day. Then he called Sir Timothy, asking him to liaise with the ship's agents in Middlesbrough on his behalf; to berth the ship, shut her down, cover her for dead ship insurance and do nothing more until further notice. Two weeks later he received a cable from Sir Timothy saying that the ship was safely tied up at Wooffendens, shut down and the crew paid off. The next day, Tresilian received all the relevant documents from Archimedes made out in favour of 'Navis Pacifica.'

He knew that the way he'd bought the ship had been foolhardy and dangerous. The first thing, surely was to get a surveyor's report on her condition and seaworthiness. Not after the
fact of sale. But he didn't want to be put off by gloomy prog-
noses, and security would be a lot harder if the ship were dry-
docked and word got out that she was being surveyed for possible sale. That was the risk. What on earth would anyone want
with a 'Samboat' in 1967?

Archimedes was the kind of shipowner who had almost as
many companies as he had ships. These were handy tax and
registration dodges — a separate company for a ship registered
by any number of obscure but willing countries. The 'Liberty'
that Tresilian bought was actually registered in the name of a
West African state that didn't even border on salt water. Glyn
realised that he'd have to do the same.

After a few days of talking and planning, Glyn and Julie
agreed that she would hold the 'office' fort and he would go to
Wooffendens to get the work under way. Once that was done
he'd return to Montreal and go about recruiting the sailing and
broadcast crews. Perhaps at or through Expo '67. It seemed a
natural and ready made clearing house. And while the people
he wanted were not necessarily going to be there at the right
time, it would be an incomparable point of contact. A lot of
the world was represented — with the gaping exceptions of
Peoples' China, Spain, some South American countries, Eire and
New Zealand.

A few days later, Tresilian landed at Manchester airport,
where chauffeur Oates was waiting. This time, Glyn declined
the hospitality of Wooffenden Hall, preferring instead, to stay
in a New Brighton hotel which was much closer to the shipyard.
Besides, he now wanted to further the business like quality of
his relationship with Sir Timothy.

They dry-docked the 'Navis Pacifica' the day after his arrival.
Sir Timothy had an independent surveyor standing by. In a white
boiler suit Glyn spent his days with the surveyor in the dry-
dock itself, in the engine room, bilges; they crawled through
double bottom oil and ballast tanks, coffer-dams and the steering
flat. They inspected the fore-peak, after-peak, fresh water tanks,
chain locker, mast-houses and hatches. They examined life saving apparatus, navigational equipment and the midships super-

structure. They went right through her. They made innumerable notes which the surveyor edited and presented in report form forty eight hours later.

Important points were these.

1. Due to neglect and large accumulations of rust, all her steel work would require sandblasting followed by many coatings of anti-fouling and anti-corrosive preparations. And then protective paint. This applied to above and underwater hull, and superstructure.

2. All life saving equipment would have to be renewed and increased to accommodate the greater numbers of personnel the ship would carry.

3. Extra living quarters would have to be built in the tween decks of the for'ard hatches 1, 2, and 3. To do this, special scuttles and ventilators would be required.

4. Because of the change in her metacentric height that would be effected through the electronic equipment and helicopters carried on her weather deck, permanent ballast would be needed in her lower holds to offset the ship becoming too 'tender'.

5. Her oil burning water tube boilered triple expansion engines required a complete overhaul — as did all auxiliaries with special emphasis on feed pump machinery.

6. The ship required a long overdue fumigation. Rats and cockroaches were rampant.

7. At the after end of the ship, the main-mast and all connected derrick rigging would have to be brought down and the hatch coamings made flush with the weather deck so that the helicopters could take off and land with the minimum obstruction. Removal of this considerable top weight with its high moment, would also help the stability problem that was obviously worrying the surveyor quite a bit. With no derricks to lift them, hatch beams would have to be of the roller type.

8. The water-tight bulkhead between hatches four and five on the after deck, would stay up; thus dividing the holds into two 'helihangars' below the common sliding hatch which when drawn to, would serve as the actual landing and take off deck. The choppers would be raised and lowered by

means of a mobile caterpillar deck crane.

9. Special antennae masts would have to be stepped mid-ships and for-ard.

10. The deep-tanks would be converted to house the massive generators that would power the ship's broadcast transmitters.

Then came a special meeting with the Wooffenden Naval Architects and a Project Manager was assigned to the 'Navis Pacifica.' He was Ray Spurling — a key man who would be in supreme charge of the conversion.

Afterwards Sir Timothy called Glyn to his office. "Everything under control Glyn?" he asked.

Tresilian bristled a little. "I thought I might have put that question to you, Sir Timothy."

The shipbuilder looked uncomfortable for a moment or two. And then reached for a file on his desk; putting on horn rimmed glasses, he looked through it. "Yes, I think I can say that things are well in hand. You will have to sign the various sub-contracting authority papers and then we can go ahead. Perhaps you'd like to do that now?"

Glyn put his signature to several documents giving Wooffendens the necessary clearances to engage electronics experts, sound proofing specialists, telephone consultants and so on. Sir Timothy put all this in the file and buzzed for his secretary. When the girl came in, he initialled it and gave it to her with an air of finality.

Sir Timothy took off his glasses. "Well, Glyn that's that, it seems. The work can now go on. I'm just as pleased that you came to us now rather than later when we'll be so busy with the American job as well as the very considerable amount of mercantile work we've got in the books and on the stocks. Getting on with Spurling?"

"Yes, very well indeed thanks. It's good of you to put one of your best men on the job."

"No need to thank me for that, Glyn. Nothing to do with me. I don't get involved with that sort of thing."

Glyn's feelings were mixed. He hated himself for the irritation that Sir Timothy's presence brought on nowadays. After all, Wooffenden had been good. He'd personally seen to it that the ship could be accepted and that the twelve month dead line would be met. Unwittingly, of course, Michael was becoming more and more the catalyst. I've a damn good mind to take him on the ship for a while, Tresilian thought. "I take it then Sir Timothy, that from here on in we'll have no further direct dealings about the 'Navis Pacifica'?"

"Quite right Glyn. Life becomes much too critical I fear when you become enmeshed with other peoples' affairs — even though they do work for you. I expect we'll hear mutterings that your ship has jumped the queue. You should get every co-operation. And if you don't then I'll hear about it via the usual channels. I trust that you will be pleased with our work. According to the pro-forma, the very rough estimate of the whole job is around the six million pound mark — or eighteen million dollars in your money. And the bulk of the designs should be ready in another month I believe; in the meantime we have plenty of other hammer and nail work to do."

Tresilian spent a few more days in New Brighton seeing to it that the main ship work got under way satisfactorily. As Michael was on summer vacation, the boy came down every day to join his father. Together they went round the ship, breaking for lunch and tea. And then they'd go round to the special gate at Wooffendens where the Bentley was waiting to take Michael and Sir Timothy back to the Hall.

At nearly thirteen, Glyn's son was now only a year away from Eton, and no definite plans had yet been made for him. It all depended of course on when his father and step-mother to be would marry. Whatever was to be done for Michael had to be done soon. It would be wrong to pull him out of Eton after a year or so and then transplant him to high school in Montreal. And yet, Tresilian determined, the Plan had first priority. There could be no other way now. He knew this as he walked aboard and around the 'Navis Pacifica' in dry dock. Everywhere there was activity. Getting her ready. Ready for the incredible task he'd set her. There was a constant roar from the compressors around the dock and this, mixed with the relentless staccato of chipping hammers and rivet guns produced a demented, earsplitting, exhilarating symphony.

On the day before he flew back to Montreal from Manchester Airport, Tresilian took his son for lunch in New Brighton. Glyn hadn't really spelled out to Michael any details of the Plan. He decided to during the meal. The boy listened with an expression of such disbelief that he couldn't really do justice to the food specialties that his father had encouraged him to order. However he recovered by the time the baked alaska arrived.

"It all sounds jolly exciting Daddy. Of course I won't tell anybody but I'd like to. Well — some of the chaps at school anyway. No. I won't — I promise. But why do you want to keep it such a secret?"

"When you're a bit older Michael," Tresilian explained, "you'll understand. But right now I don't want to bore you or disappoint you with what I think are the reasons. Let's just say that it's all to do with human nature — which doesn't always work for the general good. We can go on and hope that by the time you're of age, there won't be the slightest need for anything resembling the Plan — or the 'Navis Pacifica'."

Michael seemed to understand this and then grinned at his father. "I know you're going to say 'no' Daddy. But I'll ask anyway. Is there any chance I could come with you? After all I'm just about thirteen now — and I could come as a cabin boy."

Tresilian lit a cigarette. "And what about your education? I'd get into all kinds of trouble with the authorities if you signed on as a cabin boy — or anything else at your age. You can't be serious."

Michael looked eager and let down at the same time. Then he found something. "But I am serious Daddy. Look at it this way. Take geography. As you know from my reports, I'm a bit weak on that subject. I'm quite good at English — and I could read a lot and write essays on everything that happens. As the ship will be going all over the world, I'll be able to brush up on French and learn Spanish and Italian and German and all kinds of other languages," and now as another bit of genius floated down to him, the lad rushed on, "especially Daddy as you say that you'll have linguists of all the world's main tongues on board. Surely I can learn more languages more quickly that way than I ever could at school. And you could teach me navigation. That means plane and spherical trig. History I also could pick up as we go along. Please Daddy, think about it — and let me come. After all Julie will be going won't she? And I've been wanting so much to live with you Daddy. It's been a long time since we lost Mummy. Oh, I know I don't remember her — but I don't know — somehow, er I can't say it properly — but just lately I seem to have been missing her. Daddy, you must realise that Grandmama and Grandpapa and Mrs. Southcombe have all been very kind and I've had a wonderful time living with them — but it's not the same as having your own parents is it?

"I must say during the hols when I haven't seen you I've been quite jealous of the other chaps going home to their mothers and fathers. I don't mind about not going to Eton, Daddy. I'd rather live with you and Julie than anything else in the world. You're going back to Montreal tomorrow? When will you come back again?"

Tresilian looked away. Trying to control himself, he mumbled an excuse about having to make a phone call. He told Michael to have more of the burning ice cream and said he'd be right back.

Throwing down his napkin, Glyn went quickly to the telephone booth in the darkened foyer of the restaurant and turned his back on the people passing by. He looked up the number of the Canada Immigration Office in Liverpool. Then, just as he was about to put the coins in the box, a well of feeling overtook him. Only now did he realise what a brute he must have been to Michael all these years. And what guts the boy had shown. He'd never whined or complained.

Tresilian was ashamed and disgusted at himself for the cruel indifference that Michael had focussed so poignantly with his simple words at the table. This was it by God. He'd make it up to him. He'd check immigration and on the next trip over, before school started, he'd take Michael back with him to Montreal. With good timing, he'd be able to start high school and see quite a bit of Expo at the same time. From this point on, he'd give Michael every reason for believing that he had the best father in the world. Yes, even if it meant that the boy joined them on the ship. For a time anyway. A few months here or there couldn't do irreparable damage to his schooling. And some of Michael's arguments, especially about geography and languages, were quite sound. The first thing was to get him domiciled in Canada.

Tresilian regained his composure and found out that as a returning resident to Canada, he'd have no trouble in taking his son back with him. He returned to the table.

"What's wrong Daddy? You look upset. The ship hasn't sunk has she? No, but of course she couldn't; she's in dry-dock. Then has she turned over on her side? No, she couldn't do that either, because the shores keep her upright don't they? What is it then Daddy?" the boy asked.

"Nothing bad at all Michael, old son. Only good news. When I left just now, I called the Canada Immigration Office. I'm sorry about the unsettled years you've had to go through. It's my fault. Completely. But all that's pretty well finished now. In three or four weeks I'll be back to look at the ship. And then" — already the youngster's eyes were popping expectantly — "we'll go back to Montreal together."

.   .   .   .

During his absence, Juliana had made appointments for Glyn to see many Expo '67 national pavilion Commissioners-General. She gave as a reason for the meetings Tresilian's research work on international broadcasting which served as a sufficient half truth.

Eventually, Tresilian met every national pavilion head or his deputy. On one day he had ten separate interviews. From these people he received information and printed matter on the broadcasting systems in their various countries. Some of the Iron Curtain spokesmen were predictably suspicious and a lot more inquisitive about Glyn's motives. In answer he spoke about a book project that he was also working on.

Together he and Julie waded through the mass of material wondering what they should do next. Should they recruit the broadcast linguists this early and risk premature disclosure of the Plan? On the other hand it would be dangerous to have the 'Navis Pacifica' lying prepared but idle for too long. Her extraordinary characteristics were bound to draw attention. Ideally of course crew and ship should be ready at the same time. And then Julie had an idea.

"Why not," she asked "try to get the Secretary-General of the UN involved?" Tresilian, who had been pacing up and down the apartment, now converted to an office, stopped at the window and looked down on Côte des Neiges.

"A good thought, but then surely we've agreed that normal agencies don't work. Isn't that the whole point of the Plan?

Damn it all — who, anywhere, takes the U.N. seriously any more? Any chance it might have had was utterly shot during the early summer this year. In many ways I think it was a pity that in June, during the Arab-Israeli war the Security Council and the emergency General Assembly debates were covered by world-wide television. One thing though — and it was about all that did come out — and I hope registerd — was the Secretary-General's point about the great powers paying only lip service to the spirit of the Charter. But when you got right down to it, the big boys who could do something positive about the world situation were interested solely in nationalism. No, darling. Forget it. If the U.N. could do anything we wouldn't be mucking about with the Plan would we?"

"No, I didn't mean that," Julie countered, "or at least not about the U.N. as such. But you remember that man we met at the United Nations pavilion? That official who said he knew the Secretary-General? Yes? Well he did say that the great powers like having as Secretary-General someone from a small weak country but that the Secretary-General is not too popular with any of them because he's against war of all kinds. And that means he's against war — period. And of course the big nations consider that the ones they're fighting are justified. So, and please don't laugh dear, I just thought that if you could somehow get to see him and simply tell him about the Plan — there might be some way he could help. Surely he wouldn't disagree with it would he?"

And then she laughed, realising how naive her suggestion must have sounded. Perhaps it was the very naivety of it that made Glyn think momentarily how strong her argument was.

Enthusing suddenly, he said. "No, sweetheart. I don't see how he could be against it. The only reason he might have would be for personal empire building. But that shoe certainly doesn't fit in his case. God knows he seems to hate the job — and only a few months ago they had a hell of a time getting him to stay on. And presumably he only wanted to get out because he was fed up and frustrated — not with the idea — but with the way that the member nations won't let it work. You know something," he went on half aloud, "you may just have something there. But then — how do you get to him?"

"Why not," Julie suggested, "at least start with the same

man at the pavilion? He seemed very nice and kind."

"Yes. Nice and kind. But I'm not sure those qualities get you very far these days." Julie did not reply. But her silence, as she quietly shuffled the pile of paper on her desk, was enough.

Glyn spun around. "Let's try it. See if you can get him on the phone will you? What was his name again? Oh, yes — Bunt-horne. English, I think."

Arthur Bunthorne and Tresilian met the next day. Bunthorne, who had been a career civil servant and diplomat for most of his life was not too keen to use his influence with the Secretary-General without knowing something of the subject matter. He mildly resented Tresilian's reticence.

"You see the position I'm in. Having the S. G.'s confidence is one thing — but abusing it is another. On the other hand I'm not being deliberately inquisitive. But I must have some idea of what you want to discuss with him. Even then it'll be difficult."

Glyn considered the dilemma. Of course Bunthorne was right. Then he got an idea. "Suppose I could sell a 30 minute television interview with him to one of the networks? Would he go for that do you think?"

"He might," replied Bunthorne without much warmth, "but only might. It would make more sense than the reasons you had for wanting to talk to the people here about 'broadcast research.' How will you go about it?"

"Oh, see the networks I suppose. But that'll mean Toronto. And I don't know my way round there very well. But I won't waste much time trying to get a commitment. I'll do it anyway and then I'm damn sure they'll pick it up once it's in the can."

"I see," Bunthorne said. "You mean you'll underwrite the costs of filming or taping or whatever it is yourself?"

"Yes."

"But surely that will cost a packet?"

"Of course," Glyn replied, "but if it will get me to him then it's cheap, isn't it?"

"Well I should think that would depend on how badly you want to see him."

"Badly; very badly."

"Very well, then," the U.N. official went on helpfully, "I'll see what I can do. But if I make some arrangement and it might not be 30 minutes, you won't let me down will you?"

"I won't."

Both Canadian networks were interested in looking at an interview with the Secretary-General but neither would give financial or any other sort of commitment. Their argument simply was that their public affairs programs were adequately staffed by their own personnel and that current plans did not call for this material. Tresilian however should 'feel free' to contact them when he'd done the interview, and they'd be happy to see it.

This reaction was pretty well what he had expected. He wondered whether he should check with Yerbury about the cost of the interview.

More and more he found himself discussing all matters, large and small, with Julie. He found her utterly commonsensical approach to problems so reassuring.

"What will it cost anyway?" she asked.

"Good question. I've no idea. Let's get on to — oh, what's his name. You know the guy — that freelance cameraman. O'Hare — that's it. I'll use him if he wants it."

Freddy O'Hare did want it and quoted a reasonable price that included processing and customs clearance. Julie thought that Yerbury surely didn't want to be informed about this sort of thing.

.   .   .   .

Three weeks later, Tresilian met the Secretary-General in his suite at the U.N. Headquarters building in Manhattan. Bunthorne, who had arranged the meeting said that he had 20 minutes precisely. From 8.30 to 8.50 a.m. O'Hare stayed in an ante-room with his equipment. Glyn had long since planned his attack.

"Mr. Secretary-General, although the cameraman is standing by with his equipment outside, I must tell you that I don't want to do a television interview with you."

A flicker of surprise crossed his face, and passed. He sat upright at his desk, arms resting on the table top, fingers lightly touching. The emblematic globe behind seemed so heavy — his dapper frame so slight.

"No sir," Glyn went on, "I have deceived you and Mr. Bunthorne. The filming was a ruse — to see you, on a matter of great importance. I couldn't think of any other way. May I still have some time?"

The Secretary-General did not answer but gestured as if he were asking Tresilian to help himself to coffee cream and sugar. This was better than he'd expected. There could have been an embarrassing scene and Bunthorne might have suffered. Definitely a dangerous way to play it. O'Hare must be wondering about it all outside in the other room. Tresilian began.

The Secretary-General stared expressionlessly at Tresilian as he outlined the essence of the Plan. He did this as economically as he could having a thought for the liberty he was taking. Glyn found himself talking about it with much greater ease than he'd enjoyed at Wooffenden Hall, the Wicket or Yerbury House. A calm elation came as he relished the difference between explaining it and asking that it be done.

Toward the end of his statement he was not afraid to relate the Plan's possibilities for personal propaganda and described the meeting with Barton Mills-Cragley but without referring to the man or the World Reformation Society. Finishing, he repeated his conviction that it could become a direct and real catalyst for peace.

The Secretary-General went on looking at Tresilian for a little while longer. And then he spoke for the first time. "Yes, Mr. Tresilian — you have, as you were saying just now yourself, certainly oversimplified most of the issues. You've reduced them almost to the point of the clarity." He chuckled sadly, and went on.

"You have both experience and belief in direct communications between people. You also mentioned the difficulties facing Canadian Confederation today — and you talked about the growth of feeling for Canada to become a republic, stating that it would be better for Canada to remain within the Commonwealth rather than become a republic — why not then begin your scheme in your own country — by putting the people in touch with each other there?"

"Ah, but that's just the point, sir," he blurted out, "you don't understand. Well, no I didn't mean that exactly — I . . ."

"You may be frank, Mr. Tresilian," he smiled.

"Thank you sir. You see, in Canada we have a Broadcasting Act which is policed by the Board of Broadcast Governors. And while individually licensed stations can conduct their own open line programs — and most stations do — to connect up two or more such shows simultaneously would amount to forming a network. And while I personally have tried to obtain special dispensations to do just that as an experiment, the red tape politics become impossible. So on the Quebec independence issue for example you have the people talking alright — but only in terms of their own narrow regional and local interests.

"Because of this restriction there is no way for the people in British Columbia and Newfoundland and all points in between to talk to each other. If they could, they could understand what it is that becomes a root problem. How they can know each other better. I think they'd be surprised at how much people really want to get on — and how little they really want to quarrel. I'd guarantee that such programming — thrown wide open on a daily national basis would achieve more for Canadian unity in three months than another 100 years of the shaky parliamentary processes we now have. Providing always that the handling of such a medium is responsible and dedicated. Extend the conflict in Canada and what could be a solution — to the world, and you have the Plan."

Realising that he'd gone well over time, Tresilian got up and extended his hand to the Secretary-General. He made no move and ignored Glyn's gesture. The younger man was well pleased. There was nothing more he could do now. He'd simply ask him, in conclusion to consider the thing in the light of any assistance he could give. The S.G. looked straight ahead. Then abruptly, he asked. "Who is backing this Plan of yours?"

"I was hoping you wouldn't ask that, Mr. Secretary-General — I can't divulge this information."

Unmoved, the S.G. pressed on. "Tell me then — is it a group of individuals or a country that will be financing this project?"

"Neither a group nor a country."

"An individual then. He must be very rich?" Glyn made no comment. Tresilian was just realising how very disillusioned the Secretary-General seemed to be with the world, the U.N. and life in general when the man stood up.

"How can I contact you, Mr. Tresilian?" Glyn knew better than to press further at this moment and wrote down addresses and telephone numbers on a page of the small pocket notebook he carried.

They shook hands.

"Thank you for seeing me sir."

"Thank you for coming to see me."

Tresilian went out and into the ante-room. O'Hare sprung to his feet grabbing lights and cables. "Hell, Glyn," he exclaimed, "I've heard of preparation but this is crazy. You and he must have settled all the world's problems by now."

"Well, not quite all of them Fred — yet."

"OK. Can I get set up now?" O'Hare asked.

"No. Here, I'll give you a hand with the gear. We won't be needing it. Come on — let's go." The news cameraman looked only slightly surprised. He'd been at the game a long time and many years had passed since he thought that the unexpected was anything but normal. They took a cab to the airport and the first available plane returned them to Dorval.

.   .   .   .

Back in Montreal, Tresilian and O'Hare found the world's second largest French speaking city in an uproar. President de Gaulle had just delivered his resounding declaration — 'Vive le Québec Libre'. These words, as every French and English Quebecois knew, were the slogan of the most active separatist group in the Province — the RIN. The initials represented not, as Glyn sometimes wished, Royal Indian Navy, but Rassemblement pour l'Indépendance Nationale.

"Vhot do you think the government vill do?" Mrs. de Vries asked at supper.

"Oh, nothing very much I expect," Glyn offered.

"Why not?" the Captain wanted to know.

"Well, look at the record."

"But surely they'll have to do something won't they?" Julie chimed in. "It does seem like deliberate interference."

In a day or so the world heard the Canadian government's statement on the unacceptability of de Gaulle's call. But in the summer of 1967, it set Canadians afire from coast to coast.

What chance was there now for Confederation? People asked the question of themselves and each other, as it was being celebrated after a hundred years. What possible hope could it have now after de Gaulle's sudden and massive encouragement to separatism? Argument throughout the land raged on all media, as Le Grand Charles cut short his visit leaving for Paris within hours of Prime Minister Pearson's reproach.

Montreal Mayor Jean Drapeau, at a lunhceon given in the General's honour prior to his Air France departure later that afternoon, made a brilliant and extemporaneous speech lauding de Gaulle — but stressing also that for 200 years French Canada had paddled its own canoe without the benefit of 'La Mère' France. Pointedly he emphasised that the New and North American worlds were the 'milieux propres' for his people. By sunset, and with the French President safely en vol to Orly, Drapeau had become the most popular man in Canada. Instant pressure closed in on him from Conservative circles urging him to stand as a candidate at the Party leadership convention later in the year.

Trying to analyse de Gaulle's motives became a guessing game across Canada. Was it the raving of senility? Hardly, across Canada. Was it the raving of senility? Hardly, thought Tresilian, after Mrs. de Vries' question. He reminded Julie, who really was so innocent in political matters, that the hero of the Free French was incapable of using word or action without a studied prediction of results.

This fight with Confederated Canada then — could it be that the old ingrate would never forgive the Anglo-Saxon world for liberating his France? And that by putting up even the wispiest image of something like Cuba on the borders of Vermont and New York states he could get at Canada's neighbours? They, after all, were the real 'especes' — non?

Julie and Glyn talked again about the de Gaulle incident the next morning over coffee in their 'office'.

"You know," he said as she gave him a cup, "I'd just love to know how Churchill or Diefenbaker would have played this one."

Julie laughed. "Oh, I suppose they'd have come up with something about the French poodle's tail wagging the British Lion's teeth."

"Or bulldog. Not bad. Not bad at all. It's at times like this that we need old Dief as Prime Minister. He's quite an old lion himself when you think about it — a bit like Churchill. Do you suppose there's any way we could use him in the Plan?"

"No, I can't see how . . . what do you mean exactly?"

"I don't know, Julie. I've no idea."

She looked over his shoulder and they scanned the morning paper.

"Oh, by the way, you haven't told me yet how things went yesterday."

The previous evening Glyn had pleaded tiredness — and now he told her about the New York trip. She listened, her beautiful eyes wide with wonder as he explained the 'interview' ruse and the impossibility of gauging the Secretary-General's reaction — even if there was any. She sensed, by the way he told it, that he was disappointed. Were it not actually happening, she could never have believed that the Plan, and Glyn, would have come even close to her life.

"But you did see him Glyn. That's the main thing," then she hesitated. "Do you think he'll help?"

"Very difficult to say. There's only one thing I really want him to do. But that in itself is a pretty tall order."

"You mean the 'recruiting' as you call it."

"Yes. I just can't see any other reliable way of getting the people we want. He's in a unique position there. As far as knowing individuals in the member nations anyway. And they're all bound to have the language facility — otherwise they wouldn't be in the building. But he could sort out — well you know — the ones we'd need. Oh, hell there are going to be so many bloody problems . . ."

Finishing her coffee, she sat on his lap and played with his thick unruly mop of hair. By now she had more than an inkling of his moods. She slipped her free hand inside his shirt and gently caressed his stomach. She aroused him in seconds, and knowing this, she stopped and fastened the buttons. She kissed him and got up. He was dejected. There seemed nothing to do and no immediate course to steer.

He stood up, yawned, and paced up and down the room. "OK. Where do we go from here? There's no point in going over to Wooffenden's so soon again. God knows when or if we'll hear from the Secretary-General. It looks as if we've come to a full stop. And there's damn all we can do — for the time being at any rate. Idleness can be so bloody demoralizing. I suppose I could go to Toronto and see 'Y' and tell him how things are going."

"Frankly, Glyn, and I know I've told you this before, but I

— 234 —

think you worry far too much about 'Y'. Just look on his support and trust as a miracle and leave it that. They can happen you know. If you keep running to tell him things all the time he'll think you've got nothing to do. Which is true right now, I agree. Or else he'll think you're unsure of yourself. Don't make things deliberately harder. Now," she bubbled, "if you've got nothing to do for a week or so, I have."

"What dear?"

"Well, there's a man in my life I'm rather keen on and he happens not to be too busy at the moment and I thought I'd try and talk him into . . ."

"Julie, you're a siren. And a scheming witch. A demi-mondaine, a gold digger, a woman of leisure. Oh, I nearly forgot. You're also the loveliest girl in the world. When?"

They picked the wedding date two days later. It was to be in mid-October.

CHAPTER 3

The de Vries wanted to do it properly. With plenty of time before the wedding, and with little work to do, Julie and Glyn made the arrangements slowly.

Tresilian came out of the downtown formal dress hire store after being measured for the morning suit he intended to rent, and ran into two good, but quite disparate, acquaintances. Burt Brewster was on his way to lunch in Studio Four. And Kim Kettleby, an aged but much loved local children's TV entertainer from New Zealand also had business in the store. It was a well met but incongruous trio.

"Tresilian!" the Drom roared above the noon hour traffic. "How are you, you old bastard? Goddam it — it's good to see you. How are you Kim boy? Still wowing those little baa-lambs? Hell, this calls for lunch. On my way there now. No, never mind that crap. Come on — both of you." And he drove them along the sidewalk.

"But Burt," Kettleby protested, "I haven't time. I was just going in to rent some tails. I have to look after the 'Mums and Dads' dance next week and I . . ."

"Mums and Dads be damned, Kettleby. Plenty of time for all those horsefeathers. Glyn — you'd like a beer with the old Drom again eh?" he asked and released the shoulder grip he'd set.

"Sure Burt. Why not? I have all afternoon if you wish."

"Great Glyn. I want to hear what you've been doing. Hey, someone told me the other day that rich father-in-law of yours passed on and left you a packet. Let's you and me buy that goddam tavern haha; was that right though?" he asked, still frog-marching Kettleby.

"No, it wasn't. But I did come into a little money which helped to tide things over."

For the lunchtime crowds it was something of an audiovisual experience. Tresilian and Kettleby they recognised, but not the stern giant warder talking at the top of his considerable voice. Tresilian was amused to notice people looking around for film and television cameras. Soon they were at the door of Studio Four. At the entrance, Kettleby, thoroughly discomfited by now, took his stand.

"Really Burt, I can't go in there with you."

"Oh," Brewster's expression was belligerent, "and why the hell not?"

"Burt — please. You know very well I can't. My image after all. What would people think? Me running a kiddies show!"

"Oh, it's not that bad, Kim. I think you're doing yourself a lot more harm standing out here," Tresilian said sympathetically. "I know what Burt. Let's get inside and ask Hurtubuise if we can use that private room in the back. Maybe it's empty."

It was and the Drom settled for this compromise. Glyn couldn't understand his former General Manager's eagerness to drink beer with such an unlikely companion as Kettleby but then he remembered Burt's liking for a crowded table.

He felt sorry for Kettleby. The benign old man, after a lifetime of appearing professionally in public with children, had long since lost his feel for adult conversation. Tresilian would never forget the time he had shared the services of a garage mechanic with Kim. He marked it down as one of the three funniest things in his life. 'And what's your name?' he recalled the tots' hero asking the horror struck grease covered mechanic in an imitation child's voice. A voice which was liable to come out at any moment, quite unknown to Kim.

"OK, let's have six beers in here, Hurtoobeeze. Jeez, what a day I've had. That was a terrible thing you did to me Tresilian — terrible." Brewster reprimanded him like a testy judge.

The beer arrived and they drank. Kettleby sipped as if testing the temperature of the ale and surreptitiously cleared the coat sleeve from his wrist watch.

"I don't think that's quite fair, Burt," Tresilian replied evenly and drained his glass. He stared at the second and held it argumentatively. "What terrible thing did I do to you by baulking when a sponsor expected everything from me but wasn't prepared to go bond on his own integrity? Never mind," he said quickly. "For God's sake let's not get into that. That's all dung under the bull's foot now. Did you still get the account?"

"What goddam account?" Brewster asked dreamily.

"Well — Mathieson's. Pastoral Suburbs."

"Did we hell. And if you don't want me to go ape just make sure you never mention those rinkydink names again to me. Kim — you heard what this asshole did to me?" he asked the miserable old showman. Glyn controlled the laugh he felt coming up. The cast of this trio was getting the better of him.

"Well, no Burt. I always mind my own business and never inter . . ."

"Yea, yea. That's what I thought. Fat lot of help you are. Aren't you happy here with us or something old Kim?"

"It's not that, Burt. But I was already late and this afternoon I have auditions for . . ."

"Well, you'd better bugger off then."

An instant smile of authentic joy lit up his face and Kettleby left the table with the springy gait of a man walking off the gallows. They watched him check for a clear coast at the door.

"Can't understand people," the Drom said and he was quite morose by now. "Come on, drink up, and we'll leave this goddam cloister and go next door in the main room. As far as I know they're not laying any bodies out in there."

They settled down for what Tresilian knew would be a long session. He called Julie from the pay-phone in the corner. "It's certainly very noisy, Glyn. Do all taverns sound like that?" she asked him.

"That depends on how good they are," he laughed. "Listen, sweetie, I'll probably be late — so go home and tell your mother not to wait supper for me. OK? You don't mind?"

"Mind what?"

"Well, I know the old Drom pretty well. I'd say there's a chance we'll be tying one on."

"Just be careful though. Did you get measured for the suit?"

"Yes, I did. Met the Drom and old Kim Kettleby just as I was coming out of the store. Burt insisted that we all lunch as he calls it, in Studio Four. I don't think I ever saw anyone as unhappy as old Kim. What's that? No, no — he left. The Drom gave him an acquittal. Damned funny. Look, I've just thought of something. I've got the suit but no best man. Do you think I should ask Burt? I guess you could say he's my best acquaintance. OK then, I'll sound him out. Better do it soon — before we get too bombed. See you later dear. Take care. Bye."

Back at the table he found more freshly ordered beer and Brewster was reading the paper.

"Read this crap. Personally, I'm up to here with that goddam de Gaulle. Worse than the Brits for crissake. If that guy had piles — I'd give a year's pay to cut the painful bastards off. Jeez — how I'd envy that surgeon."

Tresilian read a feature on the front page. It explained a lot about the de Gaulle love affair with La Belle Province.

'In Ottawa and Paris, rumors have recently come to light that the French President's real interest in Quebec might be centered around the large number of uranium deposits in the Province.

'The Federal Government has so far denied the sale of Canadian uranium to France due to the French government's refusal to provide the necessary assurances that the radio-active material would be used by France for peaceful purposes only.'

Glyn folded the paper and put it on a spare chair at the table.

"Hmmm. If that's true, Burt, it could be quite a blow to separatism eh?"

"Yea. But right now I couldn't give a goddam about anything."

"Why — things that bad?"

"They're not good, and that's for damn sure. Don't get me wrong. In no way would it make sense to blame you for anything — but Trample's well on the climb again and Westall and the Silver Eminence are climbing on my back again. You know what we're thinking of doing now?"

"No."

"They're talking about applying to the BBG for a licence modification that'd let them go multi-language to a certain extent."

"Not a bad idea, I'd say Burt. Hell, there must be room for it here. You're talking about members of the Third Culture, I presume?"

"Yes, that's it. That's what they're calling it. I don't know what it is but they're trying to kiss somebody's important ass in Ottawa. The latest thing they're on is a national unity kick. They reckon they can make yards and money by bringing the many ethnic groups together and . . ."

"Let them become a kind of unifying catalyst to improve French-English relations." Tresilian broke in. The idea appealed to him. He could see the point and was agreeably surprised that CRAK had hit upon it.

"I like that Burt," he went on. "It's good thinking. You know there are all kinds of problems that have so much in common. Quebec and Ontario for instance. The two Vietnams. The two Koreas. Cyprus. French and English right here. If you could do something to bind the ethnics together and show how they can get on — I think it'd be a hell of an example to the majority of Quebecers. I think it's a damn good scheme."

"You would. As far as I'm concerned it's no worse or better than a lot of other crap you used to push out. For a moment, the way you were talking there, I thought I was listening to the car radio again. How about that? No chance I suppose?"

"No chance of what?"

"Goddam it," he shouted and bounced the table top with his fist, "do I have to communicate with you by registered mail? Forget it for crissake."

"Oh, sorry, Burt. No need to yell your bloody head off. I see. You mean I should come back to CRAK?"

"I didn't say that at all. I just 'presented it for discussion' as you used to be so damn keen on saying on that horsetrough show you did."

"No, somehow I just can't see that working Burt. Oui, encore quatre bières, s'il vous plaît, Paul. Now let me ask you something. You probably don't know — but I'm getting married again in October and . . ."

"Hell, Glyn. I did know. Heard it the other day. Forgot all about it. Congratulations, old buddy. Hope you'll be very happy. By the way, just what in hell are your plans?"

"Oh, very complicated, Burt — and thanks. I'll tell you later. But I'd like to ask you a favour. How'd you like to do best man duty for me?"

Brewster gulped at his glass. "Jeez — I didn't think you liked me enough for that, you bastard. Sure I will. And I'll knock 'em dead with a speech too. Big production?"

"Fairly big, I think. Her parents want to do it properly. Tell you what. How about you and your wife joining Julie and me for dinner sometime next week? And we can all get acquainted. Come to think of it I never did meet your wife."

"Don't know that you'd want to. She'd use your head for a bowling ball if she could. Funny thing though — she says she misses you like hell now. Won't listen to Trample and says she can't get her adrenalin going in the mornings any more. Yea, that sounds OK. Let's set it up."

A fortnight before the ceremony, they had gone to Toronto and Julie met Yerbury for the first time. They invited him to come — knowing that he would decline. He sent as presents, a pair of splendid Zeiss binoculars and a set of beautiful mono-grammed luggage. From the Wooffendens came a letter saying that a new Rover 2000 was waiting for them parked near the dock office on the berth where the 'Navis Pacifica' lay. Julie was especially touched by all this generosity.

The de Vries gave them a specially gimballed stereophonic unit with all the necessary voltage adaptation units for use aboard ship.

Weekly routine reports on progress from the Mersey told Tresilian that the 'nuts and bolts' work on the ship was well in hand as was the estimating and design for the electronics. In a private letter, Sir Timothy said that already much curiosity had been aroused about the ship's intention.

"I have been saying," the letter explained, "on your behalf and I trust this alibi is in order, that the ship will be used for satellite communications research — and that she will do most of her work in remote areas. This, so far, has worked perfectly."

Glyn appreciated this. No one knew better than he how difficult the security problem would soon become. In the mean-time he paid the 'work done' bills immediately through the account that Yerbury had opened. After writing a sizable check one day to his first father-in-law's firm, he said to Julie. "This must be a bottomless pit. It'll damn well have to be."

"Now there you go again. We've agreed the bottomless pit is a miracle. When a thing like that happens — just accept it. You know, you remind me of the cancer victim who gets cured by a faith healer — but refuses to believe it unless he can get a doctor to say there's a medical explanation. Now, do you think we should have an orchestra for the reception? The time goes so quickly you know. We'd better get a move on. I know that Mummy and Daddy want us to have the very best . . ."

"We'll get it all done. Any mail?"

"No, nothing really. I can't help feeling an efficiency expert would have fired us long ago. I don't feel too good about cashing that check you give me every week."

"Well, let's hope that we'll start earning our salt soon. I don't think we'll hear anything from the Secretary-General now. When did I go down to New York? Oh, yes that's right — in July, when de Gaulle was in town. No, I doubt very much that there'll be any action in that quarter. I've always found with this sort of thing that if it doesn't happen quickly it's not going to happen at all." He yawned and stretched. "At any rate," Tresilian went on, "it'll force us off our butts. We've got to start thinking about the bloody personnel soon. But then what the hell's the point of that — until we get a rough idea of when Wooffendens'll get that slow gutted old bastard ready."

"Don't swear so much darling. Please. For my sake. You've got a very bad vocabulary you know. I realise how frustrating all this waiting and uncertainty can be, but I feel it too. Look, let's just enjoy the wedding and the arrangements and everything. We'll have a lovely honeymoon; you'll be able to see the ship when we're over there. We'll be with Michael — he'll come back with us. Everything will be that much more advanced and you may have heard something from the Secretary-General. Come on now, cheer up. It'll all work out. You'll see. I just know it will."

.   .   .   .

They were married in the de Vries small church in Montreal's Notre Dame de Grâce. The Wooffendens were unable to attend mainly because Sir Timothy was needed at the yard. Decisions in connection with the US contract chained him to his desk.

The wedding went well. The long guest list was evenly comprised. And through a mention in a local column of the time and place, many old listeners showed up, so that there was standing room only at the sides and back of the aisles.

.   .   .   .

Julie, as he remembered her that morning, would have made a feminine products advertising agency delirious. She was right. Absolutely right. Her plain long flowing white dress was perfect, with just a hint of soft breast.

At the altar, Brewster and Tresilian watched and waited for Julie and her father. Because of the Drom's problems at the station and their trip to Toronto, they never did meet for dinner and Julie had still to be introduced.

When he had first seen him at the church, Glyn, who had worked hard at losing weight, couldn't help comparing the Drom, who had gained pounds, with an outsize penguin in the final throes of a long pregnancy. The outfit didn't fit him by a yard. Puffing, tugging, the Drom fought for a semblance of order with his costume. The white shirt refused to merge into the too small trousers. Accompanied by Handel selections on the organ, the Drom told the groom and the congregation, because his whisper carried far, what he would do and say to the tailor who had rented him the clothes. As they waited, Brewster explained.

"The trouble was I didnt have time to get the stuff fitted. Had to send the girl. Gave her measurements. Must've been wrong. Hell, I don't know what I am around the gut. And I don't want to know — that's for damn sure hahaha! But I'll chew his ass off though. Oh, hell I can't. Not until his contract's run out. We just signed him for thirteen weeks of spots. One thing anyway, Glyn. I'll make damn sure I contra this monkey suit with the bastard, hahaha!"

Tresilian gave up all attempts to 'shush' him and broke up. This spread and soon large areas of the church were convulsed and shook with silent laughter.

And then, all heads turned as the organ, just in time, announced the coming of the bride. Brewster was almost speechless at the sight of her.

"For crissake, Glyn," and his whisper was only partially muffled by Lohengrin. "What a doll. Man, you sure chose one there you old bastard . . ." He was about to roar with laughter but Tresilian dug him sharply in the ribs as the Captain handed her to the ceremony. The service went smoothly enough except for a spasm of panic as the Drom wrestled an enormous hand into his trouser pocket — in pursuit of the ring.

Later at the catered reception in the de Vries' home, the Drom excelled himself as he proposed the health of Julie's friends — the bridesmaids.

That night they flew to Bermuda. And they spent a bliss-
ful week on the golden pink sands just a few yards from
the cottage with maid service at Horseshoe Bay. After a few
hours the perfect sun did its cosmetic work basting Julie's bikini
flattered body to a turn. Shorn of worry and strife, their days
became a round of early morning island circuits on the powered
(putt-putt) bicycles, swimming, lazing and making love. The
island was so generously rimmed with beaches and privacy that
soon they would change in the cottage and run nude together
in the sea. And then they would have each other — the breakers
of the incoming tide gradually washing them inland to the
secluded cove where their robes and bathtowels lay.

"Darling, I did see some people half a mile away just now,
and I don't think we'd hear them coming," Julie said one afternoon, as he throbbed above her and the gentle depression in
the towel covered sand beneath them deepened invisibly. "Let's
finish quickly now — and start again in the cottage." And then
they heard the voices — a few yards westward of their rock.

"Quick Julie, grab the robes. Throw them right over us.
That's it. Now, just come over — on the side. Oh, lovely. Stay
like that. We're asleep." The couple passed and walked on.

"Phew," Julie sighed, "that was close. But this is nice. Let's
do it this way in case they come back."

"Or even if they don't," Tresilian breathed. "We'll make it
last longer on the side."

The Bermuda week ended and they took a night jet to London for the four weeks they intended to spend in the U.K.
Oates again met them at the airport and drove them north to
Cheshire and Wooffenden Hall. Michael was overjoyed to see
them and in view of his travelling to Canada with his father
and Julie, had left his prep school at the end of the summer
term making do in the meantime with the services of a private
tutor at the Hall.

Now that they were married, the couple handled the Wooffenden situation with much greater ease. Gone were the earlier
tensions, assisted, Tresilian thought, by the absence of Mrs.
Southcombe who had left to serve as a governess to a family
in Surrey. Dinner at the Hall that evening was pleasant and
convivial. Later, Oates would drive them to the Exchange Hotel

where they intended to stay for a few nights while Glyn inspected the ship.

"Sir Timothy, it was so kind of you to give us the car," Julie said. "I can't wait to get in it tomorrow." They were having coffee in the morning room and she went over and kissed him on the cheek. Tresilian thought the baronet flushed slightly.

"A pleasure, my dear. I only wish we could have been in Montreal for the wedding. But I'm sure the word 'radiant' fitted you perfectly. By the way Glyn, the car has already been run in and all the paper work and so on is in order. Spurling has all that — and the keys of course. He'll give them to you in the morning. He tells me that by the time you leave again for Canada, we'll have a very good idea of how long the 'Navis Pacifica' work will take. He was in the States last week by the way. Apparently Americans, when it comes to electronic telephones, do a far better job. And he tells me that you people in Canada are the most loquacious in the world on the telephone."

"Ah, that's because we don't have to pay for local calls," Julie explained. "You can talk all day long and it won't cost you a nickel."

"I think," Lady Wooffenden interjected, "we'll soon be talking about nickels and what's the other coin? Dimes — yes. Wilson was saying something the other day about Britain going over to the decimal system, wasn't he Timothy?"

"Yes, but if he goes on with any more devaluation I don't think he'll have to bother. There's very little difference even now between the worth of a pound and a dollar," the shipbuilder added cynically.

They slept well at the Exchange and after an early breakfast went by taxi and ferry to the yard at Birkenhead. Julie was looking forward to seeing the ship. Although Glyn had prepared her for the inevitable noise and dirt that clothe a ship in drydock, she wasn't prepared for the utter dismay. There she was — an aged Liberty ship — rusty and lame. The din of compressors, chipping hammers and riveting guns was deafening.

Ray Spurling roared above the racket. "How are you, Mr. Tresilian, and you ma'am? It's very nice to meet you. Welcome to Merseyside. Let's go aboard. At least we'll be able to hear each other a little bit."

They walked up the gangway where the stench of decaying

refuse, oil and sweat made Julie feel sick. Already the snugly fitting pants outfit she was wearing was spattered in grease spots. They went up two decks, through the midships accommodation structure, to the bridge flat housing the radio shack, lower wheelhouse and abaft this, the chartroom and Captain's quarters with a day room, sleeping cabin and bathroom. On the same deck and aft on the port side were the Pilot's cabin and two staterooms. Confusion and disorder were everywhere. Cockroaches, their antennae aquiver by the thousands, wriggled and darted at will. They'd beaten the fumigators easily. The Captain's bed was littered with discarded sandwich wrappings, cigarettes and decomposed food.

"Sorry about this Mrs. Tresilian," Spurling shouted. "I hope your husband warned you. A ship in dry dock's hardly the place for a lady. There's no running water either I'm afraid. Would you like to go back to the office?"

"No, that's OK Mr. Spurling — but I think I'll go out and get some fresh air."

"Fine darling," Glyn said, "go down that ladder to the boatdeck. We won't be long. I'll just have a word with Ray and then we'll take a spin in the car. Hey, I've got an idea. Let's run out to Hoylake, the three of us, and have lunch. How does that sound?"

"Fine with me," Spurling said.

"Good, that's settled then."

Julie went down one deck and the two men began their tour of the ship. In the wheelhouse the steering gear and telegraphs were strewn about in small pieces. There was a gaping hole in the forward bulkhead where the three small rectangular windows were being taken out to be replaced by a full spread of glass for better visibility. As they looked fore and aft there was chaos everywhere. Three hundred men were aboard her.

"You know Ray," Tresilian said as they went into the filthy chartroom with its burnt and torn settee, "there's one thing I don't like about these Liberty ships. I sailed on two you know — and on both of them the skippers complained about not having a for'ard view from their quarters. Still I don't suppose there's anything we can do about it. God knows we've got enough on our plate as it is."

"Aye, you can say that again, Mr. Tresilian," the ship manager agreed.

"Please call me Glyn, Ray. We're going to be bugging each other a great deal from here on in — so let's make it informal, eh?" Spurling looked embarrassed. To all intents and purposes, the north countryman reasoned, Tresilian was the owner of this bucket. He didn't really know much about it but as far as he'd been able to gather from Sir Timothy, his son-in-law was in partnership with somebody in Canada and that eventually the ship was to do something on satellite research. Whatever that might be. It was all above him. His job was just to get the work done. And damned difficult work it was already proving to be. He, Ray Spurling had certainly never been near anything like it before. He hadn't liked being taken off that destroyer conversion. Now that was work he understood. And the job was going well; and as the government was paying, there weren't too many arguments about overtime. But he was stuck with this and he'd do the best he could. Moreover, Tresilian wasn't too bad. Down to earth chap. No side. And what a looker his wife was. Even with his loyalty to Wooffenden he had to concede she could give Peta a run for her money. Spurling's grandfather and father before him had worked at Wooffendens. The finest yards in the country. He'd heard rumours that Sir Timothy wanted Tresilian in the firm. An offer most people would have snapped up. Then why hadn't he taken it? There was no accounting for some tastes, and now the same young man wanted to get on a first name basis. That wasn't right surely.

Realising Spurling's discomfiture, Tresilian came to the rescue, "Ah, Ray I must've been in Canada too long. Over there, it's a first name set up right off the bat. In the States too of course."

"Yes, I've heard that, er, Glyn and saw it too — when I was there just recently looking for those phones of yours. I suppose it's all what you're used to. But as you're the boss, we'd better do what you've become used to."

They laughed and Tresilian said. "Now you're getting the idea. O.K. Let's walk around. Things generally coming along well?"

"Oh, yes," Spurling replied. "But then it's been pretty straightforward so far. Of course we've still got a lot of work on the hull and superstructure. And we've just started on the deep tanks and after deck." He pointed to the hatch coamings as men went to work with cutting torches.

"Sir Timothy was saying that you'd have a pretty good idea of how long it'll all take before we go back Ray?" Glyn asked.

"That's right. I'm expecting a couple of Americans to come over next week — they're working on the estimates now. Unfortunately though, I can't see us finishing the job inside twelve months. And I understand you're in a bit of a hurry. The fact is that the States have much more experience with the whole business of telephone and radio electronics. The generators and transmitter mast'll all be British though. We gave the contract for that last month. But the Yanks'll do all the fiddly equipment. Oh, that reminds me. There's plenty of time but I'll make a note of it anyway. Do you want us to get the helijets?"

"Yes, Ray; please. You handle that. I'll make a note too — about pilots. In fact, as I told Sir Timothy, I want you to take care of everything. I sweated blood writing those fifty pages of general requirements and I don't suppose it was really all that helpful. And probably left a hell of a lot out. By the way, how are you getting on with choosing the color scheme for the ladies' shower curtains in the new for'ard tween deck accommodation?" Tresilian asked sternly. Spurling looked surprised. They grinned and moved off to the foredeck.

.   .   .   .

"You really like living in Canada then, Glyn?" asked Spurling as they had soup.

"Oh yes. I feel that I've taken root there now. Besides with a Canadian wife I'd better like it, hadn't I?"

"Yes" Julie chimed, "and you'd better like Holland too."

"Were you born in Holland then, Mrs. Tresilian?"

"Yes, but I was quite young when we went to Canada. My father was in ocean going tugs."

"Ah, great sailors the Dutch," Spurling enthused "and the best in the world when it comes to salvage. I ought to know. I've worked on dozens of ships in the yard brought in by — what do you call the fleet again — yes, that's right — Holland's Glory."

Then he took a sheaf of papers from an inside pocket.

"Hope neither of you mind if we talk shop for a minute? Only there's so much to cover and I know you're not over here for long."

"Go ahead — please don't mind me, it's about time you did some work isn't it, dear?" and Julie buttered another piece of bread. Spurling opened the pile of closely typed and illustrated foolscap.

"Now, Glyn. As close as I can understand it, these gadgets that you'll be dropping from the helijets will be something like those little communicators they use on that 'Man from UNCLE' business. It's amazing eh, how quickly fact catches up with fiction. All that side of it'll be handled in the States. They're already asking me about quantities — they didn't think it could be that many for research purposes."

"When you've finished Ray, I'll tell you more about it."

"I'd like that, Glyn. If you don't mind, I'd like to know as much as possible about the whole project. Now if there's some secrecy or security . . ."

"There is — a lot. You'll know why when I tell you."

"Well, it'll be safe with me. As far as transmitting work goes, we'll be doing that in this country. Got a very good firm working on it. Most of this stuff here that they've written's way above my head technically of course, but you can get the general idea."

What Tresilian read was far beyond his comprehension too. He went over it quickly while Julie and Spurling chatted and his roast lamb got cold. Evidently, 'Navis Pacifica's' bridge accommodation would end up with a maze of consoles and switchboards. There would be a special compartment for a Heaviside Layer Computer which would tell how best to use the airwaves — whether with a precisely pin-pointed beam bouncing from the moon — or by using whatever hardware happened to be in a convenient orbital position.

Or again, he read, as he tried to understand the abstruse matter even slightly, they could use a short wave signal reflecting from the 'fickle ionosphere'.

Or yet, with the massive power that they would have, there could be an all conquering output, in the order of megawatts, swamping long-wave and normal broadcast bands.

He told Spurling about the Plan as they drove back after lunch.

"My, God, I'd say that's about the most original thing I've ever heard. I'm damn glad you told me. But come to think of it why not? I quite enjoyed listening to those open line shows in New York. And that's all you're doing — extending it world-wide."

"That's all, Ray."

"Hmmmm. I wish we had that kind of show over here — but the BBC'd never agree to do it. The government'd get too much hell. Assuming of course that the bloody Postmaster General could get the damn phones working! Pardon my language, Mrs. Tresilian."

Julie turned round to look at him in the back-seat.

"Unfortunately, Glyn's got me used to it, Ray."

"Glyn, how long do you think it'll be before you have some idea of the number of those gadgets you'll be wanting? I see they call them 'Tronphones'."

"Yes, I was thinking about that myself. Frankly, at the moment I don't have a clue. But it'll certainly be in the millions if . . ."

"What?", Spurling interjected.

"Well, of course we're not too concerned about countries with proper and efficient telephone systems — they can get through to us on R/T. But we're going to concentrate . . ."

"Ah, yes. Now I've got you. Well in that case we'll need about twenty sub-contractors. I'd better get over to the States again soon. With several firms on the job turning them out, we can keep prices competitive and it'll be less suspicious too."

Tresilian knew that sooner or later he'd have had to tell Spurling about the Plan. He was glad he had done it this soon. And he felt grateful again to Sir Timothy for putting one of his very best men on the project.

.   .   .   .

They stayed on the Mersey for a further three days. Glyn spent all day at the ship with Ray Spurling, while Julie shopped in Liverpool dividing her time between the Exchange Hotel and Wooffenden Hall. Sir Timothy and his wife could not have been kinder and put Oates at Julie's disposal so that she could take Michael with her wherever she went. The two were fast becoming friends. One day as they were having coffee in a quaint old Elizabethan restaurant in Chester, Michael said, "Julie, I don't know, and I haven't asked Daddy yet, but when do you think she'll be ready?"

"I honestly don't know Michael — I wish I did. And I'm sure Daddy will tell us when he can."

The boy received this as he finished the second of two very large doughnuts — and then looked sadly at his step-mother. "You'll be sailing on the ship I expect Julie?" he asked.

"Yes, I think I probably will, Michael. But that's where I should be — with Daddy. I can tell you this; it won't be the sort of voyage that he used to go on as a sailor. And there's no knowing how long the ship will be away." Then the twelve and a half year old brightened.

"I tried to talk Daddy into letting me come when he was over last time. I'm jolly well going to try again, Julie. Hard. Very hard."

Julie poured them both more coffee. "But then there's your education to worry about Michael. If Daddy wasn't too keen for you to come, it's only because he wouldn't want anything to interfere with your schooling. As it is there'll be quite an adjustment for you to make in Montreal. It's a completely different system you know. In some subjects you'll probably be a bit ahead, and behind in others. And you'll be busy with all the fun of making new friends and getting used to Canadian ways. But I really think you'll like it there. Just be yourself."

"Yes, well Daddy likes it doesn't he?"

"True, Michael — but things didn't always go the way he wanted them to. Like everyone else he had lots of ups and downs and you'll find the same thing."

Before leaving Liverpool for their car trip, Glyn and Julie made the final arrangements for Michael with the Canadian Immigration Office. And then they drove off. Their route took them to North and South Wales, Devon and Cornwall as far as Land's End, the Southern Counties and East Anglia. The Midlands and Yorkshire. Edinburgh and a circuit of Scotland and finally the Lake District. They stayed no longer than one night everywhere they went — even at the most inviting Inns.

At the end of two weeks they were ready for a rest at the hotel in Liverpool. Michael was lyrical with excitement. The Wooffendens gave a tea party for the boy and some two dozen of his friends, and a farewell dinner for Glyn and Julie.

Julie had been at the Hall since early afternoon and Glyn who had put in a full day at the yard with Spurling arrived late and only in time for a quick drink before the butler's dinner announcement.

Over the smoked salmon and consommé, the younger couple described their trip. As the jugged hare was being served, Wooffenden asked. "What's the news from Spurling, Glyn?"

"Well I only got it this afternoon — so I don't really know how to take it yet. By the way Sir Timothy, I do appreciate that he's on the project. A fine man. And he's also agreed to let me leave the car at the yard."

"Glad to hear it. But what did he say?"

"Nothing very encouraging I'm afraid. It seems that we can't expect the ship to be anywhere near ready on time. You know the gist of the Plan as well as I do — and God knows what'll have happened if we're late. Spurling also said that the estimate of work time doesn't take into account any strikes, wild-cat or official, that may crop up. But there's no way out. We'll just have to bear with it and be patient."

"Of course you realise Glyn," Sir Timothy said tasting wine and nodding to the footman, "that nothing of the kind has ever been done on any ship before? I would say that even your famous Marshall McLuhan couldn't see your scheme working much before the turn of the century. From what I gather, no communications philosopher is more far seeing than he. And here you seem to be — scooping him by decades. How does it feel?" Wooffenden laughed kindly.

Tresilian didn't answer but smiled pleasantly as he digested Sir Timothy's bromide. They had a bad problem. A bloody big problem. The Plan was bound to leak out well ahead of time — and if that happened — well, game over. The thought of Yerbury's money, and a lot had been spent already, being wasted, was just too much to contemplate.

.   .   .   .

The following day, and after an awkward farewell at the Hall, Glyn, Julie and Michael flew back to Montreal. They went from Dorval airport to a flat near the park in Westmount that they had leased. Julie, who had discovered an unexpected flair for decor and furnishings before the wedding, had left the place in a very ready state. She had supervised the re-decorating herself and had tastefully chosen simple furniture, carpets and drapes. As the flat was large and the family few in number,

Michael had his own bedroom and another room with a desk and bookshelves. This was to be his den. Glyn also had a small nook with a separate telephone — but as they were keeping the 'office' on Côte des Neiges for work on the Plan, this was quite sufficient. Too, Julie, womanlike, wanted these pleasant and convenient quarters to be 'home' and nothing else.

"One thing sweetheart," Tresilian said, "it's just as well you've got the place fixed up so nicely. It looks as if we'll be here for quite a while. Did we sign a one or two year lease?"

"For one year dear, you said . . ."

"Yes, I know. But then I thought they could do the job in about twelve months. The way things are right now we'd better ask for another year. I don't know what we're going to do. I suppose I'll have to go over at fairly regular intervals — but I'm still going to end up with a whole slew of time on my hands. One thing's for sure — there's no hurry to get the crew. It's frustrating when you think about it — we're in other peoples' hands all down the line. Personally, I don't know one end of a transistor from another. Evidently, according to Spurling, this is the biggest job that that American electronics firm who're doing the prototype have ever taken on. Everything, or just about, has to be transistorised — and that means a hell of a lot of finnicky work. Spurling said those Tronphone things'll look almost exactly like the gizmos Messrs. Solo and Kuriyakin use."

Julie and Michael listened. They didn't understand much of this. "Yes, Glyn I see. What phones were those again?"

"Dammit Julie. Why don't you pay attention," Tresilian said irritably. "I've told you, or I've tried to explain all this stuff to you."

Then he got up and put his arm around her shoulder. "Sorry sweetheart — it's just that I'm tired and feeling a bit low. As you must be too. Forgive me. I'll snap out of it soon. I've just got to get used to the idea of it taking so long — that's all. No, the phones I mentioned are the special 'UNCLE' jobs, — the Tronphones." Seeing her puzzled look, he said. "You know those gadgets they fish out of their pockets. They look like fat fountain pens — yes that's right sweetie — and they can get in touch with and from any part of the world. Great little communicators, and it looks as if they're not that far ahead of their time as bits of science fiction."

"Forgive me darling — I'm tired too, but I still don't quite understand what . . ."

"Well, it's fairly simple really. The helicopters'll be dropping these things by the thousands in areas where we'll be working and where they don't have telephone companies. Otherwise how could . . ."

"Oh, of course. Yes, I remember you telling me all that . . . it's just that so many things have happened. My mind's a bit confused at the moment." Down the passageway they could hear Michael unpacking his things. The boy, in fine form, was looking forward to starting at a neighbouring high school for what was left of the fall term. His heavier belongongs were Montreal bound by sea from Liverpool.

Julie yawned. "I only hope the bedclothes aren't damp. I left the heating on."

"Damp or not — let's go and warm them up."

The next day Tresilian walked to the office. The early signs of winter were everywhere. Unattractively brown fallen leaves, wafted by a chill wind, littered the sidewalks on Sherbrooke street. People had broken out their overshoes and heavy clothes for yet another Canadian winter. Glyn had always found the months of November and February the most difficult and melancholy in Montreal. The one a harbinger of trials to come; the other an unwelcome guest who would not leave.

He could see that there wasn't much mail as he opened the apartment door where once he lived. A rash of circulars, some bank statements; a few publicity 'hand-outs' from public relations firms trying to get their clients free radio and TV exposure. Nothing significant. Getting pencil and scratch pad, he sat down at the desk and phoned the answering service for what he hoped would be a long list of messages.

"Hello, Phone Message Service? Yes? Oh, good. Tresilian here."

"Oh, hello Mr. Tresilian. J'espère que vous avez eu de bonnes vacances?"

"Ah, mais oui, merci Mademoiselle; ça va bien? Bon. OK. Now you know your English is better than my French haha, so we'd better play it safe. I hope you've got lots for me."

"Hold on sir, and I'll check." The girl was back on the line in less than a minute. "Not very much I'm afraid Mr. Tresilian.

Just one call but it was urgent. He phoned two days ago and I told him you'd be back today. He wants you to get in touch immediately at one of these three numbers. It's from Mr. Bunthorne." He took down the details from the girl. He hung up and called Julie within seconds. Thank God, he thought, as he dialled and heard the purr-purr at the other end, that Julie had had the phone connected before they left. He couldn't be sure of course but Bunthorne must have some news if his call was urgent. "Julie", he said excitedly, "guess what? There was only one message — but from Bunthorne. You know dear, of course you do, the guy at the U.N. pavilion who put me on to the Secretary-General."

"Oh, good; well what did he say?"

"I don't know — I haven't called him yet."

"Well, why not?"

"Blast it Julie, because I wanted to tell you first. Aren't you interested anymore?" He felt annoyed. First the girl couldn't recall one of the most important and costly technical factors of the Plan — and now she was treating this news — that Bunthorne had been trying to reach him — in a damnably indifferent manner.

"You know very well I am. Don't snap at me like that. And I do appreciate you wanting to tell me everything first — but as it's urgent, why run the risk of missing him? Keep calm, darling. We're going to have so much to worry about. We can't afford to quarrel can we?" Her reasonableness and customary good sense disarmed him at once.

"Sorry again, sweetheart. You're right. OK. I'll call him now. See you later. Bye."

For the next three hours Tresilian tried again and again to reach the United Nations official at all three numbers that he'd been given. He was certain that he'd missed him. Expo had closed six weeks before and allowing for a certain amount of 'loose ends' work, what could keep him in Montreal now? Miserable, he decided to put on his coat and go home to Julie. The phone rang as he was putting on his gloves. Tresilian leapt at it.

"Mr. Glyn Tresilian please — long distance calling."

"Yes, yes speaking."

"There you are sir, go ahead."

"Mr. Tresilian, it's Bunthorne, Arthur Bunthorne here. I've

been trying to . . ."

"Yes, I know — and I've dialled your number all day but . . ."

"Sorry about that — but I was called down here yesterday. I'm in New York. I'd rather see you in person obviously, but I don't imagine anyone will be listening in so here goes. Or rather — I hope no one's on the line. Can you come down and see me?"

"Sure! What's the word?"

"Well I couldn't say a thing about that at present. But we wouldn't ask you down unless it was positive."

The trained civil servant and diplomat was 'on duty' now. "Now," he went on, "what about next week sometime?"

"Fine Mr. Bunthorne. Sooner the better."

"Will one thirty Wednesday afternoon suit you?"

"Perfectly."

"Good. See you then."

Tresilian took a taxi and ran up the few short steps to the flat. He panted and spoke in a torrent to Julie. "Do you realise what this means? Bunthorne must have something to say. Surely he doesn't want me to go down there just so's he can say no? No, you're damn well right he doesn't. By the same token he obviously can't think I'm a crazy raving lunatic — and let's face it — I took that chance when I bent the Secretary-General's ear for forty minutes." He smiled and then grinned right across his face. Taking a spoon he scooped from a pan simmering on the stove. Julie slapped his hand.

"Now let's get this straight," she said with mock severity. "I will not have you poking about in the kitchen like that. If you do, you'll be sent to bed without any supper at all."

"Eh? Oh, that's alright. Send me to bed you say — good; as long as you send yourself at the same time. You know I'm feeling quite 'up' again." He spun around and bubbled. "If we can get the S.G. behind us — wow . . ." and he trailed off, a far look in his eyes. Julie went on slowly stirring the steak, kidney and mushroom stew she was preparing for supper.

"Just take everything as it comes. Don't build up your hopes too much until you can be sure of things. That way you won't be giving disappointments such a chance to get you down."

"You may be right. But I'm dying to see what it's all about. Where's Michael?"

"Out; he'll be back soon. He's already made friends with the boy next door. They were going on a bus to look around. Oh, I heard from the school today. He starts next week."

CHAPTER 4

Bunthorne was warm, stating that he represented the Secretary-General, who however must remain anonymous as far as the Plan was concerned. He apologized for the length of time it had taken to get together, explaining. "We had to know who your sponsor is. We now have that information. The S.G. has asked me to ask you to understand and respect his unwillingness to tell you how we got it."

Tresilian tried but failed to conceal his shock.

"The S.G. and I are the only persons here who know. Others were involved — but they only worked on one or two lines down and across. They do not have all the clues and therefore can't complete the puzzle. Now don't worry. Mr. Yerbury doesn't know and never will."

So that was it. The U.N. despite its limitations must have quite a detective ability. He spoke. "Mr. Bunthorne, I accept your assurances completely. But I won't attempt to conceal my astonishment. The vital thing about the Plan is security. We have a good cover story at the Wooffenden yards in Birkenhead where the ship's being fitted out and converted. It's simple and plausible. We're saying that she'll be doing radio-telephone communications research with broadcast orbiting satellites in remote areas of the world. There's so much of this kind of thing happening nowadays that the press don't seem to be the slightest bit interested, thank God. This story will do, I think — but it wouldn't bear much scrutiny from anyone who got wind of our intentions and really wanted to find out. To be candid — I'm scared stiff that there'll be a leak long before we're ready. Especially if there are too many delays with the ship — which I dread but expect.

"With any kind of attack or offensive there must be an element of surprise. And there's no question that the Plan is very offensive."

"I think your cover story is a good one, Mr. Tresilian," Bunt-horne went on, "and I see no reason why it shouldn't hold water for as long as you want it to. The important thing here, it seems to us, is that so very few people know about it."

A secretary brought in pots of tea and coffee. As they drank, Tresilian again went over the main points. That the ship, with her maximum transmitting power would be able to swamp local long and medium wavelength bands all over the world. That with the special 'UNCLE' type transistorised communicators, people all over the world would be able to take part in the dialogue — simultaneous translations following in all language groups and this would be done by about 50 broadcasters — the linguists and interpreters.

Here Bunthorne interrupted him, "How do you propose to recruit these people? With that large a number, the security would be very vulnerable. You'd have to take every single one of them into your complete confidence. How will you get the personnel you want?"

"I honestly don't know. A few months ago I thought of trying to recruit at Expo. But I didn't get around to doing any-thing about it, as you know. The main thing was that I met you there."

"So then it will be a case of starting from scratch?"

"Yes."

"Now, the Secretary-General himself suggested that in this regard we may be able to help. You realise the immensity of the search?"

"Of course I do, but this was precisely the help I was hoping you might give." He grinned. "Providing always that you and the S.G. didn't consider me ready for a mental hospital."

Completely ignoring the remark, Bunthorne went on. "The main qualifications for the broadcasters would be three — as we understand it. One, motive. That is they must be dedicated to the idea of peace above and beyond the interests and concerns of their own countries. Two, they must . . ." He stopped. "Why are you smiling?"

"Well, your choice of words. 'They must be dedicated to the idea of peace'. If I may say so that sounds a bit like saying that a concert pianist should have two hands."

The U.N. civil servant was not amused.

"At the risk of offending you, I would say that your observation, rather than my words, is a glimpse into the obvious."

Glyn flushed.

"To resume. I was about to mention the second requirement. They must have some broadcasting facility — microphone technique and experience. Thirdly, they should be able to speak as many languages as possible. Given time, I am confident that we can find your people through the Organization. But it will take a long time. Is that too disappointing?"

"No sir, it isn't. Because the ship will take a long time too. It will be impossible to know how long — but I'd estimate somewhere between 12 and 18 months from now."

"Very well Mr. Tresilian, we will work together as planned. Our conditions are simple and few. You will not henceforth speak to anyone, anyone at all, about the meetings you have had with the Secretary-General or with me. Neither will you telephone or write. Your only channel will be via myself, or failing that, someone else will contact you. You will take no initiative yourself — action will come from this end."

Tresilian's head was reeling. With Bunthorne acting as a recruiting agent, getting the best possible minds, voices and spirits behind the Plan, was there not a chance that it might work?

He thanked Bunthorne profusely, and through him, the Secretary-General. The Plan was now really underway.

.   .   .   .

A year went by. Much had happened. Michael, now rising fourteen, was happy and settled in Canada. All but a trace of his English accent had disappeared. He had become a good student and a popular friend at school. His natural flair for sport got him placed in both hockey and football teams. Julie and Glyn were pleased and happy that he had fitted to his new life so naturally. The boy longed to tell his friends about the Plan, but knew that he must not. He suffered frequently.

"What's your old man really doing Mike?"

"Oh, different things. He goes to England a lot. Something to do with a ship and satellite research."

"Yeah, you've said that before. But what does he know about it? He's no electronics engineer. I remember him saying once on that open line radio show he was doing that he didn't even know how a microphone works. That's easy — I knew that two years ago."

"Aw, come on Mike," from another. "Level with us. We're your buddies. What's he up to?"

Frustrated, he'd go on the offensive. "Look, I wish you guys'd quit bugging me. I don't know any more than I've told you. I wish I did. As soon as I do, I'll tell you. Then maybe you'll get off my back. Come on, let's go. We'll be late for practice."

But Michael's occasional questioning by his classmates was nothing compared to the outright inquisitiveness that came his father's and stepmother's way. Their 'satellite communications research' story was, as the 1968 Christmas season arrived, wearing thin. Very few, if any, of their friends believed them. Certainly none of their acquaintances did. And a local columnist, trusting his own well trained and experienced nose, became intrigued — and made Tresilian's activities a pet fortnightly project. He scented something from the time when Glyn, known by the trade as very promotion and publicity eager, clammed up and sheltered from press probing with a stream of uncharacteristic vacuities. Every two weeks there would be something in Wilf Wentworth's column — 'Glyn Tresilian to U.K. again . . . that's round trip number 3 in eighteen weeks . . . nothing shameful about jet-set membership Glyn . . . but be a good guy and share a little goody now and again eh?'

And then — 'Ha, a little light, but not too much, on broadcaster Glyn Tresilian . . . he's doing a bit here and there on British TV . . . must be getting lots of bread . . . When did you see or hear him last on local air? . . . And round trip jet air's not completely free . . . even when you're buying singles . . .'

Apart from helping Glyn now and again in the 'office', Julie concentrated on making a home in their flat for him and Michael. Without small chldren, she found time to take an extension course in languages and to keep up her few but good friendships.

.   .   .   .

By mid-summer of 1970 a kind of peace had come to Vietnam. The fever of war had not so much been broken as made dormant by President Johnson's de-escalation initiative in March 1968 when he announced a 90% reduction in bombing of the north. At the end of the same nation-wide radio and television speech he had shocked his colleagues, his foes and the world by announcing that he himself would not be a candidate for the presidency during the November elections.

On the night, a short time later, that he was due to leave for Honolulu to confer with American military leaders in the hope that peace steps would follow, Martin Luther King, leader of the non-violent civil rights movement in the United States, was killed by an assassin in Memphis, Tennessee. Black Power extremists called for action. 'Burn, baby, burn' became a civil war cry. Washington, Chicago, Boston, and other American cities were set alight and rent by riots as the uncontrollable rage of black millions led them to arson and pillage. Curfews could not wholly contain the uprising.

The President cancelled his visit to Hawaii. He stayed in the White House and addressed Congress. Both the Presidential mansion and the Capitol were protected by heavily armed troops. Elsewhere, paratroopers were dropping from the skies to war with their countrymen.

In the absence of any taloned hawks flying for the Presidency in the 1968 race, peace had become a safe platform issue; mainly, said the analysts, because the growing chance for a settlement of sorts in Vietnam was rejuvenating the ailing stock market and economy. They were quick to point out however that war normally brought prosperity with it, but only when the government and people of a country agreed that it should be fought. When there was division on that point, they explained, world money markets lost confidence in the currency and this would have continued to cause unbearably nervous financial breakdowns.

In his Inaugural Address in January 1969, the new President of the U.S. pledged himself to peace in Vietnam, at home and around the world. Unburdened by both commitments to the military and his own policies, the new White Houseman confidently proclaimed 'Let us have Peace for People and People for Peace.'

Also, early in 1969 it was rumoured and not denied that Peking would have all the means and capabilities it required for nuclear delivery to the United States in 1971 and not, as forecast earlier by Senator Robert Kennedy and others, as late as 1975.

In the Far East meanwhile, a second Korean war was starting. The fitful Vietnam peace agreements called for substantial withdrawals of American forces as well as the complete cessation of hostilities. The President found these obligations easy and convenient to honour, for apart from isolated skirmishes, fighting between the South Vietnamese and the Viet Cong had virtually stopped. The captured U.S. intelligence vessel 'Pueblo' had been the cause of a new belligerency by Peoples' China in Korea. Pekingologists confirmed that the Communist mainland was only about two years from nuclear equality. And that it was this confidence that brought on the provocation.

Fighting between North and South in Korea was escalating daily. The U.S. voluntarily stepped up the withdrawal program of its personnel from Vietnam, deploying them in almost equal numbers to Korea and California so that they could help to sustain another Asian war to which the Arministration was committed — and at the same time provide troops to help protect the American people from recurring civil wars, now breaking out afresh every summer in the great cities, and sometimes long before summer.

But as the guns and bombs boomed around the thirty eighth parallel, so did business. On Wall street, in Paris, London, Zurich — everywhere, brokers were jubilant. Because there was no doubt about this war. It had been officially declared. It was a conflict of the American people and in many citizens, a mood not unlike Pearl Harbour, took hold.

.   .   .   .

While he was in England on commuting trips to Wooffendens, Tresilian managed to appear on a few public affairs programs for British television as a guest commentator on Canada with special emphasis on the English speaking view in Quebec. A colleague of the Montreal columnist Wilf Wentworth, who was in London at this time, saw the Montrealer on the screen and cabled the paper. These 'guest-shots' were a good guise. And through this work, he was assigned to do a special one hour TV documentary on "Korea — The Second Time" for British viewers. This kept him in Asia for five weeks. He decided that he could well afford the time as the ship now didn't look like being ready until the spring of the following year. Despite all

Spurling's superhuman efficiency and zeal there was no way of hurrying work on the unbelievably complex and refined broadcast system that the Plan called for.

The film, when it was finally edited and cut to one hour for television was so well received in Britain that it was snapped up by networks in Canada, Australasia and the United States. It got, for Tresilian and the producer, welcome, but in Glyn's view, possibly premature international exposure. It also brought, from a variety of quarters, several assignment offers which elated the producer but which Tresilian had to decline as misleadingly as he could.

The experience of being in the war zone for five weeks, and being constantly close to injury, destruction and death by napalm, 'pine-apple' anti-personnel bombs, high explosives, sniper fire and shrapnel — sealed forever in Tresilian's mind the desperate need for the Plan. There was no other way. The film showed it all, with official sources repeating and repeating the same old hopeless stories. In the South. 'We'll talk peace any time, anywhere. Condition? That the North stops all aggressive acts.' And in Peking the same virulent refrain as always. 'We'll talk peace any time, anywhere. But the South, and the vicious, iniquitous and depraved American imperialists must stop fighting and bombing us.'

The Australians' involvement in support of their American allies had grown to the point where there was now compulsory conscription 'down under' in the armed forces. And Sydney, Brisbane, Melbourne, Adelaide and other cities felt the shock of bitter riots. Call-up papers and flags were burned all over the island continent. The friendship links between Canberra and London were rusting inexorably; while ever stronger ties were forged with Washington. More and more the world heard about the Antipodes' New America.

The Fallout Shelter was no longer an American landmark. These structures had started to mushroom all over the globe in 1970 — a time generally thought to represent the point of no return on the deadly ascent to nuclear war. The threat had loomed so large that most of the underdeveloped nations were now openly spending all their foreign aid on building the deep, protective burrows. They reasoned quite simply, when challenged in the, by now practically powerless United Nations, that there was little point in constructing hospitals, schools and roads or attempting to develop welfare programs if there was to be no humanity left to use them.

On the night he arrived back in Montreal from Korea, Glyn took Julie to dinner at the 'Montrealer.' They were shown to a good table in the corner and Tresilian ordered strong aperitifs for them both.

"Cheers," Julie toasted him. "Oh, its so good to have you back again. Let's have a really good time tonight. You're not too tired I hope?"

He looked at her, put his hands on her thigh and let the fingers roam.

"Stop it — not here," she whispered urgently and grasped his wrist. "Lot's of time for that when we get home."

"Well, what are we doing here then? I'll show you whether I'm tired or not when — oh, hello there Gilbert — how's it going?"

"Great, Glyn — just great, thanks. Didn't mean to butt in though. Saw you come in so I thought I'd say hello. Hope you don't mind?"

"Of course not. Sit down, if you've time, meet my wife and have a drink. Julie, I'd like you to meet Gilbert Morrell — my wife Juliana."

The Television Network President sat down after he had told Julie that he was just delighted to meet her and that it was great, just great, to see his old friend Glyn again. He and Tresilian had met twice before reaching for drinks at the over-crowded bars of two separate press receptions. In an ocean of sharks, Morrell was respected as an ubiquitous barracuda. In middle age, he was handsome, amusing and charming. He bustled with success and ran his network to higher ratings every year. True, there were some who likened it to a canning factory. But the President shone through as Canada's 'Mr. Communications' — at any rate, when he presented his annual reports to shareholders.

"Good to see you again, Glyn — and you Mrs. Tresilian. Skol!" He had just returned from a convention of private broadcasters in Scandinavia.

"That was too bad about you and CRAK, Glyn," he said and put down his glass. "I never did hear what happened."

"Aw, there's no point in rehashing all that Gilbert, after nearly two years," Tresilian said sadly, knowing full well that his table guest knew as much and probably more than he did about the Mathieson incident. "Water under the bridge — c'est la vie — que sera, and all that jazz eh Gilbert? Let's have another drink."

"Great idea, Glyn. Just great. But this one'll be mine. I hear all kinds of rumors about you. Just what are you doing?"

"Well, I got back from Korea this afternoon — I was . . ."

"That's right, I heard something about that. You did a documentary on the war I think."

"Yes, for the British, but . . ."

"Any of our people talked to you about it?" Morrell interrupted him again.

"No, not that I know of. At least not to me. They may've been in touch with people on the other side but I really couldn't . . ."

"Hey, wait a minute. Were you the on-camera guy? Host or whatever?"

"Yes, yes I was."

"Then wham," Morrell said writing in his diary. "I guess that'd be Canadian content, eh? Just great. Maybe we can use it. I think we're down on the quota this month. Not bad," he scribbled on and murmured to himself. "An hour you say? Ah, wait a minute — they'll edit in commercial cut-aways I suppose?"

"No," Tresilian replied, "no commercial breaks."

"Then that'd put our editing costs up a bit. Oh, the hell with it. Dammit," he said and closed the diary. "We'll run it as is. A nine o'clock Sunday morning special. I'll tell Welland to go after it tomorrow. Mrs. Tresilian, please forgive us talking shop like this. Glyn, what a lovely wife you have. Has she ever done any television? You know, honey, you'd look great — just great — on camera," he said and produced the smile that had put him first in the hearts of advertisers and shareholders alike.

Julie smiled at him sweetly and decided that she loathed Canada's Mr. Communications. He left and they went straight home after dinner.

.   .   .   .

Since his meeting with The Secretary-General in 1967, Tresilian heard periodically from Arthur Bunthorne. Every now and again Bunthorne would write or call Glyn to say that Tom Everest, the code name they were using for the Secretary-General, had been able to 'increase the club membership by two', or 'Tom Everest says a promising member who works for a big firm won't be available as he's been transferred back to head office.'

Julie was puzzled by his reticence to tell her anything about the 'recruiting' program.

"You tell me everything else. What's so secretive about this? You never did say very much about the last time you met with Mr. Bunthorne."

"I know. But I gave my word that I wouldn't say anything — to anyone. And darling — that includes you."

"But is anything happening — is there any progress?"

"Let's just say that if I'm losing any sleep it's not because I'm worried on that score. And that, my love, must be the last word on the subject. For the present anyway. Don't ask me again — promise?"

"If you say so," she said.

"That's it. Oh, I nearly forgot. This I can tell you. The trip's on. Just heard this morning." Julie tried to smile.

He'd been working on this 'refresher course' voyage for months. Long ago, Tresilian had realised that he would have to register the 'Navis Pacifica' in a 'convenience flag' country. He settled for the West African Republic, previously a British colony which had become yet another in the lengthening list of newly emerged independent nations. And fashionably, it had been swept into dictatorship shortly after in the vacuum of colonial rule. The W.A.R.'s President (the country's letters amused Tresilian greatly) a massive army swashbuckler, immediately grabbed the trappings of total rule; and with the military and radio at his finger tip control, had absolute power and was absolutely corrupt. He renamed the capital city and called it Wafrillia. Soon, the name was seen on the sterns of merchant ships in ports on every continent.

Although Wafrillia was 500 miles from the nearest salt water, the name was for sale. Shipowners wanting to take advantage of the minimal complications and tax dodges that went with a W.A. R. registered fleet, willingly paid the price. All nationalities were welcome. Foreigners found the W.A.R.'s Harold Negretto a kind of friendly despot, an easy man to deal with. Unimpressed with and by ideology, his God was money — in advance. His country's vote in the U.N. became an uncomplicated catch — going to the bloc that got its bid in first. The W.A.R.'s mineral, hydro-electric, agricultural and other natural resources swiftly resembled 'lots' under Negretto's auction gavel as buyers from East and West flocked to the palace saleroom in Wafrillia. Editorialists wondered aloud and in print if, or more probably when, Negretto would open up a slave trade as yet another 'lot'. Rubles, dollars, francs, pounds and other currencies cascaded to Wafrillia and the sound of furious industry roared throughout the country all around the clock. Negretto had become a black Midas with a bullet-proof vest of gold.

Julie put down her drink. She and Glyn were having a cocktail before supper. They could take their time this evening as Michael had done his homework before leaving to eat at a school friend's house in Montreal West. She didn't like the thought of his being away for the three or four month trip he said he needed to get the feel of a ship again.

"Glyn dear," she said slowly, "you know what I think about it but you know best. But is it really all that important? I mean you won't be sailing the 'Navis Pacifica' alone. You'll have a full crew with lots of experienced men."

"I know, but I'll be in command, and however carefully you handpick your shipmates, they've still got to understand that you know exactly what you're doing, when you're the man in charge. I'm not worried about things like navigation and ship handling, but I am concerned about discipline. And you can only get that when you're sure of yourself in all ways. Hell, in the normal course of events without this damned myopia, I wouldn't've had my own ship for another 20 years. As it is, it's only 'Y's' money that'll get me one of those phoney Master's Competency Certificates from Negretto along with the flag registration. By the way, do you realise that those two bits of paper will likely cost us more than we paid for the ship when we got her from Archimedes? But that doesn't faze me. The great thing is he doesn't ask questions and he also says his Minister of Shipping, that sounds very grand, will be pleased to have me sign on as Third Mate for a short re-training voyage 'aboard one of our vessels'. 'One of our vessels'; great — for a country that has to rent a little seaboard for a tiny naval base. That makes me laugh like hell. Here, read the letter for yourself."

Four days later, Tresilian's WARAIR jet touched down at Wafrillia's blazing new international airport. An hour later he was sitting with the dictator in air-conditioned grandeur. He was large and ebony with the eyes of a killer whale. There were no preliminaries. Negretto got down to bargaining.

"Now, Mr. Tresilian, as you're from Canada, I don't have to tell you that time is money. Let us not waste any. I understand from my man in Ottawa that you wish to register, under our flag, a wartime American West Coast Liberty ship. Correct?"

"Correct, Mr. President," Glyn answered.

"Ah yes," and the African reached for a file on his desk. "I have it all here. I like to get all the groundwork done first where the applications are made — but registrations and certificates are issued solely by me — and then only to principals. I dislike dealing with agents, charterers and middle men." He spoke in the near Oxford accent of educated Africans known as 'been-to's' — students who had graduated from the London School of Economics, Oxbridge or the Redbrick Universities in England, or, as in Negretto's case, from Sandhurst. The rich deep voice sounded, to Tresilian, incongruous — as it rolled resonantly out of the loose flowing native robes.

Glancing through the papers, Negretto went on. "I suppose you'll be converting the ship for container cargo?"

"Er, no Mr. President," Glyn started. Had the policy changed? To one of respectable investigation now?

"You see she is being modified — that is we're having certain structural changes . . ."

Negretto waved his hand. "Yes, I've no doubt," the President cut in impatiently. "That's your business. Not mine. Other owners tell me that the bulk cargo markets are lifeless, and that it's worth changing this type of ship over to containers. Personally I don't care what you do with the vessel. Maybe you're going to sell her to Abdul Amir as a block ship for Suez. They tell me he's running short — hahaha!" Negretto rocked himself with laughter.

Glyn decided to follow up. "I don't think that would be very good business, Mr. President. I hear that he's stopped sinking ships in the canal. They rot too quickly. So he has a

— 270 —

modernization plan. The President of Egypt has ordered the Pyramids to be dumped in the waterway at Port Said, Ismalia and Port Tewfiq." Tresilian knew about the row between the heads of the W.A.R. and the U.A.R. Negretto doubled up and brayed non-stop for half a minute.

"Hahohahohaho," he bawled on. "Excellent Tresilian, excellent. That is very bloody funny. Hahohaho. Damn good show, what?" And clapping his outsize hands to-gether, got up from his throne shaped chair and slapped Glyn massively on the back. Seated again still laughing and shaking, he completed the comedy. Gasping through his mirth, he shouted. "And do you know what, Tresilian? He'll mobilise the Sphinx, and that lazy inscrutable old bastard'll have to get off his arse and do some work."

The Dictator spent several minutes of money time regaining his composure. Aides were rung for, and brought in brightly hued hankerchiefs to mop the presidential tears. With a last gasp, and a throat clearing clatter, it was business as usual.

"Now Mr. Tresilian, in addition to the flag registration and your own Master's Competency Certificate, you will also require licenses for four deck and four engineer officers."

"No, Mr. President, I don't think so. I hadn't applied for those. The deck and engine room officers will all have been qualified in their own countries."

"Exactly, Mr. Tresilian. But not in the West African Republic. Our regulations insist that navigators and engineers sailing aboard ships under our registry must be certified by us."

Glyn was about to protest — but caught himself just in time. Negretto held all the cards and that meant playing the game his way or not playing at all. Package deals only.

"I see, Mr. President. If that's the way it has to be I'll . . ."

"Yes, Mr. Tresilian," and the dictator smiled, "that's the way it has to be."

"Very well; but hold it sir. It'll be sometime yet before I'll be ready for the crew. So I can't give you any information about the personnel. And I don't want to delay the registration."

"There won't be any delay, Mr. Tresilian. You will have everything you need from us today. At least I think you will. You seem to be a reasonable man — with a fine sense of humour. And we are trusting people Mr. Tresilian. We do not discriminate. You, after all, will be commanding your own ship and I rely on you to pick a good crew. I will give you the papers — 'but the task of filling up the blanks I'd rather leave to you.' Do you like Gilbert and Sullivan, Mr. Tresilian?"

"Oh, yes very much," Glyn replied and reflected to himself how much sport the great duo would have had with this negroid potentate — Pooh-Bah, the Mikado, Lord High Executioner, Duke of Plaza Toro, Sir Joseph Porter and the Pirate King — he was all of them.

"Good," and the dictator seemed pleased that he and Tresilian not only considered the same things to be funny, but had similar musical tastes as well. Negretto buzzed for a secretary. They spoke in their own language and the man left — pistol whip orders ringing in his ears.

"He won't be long. I've sent him to telephone the Shipping Ministry for the costing. I know I agreed the figure, but I've forgotten what it was. In any case we have to know the Canadian exchange rate for today. The U.S. dollar is my gold standard, Mr. Tresilian. And I adjust all our transactions to it. But I'm glad to see that Canadian funds are doing so well. Let me see. Yes. Yesterday it was at 94.7 cents. I doubt that there'll be much difference this afternoon."

"I can remember, way back in 1957, when the Canadian dollar was about 7½ cents stronger than the American," Glyn said.

"Ah, yes — well things change, don't they. Things change. The name of your ship, Mr. Tresilian, 'Navis Pacifica.' Very picturesque. And very practical too. Ship of Peace. Peace Ship. You should get lots of smooth passage with a name like that. Peace. That coveted elusive entity that everyone wants — and no one will give. Oh, good, here he is now." The secretary put a folded sheet of paper on the President's desk, and bowing, went out. Negretto scribbled on a scratch pad and put the pencil down.

"Alright, Mr. Tresilian. In your case, because I like you — and believe me that's the only reason — we can come to round figures. I am making you a slight concession on the exchange. Flag registration, your own and your officer's certificates — a total of two and a half million Canadian dollars. Your account has been checked and found to be in order. I will waive cheque certification — and will accept one on your Montreal Bank."

The dictator sat back and folded his arms. This figure was about half a million more than Glyn had expected. He decided to try.

"Is this your final word, Mr. President?" he asked bluffing firmly.

"On matters of price, where my country's interest are involved Mr. Tresilian, my first word is my final word. I did not ask you to register your ship in the West African Republic. I do not haggle. With you — or the Americans or the Soviets or the British, or the Chinese or the French. But I do good business with them all. I did not ask them to dig up and exploit my country. The price they must pay for that privilege is my price. The law of supply and demand is very simple, Mr. Tresilian. Even as they teach it in British universities."

Glyn went for one more effort. "I understand all that sir. But that's a higher figure than my research indicated it would be."

Negretto's face stiffened, and he raised his voice. "The only research anyone could conduct on this matter is with me. But now we are wasting time; and without the benefit of laughter. Only you know whether you want to operate this Liberty ship or not. Presumably you do — otherwise you wouldn't have flown out here. But I must state something we both know. It is only here, in this room, that you can be supplied quickly with the necessary documents to sail that ship and still comply with International Maritime Regulations. This is a thriving part of our economy, Mr. Tresilian. That is why we are not inquisitive. We like the business — but only on our terms. However, far be it from me to persuade you against your will. The point is that I can't see you sailing your 'Navis Pacifica' any other way."

"Very well, Mr. President," Glyn said resignedly. "You win. How should I make it out?"

"To me — Harold Negretto. That's all. No companies, limiteds or anything like that. The only difference between a lot of other people and me is that I have nothing to hide, Mr. Tresilian. You would doubtless say that I am shameless; and that's your privilege of course. Ah, thank you. And now," and the dictator handed over an official looking large manila envelope, "here is your part of the bargain. You'll find everything in order — but do by all means check for yourself."

Glyn hurriedly took out the papers and found that they were certainly in good order according to the gospel of Negretto. Inside he saw the flag registration, and competency certificates issued and signed by the W.A.R. Minister of Marine attesting that Tresilian and eight yet to be named other officers had satisfied the Board of Examiners that they were proficient to command, engineer, and navigate the 'Navis Pacifica.'

"Yes, that is all correct, Mr. President — thank you," Glyn said, still a bit shaken by the episode. Half a million more than he'd bargained for! "I'm, I'm also grateful for your arranging my voyage on the 'Lillistrata Kay.' I'm looking forward to that. Especially," and he was thinking faster now, "as my navigation and seamanship need brushing up. Where and when do I join her?"

The 'Lillistrata Kay' was the one merchant ship owned by the West African Republic although over 12 million tons of shipping sailed under the W.A.R. flag of convenience. A modern diesel cargo ship of 5500 gross tons, Negretto had won her shortly after his take over, from a Greek shipowner at a card table in Monte Carlo. At first, following the windfall, Negretto had thought of cashing in the ship as he would have exchanged winning chips. But then the idea of having a private ship succored his ego, and he returned by sea to the W.A.R.'s leased naval parking lot. As part of Tresilian's 'package', Negretto had agreed that Glyn could serve with her for a voyage without pay. The dictator had called the vessel 'Lillistrata Kay' — his beautiful and quite famous, or infamous, wife's christian names.

Like so many daughters of African Chiefs, the President's lady who was, in sailor parlance, blacker than the Earl of Hell's riding boots, had been 'French finished' at the Sorbonne in Paris. More than once she had appeared on the ten best dressed list. Time, Life, Paris Match, had all run picture spreads on the statuesque beauty. He wondered if he'd have a chance to meet her, as many shipowners had. From the latter, of whom Glyn now knew a fair number, and even from Sir Timothy, Glyn had heard more than one mouth-watering story on the fabulous Lillistrata Kay.

Negretto barked briefly on the telephone, then he swivelled round. "She gets to Casablanca to-morrow. She'll be there three days and then as, you know, she's on a four month charter. Salt from Cagliari in Sardinia to Japan, light ship to Nauru for phosphate to Adelaide. Then she goes to Brisbane for a full cargo of sugar consigned to Avonmouth. That should do very nicely I think. I'll see that you have a flight to Casablanca in the morning and you'll be my guest tonight. By the way, did you come WARAIR from Rome?"

"Yes."

"Any complaints?"

"No, Mr. President. It couldn't have been a better flight."

"Good. Those aeroplanes are very fine ambassadors. I keep a close watch on them. And now my good Tresilian," Negretto expanded and rubbed his hands together joyfully, "enough of sordid commerce. In the words of your P.G. Wodehouse's Uncle Fred — 'let us sketch out rough plans for the evening.' Actually, there's very little for us to do — my wife's done it all. She's arranged one of her soirées. The room will ring with culture — which I personally find tedious, but the little woman thrives on it.

"At the moment she's in love with Spanish Modern and she's soaking the whole palace in it. There'll be some Ambassadors of course — there always are. I find it fun to listen to their lies. But most important of all — I insist on this Tresilian — we'll have lots of vulgar foreign businessmen. After all life would be pretty hard without them, eh? I include you in that category of course. Come, I'll have someone take you to your suite. You'll want to bathe and freshen up."

Glyn unwound for an hour in the sunken marble bath with silver fixtures, attached to the luxuriously large guest room. And then a valet took him to the Public Rooms of the Palace. The cocktail party, when he arrived, was just reaching that satisfying crescendo beloved of hostesses the world over. Platoons of waiters bore glittering trays of food and drink darting everywhere so as not to be more than a half-full glass away from anyone. Tresilian, himself an efficient performer on the 'freeload circuit,' reflected that even the most critical consumer in that set at home would have given this event full approbation.

An African band throbbed sensously in one corner. The sound grew and grew. He was enjoying it thoroughly. Normally he didn't very much like the press conference and cocktail reception affair because of the strain that went with being 'on'. Here, in Wafrillia, no one knew him and there were no press agents to ram him with clients craving free broadcast exposure. Negretto was at the top of his form.

Tresilian couldn't imagine anyone being a better host. Dividing his time perfectly, and followed constantly by two servants, one carrying a bundle of scented hand towels for his sweating face and underarms, the African mogul talked and laughed his way from group to group. The culturalists, diplomats, money men — he rotated among them all like crops. And then he saw Glyn.

"Ah, Tresilian," he bellowed from a few yards away, "enjoying yourself?" He came over and battered his guest on the back. "Have you met my wife yet? No? Then follow me."

They crossed to the other side of the giant room and found Lillistrata Kay in an animated group. Encompassed by black and white painters, sculptors, musicians and writers, the luscious black mistress of the republic held her audience captive. As he saw her for the first time, Glyn realised how true to her magazine image she was. A six foot three Venus set in pulsating ebony.

"Now, my queen," Negretto broke in. "I want you to meet Glyn Tresilian from Canada. We have just concluded a little business and he leaves tomorrow for Casablanca to join your namesake for what he calls a 'refresher course voyage'. He's registered his own ship with us and will command her himself."

The W.A.R.'s first lady eased herself a few feet from the artists' cell.

"Oh, how interesting. It's a pleasure to meet you Mr. or should I say Captain — Tresilian?" she said sultrily in her English English. He flushed. This hadn't occurred to him. But by God, she was right. In command he'd have the courtesy rank. Not bad. He'd like using it too.

"That's very kind of you Madame," suspecting she liked the sophistry of French address, "but a bit premature I fancy. On your namesake I'll be but a lowly third mate."

Negretto had moved off and they were alone. Glyn swallowed her with his eyes. Especially her welcoming scarlet painted lips. The only W.A.R. woman not in native dress, the revealing low cut white sheathy Paris creation gripped her handsomely proportioned body. She was a big and tall woman, a feminine Charles Atlas. The top of her extreme decolletage was only slightly below Glyn's eye level. His gaze swooped down the fleshy ravine. My, what voluptuous tits she had, he caught himself musing. Full, upright, gently heaving and exposed. He couldn't take his eyes off them — and she seemed in no hurry to spoil the view. Taking a glass she turned, and the movement for an instant revealed all for him — including a glimpse of the slightly pinkish nipple on her left breast, unhidden by bra or slip.

She raised her drink and smiled invitingly.

"Were they worth looking at?"

"Madame," and he knew there was only one tack to go on, "you have the most beautiful bosum I've ever seen."

"How very sweet of you, Captain. I must call you that now, mustn't I? Or would you prefer Monsieur le Capitaine? I take it that you speak French, coming from Montreal?"

"Not in the way that our Prime Minister Trudeau speaks it — but serviceably."

"Ah, you are lucky to have him as your leader. Come then, let us speak French together. I knew two boys from Quebec City quite well at the Sorbonne," she continued in French, Tresilian translating her voice back to English as was his custom when listening to spoken French. "I think they were nationalists, or I think you call them separatists? As a matter of fact even though I haven't been there, I have a soft spot for Canada and the Canadians. They're such peaceful people I think — and wonderful businessmen my husband often says. Now let me return the compliment. Unfortunately you are dressed in such a way that I cannot give you an anatomical once-over, so I'll say that you have one of the nicest speaking voices I've ever heard."

Tresilian was glad that he'd lost weight and been in the sun a lot. He flattered himself that the ravishing Lillistrata Kay seemed to have her eye on him. He'd be game and try it.

"Très bien, Madame," and he picked his words carefully, "l'autre jour un homme m'a dit que je parle Français mieux que Diefenbaker, et mieux que Pearson mais pas mieux que Madame Lillistrata Kay Negretto."

She looked at him fondly. "I'm sure you won't mind my saying, Mr. Tresilian," switching to English, "that your French pronunciation hardly qualifies you to teach at Berlitz . . . I much prefer to hear you in English I'm afraid. But you're missing so much. I was brought up you know in a French colony —

although my family and the President's are distant relatives. Over the years I have gotten to know both Paris, where I spent my formative years, and London very well."

They talked and Tresilian explained the difficulties of learning French in Montreal. All the time he was talking, Lillistrata Kay smiled knowingly, even understandingly, and said that her French upbringing forced her to side with the French in Canada and de Gaulle — she admired him greatly — but the practicality of her position in a former United Kingdom colony was another matter. Her heart and mind were two quite different things. The French colonies in Africa had created an African love of France.

At the same time, she told him, she and her husband were 'acceptable' members of the Church of England — as were nearly all members of the W.A.R. establishment, educated as they were at missionary schools and then sent to England for finishing.

"That was a switch for me of course, Captain. I was born a papist naturally — but changes of that sort are of minor importance in Africa. Why continue Europe's religious wars on this continent?" she asked, and went on.

"Oh, I think you'd like this. We've decided to form a morale building women's branch for our mini navy. I am Commodore-in-Chief. I think I'll ask Dior to do the uniform. I'm very suited for the job — I took a course in coastal navigation once, and know all about running fixes."

They both laughed. Then she returned the discussion to herself. It was obvious to Tresilian that she was completely self-centered and as proud of her intellect as her great beauty. She asked Tresilian for his impressions of the W.A.R. and the party. Glyn complimented her enthusiastically on everything . . . decor, food, drink, flowers, decorations. He almost drooled when he told her of his feelings for the W.A.R. women whom he found 'sexy and stunning.'

She wanted and expected these reactions as she herself was practically wholly responsible for bringing the fashions and styles of Paris to the W.A.R. Then asking for a light for her gold cigaret holder from a passing waiter who seemed oblivious to the scene, Lillistrata Kay leaned over, demurely lowering her eyes to inhale from the bright flame, and purposely allowed

Tresilian to note the fall of her other breast. She turned and looked at him.

"I hope you liked the starboard side as well?" and Glyn's eyes glowed.

"But seriously Captain, I appreciate a man's frank assessment and attention, as any woman should, and I believe you will find the evening as enjoyable in reality as you now find it in anticipation . . . . " Savouring Tresilian's perplexity, she hurried on with her point. "Note the white women here," and her arm swept the room, "their sickly features. Just look at the tall American Ambassador's wife over there. She was a year behind me at Neufchatel. She has that dutifully conservative late 1930's gown trapped in a steaming hot corset. And what about that ancient hair-style? Typical foreign service officer's haybag. Over there — in the corner; UK and French Ambassadors' wives — same thing. They're all frigid and I know — that's their trouble. Imagine that, Captain, in this heat. I don't know why but they just seem to be afraid to be and look like women. Out of all the foreign, stiff and dowdy cows here, about the only one that's worth peeking at is the Indonesian Ambassador's wife. See her? There, by the orchestra in that gorgeous sarong."

Tresilian had to agree. My, she liked rubbing it in. But Lillistrata Kay thundered on, in full flight, declaring how lucky it was for the Captain that Canada didn't have regular representation in Wafrillia yet! "I know your men and know of your women. Now look at my husband's ministers' wives," and Glyn's eyes, now shot with champagne and sensual anticipation, were already fixed on the objects of the African queen's attention. "It's too hot for corsets and bras . . . so we go without. That's why you can see their breast nipples through the cloth, and why not? . . . They're women and here to proclaim it," she said half in French and half in English, as if rapturously intoxicated by the force of her own argument.

Fortunately for Tresilian's resistance to temptation, the French Ambassador happened by. As suddenly as the conversation had begun, it ended — as if he were dismissed. Yet there was something there. Glyn wondered about Lillistrata Kay's feeling for him, and especially her 'anticipation' inuendo, for the rest of the evening. He was going to wait this one out, with all thought of Julie left far behind in Montreal.

His head still reeled. The tête-a-tête was over. Tresilian munched on a caviar canapé. He'd often heard about what his grandmother would have called 'goings on' in self-governing African circles. But had she, or hadn't she, suggested something for tonight? As he watched her begin a new round, he was sure that he'd never know. But by heaven what a bedmate she'd be.

The cocktails flowed for another three hours and it was well past eleven when dinner was announced. The enormous feast ended in the small hours. Glyn, over full with food, was also extremely drunk. At the end of the gorging, Negretto waved away his guest's thanks.

"Think nothing of it my dear Tresilian," he said winking heavily. "Bon voyage. It's been a pleasure and a privilege doing business with you."

Glyn, his mind clogged by excessive liquor, knew only that inhibitions had long ago left him. He opened the door of his suite and was greeted by three nubile African beauties wearing the bottoms of TV white bikinis, and nothing else but strings of pearls around their necks. He blinked at the dazzle and blearily noticed that they were very young and statuesque and approximately three-quarter size models of Lillistrata Kay. She'd probably picked them, by God!

He stood and swayed at the door and the girls covered themselves with brightly coloured bath-robes. On the four poster bed were a guitar and bongo drum. A trolley bar, laden with bottles, ice and glasses had been pushed to a corner where a small buffet table was set out.

"Good evening sir," one of the girls, who couldn't have been more than seventeen at the most, said. "We've come to make you happy. We want you to have nice memories of the W.A.R."

Tresilian blurrily took in the scene.

"My God," he croaked, his voice thick and muddy with intoxication, "an orgy. A bloody orgy. I've never been to one of those l'il things before. Let's dance, girls eh?"

"Sir," the spokesgirl said, "wouldn't you prefer the bath first? And then we can have some music and dancing. And then some food if you're hungry. And after that we three girls will please you very much in the bed."

"OK," he jollily intoned. He was never further from a quarrel in his life. "Whatever you say."

Delicately they undressed him and themselves, then ran the bathwater in the sunken marble tub. They soaped and rubbed and dried him and each other. The bath had done him good. Erect and pulsating out of every pore, he panted for the play and hoped with all his heart that he could please all three. Never mind the music, food and drink. His throat choked as he breathed, rather than spoke. "Alright. Now. Right now. On the bed. One at a time. Never mind the other stuff."

"But sir."

"On the bed, goddam it."

"Yes, but sir, we don't do it like that. We do it together so that we can make you most happy. You come into me and the other two stroke you nicely all over like this and . . ."

"Oh, hell," he shouted, "damn and blast the whole bloody world." It was too late, too early. The girl had barely caressed his groin in demonstration. She wiped her hand and then the floor. He felt ashamed and went limp. Motioning the women out of the room, he took a Scotch bottle from the portable bar, put it to his mouth and drank himself insensible.

CHAPTER 5

Four and a half months later, Glyn Tresilian worked the bridge telegraphs on the 'Lillistrata Kay' for the last time as she made her way to a dock at Avonmouth in the Bristol Channel. He had enjoyed the voyage and now felt confident at the prospect of command. The W.A.R. ship was a floating United Nations in itself. And he'd noticed that, apart from the odd drunken brawl ashore, the polyglot crew got along with itself very well.

He took a train from Bristol Templemeads station to Lime Street, Liverpool, had a quick visit with Ray Spurling to the 'Navis Pacifica' and got a plane from Manchester to Prestwick for the direct flight back to Montreal.

Julie, who had some time before learned to drive the Black Panther, met him at Dorval airport with Michael.

St. Patrick's Day, 1970. Official spring was only four days away. Tresilian had put in a good day at the Côte des Neiges office finalising Articles of Agreement for the sailing crew. He was indeed glad that he'd taken that voyage on the 'Lillistrata Kay.' The benefit to himself apart, he'd also had time to watch the work and characters of men in all departments.

He had deliberately befriended the German Bosun, Polish Second Mate, and Glaswegian Second Engineer. Without actually telling them about the Plan, he had offered them well above normal pay and good prospects for a happy ship. He said that he'd promote them all in rank, 'commissioning' the Bosun to Third Mate. They accepted his offer to sail and agreed to recruit their own personnel. Glyn had also tracked down a very good Chief Steward he'd sailed with in the Baltic once, so he knew that the enlarged galley would be well run and that the food, which could make or break a ship's morale, would be good.

Things seemed to be going well. Sir Timothy's yards had finished the U.S. naval contract in record time and Wooffendens were singled out by a fiscally harassed government as an example of dollar-earning productivity, and by protest groups as a lackey shoving and pushing on the steps of a nuclear warmonger's escalator. Peace pickets and demonstrations outside the main gates and in view of Sir Timothy's office were now a daily occurrence. On the other hand, there had never been prosperity quite like it on the Mersey. As the shipbuilder put it in a letter to Glyn:

". . . You will remember that talk we had in the library at the Hall. War is most certainly good for business. We have had to and will continue to expand. Already we've taken on six thousand more men — and we bought Kilby's, the next yard to us up the river. As you probably know, I have become the Prime Minister's industrial 'blue eyed boy' — which I don't have to tell you, my dear Glyn, gives me embarrassment as well as pleasure. The Americans are absolutely delighted with our work and we have a contract with them, as a result, to build nuclear tonnage of such quantity that I can't see us doing anything else for about 15 years. Consequently the board has agreed that we 're-tool' ourselves totally. Your 'Navis Pacifica' is now the only mercantile work we have on hand, as you've probably seen for yourself. The rest we've either finished or passed to the Clyde.

"Of course as you know, I'm no philosopher. The rough, tough, philistine work of shipbuilding and the worlds of intellectual exercise are very far apart. But I cannot help reflecting, as your 'Navis Pacifica' nears completion, on the irony of fitting her out so that she can pursue her purpose of making our other work redundant!

"You know, Glyn, that we shall wish you God speed. Candidly, I believe you to be facing an impossible challenge. You know far more about idealism than I do, but I cannot see you taking on the unfortunate realities of human nature single-handedly. However I realise that you must have a rich and powerful sponsor who wouldn't be in a position to support you unless he had conducted his business affairs with the utmost realism.

"You will, I'm sure, not be surprised to hear that Diana and I are concerned that Julie and Michael will be sailing with you. Is it a wise decision? With so many unknown factors to confront, and the enormity of the task itself, will not their presence aboard give you added worry? Do please reconsider this . . ."

.   .   .   .

The following day Tresilian took the new Montreal-Toronto train to see Gaston Yerbury. This was their third meeting. They lunched, as they had when the billionaire agreed to back the Plan, in the same private dining room.

Over the one pink gin they were again having as an aperitif, Yerbury said. "Now Glyn, you doubtless feel that on this occasion I expect you to give a detailed account of yourself. Please don't. Let us talk about other things. Music, for example. Dame Gwynneth told me the other day that she'd be meeting you on her way back to London and that the Company would be doing some performances from the ship." Tresilian gulped. He knew, as he'd known hundreds of times since the birth of the Plan, that no one would ever fathom Yerbury. No questions, no queries, no doubts. And so far his judgment had cost over 20 million dollars and the 'Navis Pacifica' wasn't at sea yet. But Wooffenden's monthly bills had all been paid promptly and not a nickel was owed anywhere.

They took their places at the table. "Yes, sir. We should be in Hong Kong at the beginning of November and they'll have just finished concerts there. It should all fit in very well as I'd like to spend a few days at anchor to rest the personnel and to get any repairs done that may be necessary. And of course when we leave Hong Kong we'll have our hardest work ahead of us in Asia."

"I think," Yerbury said putting down his spoon, "that the 'Pueblo' affair was the most unfortunate thing since the Cuban crisis in 1962. In fact, I believe that, in many ways we were closer to a nuclear outbreak over that in '68, than during the Caribbean confrontation."

"Mmm. Yes, perhaps you're right. By the way, Mr. Yerbury, do you know the difference between 'tactical' nuclear bombs and nuclear bombs?"

"No, I don't think I do. Unless it means that they're 'tactical' when you drop them — and not when your adversaries use them. But tactical or not, I'll never know how or why they haven't been triggered yet. God only knows how much more time, if any, we have. The world situation at the moment would certainly suggest that we must be very close to Armageddon. Look at it. The 'Pueblo' got the United States involved with conventional war again in Korea and even they can't stand the strain of thinning themselves out on two Asian fronts for much longer."

"Yes, I know," Tresilian said as he picked up the dismal review. "They're trying to keep this quiet, but I heard that they're having to deploy huge numbers of enlisted men to the home front. Police and national guardsmen just can't handle it. And naturally they'd like to have them out in the far east. Britain seems to be on her economic knees permanently. And no one knows how much longer de Gaulle can go on. The British probably think forever. It's one thing keeping them out of the Common Market but to have cut off all U.K. trading is something else again."

"Of course I'm not sure just how miserable we want to make ourselves Glyn — but take the middle east," Yerbury continued. "The refugee problem remains unsolved and the Israelis are still occupying the territory they captured in '67. Amir's just as obdurate over the canal and as usual the U.N. seems so impotent. A Peoples' China type communism is firmly rooted in the political life of all the South American countries. The American-supported military regimes just can't seem to dig the guerillas out. By the way, had you intended to use the Panama Canal?"

"Oh, yes. But the only way we could get through now would be to convert the 'Navis Pacifica' into a hovercraft." Glyn alluded to the communist Central American dictator who had recently upstaged Amir as a canal blocker. The media called him 'the Maestro.'

This 'Maestro', following his armed takeover of several neighbouring republics in the Canal Zone, had emptied the Pedro Miguel, Miraflores and Gatun locks; and then poured thousands of concrete tons to seal them against navigation. The amount was so huge that they could only be freed by massive aerial bombardment with such explosive power that portions of the waterway in the vicinity would be unbanked beyond repair.

"So, you'll have to round Cape Horn?" Yerbury asked as he helped himself to mushrooms.

"Yes," Tresilian replied. "I think I'd better have a word with Sir Francis Chichester!"

"Did you ever sail that route?"

"No sir. But if 'Gypsy Moth IV' could do it, I'm sure we can too."

They finished lunch and it was time for Glyn to go.

"I think this is the last time we'll meet before you leave, Glyn?"

"Yes, Mr. Yerbury, I suppose it is." Tresilian felt awkward and embarrassed. He could think of nothing to say that made any sense. The tycoon stood up, walked Glyn silently to the door and wished him 'God speed.'

.　　.　　.　　.　　.　　.　　.　　.

Flying the West African Republic flag, registered in Wafrillia, and under the command of Captain Glyn Tresilian, the 'Navis Pacifica' sailed from Birkenhead on the night of April 15th, 1970. Other than her name and registration, she carried no markings. She had been painted a gleaming white on her hull and superstructure. Wooffendens, and the scores of sub-contractors, brilliantly co-ordinated and misled as to purpose by Ray Spurling, had done a superb job.

Aboard her, as she approached the Mersey pilot cutter, were 52 crew members representing 20 nations to man the deck, engine room, and catering departments. They had been screened and selected with great care by Tresilian's former shipmates. Recruited by Tresilian himself were 12 broadcast technicians and operators, many of whom had served aboard commercial radio pirate ships off the British coast, two helicopter pilots, and three computer experts, who would be working in eight-hour shifts around the clock so that precise 'bounce off' satellite information suggesting what frequencies and wavelengths to use could be fed at all times into the Master Control Room and studios, all of which had been built abaft the upper bridge and wheelhouse. Her foremast had been transformed into a hydraulically powered telescope antenna tapering to a fine maximum height of almost three hundred feet above the weather deck.

As the ship would be their working base for such long periods and because the 'Talkers,' as he'd call them, would probably be poor sailors, and due to the sensitivity of the electronic mazes all over the ship, Glyn had decided to install stabilizers for comfort and efficiency. Normally this luxury was reserved for passenger ships.

"Stop her sir, please," the Pilot called to the Third Mate at the telegraph. "Midships and steady. Let me know when she doesn't answer."

"Aye, aye sir."

The Pilot vessel came on and lowered the small pinnace.

"That's it then, Pilot, off you go and thank you very much," Tresilian said.

"Good, Captain. She's stopped and steady. Where are you bound, sir?"

"Cobh, right now; to pick up some people — and then we'll see." The ex-Master Mariner buttoned up his heavy overcoat. "My word Captain, I've handled thousands of these 'Sam' boats in and out but this is the rummest one I've ever seen. What does all this satellite research that they told me you're going to be doing mean exactly?"

"God knows Pilot, I don't," Tresilian laughed. "You'd better ask the experts. That's why they're aboard. I'm only a sailor like you."

"Well, good luck anyway Captain. Have a good trip — wherever you go." The Pilot went down the rope and wood-stepped ladder and waved from the pinnace.

The 'Navis Pacifica' lay still off the Mersey estuary. The night was clear, heightening the flashing lights of buoys, headlands and ships signalling by Aldis lamp. Glyn, dressed in serviceable khaki and peaked cap without insignia, stood by the port clear view screen for several moments. Julie and Michael, came in through the chartroom and stood back in a corner of the wheelhouse. There is something about the bridge of any ship that makes it inviolate. It is the Master's territory — where his business, and his alone, is done.

Michael sounded an attention getting cough. Tresilian turned around suddenly. "Oh, I didn't know you two were up here. Come with me a sec, will you," and he led them back to the chartroom.

"Now, look, I should have mentioned this before, but from here on in I don't want either of you to come on the bridge while we're at sea unless you've checked with me first. I'll explain later. You can see everything just as well from below anyway. O.K. monkeys, off you go. I don't want you to be the first entries in the punishment log-book." He went back and stood in front of the helmsman.

The telegraph clanged and drowned the shouted repeats of his commands. "Half ahead and hard a-port," he ordered. My God, he thought, command. And felt the jubilation that he'd envied so much as a junior officer when a ship shuddered with way upon her and steered to her Master's calls.

"What's our E.T.A. Cobh Second Mate?" he asked the Navigator.

"0930 sir."

"Right, get some bearings will you? Ease your helm. Midships. How's your head quartermaster?"

"Coming round to 285 sir," the Welshman at the wheel called.

"Meet her now. Steady as she goes. Nothing to port."

"Steady on 281 sir, nothing to port." "There you are Third Mate. Check your courses with the Second Mate, keep five miles off everything and blow down if you want me. No point in having three good men on the bridge, eh?" And he went below to have supper with Julie and Michael.

"Sorry if we did the wrong thing darling," Julie said.

"No, you weren't to know. But the fact is we can only be 'family' right here in our own quarters. It's going to be a long trip and while I've no intention of doing a 'Bligh', I'll be keeping a very close watch on discipline and morale. And don't forget there'll be a lot of other women aboard tomorrow. The bridge'll be absolutely out of bounds."

.   .   .   .

Since the New Year, Arthur Bunthorne had been in almost daily contact with Glyn. For nearly two years he had worked carefully and slowly behind the U.N. scenes as promised, and all the Talkers had been found. They had agreed to serve on a mission that the S.G.'s man had described as 'one of the last hopes for world peace, by-passing governments.' But they had been told nothing about the essence of the Plan.

As the 'Navis Pacifica' steamed down the Irish Sea, the 48 Talkers were crossing the Atlantic from New York to Shannon airport on four different flights. They had all been able to get indefinite leaves of absence from their countries' missions to serve with a special 'Nuclear Peace Research Committee' that the Secretary-General had set up as a camouflage for them. This had met the usual resistance in the Secretariat, but as there were already so many committees and groups at the U.N., one more or less made little difference.

Bunthorne had made all the necessary arrangements and was already in Shannon standing by the two chartered buses that would take the Talkers and their baggage to Cobh. A tender would ferry them to the 'Navis Pacifica.'

Tresilian was too excited to sleep. He went to the bridge and spent most of the night there. To the first mate, who came on watch at 4 a.m., he said. "Don't mind me, Mr. Karabewski. I couldn't get to sleep. So I thought I'd come up and get the feel of her. My, but it's good to be at sea again."

"You've been ashore a long time sir?" the Polish ex Naval officer asked, as the standby man brought up hot tea from the galley.

"Yes, quite a few years," Glyn replied and went out onto the starboard wing of the bridge. He paced up and down, thinking out the words he'd speak to the entire ship's company after they had cleared Cobh Harbour. For the first time more than a small handful of people would know about the Plan.

The Irish Sea was calm as the ship made her way SSW at 12½ knots. At 6 o'clock he went down to the stateroom and looked at Julie sleeping peacefully in their bed. Not wanting to disturb her, he took a blanket and slept for an hour on the settee in the day cabin. The Malay steward brought in tea at seven. Tresilian showered, shaved, and asked the steward to bring breakfast on the bridge. He brought the 'Navis Pacifica' carefully to just outside the harbour entrance at Cobh. The Pilot boarded and 15 minutes later the Swedish carpenter, with the Chief Officer supervising on the foc's'le head, knocked out the windlass anchor brake and three and a half shackles of chain rattled and sparked down the hawse pipe. The cable took the strain and the ship brought up.

Using the powerful binoculars that Yerbury had given him as a wedding present, Tresilian could see Arthur Bunthorne sitting in the stern sheets of a small launch racing to the ship.

"Well, hello, Arthur," Glyn said a few minutes later in the day room. "Quite a surprise. I didn't expect to see you. Decided that you want to come with us?"

"No, that's not it Glyn," he smiled, "but Tom Everest asked me to see them safely aboard. I fly back tonight. But I'd certainly like to be coming with you — nothing like a good sea voyage to tone you up. Now, as I told you before, we've got some first class people for you. As far as I know, security at our end has been airtight. They're all at the tender now which I've ordered to leave in half an hour. I wanted to have this chat with you before they board and to have a quick look around the ship so that I can make some sort of a report to Everest."

Beginning with the bridge, Tresilian showed Bunthorne through the studios, Master Control Room, officers and sailing crew accommodation admidships, computer room, generator spaces, the heli-hangars aft with the choppers stowed below and then the special living quarters that had been constructed for the Talkers in the for'ard tweendecks. Air conditioned throughout, every cabin had a single berth with private bathroom. In the same area were dining and recreation rooms with a well stocked library. Bunthorne was impressed.

"Damn nice, Glyn. By God, this must have cost a packet," he said.

"Yes, it certainly did," Tresilian smiled in agreement. They finished a quick tour of the ship and went to the gangway to receive the tender. As it approached, Glyn watched the men and women standing at the rail. They appeared to be all ages and colours. There were gaily coloured saris, native African robes, turbans, short skirts, western suits, sarongs, and a bowler hat or two. The faces were black, white, yellow, coffee, Latin and Semite swarthy, red and eskimo.

"Ah, there he is, I see him now," Bunthorne said suddenly. "You see that tall chap at the back? Yes, with the trilby and sun glasses. He's Alan Digby. Everest chose him to be your liaison man. A hell of a nice fellow. Australian — from Adelaide. He's really seasoned. Been with Everest on his personal staff all the time since he took over. But even he doesn't know the full score yet."

The tender bumped gently against the 'Navis Pacifica's' starboard side at the anchorage in the pastoral harbour. Tuneful

Irish voices heaved the small passenger vessel's lines up on the peace ship's deck where their eyes were quickly slipped over the mooring bitts in her waist. The accommodation ladder went down and embarkation began.

The Talkers and their baggage were all aboard an hour later. The ship came to life and rang with excited voices in over 20 tongues. Julie and Michael introduced themselves and helped the new arrivals to find and settle down in their cabins. The alleyways and ladders to the Talkers' rooms soon became congested with people, trunks, suitcases and, Tresilian noticed, quite a few musical instruments. At this rate Dame Gwynneth wouldn't need her orchestra in Hong Kong for the company's performance. He went back to the day room ready to welcome Digby. Moments later Digby was at the door escorted by Bunthorne.

"Alan, this is Glyn Tresilian — Alan Digby." They shook hands. Instinctively Glyn knew that the Secretary-General had chosen well. Tall, bronzed, spare and greying, Digby reminded Glyn of some of the many Australians he'd known during his sailor days 'down under.' Salty, direct and fun loving. To him and his sort, the only possible other name for a spade might be a 'bloody shovel.' But nothing else.

"Very glad to meet you Cap'n," Digby said, his set steel blue eyes sparkling, "but can't wait to find out what it's all about."

"You will in just a minute or so. A pleasure to meet you too, Mr. Digby. Look, you and I'll be working very closely indeed. Lets make it informal, shall we?" Tresilian suggested.

"That's just fine with me, Glyn. Now, you see Arthur, I've only been aboard half an hour and I've got him shaping like an Aussie already," he laughed.

"Ah, but he's more Canadian than anything else, Alan. Don't let the voice fool you," Bunthorne said.

"Well, well, you'd never know it. I thought I was saddled with a couple of Pommies in here. You were born in Canada?" Digby asked.

"No, not born; but I've lived there a long time. And my wife's Canadian. She's aboard too with my son. You'll meet them shortly. But we'll have lots of time for the life story. I'll bore you with it in installments later on. Now Arthur, I'd like to get under way in about an hour so let's fill Alan in right now.

We'll have a drink while we're at it. Pink gin? Good. Might as well start with a sailor's gargle, I guess."

Tresilian went to the liquor cabinet in a corner of the day room and flicked a few drops of Angostura bitters into three glasses which he rolled in his hands. Shaking the glasses free, so that only the oily reddish liquid stuck to the sides, he poured the gin, dropped in some ice cubes and took a water carafe to the table bolted to the deck in front of the settee.

"Well, here goes," Glyn said and raised his glass. It took him fifteen minutes to give Digby a concise summary of the Plan. The Australian listened with growing astonishment. In over 30 years' diplomatic experience, he'd heard nothing like it.

"As soon as we clear the land," Tresilian wound up, "I'll explain the whole thing in detail to everyone aboard. It'll come as news to the sailing crew too. But I wanted you to have the guts of the thing first." Digby toyed with his empty glass. Several seconds later he spoke. "That's quite a mouthful Glyn. I don't know what to say. Do you think it'll work?"

"How can anyone tell?" Tresilian shrugged. "But what's a better idea to try?" and he looked out through the scuttle. The low, soft Irish hills moved by as 'Navis Pacifica' swung gently round her anchor with the tide. Afternoon showers came and went; the sun popped in and out, and sea birds sang between the rain.

"Mmm," and Digby shook his head from side to side. "Yes, well there I admit you have me, Glyn. I suppose you've got a point. But, I don't know, it just seems so, so fictional. 'Incredible's' just about the right word, I'd say. I should have guessed something of the sort though when we were coming out in the tender. That transmitter mast and all that electronic gear. She looks like a Christmas tree from a distance."

"Ah, but a white Christmas tree at least," Bunthorne added.

"I only hope Alan that you're not so staggered that you want to go ashore with Arthur?" Glyn asked.

"God, no. But I'll tell you this Glyn. If anyone but the S.G. had tried to persuade me to agree to do something I knew nothing about, you can be damn sure I wouldn't have gone along with it. Oh, my word. You can bank on that," Digby finished firmly.

"Well said," Glyn countered. "Now we understand each

other," and they grinned.

"Of course there's one obvious question," Digby said with considerable warmth. "Just who the hell's the money behind all this? I know damn well it isn't the S.G. or the Organization."

"In many ways Alan, you're going to be the most important man on the ship. But I can't tell you even. Sorry. When it's all over you'll be the first to know though," Tresilian assured him.

"When it's all over . . . you can say that again," the Australian said quietly and changed the subject. "I imagine you heard the Ottawa news last week? What do you think of that?"

Digby was referring to what the world press was calling The 'Great Canadian Compromise.' The 'compromise' was the work of a former Prime Minister of Canada, Richard Duncan. Into his seventies, Duncan, free at least of a party label, devoted himself as a Senator to the consuming cause of national unity. Unburdened, he tested and felt his way along the sensitive quicks in Quebec City, the other provincial capitals and London. Working privately, he made neither sound nor headline and eventually produced a formula.

1. Quebec, all the other nine Provinces and the Northern Territories opted to stay within the New Confederation as set out in the repatriated and newly written Constitution of Canada, which incorporated all the language rights recommended in the Royal Commission on Biculturalism and Bilingualism presented to Parliament late in the Centennial year of 1967.

2. Canada had to become a Republic, replacing the Governor-General with a President as head of state. There republicanism ended — the country holding on to the Parliamentry system. The Crown and all Royal symbols — abolished. The Sovereign was no longer Queen of Canada.

3. The Republic of Canada was not now a member of the Commonwealth. But the country had become the first of a new order — 'Friend of the British Commonwealth.' This last was devoid of all commitments and obligations and was nothing more or less than an emotional comforter.

The 'Duncan Points' had subsequently become the 'Instrument of Canada' copies of which had been signed simultaneously in Ottawa and London on April 11, 1970. Despite predicted storms, a typically enigmatic contentment settled on Canada as the Instrument became inevitable and the country's unity assured.

"Oh, there"ll be some more wailing and teeth gnashing for a while yet in places like Westmount and Victoria, but it'll fizzle out. Just as the rows about the flag and unification of Canadian Armed Forces did," Glyn said, answering Digby. "I remember that row well. About the Services changeover I mean. Let's see, it was in 1968 and I'm positive I was in Montreal at the time. And do you know I can't remember anyone even talking about it. It must have been early February — on or around Groundhog Day. And that was a fairly significant change — no more Royal Canadian Navy or Air Force. And of course we don't even have the Mounties with their Royal prefix any more."

What are they called now?" Bunthorne enquired.

"Just CMP — without the R," Glyn replied.

"The poor old Pommy Empire," Digby ruminated. "As sure as hell the sun's not setting on it now. Oh, my word no. Look at our country. Getting more like America every day."

"Oh, I nearly forgot," Glyn said, motioning to Arthur and Alan with some papers. "Could you take these Articles of Agreement down and get all your people to sign as supernumeraries? They'll be paid a dollar a month from the ship — yes I know the special committee arrangements and that's fine, — but we have international agreements to comply with. Even in Wafrillia they're against slavery, believe it or not. And by signing on a ship for even a dime a month, a person, technically and legally is working for payment. I know it sounds crazy but we have to do it."

Bunthorne and Digby returned with the signed Articles and Michael was with them.

"Michael, tell the Chief Officer to stand by for'ard. We'll heave away in five minutes," Tresilian ordered.

As the anchor broke surface streaming mud and water, the Mate rang the foc's'le bell rapidly to and fro signalling that the flukes were aweigh. Ten minutes later, the pilot launch was alongside as 'Navis Pacifica' slowed to steerage way.

"I'll be off then, Glyn. Good luck," and Bunthorne was already on his way down the ladder.

"Thanks, Arthur — for everything. Give my salaams to

Everest. And Arthur, don't forget to listen," Tresilian called after him.

"Take her to half, full and then ring her away Second Mate. Quartermaster, keep the sea ahead."

CHAPTER 6

With the ship well out in the open sea, Tresilian went below to gather his notes. All was ready in the studio where Digby was also waiting.

"Oh, my word, this takes me back a few years, Glyn. Mind you we didn't have all this modern equipment in those days back in Adelaide, but a microphone's still a microphone, isn't it?" Digby reminisced.

"How long were you on the air?" Glyn asked.

"Oh, about five years. News and commentaries — that kind of stuff. And then I got into the Government broadcasting empire in Canberra, and then into the foreign service. Will you want me to say anything now?"

"Yes, a few words when I'm through. You've got your Divcords selected?"

"Right. I did that in New York. Long before I knew what this craziness was all about. Two men and one woman. Twenty languages and 30 years broadcast experience between them. God knows what the total among all forty eight would come to. But they've been air or producer people at one time or another. Everest told me about the sort of qualifications required. Damn it, I should have twigged it then!"

Many months before, during talks in Montreal, Bunthorne and Tresilian had coined 'Divcords.' These were to be the three Divisional Co-ordinators acting as 'company commanders' to 15 Talkers each, and they would report to Digby.

"Fine," Glyn said, and hit the P.A. microphone switch. This system was a new type with automatically governed amplification. It eliminated the problem of 'feed-back' whistle and meant that in the engine room for example, the sound boosted itself on its own to rise above the roar of machinery, and fell to minimum decibels throughout accommodation spaces.

Tresilian began: "Good afternoon, Ladies and Gentlemen.

This is Glyn Tresilian speaking. This is the first time that I will have spoken to both the sea crew and those of you who embarked today at Cobh about the real purpose of our voyage. We shall call you, the U.N. people, our 'Talkers.' As I explain it to you, you will understand how great the need for security has been. The camouflage story about the ship being converted for satellite communications research' worked perfectly . . . 'Navis Pacifica' has aroused very little interest. Now all that will change, as we begin our work. In a few days, this old, converted 30 year old wartime ship will be known all over the world." He paused, and saw some of the Talkers on the boat deck below as they watched the distant shore line fade. He continued. "About two-and-a-half years ago, without searching for it, I hit upon the idea that has brought us together. If simplicity is the essence of good ideas, it must stand a good chance of working.

"I will not presume to talk about the history of recent world politics with you Talkers. But all of us have in common an overwhelming fear that life may not last much longer on this planet. How many more months, weeks, days, or even hours are there? In Churchill's words, is God 'weary of mankind?' Will He intervene? If we leave it to governments, and that means government on both sides of the ideological blocs, the earth will surely explode in a nuclear holocaust.

"The Peace and Friendship Pact of 1969 was signed in Washington and Moscow. About the only common denominator that one can see between the New West and mainland China is that they are both eager to talk about their 'limitless manpower'."

As Glyn explained the Plan, 'Navis Pacifica' leaned into the building westerly swells when she altered course to round the south coast of Ireland. She began a tender roll, but the stabilisers caught her when the fish-like fins extended out on either midships side.

"For some years in Montreal, as a broadcaster," Glyn elaborated, "I moderated an 'open line' program. In North American commercial radio, you do this most successfully when you pit yourself and your listeners against each other. This is necessary in order to secure the largest possible audience over your competitors. Advertising sponsors want their sales messages to reach the maximum number of people. And so you get your program talked about, and therefore listened to, by getting people to react. The surest and quickest way to do that is to arouse as many of their hostilities as you can. You become, in a sense, a kind of 'hatred broker.' Using all the skills at his command this 'hatred broker' will build a sizeable audience. The shows are successful because there is nothing so fascinating to people as other people."

Tresilian smiled inwardly. God, what wouldn't he give to have the old 'Drom' listening to him now. From the studio porthole he looked down and saw small groups of Talkers chatting hurriedly with each other during the few seconds break that he took to light a cigarette. He guessed that they already knew the Plan.

"I think, as I watch your expressions from up here, that you get the idea. Our mission is to conduct an Open Line program of the World. It has taken well over two years to prepare, and we have called it The Plan. You are all intelligent, experienced and mature people. So I will not doubt you for thinking at first that the scheme is naive. You will also understand that the purchase, conversion and manning of the ship has cost a very great deal of money. The person who has supplied that money might well have been considered naive as well. No one, who thought that, could be more wrong. Commercial fortunes are not built by childish frankness.

"Now, we are not going out to try and reform the world — or change it. But halt it — yes. We are going to talk and we are going to let the people talk — to each other. When I spoke to your Arthur Bunthorne once, he asked me why the idea had not been used for the unification of my own adopted country, Canada. To bind French and English together. It couldn't be done because of the restraining broadcasting laws of a country that needed a good bi-lingual coast-to-coast program more desperately than anything in its history. It needed then, as the world needs today, a tool that can make people, rather than government, sovereign.

"I am convinced that, if the people of Canada had been able to talk to each other in this fashion, air their grievances and problems publicly, wash away prejudices, and in so doing find out how much they had in a common cause, the country would have been united a long time ago.

"Now, the 'Navis Pacifica' is of course, a pirate ship. But without contraband for profit. It is true that we shall be swamping wavelengths and frequencies — but our programming will be free. We have no rate cards on board.

"Get the world talking, listening, understanding. I think you all know Alan Digby, who's in the studio with me now. You'll be under his general broadcast direction. What follows is vital. We shall make no attempt to foment insurrections or to upset any status quo's that could harm anyone anywhere. We shall make no calls to civil disobedience. We shall not foster revolt. But we shall mobilise public opinion throughout the world so that maximum pressures will be brought on governments everywhere to recognize the prime need of people — to be alive. Somehow governments must be told by those they are supposed to serve how wrong their policies of nationalism are. They must be told again and again and again, that their employers — not they — are supreme.

"Nor shall we stray or wander from the main point. It will not be our aim to argue regional domestic politics. If there is no world, there will be no local issues. Nor shall we propagandize. This is no Radio Moscow, Voice of America or any other one-directional pulpit. 'Navis Pacifica' has been transformed into the greatest communications switchboard in the world. We will soon explain the technology to you. But we are able, with your linguistic and broadcasting talents, to air simultaneously translated conversations between the world, transmitted to the world. The computers we have on board put us in a unique position of being able to bounce our signals off orbital space satellite hardware right round the clock.

"As soon as I have finished these remarks, I look forward to meeting you all personally. And I know that you'll have a great many questions. But there is one that you're probably asking now — how do you conduct such a world dialogue with people in countries where telephone systems are primitive or non existent? We've been able to solve that problem with an idea from the old 'Man from Uncle.' Basically those little communicators that Messrs. Solo and Kuriyakin used will be dropped in large quantities by the two helijets we have on board.

"Highly transistorised and powerful, they are easy to operate

— even by the illiterate.

"Even in the most primitive areas in the world today, small transistor radio sets abound — and as we swamp them, you will be required to explain the simple instructions for the operation of these little electronic telephones. You will also ask the people to pass them from hand to hand, in an inland direction so that we can get the maximum possible penetration.

"Ladies and Gentlemen, you are all schooled, in one form or another, in the broadcast medium. We all know that when it comes to programming, nothing succeeds like the word of mouth. We must work quickly, so that the Plan can become a Domino Theory too."

It was time to stop; the Talkers were restless. Either they thought he was mad, or, hopefully, they wanted to put the Plan to work.

"To conclude, here is our schedule. For the next two days we shall proceed to and steam off the north of Scotland in the vicinity of the Shetland Islands. This will give us all an opportunity to get acquainted — and you'll be able to familiarise yourselves with the equipment and studios. Then we will start. The itinerary is as follows. The Gulf of Bothnia to work Scandinavia, Northern Europe and the Soviet Union; then through the Mediterranean to work on the Middle East area off Israel and Egypt; I'm hoping that President Amir might give us dispensation to go through the Suez Canal — there is a channel of sufficient width for a ship of our size to use. After that we'll go down the Red Sea, working the Persian Gulf and the west coasts of India and Pakistan; then it'll be south down the Mozambique channel to East and South Africa. There's no more Panama Canal, so we'll work right round the South Americas passing through the Magellan straits. The Californian coast will be next, then across the Pacific to Japan, Gulf of Pohai off Taku Bar, Peoples' China. From there we'll go to Hong Kong for a rest and repairs. We'll need it, because after that it'll be Vietnam possibly — and Korea definitely.

"You may ask why we don't go to Asia now, because that's where the greatest danger is. True. But I'm convinced that we'll have an altogether better chance, if behind us we've got a tidal wave of mass reason going for us. Especially if we're able by that time to show actual examples of loosened tensions.

"This is my first command. It will be the only one. I know from experience how good a happy ship can be. Let us all do everything we can to make this voyage the most enriching thing we have ever done.

"Thank you, and bon voyage. Now, here's Alan Digby."

Glyn got up to stretch his legs. His hand shook slightly as he fumbled for a cigarette. How had they taken it? Was it too long? Digby began.

"Thank you Captain. I know I speak for all the Talkers, as you call us, when I give you our assurance that we shall follow you wherever you're going to take this ship. There will be a general meeting in the lounge after dinner. I'd like to see the Divcords there now. Thank you."

.   .   .   .

'Navis Pacifica' rounded the island of Bornholm in the Baltic sea and set course for Kokkola on the Finnish side of the Gulf of Bothnia. The Plan was about to start. Lying off the port, called Gamlakarleby in Swedish, Tresilian ordered the telescopic transmitter mast extended. The helijets idled on the after deck. Talkers manned the microphones in their sound proof booths in two rows of twelve in the Main Studio. Digby checked that they all had their opening scripts at the ready and that their headphones were comfortable. Behind the glass in the Master Control Room, the Chief Operator dropped his hand in cue. The 'Navis Pacifica' was on the air.

And at that instant, radio listeners from Murmansk to the Falkland Islands, from Yokohama to Lisbon, in their cars, in their homes, on their bicycles and as they walked carrying their sets, heard these words, in their own languages.

"People of the world. The voice you are hearing is coming to you from the studios of the 'Navis Pacifica' lawfully sailing under the flag of the West African Republic.

"At this moment we are between Kokkola and Umea in the Gulf of Bothnia. Two minutes ago, our helicopters with special electronic telephones left the ship for a drop on the Swedish and Finnish sides of the Gulf. You can also reach us by phoning our special international telephone number: 99-405-999-9999. These communicators will be used so that we can bring the people of the world together for a global discussion in all the principal languages.

"By this means we hope to destroy the barriers of suspicion and hatred and so lessen the ever increasing chance of nuclear war. We are a group of internationalists who believe that man, if not his governments, can live in peace. We are supra national and supra ideological. We apologise in advance to those who own the frequencies we shall be pirating as we go about our mission. But we shall not cease to use the airwaves until we have exhausted the formidable human and technical resources on this ship, so that the human race can express itself. Our aims are: understanding; tolerance; and co-existence. As soon as we have some Scandinavian people speaking to us from the shore we will interrupt your programs again. Please stand by."

In Master Control, the operators 'cut' all output except in the pre-planned areas where the helicopters were dropping the Tronphones in parcels of fifty.

People in those parts of Finland, Sweden, and the Soviet Union were asked to turn the dial switch until the distinctive high pitched beep . . . beep . . . beep had disappeared. This would tell the 'communicators' that they were tuned to the ship, and they could listen through the tiny ear piece attached. When their turns came to speak the cue would be one long 'beeep.'

Men, women and children came running out of houses and cars. The canisters with 50 fat pen like objects in each of them were hastily opened as the helijets soared away. Soon, the first caller, a school teacher, was on the air and the rest of the world heard the conversation as it was simultaneously translated into 23 other languages by teams of two Talkers — working the ship-shore dialogue at the same time.

"Talk of the World, you're on the air — go ahead," the Talker said in Swedish.

"Yes, what's this all about?"

"Exactly what we said in our introduction a few minutes ago."

"But it's illegal, surely."

"No, sir. We're outside territorial limits."

"Even so, you can't take over frequencies just like this. Doesn't the U.N. control communications through one of its agencies?"

"Yes."

"Well what about it? Surely they haven't sanctioned this."

"No sir. They haven't. And you're right in saying that we are pirating radio wavelengths. And we're prepared to take the consequences of that as an alternative to annihilation. Anyway, sir, what do you think about the world situation?"

"Do you mean to say that my voice is being heard all over the world — just by speaking into this thing?" the Swede asked.

"It could be — but all your words and mine in Swedish are being instantly translated into the world's principal languages — and that of course is being heard right round the earth. In your own country they're listening to us direct of course. But that shouldn't startle anyone as our scientists receive radio signals from planets several light years away. But what views do you have on the prospect of world peace?"

"I don't know that there are any prospects. Certainly the danger is very great. But I can't see any progress being made until Red China gets a seat in the U.N."

"That seems as unlikely now as it was years ago. Because they won't go in unless Taiwan gets out."

"Who's paying for that ship you're on?"

"That can't be divulged."

"You say the vessel's registered in the West African Republic. Are they behind it?"

"No. But thanks for talking with us." Glyn had instructed the talkers to cut them off gently when talk veered from peace.

"Yes, hello?" a perturbed female voice came on the air.

"Go ahead."

"Am I on?"

"Yes, you are, madam. Go right ahead please."

"Now then. Is this some communist plot? How dare you interrupt the radio like that. But you won't last long. I hope they bomb you. Quickly."

"Talk of the World. Go ahead please."

"Oh, good; thank you," said another woman. "This is the most wonderful thing that's happened. Will you be going all over the world — letting people speak like this?"

"Yes, that is our intention."

"Well God speed to you all, whoever you may be. I graduated in communication arts at Uppsala and I can see the enormous impact that this global dialogue will have on governments. And about time too; I take it that you'll be asking people —

literally — to drive their leaders to peace. To forget about the rights and wrongs of offence and aggression if only for a day, and concentrate on the dehumanisation of war for a change."

"That, madam, is the essence of our scheme precisely, but then, with your background you should get the point fairly quickly, eh?"

"OK," and the pleasant sounding woman laughed. "I won't keep you any longer. Not with the whole world waiting to talk to you. But I'll get the ball rolling here at Umea. I'll write the Prime Minister at once. Although I think you'll agree that as a country, our peace record hasn't been too bad. But I hope everyone in the world will bring every possible pressure to bear — and we may still have a chance. Did you read 'On the Beach' by Nevil Shute?"

"Yes, and I saw the movie too." Svensen, the Swedish Talker replied.

"Good. Well I would say that what you're doing on that ship, 'Navis Pacifica' — what a lovely sounding name, will do more than anything to keep 'On the Beach' in the fiction category."

The helijets ran their shuttle services dropping Tronphones as the ship steamed south down the gulf at half speed. Using the special 'add-on' device in 'Navis Pacifica's' Master Control, Swedes, Russians, and Finns, up to five at a time were able to speak to each other and could be heard by the world.

Russian: "If this is some propaganda plot to infiltrate the Soviet Union then . . ."

Finn: "Why don't you people listen for a change? Didn't you hear what they said? That's exactly what it's not."

Swede: "I understand the point clearly — I heard the opening statement in my car. All I can say is that if all governments behaved like ours have done for so long, there'd be peace alright. When did you last . . ."

Russian: "That's a typical Swedish myth! You're not without imperialist aims. What about the unfair system . . ."

Talker: "That'll be all thank you, gentlemen. You're on the air to get on — not to quarrel. And we don't care how many times we have to say that either." He broke the 'add-on' connection and went on to the next Tronphone cue.

"Talk of the World, you're on the air — go ahead please . . ."

The Helijets had managed to drop some canisters just inside the Soviet frontier. Other Tronphones had been passed by hand across the border. At intervals of not more than ten minutes, the Talkers urged the people who had the little communicators, to circulate them quickly, or to get on the nearest telephone.

Within hours, the Plan became front page and headline news everywhere. The Headquarters of the International Telecommunications Union in Geneva were bombarded with protests from member nations. Private and government communicators dropped other business to deal with, as one put it, 'this abominable piracy — this monstrous liberty.' Some called for an immediate arrest and or sinking of the ship. Others hurriedly tried to devise technical obstacles to block the ship's power.

All naval shipping in the area was told to proceed at utmost speed to the 'Navis Pacifica' and stand by. Soon the warships were joined by airplanes of neighbouring European air forces.

"Well, how about that Glyn?" Digby said to Tresilian on the bridge as more and more ships and aircraft approached. "I always did like company. We Aussies are very sociable people — as I've told you before."

"Mmm. I only hope they don't want to stay the night though. They must know where we're bound. See — there's Hangô, there to port. We're just about in the Gulf of Findland now. And I really want to make some drops over Leningrad, Tallin, Parnu, Riga, and Gdansk. That's about as much as we'll be able to do on the Curtain side right now. But it should be enough. We're only the spark plug; sorry if I've been over-working that one. Any doubts about radio, Alan?" he asked.

"Well, I never did have any doubts about radio — if that's what you mean. But I just couldn't see this lot working — you know, the Plan. It's working — but I'm not sure this is what you had in mind." And the Australian waved his arm at the gathering air and sea armada. "Well, well, look at that. With all these electronic marvels we've got aboard you still need the old morse code eh?"

"Yes," and Glyn grabbed the Aldis signalling lamp from a shelf in the wheelhouse. The low flying piston engined reconnaissance plane circled and made a series of short and long flashes. Tresilian aimed the light and replied with one long 'T'.

"Where bound?" the NATO marked aircraft asked.

"Gulf of Finland and Baltic Sea. Then English Channel," Glyn answered.

"What ports?"

"None. Off shore cruising in international waters."

"What intention?"

"Dropping Tronphone canisters for 'Talk of the World'," explained 'Navis Pacifica' at six words a minute. The plane flew off.

The ship was followed to the Skagerrak as the talk grew and grew. In the small newsroom alongside the studios, the Talkers saw reams of wire copy about themselves spewing out of the teleprinters.

One government, it was rumoured, had already asked for an immediate session of the Security Council. The Secretary-General was reported to have requested detailed accounts from all pro-testing countries, setting out the precise threats to world security that the ship was posing.

On a Tronphone from Kristiansand, a Norwegian caller asked. "How many languages can you use?"

"Twenty four principal tongues and the lesser spoken ones as well," came the reply from 'Navis Pacifica.'

"Will you list them please?"

"Certainly. In order of most usage they are: Northern Chinese (Mandarin), English, Great Russian, Hindustani, Spa-nish, German, Japanese, Bengali, Arabic, Portugese, French, Malay, Italian, Urdu, Cantonese, Javanese, Telegu, Ukranian, Wu, Tamil, Min, Korean, Marathi, Polish. Those are the world's principal language groups — but as I said before we can, bet-ween us, speak every language there is — but can't guarantee our accents all the time." Svensen said.

"How many are there of you on that ship?"

"Forty eight linguists — but then there is the crew as well. And the satellite computer experts, and the helicopter pilots, and the broadcasting operators and technicians. We also have with us a doctor and two nurses. And there are many cooks and stewards too. Hold on a minute. The Captain's just come into the studio. I'll ask him how many people there are on the 'Navis Pacifica.' You speak English? Yes, good."

Glyn leaned over Svensen's shoulder. He'd be on the ship's air for the first time. He grinned as he considered the size of the vast world wide audience that would hear his words before they reached the other end of the studio. What old Burt wouldn't give to have ratings like this.

"It's good to be talking to you sir, in Kristiansand. All told we have 136 people aboard. But that includes my wife and son. What kind of work do you do sir?" Tresilian asked, tasting again the urgent flavour of an 'open line.'

"I'm a clerk at the town hall here. In the rates office. I think this is a great scheme you're working on — but I don't know how far you'll get with it. I suggest you get those helicopters to pick up some newspapers. They're just full of it. It looks as if you've got the whole world up in arms. The government radio says you have no right to fly helicopters over people's coasts; and certainly not to take over the radio wavelengths."

"Do you think we're doing a bad thing then?" Glyn asked him.

"No, I don't personally. After all, as your people are telling us all the time, if governments would make the world secure, your idea wouldn't be necessary. But that's just my idea. And who am I? No, you'll never get away with it. They won't let you get very far. You'll be lucky to get past the straits of Dover," the voice from the Tronphone said matter-of-factly.

"Who are they, sir?" Glyn asked.

"Well, you know. They. The people who can blow you up, or sink you, or stop you. Or something."

"Why should they want to do that?"

"Because, well. I don't know. You're stirring people up I suppose."

"Why are we stirring people up, sir?"

"Yes, well, that's the point, I agree."

"You see, just a moment ago you said, 'but who am I?' You sir," Tresilian said, "are millions and millions of people. And you are that at this very instant. Because that number of human beings are listening to every single word you're saying. And if we're stirring them, and I agree we are, and we're going to go on stirring them, it's because we want them to stir their governments. There is no other way that I can see of forcing governments into political sanity," warming to the old 'Crakkerjack Line' style. "One thing is certain. I was not born, and you were

— 308 —

not born and our children were not born to stop bullets in Asia and Latin America and the Middle East. And I'm more than damn sure, that every single human being who's alive today wasn't born to die by the blast or the burn of an H-bomb. When it comes to global suicide, the rights and wrongs of who started the bush fires and who didn't, of charge and counter charge, are as out of place as a doctor at a Christian Science convention," Tresilian said feelingly and left Svensen with the microphone.

"That was great stuff, Glyn," Digby said a few minutes later in the chartroom. "Heard it on the lounge monitor. That must have been quite a show you did in Montreal."

Tresilian, noting some bearings on the chart, said. "Oh, I don't know. I think it wasn't too bad towards the end — but it was bloody awful at first. I loved it though. Do you have any open line shows 'down under'?"

"I'm not sure. I heard a little talk about it a year or so ago. I think some stations did send people over to the States on look-see assignments," and he followed Glyn out to the starboard wing of the bridge.

Tresilian shaped the ship down on courses that took her close into the West German and Dutch coasts — but always outside territorial limits. Due to the low lying terrain, the helicopters with their special long range tanks were able to make drops at considerable distances inland. On reaching the Hook of Holland, they started the 'Tronphone service' over East Anglia, the Thames Estuary and Belgium. A few hours later, they were flying over France between Calais and Cherbourg. By this time, 'Navis Pacifica' was surrounded by units of the British Home Fleet as she steamed down Channel to Ushant and the Mediterranean. And all the while consternation, rage and puzzlement grew in official circles everywhere around the globe.

In South East England the Tronphones went rapidly from hand to hand. Glyn was annoyed to find that exchanges between French and British listeners became vituperative. Many fought Vichy and Laval again. Arguments raged to and fro across the Channel as Englishmen hurled what they doubtless thought was justifiable abuse at the aging, but still very much alive and stubborn President. de Gaulle in keeping Britain out of the

E.C.C. had also provoked the U.K. into a total trading halt with France. All the rancour of Dunkirk, ingratitude and misplaced arrogance was repeated many times over.

"This isn't the idea at all," he said to Digby as they listened in Tresilian's day-room. "We'll have to speak to those Talkers again. They must get rid of this crap. I'm taking over for a while", and he left for the studios. Motioning the French Talker, St. Onge, out of his seat, he sat down and spoke in English.

"This is Glyn Tresilian speaking, Master of the 'Navis Pacifica.' I want to tell our British and French listeners that our purpose in this venture is to help people in the world to get on. Not to fall out. And above all our aim is to persuade human beings into forcing governments to stop the senseless and wanton killing in Asia, and then to see to it that every single nation has a seat at the U.N. Furthermore governments must be led, and if necessary driven into giving the Organization full powers to police compulsory multilateral nuclear disarmament . . . the whole point therefore, of 'Talk of the World' is to set an example to governments. The Plan that we have evolved is rooted in the premise that governments either cannot or will not coexist — but that people can, want to, and will. This can't be emphasized enough. Now, obviously, we must have government in some form. Without it, there is anarchy and mob rule. That is why we are stressing that the very last call we want to make and will never make is to disobedience and insurrection. But we do want you to talk to each other and to your legislators and argue. But do so constructively.

"I was listening, just now, to the quarrels between Frenchmen and Englishmen. We didn't drop the Tronphones and open our telephone lines so that you could bicker like children. We can't set the clock back to 1939. I'll take the next call. 'Talk of the World' — go ahead please."

"Yes, I will," a man in Sussex said. "Look you silver tongue bastard — tell me something will you? Just who in hell do you think you are, coming . . ."

"I don't have to think about that, sir. I happen to know," and Tresilian tasted the relish of past battles. As long as they took it out on him and the Plan — it would be alright. He'd warned the Talkers to encourage listeners to use this safety valve. He'd learned its value long ago.

" 'Talk of the World,' go ahead," Tresilian said.

"Mr. Trevelyan — or whatever your name is. You have no right to be doing this. I'm not going to swear — as that rude man in Sussex did just now — but I do agree with him. You're cutting into people's favourite radio programs all over the world. And while I expect you're probably quite sincere trying to promote peace in this way — you're still breaking the law. There was a TV program about it last night. They showed aerial films of your ship, and the man said that you're definitely operating illegally. It was on the BBC for an hour and they had lots of experts. One of them said that even though your ship wasn't actually sailing in anyone's territorial waters, those helicopters you've got were actually a part of the ship. And by flying over land they were committing violations. He said they were dijury extensions or something like that. He said the International Telecommunications Union will have to act," the woman said.

"Really?" Glyn came back. "This is very interesting, madam. Tell me more."

"Well, one of the MP's said that the Navy should seize you. And open fire if you didn't stop."

"Who was that?"

"Iain Partridge."

"Oh, I see." Tresilian recognised the name of the opposition party's best known hawk. "Tell me, did anyone think the Plan might be a good idea?"

"No, I don't think so. In fact I'm positive they didn't. I watched it all very carefully."

"Who were the experts you mention?"

"Well they were politicians mainly. And there were a couple of international lawyers. But they only answered questions about the regulations and things."

"Thank you very much madam and goodbye. We apologise again to everyone for interrupting their favourite programs from time to time. And now, I understand, we've just been joined, on the radio telephone from New York, by Dr. Franklin Gunter. All those with Tronphones can speak to him direct in English or through our simultaneous translations. How do you hear us Doctor?"

"Clear and well, thank you."

"How is the Plan being received in the United States?" Glyn

asked the world famous urologist, so closely associated with the work of peace movements.

"With very mixed feelings," Gunter answered. "There seems to be no other topic of conversation here. The three networks have already urged the President to 'have done with this flagrant piracy' as they call it. You're cutting into their key stations. Personally, as a result of what you're doing, I feel more optimistic about the world's survival than I have for some time."

"Some years ago you were very pessimistic weren't you?"

"Yes. In 1968, when we marched and demonstrated, people would tell me to behave and wait for the election of that fall. My answer to that was 'I don't know if there will be a United States in the fall of '68.' But in those days the main difficulty lay in trying to persuade the U.S. and USSR to give up some of their sovereignty to strengthen the United Nations. That's all changed of course since the Peace and Friendship Pact as we're all on the same team now. But the merger just makes the ultimate conflict with China twice as dangerous."

"A lot of us know, but I'll ask the question again, Dr. Gunter. Why, when you could have retired comfortably, did you take on this crusade for peace and all the confusion and commotion of protest politics?"

"I'll be glad to give the answer again. It's because I don't see the point of parents working and sacrificing to bring healthy, well adjusted children into the world if the children are going to be incinerated. I said that in the sixties — and I say it again now in 1970. But I don't know how much longer I'll be able to go on saying it."

"You know, and the whole listening world knows," Tresilian declared, "that we're persuading people to rise above their governments and settle for co-existence, a strong and fully seated United Nations and then of course, if it's not a pipe dream, compulsory multilateral nuclear disarmament. Now we know that nationalism, and as Eisenhower put it, the military and industrial complexes are the real devils, but what is a specific target that the people in a new mobilisation could attack? Through our ship you can reach the world. What advice will you give?"

"That's fairly simple," Gunter came back. "I mean the right advice to give. Let's hope to God some people will take it. You see, the whole defence thing all around the earth is a self-perpetuating escalation. And governments will always vote the money for more arms. It's a good way of being patriotic; and it's always good politics to bring more defence industry into an area. And the press is nearly always in favour. Municipal government is eager for more defence industry. But, and this is where you come in, Mr. Tresilian. It is only the people who are going to be burned up by this, who have an interest in keeping it down. I think they can best do this by letting their governments know that they're listening to you — and if they take a sane view of the world situation, then surely they — governments — will support what you're doing. The immediate pressure that people should apply now is to ensure that their leaders don't stop your voyage by force. I never did fully understand what your Pierre Elliott Trudeau meant by the 'tyranny of public opinion,' but if that's the kind of tyranny that'll get some peace going in the world, I don't think we can ever get enough of it.

"But," Gunter went on as millions listened, "with every hour that passes, I think your operation becomes safer. It would have to be a very foolhardy or insensitive government indeed that would order your capture now. A few days have been enough time for you to light the fuse. That's obvious. Despite the fact that you may not have a legal leg to stand on, you can't be aware of the world wide impact you've already achieved. I think you've really caught governments with their trousers down. God knows how you did it. But I'm delighted. Of course you realize that had you people tried this in sixty eight or last year before the Peace and Friendship Pact was signed, you'd have been branded as Kremlin agents on the one hand — and CIA men on the other. Governments are the same the world over — and so, thank God are people. It's only from them that the solution may come." And the controversial kidney specialist was off the air.

"Talk of the World — go ahead please."

"Oui — bonjour, Monsieur, je . . ."

"Un moment, s'il vous plaît, Monsieur," Tresilian said and put on his head-set as Jean-Pierre Malenfant, the French Talker, took over.

"Bon," the Tronphoner from Caen continued. "Tell me. What is your range? For how long can you sail without a port of call?" the Frenchman wanted to know.

"Er, wait a moment please," Malenfant hesitated, as Tresilian

— 313 —

waved him off. There was dead air for a few seconds as Malenfant tried to interpret the signal. Quickly Glyn gave the 'cut'
sign to the operator in Master Control who despressed the main
output switch killing all microphones instantly. The world waited
for the answer. He spoke to the Talkers urgently.

"Look, that's a curve, don't attempt to answer. Just say,
Jean-Pierre, that we don't know our precise maximum range
and for obvious reasons wouldn't want to divulge our first port
of call anyway. For God's sake don't say anything about Hong-
Kong. O.K." he said and pressed the talk back button to Master
Control, "get back on the air."

.   .   .   .

In Montreal, Glyn's old friend Burt Brewster, wrestled with
the same problem that had come to the managers of all similar
broadcasting operations in North America, Europe, Australia,
New Zealand, South Africa, and in every country with commercial radio. Wholesale cancellations of advertising contracts
by local and national sponsors and their advertising agencies
threatened the survival of the stations. 'Navis Pacifica' had
shown herself to be indifferent to the sanctity of commercial
messages which, all over the world, were often cut off in mid
jingle or sentence. Brewster himself had bordered dangerously
close to apoplexy when he heard first the name, and then the
voice of Tresilian. Good, safe accounts were flying out of CRAK
and into competitive stations not affected by 'Navis Pacifica.'
The same thing was happening everywhere. Private radio asso-
ciations in Canada and the U.S. met hurriedly in convenient
centres to plan retaliatory action.

Out of one of these urgent councils, came an agreement to
request international and all oil companies to withold fuel from
the ship. In this way, whether governments or the I.T.U. acted
or not, the piracy, it was felt, could only last for a limited and
roughly predictable period. The oil companies, believing they
would score one of the greatest public relations coups in history,
agreed.

Brewster wasn't at all sure that this oil ban would work.
He'd have to think of something better. Desolate, all alone, he
went for beer.

"Yeah, four beers. Might as well order 'em while we can,"
he said mournfully in studio 4. "If that goddam Tresilian keeps

— 314 —

that bastard ship going another day, I'll be in here tomorrow washing dishes," he said to Henri, the waiter.

"What're you talking about Burt? Hell, Tresilian's got it made for you," the genial French Canadian said putting the glasses on the table.

"Now, what's that crap supposed to mean?"

"Well, you like listeners don't you? Yes? Well, you sure got 'em now. The whole town's tuned to you."

"What the hell's the good of that if all your goddam sponsors are taking off," the Drom drank deeply and put the glass down. He picked it up again, put it to his lips but stopped short of the swallow. He banged the glass down loudly, and stared at Henri for several seconds. Then he banged the glass again. "Goddam it, Henri," he roared and grabbing his hat, left the tavern, and three full beers untouched. He ran the short distance to the station, and reaching for breath, shouted for his secretary.

"Get me Westall on the phone," he gasped, "right away. Pull him out of lunch, bed, the can — I don't give a damn where he is. Just get him. Now."

Half a minute later, the General Cosmetics executive was on the phone.

"What's up Burt? I've got an important lunch and I'm late already. Just going out of the door when you called. Can't it wait till I get back?"

"No, it sure as hell can't, Bob," the still breathless Brewster pressed. "I just left a table full of beer in Studio 4. That'll tell you how important it is. Look, Bob. I want you to let me have $2,500 over budget right away."

"What? With all your sponsors can . . .?"

"That's the whole goddam point, Bob. Just let me have it — that's all. I want to call a special rating survey. Now listen. I wasn't wrong about Tresilian before. Right? Right. Then just trust me this time. If it doesn't work, I'll pay the whole goddam lot back myself — and I'll give you that in writing. It's the most surefire hunch I've ever had."

Brewster got the money. A week later the audience measurement company that had conducted an unusually large sample survey confirmed that 70 per cent of sets in use in the Greater Montreal area were tuned to CRAK. And this included both

French and English speaking listeners. For the first time in history, Montreal was no longer a 'split' market. Within hours of the figures being published, similar surveys were taken everywhere and usurped commercial stations around the world retrieved not only the accounts they had lost, but because of watertight guarantees to 'make good' any and all interrupted commercials, ended up with more business than they had ever done before. As always, the 'numbers game' proved the most popular to play. Every thirty minutes, the affected stations broadcast their warning disclaimers. These recorded announcements freed them from all association with 'Navis Pacifica's' program content.

At CRAK, Brewster took special relish in promoting the broadcasts as coming from "our own Glyn Tresilian." Once onto the thing, the Drom didn't miss a trick. In fact, in both Canada and the U.S., the Drom gained a certain esteem among radio pros for having discovered the 'peace nut.'

CHAPTER 7

'Navis Pacifica' steamed south across the Bay of Biscay, down the coast of Portugal, through the straits of Gibraltar and into the tideless Mediterranean. As the weather warmed, so did the spirits of those aboard the peace ship. Tresilian took her close into Sardinia, and then south through the Messina straits, dropping Tronphones everywhere. From the Ionian, Adriatic, Aegean and Black seas, the helijets made long range flights servicing the 'soft under belly' countries of Europe. Soon, 'Talk of the World' carried the voices of people in Bulgaria, and Romania; Yugoslavia and Hungary, Austria and Czechoslovikia. The 'curtain' countries were all parties to the Peace and Friendship pact. There were Tronphone drops as well over Turkey, Cyprus and Crete. Ships and aircraft of all the nations whose coasts she approached circled and watched 'Navis Pacifica' and her jet helicopters without pause. Tresilian and Digby knew, as the haze of Port Said lifted, that the first real test was upon them.

"Well, do you think he'll let us through?" Digby asked Tresilian as the ship closed in.

"I hope so. I think it'll depend on how we get on after some Tronphone work. Half ahead. Get some bearings, Second Mate. Keep her 15 miles off everything — not an inch closer. Ah, there he is — see him?" and he passed the binoculars to Digby.

The Australian made the fairly considerable focus adjustment to suit his own normal eyesight. "Well, so he is. The old bastard's lasted a long time eh? Must be symbolic." The statue of Ferdinand de Lesseps, creator of the Suez Canal, came clearing through the powerful lenses.

"Did you get through to Amir on the R/T just now?"

"Well, I got through to his press officer. He was obviously pondering what to do. This guy sounded pretty non-committal. Said they had a feeling it was all an Israeli plot and that American Zionists were probably financing us. But he did say

Amir would probably go on the air. And for the time being at least they wouldn't take any action against people who talked on the Tronphones. If he does let us pass it'll cost a packet. And to make it even easier he's got no pilots. I'd have to take her through myself — but there's one consolation — we won't have to tie up anywhere for convoy passing. Only at night. You know Alan, I'm a damn fool. I had about two and a half years and unlimited funds to prepare for this junket. And I was absolutely sure that by the time we left the Mersey I hadn't forgotten one single bloody thing. Big or small. I've got information charts on every inch of the Suez Canal — but I didn't think of the searchlight. In normal times the Canal company did all that for you of course. But no more. On the very rare occasions that they'll let you through, you're on your own. No pilot, boatmen, or searchlight. And if anything happens — well, goodnight. Frankly it scares the sh . . ." Before he could finish, Tresilian and Digby were interrupted by the Irish Chief Master Control operator who came running into the wheelhouse.

"Excuse me Captain — and Mr. Digby," he said, as he gulped and caught his breath, "but we have a Monsignor something or other from the Vatican on the R/T. He says he's one of the Pope's private secretaries and," he rushed on with mounting excitement, "he says that the Holy Father has been following our progress with the greatest interest and he says that if we would like it, he'll go on the air himself. The Pope I mean. Now, if you wish."

Astonished, Tresilian and Digby looked at each other for an instant. "Second Mate," he shouted to the officer-of-the-watch at the compass platform on the Monkey Island above, "take her will you? Stop her when you get to that position. I'll be in the studio if you want me."

Digby went into the Italian Talker's booth while Tresilian rapidly checked that all was well in Master Control. Particularly the documentary disc recording system that caught and filed every syllable of the Plan.

Here would be something to play back . . . The Pope's personal blessing. Things can't be going too badly. And how good of him to be the only one besides Gunter to accept the ship's repeated invitations to world figures and everyone else to join 'Talk of the World' at any time through regular telephone.

"Stand by please, 'Navis Pacifica'," an Italian voice said from the Papal apartments in the Vatican. "His Holiness is ready to speak."

The Pontiff's slightly high pitched voice bounced off the 'Navis Pacifica's' complex nerve centre, soared to the ionosphere and sounded in a billion ears. His words were flung around the continents as orbital satellites swallowed and spat them back to earth.

"People of the world. We give our heartfelt blessing to the work of the 'Navis Pacifica.' We give it unhesitatingly and unconditionally, and we shall pray for those who sail with her. We are glad mankind is capable of such technological excellence in the field of world wide communications. And we rejoice at the use to which it is being put on the 'Navis Pacifica.' Like one of our predecessors, we are also 'afraid for our children.' But with every passing hour we are encouraged that the peoples of the world are trying hard to break down the barriers of hatred and prejudice, and are finding through their talking together that the Saviour gave to his children the grace to forebear and to love. Although our words do not comprise an encyclical, we ask mankind to respond to the warming influence of the peace ship's broadcasts. And from the Eternal City of Rome, we ask our Bishops, Priests and laiety to pray for the success and safety of the ship. Pacem in Terris. In the name of the Father, the Son and the Holy Ghost, Amen."

The Holy Father's imprimatur hit with unparalled force. Tresilian returned to the bridge, verified that the 'Navis Pacifica' was well within international water, and went down to his dayroom. Julie put down her knitting and poured a cup for him from the pot of tea she'd brewed.

"Well, how about that?" he said and took off his cap.

"Marvellous. I wonder what'll happen now?"

Glyn turned up the volume control on the cabin speaker which always carried an English translation of whatever was being transmitted. As the sound came on, they listened to a tirade from a Tronphoner in Algiers who now knew for certain that the whole sinister scheme was hatched up and paid for by the Roman Catholic Church. Only they, the near hysterical man screemed to the world, would have enough money and wickedness to do it.

The Pontiff's statement brought the first massive editorial reaction. While the 'Navis Pacifica' had been front page news on a sporadic basis, even a curiosity item to some newspapers, the Pope's declaration changed all that.

In Dublin, one commentator put the Pope's approval this way.

"Whatever else the 'Navis Pacifica' will or will not achieve, it may have put God, temporarily at any rate, on His feet. If the ship's voyage were not a prime topic of world conversation today, people would discuss the second Korean and Vietnam wars, the conflicts in Central America and the racial strife in America. Too, they would agonize over the Arab Israeli fighting, the terrors of the H-Bomb, and the 'Is God dead?' issue.

It is true that since the new reformation, the churches of all denominations have done little or nothing to answer that question for a confused and troubled world. Until, perhaps, an hour ago when the Pope took his unprecedented stand.

Be sure that his short statement was a model of directness. The Holy Father offered not a word of apology or explanation.

For governments there was the icy vacuum of being ignored. But did not governments themselves ignore him after his 1965 address to them at the United Nations — when he exhorted them to search for peace and an end to hunger?

Had he, before his broadcast through 'Navis Pacifica,' consulted with the Sacred College or the Curia? One doubts it.

For it is no secret that His Holiness has long regarded the international situation and the survival of mankind as matters 'In Extremis.' We believe he acted arbitrarily on the strength of divine inspiration.

How will the churches react? Will we, today or tomorrow, as the 'Navis Pacifica's' broadcasts swamp our wireless programs, hear from the Archbishop of Canterbury? And Archbishop Makarios? The Moderator of the Church of Scotland? The Chief Rabbi and other religious

— 320 —

leaders? And will they as readily support this talk of the world?

We are pleased that the Pontiff took this action. We are glad if only because here at long last is an example of uncompromising definition.

Leadership, Your Holiness. We crave it. You have given us a good taste. And like Oliver, we want some more."

After the ship's first transmission from Scandinavia, the world press had generally rolled over and winked at what one called the 'virtuous pirate.' Leading articles almost without exception mildly scoffed at the seriousness of the Plan's objectives — but all conceded the brilliant electronics technology behind it. The Editor's letters pages were filled with questions and some very amusing explanations. One German correspondent insisted that the ship's transmitters could only get their enormous power from a 'boost' supplied by a shepherding interplanetary spaceship.

Other writers urged their governments to increase the weight of their protests through governing bodies like Canada's Radio and T.V. Commission, the United States' Federal Communications Commission, and through North America's NORBA — a Canada-US-Mexico agreement. But nearly every country was complaining furiously to the ITU in Geneva and readers' encouragement was unnecessary.

With the Papal imprimatur, journalistic winking ceased. Several newspaper stopped their presses just in time. A Montreal paper, with an editorial put to bed declaring that at least 'Navis Pacifica's' open line programming was more civilised than Tresilian's previous offerings, hastily did a rewrite affirming that the Pope's hortatory words were in the spirit of Cardinal Leger's brave example when the former Archbishop of Montreal cast off the grandeur of episcopal office to work for lepers in Africa.

Other editorials:

CHICAGO GAZETTE

"In God We Trust — yes. In letting the church meddle in international politics — no. With offence to no one, we reject the Pope's encouragement to violators of international agreements. That the world wants peace we accept. That the world can achieve it by the illegal broadcasts of a cast-off wartime cargo ship, we do not accept. As leader of the free world, the President must take immediate steps to have done with this floating electronic bauble."

MOKBA

"The Roman Catholic leader should know better than to preach in illicit pulpits. He will have shocked people all over the world by his endorsement of piracy. The Christian house has stood for some time on the shakiest of foundations, ever sinking in the crevasse of its own credibility gap. We suspect that the contraband vessel is in reality geared to some profitable commercial enterprise. The possibility of it being a water-borne collection plate for Roman pomp in dire circumstance should not be ruled out."

WASHINGTON MORNING NEWS

"Predictably governments everywhere have concentrated on the 'Navis Pacifica's' sheer illegality. The United States has had to face this charge many times — the only exception seeming to be our official second war declaration in Korea. If this ship, which we think should be renamed 'Argosy,' can do something to make governments see sense, does it really matter that she is liable to international prosecution? And are there many who would not willingly share the same dock as the Pope — charged as he could be — with aiding and abetting?"

Tresilian and Digby decided to wait until the next day before dropping Tronphones over Arab and Israeli territory. This would give the area a chance to get used to the ship's presence.

So far, President Amir was the only political leader in the region who had agreed to join Talk of the World — and the R/T operators were waiting for the others' replies. By morning, the Israeli, Syrian and Jordanian heads of government signified their willingness to broadcast — but only in the form of direct statements. They would, in no circumstances, consent to dialogue.

'Navis Pacifica' circled at slow speed through the night. To cool off the effects of their transmissions to date, Tresilian ordered an 18 hour hiatus and the ship went off the air for the longest period since the Gulf of Bothnia. When normal programming had not been interrupted, radio stations speculated that this was the end as the ship had not given any notice of prolonged silence. Glyn decided to say nothing about the pause from a basic radio lesson that Brewster had taught him. 'You gotta keep it immediate. Never let the bastards know what you're gonna do next. Catch 'em with their goddam threads down all the time.'

Glyn, along with everybody else on board, welcomed this respite from the microphones. He met Julie, looking lovely and tanned in her swim suit, with Michael on the lower bridge. They sat in deck chairs, enjoying the cool balmy evening.

"Well, Michael — what do you say now old son?"

"Great, Dad. But boy, would I ever like to get to know some of those chicks a bit better. You won't let me in the studios and their cabins are out of bounds so all I can do is ogle them from up here when they're sunbathing. You should've seen the Pekingese in her bikini. Lying on the foredeck this afternoon. Wow! You know her, Dad — Soong Lee."

Tresilian knew her all right. How could he have missed?

"Don't you think she's the greatest looking little . . ."

"Yes, never mind all that. How've you been getting on with your school work?" his father wanted to know.

"Fine, but I get stuck at times. I sure could use some of those Jesuits now and again. I think they credited me with more brain power than I've got." The boy was talking about the special comprehensive one year syllabus that had been prepared for him by Loyola College in Montreal. He worked at this in the study next to his own cabin at the after end of the lower bridge.

"If you've got to dig and think it out for yourself that much more, it'll probably stick better in the end," his father told Michael. "Anyway, just keep at it. I'm afraid I'm not much help. No time. And in any case I must've forgotten the very little I ever knew. By the way, the Bosun seems to be very pleased with you. Apparently you're a big help to him on deck. You certainly look very well on it." He paused a few seconds. "But what do you really think about it all now Michael?"

"Fabulous," the boy replied, his wide face shining now. "It's the most exciting thing that could ever happen to anyone."

"Feel a bit scared sometimes?"

"Just a little — now and again. I think the planes swooping

down are the most scary bits. You wonder how much closer they can get without crashing into us."

"I think that's about the only thing we forgot to bring with us — ear plugs," Julie said and took Glyn's hand. "Now I know why people living near airports complain so much about jet noise."

"Dad, be honest now. Do you think they'll do anything to the ship?"

"God, I hope not Michael. I know we're breaking all kinds of international regulations — just about everyone in the world knows that. But are we doing any harm or damage? We can only do good, if we do anything at all. In that case, even though a hell of a lot of people, no — that's wrong, not people but governments, would like to have us sunk and off the air, I don't see what country, now that the Plan's beyond the point of no return so to speak, would want to be seen getting us off the air. That's about our best — and only security. Anyway, let's enjoy the rest tonight while we can."

.   .   .   .

.In the Wicket Club, St. James's London, Barton Mills-Cragley was reading the stack of newspapers in the Morning Room. The Plan was having more effect, he considered, than he or anyone could have foreseen. Competing with television, he was amazed that radio still had this kind of power. He read the headlines of all the British national dailies and followed on to the editorial pages. Nothing but Vietnam and Korea had received more ink than the 'Navis Pacifica' since the Pope's support. Especially now that the ship was in the Mediterranean. He hadn't told any of his colleagues in the World Reformation Society about the option he himself could have had on it. And now, as he went to the bar and heard the Plan discussed from a great many points of view, he became increasingly annoyed that he had not negotiated some sort of compromise with that Tresilian.

Maybe there was still time. After all, one take over bid was much like any other. But who was behind it? If it really was the Vatican, as a lot of people were saying, then the deal would be a tough one to close. If on the other hand it turned out to be that kidney doctor, Gannet or whatever his name was, the W. R.S. surely was already in business. But could a medic, even with huge private means, find the necessary millions? He,

Barton Mills-Cragley, didn't think so but he'd damn well find out.

Yes, he'd still take the whole thing over and then, by heaven, he'd make the chaps at the club sit up. Put some spunk in them. Tresilian had it all wrong. Far too much waffle about 'peace and understanding' and all that. He should be calling on the people to get some good strong men in government instead of condemning governments all the time. Good men. Straight-shooters, his American associates would say, that's what's needed. Sound, solid business men. Physically and mentally fit as fiddles. With backbone. That's the trouble with the world. Too many soft bellied creeping socialists coming at you like termites eating away the guts of society. Want the state to do everything. Having the man with initiative and enterprise pay. Subsidizing idleness.

"Yes, Mr. Mills-Cragley, the usual for you sir?" asked Walker who had been at the Wicket behind the bar for 40 years. The WRS Chairman nodded, looked around the room and went over to a table where he sat by himself as he did most of the time on his visits to the bar. Walker brought his tomato juice, sauce and lemon. He stirred the thick liquid and drank. Yes. That's it. He could do it without having to buy the ship. Every few minutes they were inviting, what was it again, prominent world figures and others to go on the air by Radio Telephone, weren't they? Well, by jove, he'd go on. Leaving his chair he went to the leather padded 'phone booth in the Main Hall, telephoned the Secretary of the WRS in London and told him to call an Extra-ordinary Annual General Meeting at once. There, he'd tell the members about his own Plan. They would call the ship and talk to the world and give the human race the real formula. They'd close the brothels in Saigon and Seoul, and they'd inject some fibre into the fighting men out there. And then they'd beat the communists once and for all. That should have been the real Plan all along instead of all this wishy-washy rubbish Tresilian had told his people to push out.

. . . .

Sir Timothy and Lady Wooffenden listened daily to news reports about the 'Navis Pacifica.' Like Mills-Cragley, the Woof-fendens were surprised and shocked that the Plan had made such an impact.

"I have a feeling, Diana," Sir Timothy said to his wife, "that

Mills-Cragley might be a bit sorry now that he didn't back Glyn's scheme after all."

"Oh, why?"

"Well, he's a vain blighter you know. And I'll bet he'd revel in the doubtful glory of being known as the man behind it. And he's certainly got the money."

"Then why didn't he?" Lady Wooffenden asked.

"That depends who you listen to. Glyn said they were poles apart philosophically I think. But Barton told me that after sleeping on it he thought the whole thing was too impossibly idealistic — as I did of course."

"Are you sorry you turned it down, Timothy?"

"Good God, no. Not in the least. Especially now. Wouldn't touch it with a bargepole," the shipbuilder stated emphatically.

"But you know dear, I heard a man on the wireless this morning saying that no one should be too surprised if Glyn's ship does do something to help promote world peace. How do you say the name again? I never could pronounce it properly."

"Navis Pacifica. Navis as in Narvik and Patchiffikka."

"But what do you really think dear? What will happen now?"

"Oh, nothing very much I expect. I must admit though that the impact seems to have been enormous. But one shouldn't be too surprised. What else do you expect when over a billion sets, I think they estimate, are being taken over daily for hours at different times by his, er, 'world talk'."

"But they are breaking rules aren't they?"

"Yes, of course."

"So won't they be stopped?" Although she wouldn't think of saying so to her husband, Lady Diana was becoming more and more intrigued by the Plan and hungrily waited for the daily 'Navis Pacifica' transmissions to blot out the BBC Home Service on the Northern Region wavelength. The day before, she had been particularly impressed at the way Greek women spoke through their Tronphones to an internationally famous Athenian actress, connected to the ship by R/T from Los Angeles, who since the military coup in 1967 was still trying to rally support for the Royalist cause and the return of the Monarchy to Greece.

The film star implored the women of her country to act. She reminded them that every human killed by bullet, flame or H-Bomb was conceived and carried by women. Did the Creator ask that women bear mankind only to have it slain? The well-bred Englishwoman found herself caught up in the passion and emotional simplicity of the wail.

"Well, obviously, they'll be stopped, m'dear," Sir Timothy said with a trace of impatience. "No one's going to put up with having their broadcasts interfered with indefinitely."

"Yes, Timothy. Forgive me, but how are they going to be stopped. Don't forget Michael's with them. And I must say I'm . . . "

"Now, now Diana, don't start worrying. As far as that sort of thing goes, they're as safe as houses. No one would want to bomb or torpedo them or blow them up or anything of the sort. That'd be political dynamite. That's the trouble with public opinion. Damn difficult to control once it's aroused. Exactly the same thing applies to us of course — and all industry. Once the public get hold of a strike for example, and it becomes what the press call a hot story, we usually come off second best, and get involved politically. Usually the government arbitrates more for the unions than for us. Why? Because you'll notice that big wage increases are somehow magically arranged to be argued out close to general election times and the workers have more votes between them than we do," Sir Timothy wound up sadly.

"Yes, darling, I understand all that. I have heard you say it all before," Lady Wooffenden held out her sherry glass as her husband poured. "But if you say that the ship has strong enough public opinion to stop countries from harming her, because that's what you said Timothy, then perhaps the same public opinion will be strong enough to make Glyn's idea work. I mean that the people will be able to force their government to stop fighting and throw away those horrid H-Bombs."

Lady Diana sipped her aperitif. The Baronet, standing with his back to the large fireplace, looked at his wife, mild amazement on his face.

"Good God, Diana, what on earth has happened to you? You're beginning to sound like Glyn for God's sake. Of course, much as we love him, he's still a socialist through and through.

"I've known that much about him for years. He's not just a socialist; to make it worse, he's a dreamer too. And that's a very unfortunate combination."

"But you still haven't answered my question Timothy," Lady

Diana persevered. "How far will the ship get and how will they stop her?"

"Really Diana, I find this a bit exasperating. I've put in a hard day at the yard and merely want to enjoy a quiet glass or two of sherry before dinner. It's not often we have an evening without guests, so I propose we drop the matter.

"Nothing will happen to the ship. In all probability it'll just carry on until everyone gets tired of it. After all there are other stations on the dial that people can listen to if they wish. And then when it's obvious that nothing's going to change and it's all been a colossal waste of money — yes I admit we did very well out of it — whoever's behind the whole thing will say 'enough' and that will be that. Mind you, with all those special fuel reserve tanks we fitted they do have an enormously long cruising and operating range — but I think it'll all fizzle out long before the tanks run dry." He held up his hand before Lady Wooffenden could say anything. "And a last word. No one's ever going to use the H-bomb. They'll eventually sort out the Vietnam and Korean messes and the world will get back to some sort of normalcy. In the meantime, although I regret the rather disturbing look of things, I must say that business has never been better. And with yet another American naval nuclear contract on our books, we have easily become the busiest and biggest shipbuilders in the British Isles. And now let's have a pleasant dinner. I think you said it was venison."

In Toronto, Gaston Yerbury had not gone to his office since 'Navis Pacifica' began to transmit. Instead, he spent all the time near the radio loudspeakers in his home. Senior members of his staff came with important business for approval.

"What do you think of it, sir?" a vice-president asked him.

"I'd say it's as imaginative a peace project as any we've seen for some time," Yerbury replied.

"Then you approve of it sir?"

"Don't you, Mr. Williams?"

"Well, that is, I'm not really sure, Mr. Yerbury. It seems a bit much — all this constant breaking in on radio stations all over the place. Perhaps," and the executive laughed, "I'm being a bit selfish. I normally listen to CORK and that's the station the ship takes over in this area."

"But then you can always tune to the CBC or something else can't you?"

"Yes, but oddly enough I don't. I usually only listen while I'm driving anyway; and I must say there is a fascination about the break-ins. Just the sheer technology of the whole thing. Did you hear that Greek actress talking to the women in her home town? Incredible when you think about it. And the funny thing is that a lot of my wife's friends who never used to listen to CORK are switching over like mad — just to hear what'll happen next."

"Really? Yes, I suppose you could say it's all a bit fascinating. But then people always are. Now, let's get down to this Argentine contract Mr. Williams."

.   .   .   .

At the de Vries' home in Montreal, the door and telephone had rung with human-interest-hungry journalists so often that after a week, the Captain and Julie's mother locked the door and moved to the Queen Elizabeth Hotel for sanctuary. As the 'Navis Pacifica' story developed in size and importance, Glyn's former associates and Michael's classmates found reporters waiting daily for 'background' material on Tresilian.

In their villa on the outskirts of Madras, the senior Tresilians found their quiet retirement abruptly interrupted as new-gatherers closed in. Their correspondence with Glyn had become increasingly sporadic over the years, and although Julie had written — warning of possible publicity, the extent of their son's venture so staggered and shook them that they decided to leave, without delay, for a Hill resort in Simla until the madness blew itself out.

Dame Gwynneth Rhondda-Llandaff was filled with joy when news of the 'Navis Pacifica's' inroads came, as she thought of the special concert they would give from the ship in Hong-Kong. The Secretary-General for his part was pleased to see that very little progress had been made by the International Telecommunications Union to deal with the 'Navis Pacifica's' unlawful wavelength piracy. For once, since he took over the Secretary-Generalship, the internationalist was glad that no positive agreements would come out of the endless stream of charges and counter-charges. The new U.S. — U.S.S.R. entente was not so warm that every move by one wasn't watched with the closest vigilance by the other. But the U.N. executive knew precisely what he would do if the great powers found a way of truncating the mission. For the present he'd bide his time.

.   .   .   .

The 'Navis Pacifica' went on the air again the next morning. With the ship steaming slowly between the vicinities of Damietta and Haifa, the helijets began their Tronphone drops and soon the air was filled with argument.

It was the same old conflict — from Israel. Tronphoners, determination not to relinquish an inch of territory gained in 1967 and through border clashes, until their sovereignty was recognized by their adversaries; and from the Arab side an equally resolute declaration that recognition was unthinkable until Israel returned to Egypt, Syria and Jordan the land that rightfully belonged to them. On the R/T, President Amir spoke menacingly of new agreements with Peoples' China and condemned the Soviet Union's perfidy to the Arab nations following the Peace and Friendship Pact with the United States. It was incredible to note the degree of unanimity on both sides between leaders and people. No one, absolutely no one, was budging.

As they listened to the boringly repeated points, for the first time Tresilian and Digby were at a loss. This wasn't the age-old, barely vicious diatribe heard in the Channel. This was real and live hate. "Go on the air for God's sake, Alan," Tresilian, irritated and exasperated, shouted at Digby. "Tell the bastards on both sides to get off it. This crap won't get us anywhere."

The Australian did well. Under the most trying conditions of the voyage. After an hour of slugging it out he finally scored with an Israeli born Arab in Tel-Aviv.

"Now sir, let's get one thing settled. No, don't interrupt and don't give me all the tired stuff we've been hearing all day long. If that's all we wanted we could get government statements. Remember that we see the way out everywhere on the basis of people talking to people; not governments talking to governments. If that worked, we wouldn't be aboard this ship. Now, you're an Arab living in Israel; do you have to join the armed forces?"

"No."

"Did you fight in the June war of 1967?"

"No."

"You weren't conscripted. Why not?"

"Because as an Arab I can't be called on to fight my brothers can I?"

"What do you mean, your brothers?"

"My fellow Arabs. They're my brothers."

"Precisely. But by the same token, is not every other human being in the world also your brother?" Digby bored in, and waited for the man's reaction.

"That's a very idealistic way of looking at it. A religious point of view in fact. But yes, I agree, from those standpoints, you're right. I suppose we should all be living as brothers."

"Of course. Never mind the religious aspect for the moment because it comes to the same thing anyway. But you mention the 'idealistic way of looking at it,' in your words. How does the realistic view, past present and future look to you?" Digby next asked.

"Depressing and frightening. But I still don't think your scheme will work. Like most other things nowadays it has some novelty value — but it won't last long. And then people will stop listening, if you're on the air for much longer that is; and they'll just tune to other stations than the one's you've been talking over. Sorry to be so cynical, but that's what I think."

"Right sir. Thank you for your comments. I hope you're very, very wrong. I next want to hear from any Jewish person living in an Arab country who has a Tronphone or can get us on the Radio Telephone. If you're on the Tronphone, please turn on the small dial to the mark that says 'cue' and stand by."

After two other conversations, the world heard from a Jew living in Port Said. Like the Arab in Tel Aviv, he had not been called to combat duty in the Egyptian forces on the same 'brotherhood' grounds that applied to Arabs domiciled in Israel.

"Very well," Digby continued. "We now want to apply a practical test to the whole idea of brotherhood on a very small scale. In the last 24 hours, a total of 34 people have been killed in this part of the Middle East. Without calling on servicemen to disobey officers' orders, we call on commanders and men alike, on all sides, to pause before they fire their next shot, or hurl their next grenade, or drop their next bomb; and then think about the things that have just been said and agreed upon on 'Talk of the World'. If we can get through the next 24 hours without a single deliberate death; without blinding another human being; without bringing battle bereavement to a wife and small children; if we can get through just one day like that, it will be a glorious tomorrow. When people are addicted to war, as alcoholics are to drink, the treatment must be the same." The Australian left the studio while the Semitic Talkers carried on.

"Bloody good, Alan; great stuff. Let's see what happens now," Tresilian said and shook his hand vigorously.

"Whew," Digby exclaimed, sweating and shaking slightly. "I got a bit carried away. Radio was never like this in my day. Oh, my word, no."

Many more R/T calls were now coming into 'Talk of the World' as people realised that they could join in the dialogue simply by calling from their own phones via the overseas operators at no cost to them. 'Navis Pacifica's' credit with the telephone systems had been established a year before. But, Tresilian wondered — for how much longer? Not because of payment defaulting, but possibly through government pressures. But, he sighed to himself, they'd still have the Tronphones.

An insoluble problem with the Plan was the waiting time involved. The Talkers had been instructed to take every call in strict order — with exceptions made only for world figures. This meant that someone in Milwaukee or Buenos Aires using R/T might have to wait on the line for an hour while the ship cleared the people in a local area who had just picked up Tronphones. Irrespective of language, only one conversation was heard at a time, and so at the point of transmission from the ship, verbal traffic was single-file-out.

The only calls so far to 'Talk of the World' from the Soviet Union had come in by Tronphone. While not officially condemning participation, the Praesidium had instructed the state telephone chiefs not to provide R/T service to the ship. But one Tronphone at least had evidently reached Moscow from the Baltic coastal drops. However, since the renewed Czech liberalisation, R/T connections from Prague were frequent.

"'Talk of the World,' go ahead please — I think we have a connection to Moscow."

"That is correct. I am speaking on this gadget from a vantage point near the University. From the Lenin Hills I can see our beautiful Moscow spread out below. But I am not trying to get publicity for Intourist. The Soviet people agree with our Mokba. We are convinced that your illegal transmissions are sponsored by the Vatican and we have reason to believe that the culmination of a long laid plot is near at hand."

"What plot is that, sir?" the Russian Talker asked.

"The one that began when the first Catholic missionaries bedevilled the Far East. They saw it all coming. They knew that evil forces would mesmerise and then sway the workers back to slavery under capitalism camouflaged by the twisted cloak of christianity. They knew that . . ."

"Tell me sir," the Talker cut in when he heard the distinct rustle of paper. "Are you reading a statement — because that's not the . . ."

"People everywhere — listen to me. That ship," the man shouted and distorted the sound momentarily, "that ship is not only unlawful — it is also wicked. The Pope is manipulating it not for peace — but for the total conversion of the Far Eastern peoples who . . ."

Digby was livid. "Cut that bastard right off," he roared in the studio.

" 'Talk of the World' — go ahead please."

Bostonian on R/T: "You're a bunch of time and money wasting dreamers, aren't you?"

Talker: "You may think so — and that's your privilege. We don't."

Bostonian: "Well, just let me tell you that you're a raft of sentimentalists and idiots. I'd like to get my hands on whoever's backing this load of weepy garbage. Actually, I'm not too worried — you're creating confusion, but already people are getting tired of your super-internationalism and frustrated idealism. Too bad. Soon as your ratings slip and all you have left are Dr. Gunter's friends you'll have to take that boatload of bawling crap back to port. Now . . ."

Talker: Do you have anything constructive to say? If not we'll cut you off right now."

Bostonian: "Now just listen to me flannel mouth! You had the Pope on blessing you all over the lot, eh? And I suppose you think that's just great."

Talker: "That's putting it much too mildly."

Bostonian: "Well, just let me refresh your memory. You're

— 333 —

that taken with sloppy do-goodism. Some years ago a Canadian woman wrote to the Pope suggesting that he ought to go and stay in Hanoi as a hostage as no one would bomb the place if he was there. Right then. Why didn't he take the Papal Bull and set it up in Ho Chi Minhsville, eh? Can you answer that? No you can't. But I can. I'll tell you and I'll have you know I'm a Catholic too, but one who doesn't forget he's an American as well. The reason my dear sir, is because he's also running a multi billion dollar corporation — and war's as good for his business as anyone else's. That broad's idea might have worked. It was a goddam sight more practical than this crap you've got going — but it's a lot easier and safer just to mouth a few words on the phone, eh? And now, it's my pleasure to cut you off — you tear-eyed clutch of grieving bastards."

Unlike all other open line programs, 'Talk of the World' was not delayed by the customary censor procedures which gave a station several seconds in which to delete obscene, offensive and libellous material. Tresilian had decided against delay mechanism, not for technical reasons — that, when compared to the rest of 'Navis Pacifica's' equipment would have been elementary, but because he judged that the Plan would carry even more impact if the world could hear at first hand the depth of feeling the peaceship generated.

After the Boston call, follow up R/T conversations were with two American mothers from San Antonio and Detroit who had lost sons in South East Asian fighting. The disparate views they expressed seemed inexplicable. On the one hand there was the bitter mood of unforgiveness and the call to 'nuclear bomb those red yellow bellies back to the stone age.' On the other, the sad and compassionate reason of one who had borne a child and lost it, but who didn't wish her tragedy on others.

The good news came a day after Digby's appeal. Only four persons had been killed in that period through rifle fire in Arab-Israeli border battles. And reports from U.N. observers said that infantry and aircraft in good firing positions held back and flew over. At the United Nations in New York, the Secretary-General seized the opportunity at once, addressed the General Assembly already in session and called a press conference. On the following day, the Secretary-General's statement was front page and headline news everywhere.

'I wish as Secretary-General of the United Nations, and as an individual, to announce my complete approval of what is being done by the 'Navis Pacifica' in the cause of world peace. In this expression of confidence and hope, I join the Pope together with millions of ordinary men and women on every continent. News of the response in the Middle East to the ship's appeal to commanders and men on the battlefield to meditate before they mutilate is the most encouraging of any we have had in the Organization's history. It is positive proof of the individual's sovereign excellence — sense of personal responsibility and craving for peace.

'And now I wish to state this with the utmost clarity. Any attempt by any government, be it of a member nation or not, anywhere at any time to impede the progress or work of this vessel will result in my resignation within the hour.'

On the following day, there were no casualties at all. With another moving appeal, Digby suggested that those Israelis who could, might seek out refugees near their homes or in camps and give them friendship and succour. And again, UN reports of actual results came in. 'Navis Pacifica's' Middle East prize came, when after three more bloodless and comparatively calm days, President Amir spoke to the world through the ship on one of the thousands of Tronphones that the helijets had dropped over Cairo.

"People of the world," the leader of the United Arab Republic said with unusual kindness in his voice. "I wish to make it known that the UAR, satisfied that the 'Navis Pacifica' is not after all engaged on a hostile mission, has granted to the ship a special dispensation to pass through the Suez Canal. My government has never desired to halt the progress of peaceful adventures."

And so Amir became the first head of government to endorse the Plan, albeit obliquely.

It took Tresilian two nerve-wracking days to get the 'Navis Pacifica' past the block ships in the one ship channel of Suez. Proceeding by day only and tying up to the lonely bank at night, he closed down transmission during passage. No attempts to molest the ship were made by either side. He felt elated and relieved when the generators hummed again as the ship cleared Norfolk Rock off the southern end of the canal. The old 'Liberty' shook herself free and headed down the Gulf of Suez for the Red Sea. The helijets took off in the unbearable heat and made Tronphone drops in Saudi Arabia, the Sudan, Yemen, Ethiopia, and French Somaliland.

News of pressures by the world's private broadcasters whose wavelengths the ship was plundering, had reached listeners by Tronphone from Luxembourg. The fact was that the Drom's sales strategy based on the ship's success was both ill-timed and embarrassing.

The move had been too quick. Would stations like CRAK now want the 'Navis Pacifica' to be without oil fuel? Who could possibly want anything but full tanks for the ship that had brought just about every listener in their markets to the right spot on the dial?

Not knowing about the Brewster stratagem, Glyn decided to work on the problem of a crippling bunker embargo and instead of going to the coast of India direct, altered course for the oil rich Persion Gulf. But while the Tronphone talk was encouraging, there were lean pickings from a local Oxford educated Sheik, who when asked to provide oil fuel, told Tresilian concisely on the R/T to 'Bugger off and leave us alone.'

As the ship worked south along the Indian coast from Karachi to Cochin, Tronphone-dropping and talking not less than eight hours a day, there was a noticeable decrease in the amount of sea and air surveillance. And by the time she'd cleared the Laccadive Islands, en route on a south westerly course across the Indian ocean for East Africa and the Cape of Good Hope, the vessel had no company at all. To top it all, the Middle East news continued to be good. Since the ship had left, there had only been minor flare-ups among individuals — but no organised armed hostilities. The Argus of London boomed in a leading article:

> "Whether we like it or not, and there is every reason why we should like it, the 'Navis Pacifica' is sailing towards a checkmate hold on the world. Official fulminating at the United Nations headquarters and in the national capitals should be encouraged and prolonged.
>
> If there are to be explosions, we prefer that they should come from furious statesmen, rather than from H-bombs. Let official East and official West bristle and blus-

ter. And let the ship have time to achieve her relatively simple purpose, which is to encourage people everywhere to disarm their own governments of aggression and war neuroses. In the light of twenthieth century history, and the long trail of diplomatic failures in its wake, we support and recommend the 'Navis Pacifica's' aims, objects and methods. International laws aside, the saying that 'the end justifies the means,' was never more worthy of being stated than it is today."

When the ship was two days out of the Mozambique Channel, and the helijets were again readied for Tronphone dropping, the South African and Rhodesian governments simultaneously proclaimed a Contraband Wavelengths Act, emergency legislation which made listening to, or participation in programs such as Talk of the World treasonable offences punishable by death. Then, as 'Navis Pacifica,' after Tronphone dropping in the Mozambique region, neared Durban in Natal Province, the Capetown government issued the following ultimatum, and became the first country to move positively on the " 'Navis Pacifica' problem."

'Attempts by the contraband wavelength vessel 'Navis Pacifica' to violate South African air space through dispatch of aircraft will be regarded as an unfriendly act. The South African government warns that these machines will be shot down and destroyed.'

The announcement became a main topic for several hours on Talk of the World. Tronphoners from Gothenburg to Beira wanted to know what Tresilian would do. After a day of sweating out the problem, he and Digby gave the Talkers this bulletin to announce:

"In view of the South African Government's decision, the Master and internationalists of 'Navis Pacifica' agree not to helifly over and drop Tronphones in the coastal regions of South Africa. The ship's personnel make this decision with regret but are convinced that the agonies of violence and death that would follow Tronphone users is an unthinkable price to pay."

CHAPTER 8

With jet aircraft screaming around her at masthead level, 'Navis Pacifica' rounded Cape Agulhas and began her composite great circle sailing to 40° south latitude for the long South Atlantic haul to the Magellan straits. The ship settled down to the routine of a long sea voyage. Tresilian and Digby decided to cut back the number of transmitting hours from eight to four in order to 'pace' Talk of the World more slowly. The Talkers, who had worked a furious schedule up until now, needed and welcomed the shortened workday.

On June 2, 1970, 'Navis Pacifica' felt the roaring forties on her bluff bow. The strong winds blew out of a cloudless sky, and brought with them a healthful invigoration. Tresilian, Digby and Michael were painting deckheads on the lower bridge in the late afternoon. Soon they would call it a day and Glyn was looking forward to drinks with Julie and Digby before supper. In the last few days since South Africa, this had become a genial routine.

"That's enough for now, I think," Tresilian said wiping his hands with cotton waste. "Michael, square off around that knee frame and tell the Bosun we're finished at least for today. If the weather's good, we'll have another go at it in the morning. Take these pots and brushes down at the same time. Now Alan, what about some gin?"

"Ah, that's more my line of country, Glyn. Oh, my word, yes."

"O.K. Tell Julie I'll be there in a minute, will you? I just want to check if they got that Venus latitude. Don't want to get too far south yet." And Tresilian went up to the bridge.

By pre-computing the maximum altitude of Venus on his sextant, the second mate had been able to verify accurately the ship's latitude some three hours after the sun passed over the vessel's meridian. Satisfied that the Navis Pacifica was not being set too far to the southward, her Master went to his quarters.

"Oh, good to see you Glyn," Julie said as he came in, "the Doctor wants you. He seemed to think it was important."

"Oh?, I hope to God it's not appendicitis. We'll have to heave to if it is. I'll go down," and he left for the small dispensary and surgery in the for'ard tween-deck accommodation.

"Sorry to trouble you, Captain," the Pakistani surgeon said.

"What's the trouble? Appendix?"

"No, nothing like that. Not even medical as far as I can see. It's Soong Lee. She came in here a few minutes ago and said that she must see you urgently," the Pakistani explained. "Naturally I told her to see you herself but she wanted me to act as an intermediary. I asked if she was feeling alright and she said that she was perfectly well. But the only time she ever saw you was in the studio and didn't want to say anything in there. So that's all I can tell you, I'm afraid."

"That's easy enough," Tresilian said and looked at the cabin list on the bulkhead. "Port 17. I'll go and see her now. No other problems Doc?"

"No, Captain. We seem to be quite lucky. A few coughs, colds and cuts, but nothing serious."

"Good. You must join us for dinner soon. Now things are less hectic, my wife and I are trying to get acquainted with everyone a bit better."

Tresilian knocked on the cabin door, numbered 17, the most for'ard one on the port side of the Talker's accommodation. She opened the door.

"Hello, Soong. You wanted to see me?"

"Yes, Captain, come in please." He glanced down the alleyway and was relieved that no one was there.

"Soong, it's perfectly in order that you want to see me. But I'd rather not discuss whatever's on your mind in here. Why don't you come to our quarters? Or if it's private we can talk in the ship's office." There was a delicious scent in the small but tidily arranged cabin. The Chinese girl was wearing a silk embroidered blouse and tight, seductive slacks. She sat down on the edge of her bunk.

"No, Captain that wouldn't do I'm afraid. And you see it is private. Very private. Please sit down," she asked.

Irritated, Tresilian declined. "No, Soong. This won't do at

all. You can see me about anything you want, at any time, —
but in the right place. And that's not here — in your cabin.
Anyway, Alan Digby's your man. That was all agreed in New
York, wasn't it? That he's the liaison between you people and
me." And he went to open the door.

"No, don't go, Captain. You'll be sorry if you do. And Mr.
Yerbury wouldn't want anything to go wrong with the Plan
would he?" Tresilian tautened and felt much as a man driving
at speed on a freeway feels when he brakes for an emergency
stop and nothing happens as his foot floats to the floor board.
His throat went dry.

"What did you say?" the words stuck to his lips.

"You heard me. But I'll say it again. Mr. Yerbury wouldn't
want anything to happen to the Plan, would he? Now Captain,
I think you'd better sit down, and I'll tell you all about it. Oh,
you forgot your cigarettes? Never mind. I have plenty. Have
one of these," and she offered him one from a carved box on
the table.

"No, thanks. How do you know about Mr. Yerbury?"

"That's not important Captain," Soong said, now completely
in control of the situation. "But you can set your mind at rest.
I knew all about it a long time ago. So you needn't be afraid of
a ship conspiracy. I'm still the only one on the ship apart from
you and your wife I suppose who knows what everybody in
the world wants to know. I couldn't count the number of Tronphoners who've been asking for the name of the person or
people who are backing you. It's quite a valuable piece of information, isn't it?" she asked and took him with her eyes.

"You'll gain nothing by fooling around Soong. What do you
want? Money? It's bound to be blackmail of some sort," he said
angrily.

"Blackmail? Oh, come Captain. I'm a civilised girl. And
money doesn't interest me. So you're wrong there," and she
kicked off her sandals and lay back on the bunk propping her
head against her small, manicured, right hand.

Tresilian stood up. Was it all going to be spoiled now? The
thought set him alight and he raised his voice, shouting.

"Then what the hell are you after?"

"Don't get excited Captain. It's not good for you. I'll tell
you soon, but first I'd better tell you something else. You see

— 341 —

Captain I'm not on your side at all. You know that saying about the one rotten apple in the barrel? Well, I'm the one in yours. The recruiting was nearly perfect, but not quite. And I don't care about your ship or your famous Talk of the World. I'm supposed to sabotage it, but I hope this makes you feel better. The fact is I don't care about that either."

The girl paused without taking her eyes off him. Tresilian was speechless. She went on.

"No, Captain I don't care about anything very much at present except one thing. But to continue. I was at the United Nations as a Peking defector under entirely false pretences. That was very easy — to work as a linguist in the Secretariat, I mean. However, in real life, I'm a secret agent with the Peoples' China equivalent of the C.I.A. And I'm a very good one too. You could call me a sloe eyed Mata-Hari. Or I should say I was. I was expected to end your voyage before you even began it. My people in Peking were convinced that Mr. Yerbury, once I'd told them about him, was hand in glove with an American plot. They made no allowance for his being a Canadian. In Peoples' China, Canada is just another profiteering lackey of the United States."

"I don't have much patience left," Tresilian muttered and moved to the door again. "But I'll tell you this. I'll imprison you for the rest of the voyage before I'll let you ruin it."

"Captain," she said coolly and precisely, "you're being silly now. I did think you'd have the intelligence to know when you're in a strong position and when you're not. You certainly are not now. As I had anticipated a little trouble with you, I took the precaution of doing what I was originally assigned to do. Unless you do as I ask, all the equipment on this ship will be put out of action in about," she looked at her wrist watch, "in about 15 hours from now. I said all the equipment and I mean all the equipment. Satellite computers, generators, main and auxiliary transmitters. Nothing will happen to the helijets or Tronphone containers. But they won't be much use if all your microphones are dead," she smiled.

He hadn't felt this perverted quality in the seemingly gentle Chinese before. With his mind in a whirl, Soong Lee became positively charming. "Please understand that nothing will happen to the ship itself and no one aboard will be hurt. Unless you foolishly alert the technicians. In the unlikely event that they should discover it, let's call it the arrangement I've made, they'll die painlessly — but at once. So I wouldn't say a word to anyone. I think you'll agree that I hold all the cards, Captain. A dreadful expression but it'll do. Now what do you say?"

Tresilian said nothing. He weighed the desperate way out that had suddenly come to him. Unconcernedly, he looked at the cabin scuttle. It might work. No, you bloody fool. She's the only one who can stop whatever's going to happen. Forget it.

"Well, Glyn?" she now asked familiarly and got up from the bunk. Emotions spinning, totally confused, Glyn was in no position to think.

"What the hell can I say when I don't know what you want? And don't call me Glyn!"

She ignored the outburst. "I saw you looking at that thing just now," and she waved at the scuttle. "I have a vague notion that for a second or two you considered throwing me out of it. But," and without loosening him from her eyes, she stooped down and whipped out a small revolver from under the pillow, "I'm glad you didn't try Captain. I'm sorry if the thought of this thing being aboard your peace ship upsets you, but one can't be too careful."

"I see," and Tresilian's hands shook as the aggresive temper in him took charge. "You win. Even though I don't know what bloody game you're playing. But you win. Now," he yelled again, "what the hell do you want?"

"Shush, Captain, not so loud, we don't want the others to over hear do we?" She took the few steps to the single cabin chair and put her hand on his forehead. "And besides I rather hope that you might enjoy giving me 'what I want', as you put it. Glyn," she said pointedly ignoring his shouted admonition, "you've fascinated me ever since I saw you for the first time in New York. No, you didn't see me. Shortly after that, I found out what you were up to and I was even more intrigued. I told you I was very good at my work because I made it a habit of getting what I wanted. Now I want you. Surprised? Oh, it's not that I'm a nymphomaniac. You won't be surprised to learn that the Talkers' accommodation hasn't turned out to be a monastery. No its not that. It's you. And you're the price. I can't explain it either. You're no glamour boy, but then I don't

- 343 -

go for that kind. I guess I like my idealists, though you can have your ideologies, and that goes for the thoughts of Mao too. I agree with Westerners that life's for living. I've worked out a little scheme. I'd like to have you about once a week — now that's not asking too much — and when I go off shift and I need you, I'll leave a note by the scratch pad in my studio booth. I'll always write some meaningless sentence with the rest of my notes but the ones for you will include the words 'almond', 'orange', 'sandal' and 'relief'. It was very thoughtful of you to put these inside bolts on the door."

. . . .

Dazed, Tresilian strove to compose himself as he slowly walked back to the bridge. Julie, Michael and Digby were in the middle of a lively talk about sheep grazing, aborigines and the outback of Australia.

"Where have you been? You've been gone long enough to have your own appendix out. Nothing wrong is there?" Julie asked him.

"No, nothing wrong. But as it's a long passage, the Doc wanted to know how steady we could keep her if he did have to operate. And we had a bit of a chat at the same time. I told him he must have a meal with us soon," Glyn said, and with his back to them poured a shot of gin. He tried but couldn't prevent his hand from shaking as he held the glass. Julie knew there was something wrong.

"Look, darling, if you're worried about anything and want to talk to Alan, Michael and I can sit outside. It's quite warm on the lee side, even though there's a stiff breeze to windward! See, I can speak like a sailor after all," she laughed.

"Yes, Glyn. You look as if the Doc told you we've all got small-pox or cholera," Digby added.

"No, really. No problems. Sorry. Probably a bit tired. That's all," but he knew Julie didn't believe him. They carried on with Alan telling stories of Australian graziers. Tresilian laughed, nodded, shook his head in disbelief at the appropriate times, but when they went to eat, he had no idea about anything the man from Adelaide had described.

Two days after his first meeting with Soong Lee, Digby called Tresilian into the studio.

"Glyn, there's some joker with a plummy voice and a double

barrelled name on the R/T from London. Says he knows you and won't speak to anyone else. Mills-Cragley or something I think he said . . ."

"Oh, yes. I'll handle it," and Tresilian went into the English language booth.

"Hello, Mr. Mills-Cragley. Tresilian here. You're on the air; go right ahead please."

"Ah, Tresilian, how are you? I'd like to speak to the world if I may . . ." "Go right ahead," Tresilian said.

"To begin, I think people should know that you did approach me as an individual to back your scheme; and secondly that I am Chairman of the World Reformation Society whose members have recently met to discuss the best way in which we can participate in your Talk of the World.

"As I said to you before, we are all in favour of using technology for the purpose of putting people in touch with each other. At the same time we feel that there must be a strong central theme to all the dialogue. We, like millions of other people, have been listening to your transmissions with the greatest attention. Without wanting to discourage you, however, we do think that a lot of the enormous potential you have at your command has been wasted and . . ."

"Specifically?" Tresilian interrupted him, knowing what was coming and deciding to hit back. "Do you say that exploiting a sense of brotherhood is a wastage? Is the fact that there has been no major fighting of any kind in the Middle East since we left the area a complete co-incidence? Is it a total accident that athletes of countries that had intended to boycott the Munich Olympic Games in two years time are now forcing their governments to let them participate? Is it by sheer luck alone that we hear of fighting men on all sides in Vietnam and Korea looking forward to our arrival out there — human beings who have long since given up all hope of a settlement by any other means?"

"Well now, you're rambling of course, Tresilian. Let me make my point to the world — and I'll thank you not to interrupt. To be frank and truthful about it, your scheme is much too dreamy. Oh, it's bound to have a little emotional novelty appeal but that'll soon wear off. The thing that disturbs us most in the World Reformation Society is the way you keep up a sustained attack on governments. And your negative preoccupation with established systems.

"There is nothing to replace the system of governments, as we know them, in just about every part of the world. But instead of encouraging people to by-pass legislative authorities and filling them up with cynicism, you should be stressing the positive roles and opportunities that governments should be working on. And above all you should be encouraging the right types to run for office.

"That's the real target, Tresilian. That's what the world needs so desperately. Men, who through personal example of purity and clean living, whose success by their own initiative and enterprise has been proven, are the only people truly capable of giving great leadership. And to that end, we in the W.R.S. would like to offer our services at no charge to any country where we can be of use. By that I mean that we shall finance the setting up of local chapters in . . ."

"No, thank you Mr. Mills-Cragley," Tresilian cut in. "I" — and he angrily underlined the word — "am in command of this ship and the entire broadcast operation. My judgment tells me that I must deprive the world of listening to your proselytizing."

"Now, look here Tresilian," Mills-Cragley exploded, "I'm not calling to be cut-off by you . . ."

"And neither are we sailing the 'Navis Pacifica' to be preached at by you, Mr. Mills-Cragley. You are an extremely arrogant 'naked ape,' and that — animal arrogance — is the root cause of our troubles. Arrogance, Mr. Mills-Cragley. And the type you personify is the worst kind of all. Instead of glorifying governments, and thereby adding to those repositories of arrogance, I suggest that instead we purge ourselves as individuals — myself, yourself, everyone — with large doses of humility. Because, Mr. Mills-Cragley, there is no other medicine that will work." Tresilian said "Good day" and left the studio.

After Mills-Cragley, other representatives of various movements, religions and sects called Talk of the World on the R/T. These conversations deteriorated into fruitless arguments leading nowhere. Digby banned 'cause recruiting' on the grounds that it was divisive, and therefore useless to the Plan. The policy backlashed when from pulpit and platform, charges of prejudice and discrimination were fired at the ship.

"It is not enough evidently," one man in Scotland thundered

at a meeting of his group, "that this band of brigands and pirates brazenly pillage the airwaves. Oh, no. That is not enough. They must also have control over what is said. Which makes theirs an evil trumpet, my brothers and sisters, out of which comes not The Word's sweet harmony — but the destroying damnation of the devil's discord."

. . . .

In spite of everything he could do to reassure her, Julie was positive that there was something wrong. At first Tresilian thought of telling her about Soong Lee but then he realised that, far from dreading the words 'almond', 'orange' and 'relief' on her note pad, he was beginning to look forward to them. Physically, he doubted that any woman could be as exotic as this rapturous oriental. Emotionally, he was tense, constantly feeling remorse. When the guilt became unbearable, he allayed his conscience by telling himself that it was either this or the end of the Plan.

At times Julie worried frantically that he was heading for a breakdown. She thought that perhaps the strain and the fact that they themselves evidently could not have children had forced him to an outlet. But, being the type of level-headed girl she was, (Glyn assured himself repeatedly on that point) she worked hard to win him back. Somehow her instincts told her that if he was having an affair on the ship, there had to be a reason — and one day he'd tell her. She was sure his conscience would never rest for long though, and that he was constantly questioning himself and his loyalty.

One day, as they were nearing South America, there was amusing relief. They wanted Glyn in the studio, and on the air.

"Talk of the World — Tresilian speaking — go ahead please."

"Mr. Tresilian?" a joyful female French Canadian voice came through on R/T. "How are you, chéri? Remember me? I used to give you a hard time on your Crakkerjack line in Montreal. I just can't get over it Mr. Tresilain I think it's . . ."

"Tresilian, Madame, Tresilian. T-R-E-S-I-L-I-A-N. You still haven't got it right. How've you been then my darling? Aimez-vous La République du Canada?"

"Oh, mais oui, chéri. We'd better speak in English, non? Of course I like it better — you should know me better than to ask. I'm the one you used to call the Broad on Van Horne — especially when I made you mad, hahaha."

"I remember it well, chérie," and he sang it to her à la Chevalier.

. . . .

'Navis Pacifica' sailed on and her helijets made Tronphone drops, as soon as they were within range, on both sides of South America. She made a surprisingly quick and calm passage through the Magellan straits, and, although watched again by aircraft and ships, had still not been troubled or halted. Apart from the South African declaration, things were proceeding more normally than Tresilian had dared hope. Using the Peru current to good advantage, the ship made fast time steaming north to the coast of Americus. Her helijets made the first Tronphone drops over the capital on July 1.

Following the Southeast Asian pattern, a military dictatorship had been bolstered in Americus by American advisers and arms to the point where guerilla warfare had rapidly progressed to full scale burning and bombing. On the one hand the South Vietnamese, South Korean and Americusian government forces were being nourished at the bottomless well of the U.S. and Soviet Union Peace and Friendship Pact countries. While on the other their breakaway adversaries, poorly fed with war material, somehow kept revolution alive.

Father Bonpane, in the 1960's Tresilian remembered, had foretold of a similar situation with reference to Guatemala. He had said.

'The peasant has a catalyst of revolution in his hand, the transistor radio. He realizes something is wrong with his life and he knows that it can be better . . .

'I think the United States is the greatest country in the world, and I don't want to see it on a self-destruction course. These new five, six, seven, or eight new Vietnams that could erupt in Latin America would be the end of the United States because we would find that our boys wouldn't go.'

A few minutes after the first Tronphone call from Americus City — a peasant vividly describing the distress of his own refugee family — a call on R/T came through from the local government's military H.Q.

"This is the General Officer Commanding Americusian Republic Forces," an angry voice in Spanish said. "We give notice to the contraband vessel 'Navis Pacifica' that it will be sunk and its helicopters shot down if there are any further violations of our territory. This is the first and final warning."

Tresilian and Digby looked at each other.

"How many have they dropped so far?" Glyn asked.

"I'll check. At least they're both on deck. We'd better hold them now eh?"

"Yes. Just to be on the safe side have the Bosun hangar — stow them will you Alan? What's our distance off, Third Mate?"

"Seventeen and a half miles sir. Got some bearings a minute ago."

"Right. Keep the sea ahead. I don't like this much. Take her out another 25 miles. We'll do what we can from there."

"Aye, aye, sir," and the officer went into the chartroom. In a minute Digby was back on the bridge.

"Three trips each Glyn. That means they've got, let's see, 50 per canister by ten each load — 500 by three trips. Fifteen hundred each comes to three thousand between them. Not a hell of a lot I'm afraid but 3,000 better than South Africa," the Australian said encouragingly.

"O.K. Let's try. We'll play it just as we did in the Middle East, Alan. Mind you, it's a lot worse here. But we should be able to get the brotherhood bit going again. It ought to be something of a Holy Land in itself — it's a 90 percent Roman Catholic region. Julie gets mad when I get on to that. In you go and give 'em hell."

Using the relative Middle East tranquility — holding now for weeks — as an example, Digby and the Talkers worked twelve hour stretches for the next three days. Despite death ultimatums from both government and breakaway rebel leaders, the Tronphones were used and circulated. After a few hours, Father Bonpane's reasoning came to life as in the hills and the streets of Americus, individuals, then small pockets of soldiers, and finally scores of fighting men paused at their arms.

Although at first these voluntary, individual acts of peace had a negligible effect on the total war, the government Military Commander sniffed the virus of an uncontrollable epidemic that would spread the vile germ of communism through Americus and beyond. He encoded a cable to the Pentagon in Washington:

"NAVIS PACIFICA SUBVERSIVE STOP MUST BE SUNK STOP WILL BOMB AND DESTROY TONIGHT STOP AM PRESUMING YOUR FULL APPROVAL."

Within the hour the General was reading the decoded reply:
"IMPERATIVE YOU HOLD NAVIS PACIFICA FIRE TODAY. STOP. REPEAT IMPERATIVE. PROPAGANDA GAINS BY PEKING INCALCULABLE THROUGH SUCH ACTION STOP U.S. OFFICER FLYING IMMEDIATELY WITH FURTHER ADVICE AND EXPLANATION. STOP. REPEAT REPEAT TAKE NO ANTI VESSEL ACTION TODAY."

The General waited a week, but no high ranking officer from the Pentagon arrived. And in spite of increasingly urgent cables to Washington, the joint Chiefs of Staff seemed disinclined to discuss the 'Navis Pacifica.'

The ship was now well on its way to Californian waters and therefore safe from Americusian hostility. Also, Washington was finding that with slow but steady daily reductions of fire, the Administration could begin thinking about taking men out of the area and deploying them home and to Korea, where although there were already a million U.S. servicemen under arms, more were urgently needed. By the time 'Navis Pacifica' was 20 miles off San Pedro, the battle death rate in Americus had fallen 25%. And in official and unofficial circles everywhere, there were no more condescending sniggers.

Too, for the first time since 1945 in San Francisco, the Secretary-General at the United Nations found himself with power. He now pointed to the Plan unashamedly and when blockages loomed anywhere in the Secretariat or Assembly, he more than once suggested that the problem be aired on 'Talk of the World' for, as he put it. "It has more meaningful and constructive exchanges than we appear to be capable of providing."

Tresilian and Digby determined, with this kind of progress at the U.N., to follow up and make the admission of Peoples' China to the Organization a main issue on 'Talk of the World' as they cruised the waters off Los Angeles. Here — Tronphone drops were unnecessary. They could conserve the remaining thousands of crucial little cylinders for the big job in Asia.

"OK boys," Tresilian said to the two helijet pilots, "you

can take it easy for a while. No more drops till we get out there. You've done a hell of a job already. And you can see the results. You'll probably want to work on the birds though. Make damn sure they're in good shape."

People from all over the United States and Canada called 'Talk of the World' on R/T. Much of the dialogue was hysterical. Since the last Presidential election the North American continent had, in just about equal parts, become extremely left or extremely right wing. By a slim majority, the administration was still in hawkish hands. The Domino Theory and Red containment in Asia were still the official policy.

"If you let those red and yellow bastards from mainland China get in, they'd subvert the U.N. in minutes. Not that it isn't a communist club already," an elderly-sounding gentleman from Galveston declared in a deep, slow, resonant voice. A kind of Deep South Oxford accent, Glyn mused in admiration, listening at his Captain's post. Even swears with a certain cultured finesse, Tresilian allowed.

"But," the ship's Talker countered, "if they don't get in, how are you going to talk to them and come to some sort of understanding?"

"Talk? Understanding? With those people? Who needs it? Who wants it?"

"But that's exactly what we've been trying to do for the past few months. To get people, not governments, talking to each other, and then understanding's easier. Look around you — the Middle East, Americus . . ."

"Ah, there you go you see. Your lot aboard that ship will get us so much 'understanding among peoples' that the freedom and liberty our forefathers fought for on this continent will have been compromised out of existence. You may call that arrogance, as you put it to that fine Englishman. I call it Americanism."

"Tell me sir, if there's to be no talking with Peking at the U.N., how do you predict the future?"

"If I'd had my way, the future would have been predicted a long time ago. Back in the sixties — when the Cong started those offensives in the South. I'd have used nuclear weapons to wipe out Hanoi and Peking in one day."

"But in those days Peking didn't have any long range nuclear delivery systems to reach the United States. Now they do.

Would you drop H-bombs today on Hanoi and Peking?"

"You'd better believe it. Because I'm not one of those who'd rather be red than dead. Communism's the worst evil the world'll ever know." And the Texan shook his fist while listeners in his office beamed him on.

"Is it a bigger evil than global suicide?"

"What the devil's that supposed to mean?" the Galvestonian asked to hoots of approving laughter.

"Quite simply this. If communism is the evil thing you say it is, is it still worse than the destruction of all life on this planet?"

"Nothing — nothing is worse than communism — the loss of our liberty. Those who haven't enjoyed the benefits of liberty are always the first to give it away."

"What about people who don't share your views? People who want to go on living? About a billion and a half already must prefer being red to dead. Where do you get your right sir, to make a death wish for the whole human race?" the Talker persisted with scribbled encouragement from Digby in the studio.

"I don't have a right to speak for everyone in the world, but I believe I can say something on behalf of most Texans, and even today, most Americans." The Texan was at his best now, the 'r's rolling off his tongue. It was, regardless of anything else, great theatre.

"We in the United States, believe in the rights, the freedom and liberty of the individual. If these are to be denied us, what is life worth? For nearly 200 years we have fought to expand liberty. Are we to give up now? Tell your Mr. Tresilian not to compromise his inherited values. We are of the same stock, and together we have contributed much to this world. In the face of the Marxist challenge it is our duty to stand firm once more. I have a choice, and I choose men who are ready to die for liberty, in preference to your Dr. Gunter who isn't . . . well, I don't want to get into personalities now. That is what Americans believe."

Digby asked the Talker to thank the caller and go into the next conversation. A good example of the old 'Anglo-Saxon' spirit, Digby said to himself. How can we cope with that when we're not even on the same wavelengths? They'd been psychologically beaten on this. There must be tears in every American's eyes, he thought. God, he pronounced 'American' just like the legendary Senator Claghorn! Obviously Glyn with his supreme idealism would have wanted us to debate the old fellow. Maybe it was best he wasn't in the studio. Glyn would have bombed badly on that one.

Digby was right. Tresilian was annoyed. In his way, however, the Texan had put a certain intellectual balance in the calls, allowing the conversations — many calls were now coming from 'new left' professors answering the Texan — to maintain a high level, at least for a while.

Tresilian went on the air finally and asked if there were any moderates left. He encouraged them to call. A few did react. But it seemed that in 1970 America, a moderate was regarded as subversively red or facist by the encampments on either side of him.

'Navis Pacifica' altered course on the first leg of a great circle sailing across the North Pacific.

CHAPTER 9

It was August 1. The ship had entered fog off the Kuril Trench. She was just over three days away from a Honshu landfall. Neither Julie nor Michael could sleep that night — as the prolonged fog-signal blast at two minute intervals shattered ear drums and nerves to insomnia. The Talkers could neither hear nor concentrate properly in the studio housing only a few feet from the funnel, atop which the steam whistle brayed and jarred through the dank grey night. Tresilian was on the bridge. His wife and son were playing chess in the day room. In the wheelhouse, the Engine-Room voice pipe shrilled.

"Captain speaking," Glyn called urgently and moved his ear to the brass mouth piece.

"Aye, Cap'n. It's the Chief here. I'm coming up to see you right away," the Scots voice came on the tube anxiously.

"Why — what's wrong Chief?" but already Glyn heard the thuddy rattle of the whistle piece below as the Engineer banged it home. They met at the chart-room table. The Chief wiped his hands with a wad of waste and filled his chipped and bitten briar pipe from an oil blackened old pouch.

"How far out are we now, Cap'n?" the Chief said setting his bowl on fire.

"From Hong-Kong?"

"No, anywhere. The coast. Japan." Tresilian reached over the chart table for a pair of dividers, measured off an estimated day's run on the latitude scale and 'walked' the ship from the last dead reckoning noon position to Kamaishi.

"A bit over three days as near as I can tell Chief. But that's a bit dicey. We haven't been able to get any sights for a couple of days. The last two noon positions were both D.R. That's the trouble around here at this time of year. Too much damned fog. Warm current and cold air. Same thing off the Newfoundland Banks. But we should be getting into D/F range soon," Glyn explained chattily, dreading and putting off whatever bad news the old Scot wanted to give.

"Aye, Cap'n. I know a little about all that myself. Even though I am just a silly old pig iron polisher. No, no, no offence meant," he said quickly as he noticed Glyn's look. "I'm afraid we're up the creek Cap'n. There's nae easy way of putting it — so I'll let ye have it straight. And of course I take full responsibility. But what I'm going to say to that Second Engineer of mine," he said ominously, "well that's my responsibility too . . . Cap'n, we only have bunkers for about another six hours steaming." Tresilian, who had expected something of the kind, walked in to the wheelhouse, and checked with the second mate that there were no echoes on the radar screen and returned to the Chief in the chartroom.

"It won't help us Chief, but what went, oh damn and blast," he yelled and waited five seconds while the whistle roared. "Let's talk while we can. What went wrong, was what I was trying to ask."

"Aye, Cap'n, you're right. It won't help us. I'm surprised you keep that damn thing going when you've got two radar scanners and all that other fancy equipment."

"I'll take care of that thank you Chief. But for your information we ran a fisherman down out here once on a ship I was on. A wooden bastard. You don't get an echo from them — so they don't show up on the screen. So radar or no radar, we keep that racket going," he said testily.

"Sorry Cap'n. Well you probably won't believe this, and again it's my fault — I want you to understand that ye ken — but half of the specially fitted oil fuel reserve tanks were never filled in the first bloody place."

"Oh, my God!" Tresilian's face turned white. "You mean they weren't full when we left Liverpool?"

"I know Cap'n, I know. How do you think I feel eh? I admit it. In 40 years at sea this the worst case of downright negligence I've known. But you see we've only just needed those tanks — and we hadn't sounded them up until now. I told the Second to open the valves into the settling tanks a few minutes ago and then nothing happened." The old Scot trailed off forlornly and looked away, puffing savagely on his pipe as an upset child devours a comforter. Tresilian felt sorry for the small man.

He brought himself up short.

"Right Chief. Spilt milk rules apply. Six hours you say. That won't get us much closer. I'll call Digby, but I think we'll stop her anyway. The bad part of it all is that the bloody oil companies announced a long time ago that they wouldn't give us a drop. The lilywhite bastards couldn't think of supplying a contraband vessel. Haha! Can you hang on up here a minute? Good. I'll rustle Alan out of his bunk."

Two minutes later the Australian, who like just about everyone else aboard couldn't sleep through the incessantly intermittent fog signal, arrived in the chartroom wearing a dressing gown. Tresilian told him the news. He sounded jovial.

"Nothing to worry about, men. I was a bonza oarsman at college in Adelaide. Know a bit about sail too. Went on the Sydney-Hobart once. And we won. What's the score then, Glyn?" and he poured tea from a tray on the sextant rack.

"Pretty low, I'd say Alan. But we'll stop her now. We can't get anywhere close — and that way at least we can keep the generators and auxiliaries going. For how long do you reckon, Chief?"

"With main engines shut down? Oh, about three days I'd say."

"OK Chief. Down you go. We'll stop her." A minute later the telegraph clanged, the ship lost way and the devilish one blast multiplied to the fog signal for a vessel not under command. 'Navis Pacifica' sat ducklike in the Kuril current. Tresilian and Digby anxiously sought alternatives.

"I don't know, Alan. I just don't know, and I can't think straight. Here we've been worrying all the time about what the famous 'they' would do, and let's face it, they haven't done a hell of a lot to us so far, and we can't even fill all our own bloody fuel tanks." Tresilian spat the words, throwing a pair of parallel rulers down the chart.

"We'll be a floating laughing stock. Oh, my word yes. But then surely we're not going to say anything on the air, eh?"

"Oh, hell, no. Not until we absolutely have to. Unless they monkeyed up the stores and fresh water, we could wallow on out here for weeks. Bloody uncomfortable and cold. But we could survive." There was a knock on the inside chartroom door. Tresilian opened it and found Julie and Michael in their night clothes.

"Come in both of you. Michael, make some fresh tea will you?"

"OK Dad; what's wrong?"

"Well, to put it plainly, we've just about run out of gas."

"What?" his wife and son spoke together.

"Yep. The why's and wherefore's don't much matter right now. But we've stopped her to conserve the little we've got left. It's not enough to get us to any port and even if we could reach one it wouldn't do us any good. You know the agreement they've made not to supply us with any fuel?"

No one said anything for a few seconds. Then Julie asked quietly. "Is the ship safe? I mean will anything . . ."

"Oh, the ship's fine. She'll stay afloat for ever of course. And we've got provisions and fresh water for a very long time. We're adrift — that's all. We'll have a cup of tea and then I think we'll all try and get some shut eye. I'll tell them to cut the whistle down a bit."

The ship sounded oddly quiet. Soon Michael brought in a large pot of newly brewed hot tea. They all had a cup. Julie motioned to him and excused herself. Glyn told the second mate that he was leaving the bridge for a minute or two. In the day-room he said. "Julie, I can't sleep here darling. I'll get my head down on the chartroom settee."

"No, dear it's not that. But I've just thought of something. Maybe I can make myself useful again," saying the words with determination and longing. "Whatever happens, sooner or later we'll have to be towed — right?"

"Er, yes. Right. Why?"

"Well — don't you see? Daddy. I think they must still be in Osaka. You remember, they said . . ."

"Of course. How about that. Yes. He was sent over to look after the display of the ocean salvage stuff at the Expo 70 Dutch Pavilion, wasn't he? Hmmm. Good. Very good Julie. I wonder if the Japs'll give us R/T service. We haven't asked anyone to use it since California. We'll try and raise him at daylight. Try and get some kip now." He kissed her and went back on the bridge.

.   .   .   .

"Ya, hello, Glyn. I hear you very vell. Are we on the air now?" the voice of Captain Jan de Vries came through clearly on the R/T from his hotel in Osaka at 7 a.m. local time.

"No, Captain," Tresilian replied, "this is private. Why don't you and Mrs. de Vries speak to Julie and then I want to talk to you urgently," and he passed the headset. She spoke to her parents briefly.

"Right then Mummy. Get Daddy, will you? Here's Glyn."
Julie mentioned nothing about the fuel problem.

"Captain, we're in the soup. Just about out of bunkers. I won't go into details. Yes, er, no. Nothing damaged. No leakages. Didn't have the damned stuff aboard in Liverpool. Yes, I know. Negligence. But we can't do anything about that now. I don't want to break it on the air though."

"I'm very sorry to hear this Glyn. Naturally, we'll do the job if you want. We have a tow due at Yokohama in a couple of days. What's your position? Alright, we'll send the same tug out to you," the Holland's Glory man said reassuringly.

"What is the tow, Captain?" Tresilian enquired.

"Believe it or not," and his father-in-law laughed, "it's a damn great super tanker right down to her marks with crude oil. Unshipped her rudder in a China Sea typhoon last week. Couldn't do anything with a jury rig. So we sent the 'Lies Beatrix' out to her from Manilla. She was bound for Yokohama, anyway."

"Where's she registered?"

"Where do you think? Wafrilla, of course. What ship isn't these days?"

"Same ship and cargo owners I suppose?"

"Ya, World Oil," de Vries replied.

"They sure as hell don't come any bigger than that. You've heard about the total oil embargo on us eh?"

"Of course. Now I want to say something to you, Glyn," a note of pride coming into the Dutchman's voice. "Despite our early doubts, you're doing a good job. I don't think there's ever been world-wide news like it. We still can't get used to the idea of having you as a son-in-law. But we don't mention it any more. As soon as we do, the press come flocking round. Julie's mother's quite overwhelmed by it — and so am I."

"Thanks, Captain, for the kind words. But right now I've got a problem. Rudder trouble you say — on this World Oil tanker? Her main engines and pumps must be OK then?"

"What? Oh, yes, I imagine so." Shocked by the implication, he gasped. "Why surely you're not thinking of taking fuel from her?"

"Yes. That's exactly what I was thinking. I know World Oil would never agree to it. So let's find a way. How about this? No, no. First — what crew does she have — and who's commanding her?" Still stunned by the incredulity of the idea, the Dutchman replied with fast-waning enthusiasm: "Oh I don't have that kind of information with me here Glyn, but I could get it from our Yokohama office, I think, if you really need it. It might take a few hours though. Call me here on the R/T again at noon. I'll see what I can do. Now what exactly do you have in mind?" he asked suspiciously.

"Fun, Captain. Fun. For you and all the family. I'll tell you later. But if she's Wafrillia registered, I'll bet she's a mixed bag. Bye for now."

After breakfast, Glyn spoke to the ship's company on the public address. It was a brief explanation, and he finished:

"I can't emphasize enough that the ship it not in any danger. We have a practically indefinite supply of fresh water and provisions aboard — and the worst that can happen is that we might feel a bit chilly in a few days — if we're not under way again by then. So carry on as usual; and again I remind you not to make any broadcast mention of our being stopped through lack of fuel. the only real pain I can foresee is having to shave in cold water. This afternoon I'll be in a better position of knowing whether we can work something out fairly soon."

At mid-day Tresilian spoke to his father-in-law again on R/T.

"You were right, Glyn. The 'Oil Constellation.' She's a mixed bag, sure enough. German and Italian Deck and Engineer Officers — and a Greek Master. Captain Nicholas Phrixos; he's a very experienced Tanker man they tell me."

"Thank you, Captain. Now listen and please listen hard and don't say anything until I've finished. We'll have to risk security I'm afraid. What I'm going to propose is just about the only way out that I can see . . ." Tresilian outlined his scheme.

When he had finished, de Vries said quietly. "You realize of course that this will finish me?"

"Yes, I do Captain. But I realize even more that unless we can get down to Vietnam and Korea damn soon, everybody else'll be finished too . . ."

.   .   .   .

Twelve hours later one of the helijets with spare fuel aboard
to augment its special long range capacity, thrashed and screamed off 'Navis Pacifica's' after deck bound for the coastal town
of Shingu, some 70 miles south-east of Osaka. Fifteen miles off
shore, it hovered low over a powerful sea launch, paid out a
man harness and winched Captain de Vries up to the flight
cabin.

There was a brief re-union aboard the 'Navis Pacifica' with
Julie, Glyn and Michael while the helijets refuelled and then
the Dutchman took off again for the 'Lies Beatrix.' The tug's
Master and de Vries had sailed together many times before
when Julie's father had been in command. Fog in the area had
lifted and the sea was calm enough for the helijet to float on
it's amphibious landing cushions. The two ocean salvage men
discussed the operation. An hour later de Vries called Tresilian
on the R/T.

"Everything's fine so far, Glyn. I'll call the 'Oil Constellation'
right away. And I'll be back to you as soon as there's news.
Stand by."

The Rotterdam registered tug blinked Morse Code on her
Aldis lamp. The German officer of the watch on the super
tanker's bridge, several ship's lengths astern, replied immediately
with a long 'T' to proceed. The Tug flashed:

"MARINE SUPERINTENDENT HOLLAND OCEAN SAL-
VAGE COMPANY NOW ABOARD LIES BEATRIX RE-
QUESTS URGENT PERMISSION LAND BY HELICOPTER
YOUR DECK."

Captain Phrixos, who had read the signal in his cabin, rushed
into the wheelhouse, grabbed the signalling apparatus and made
"PERMISSION GRANTED."

Captains de Vries and Phrixos bargained, over wine and
black olives, in the Owner's private dining room for several
hours. The supply and demand factor was simple enough.
Phrixos had sufficient fuel aboard the 'Oil Constellation' to fuel
a fleet of Liberty ships, but a direct order not to fuel the 'Navis
Pacifica.' What price had to be paid then for Phrixos to con-
travene his owner's orders? The demand was great, but had to
meet Phrixos' price: sufficient cash to atone for loss of job, and

dismissal in disgrace; in effect, instant retirement for life. de Vries knew all this.

On the premise that each man has his price, succinctly outlined to him by a now seemingly unscrupulous Glyn face to face with an obsession, de Vries started with a figure of $250,000. They finished at Phrixos' figure of a million dollars — in United States funds. At the end, the small Greek seaman's moustache was sodden with olive oil, wine and sweat. Exhausted from endless arm waving and shoulder shrugging, he jabbed a forefinger at the stolid Dutchman's head.

"This is most dangerous thing I ever been asked to do Captain. No, never mind seamanship. I am one of best tanker sailors in the world. That's no point," and he lit a cigarette furiously. de Vries was tempted again to convince the little Master that the 'Lies Beatrix' and not his disabled leviathan, would be doing the manoeuvre. But he'd known for sometime how futile the effort would be.

"You understand Captain," Phrixos went on with his haytosser hands, "that to me it's finish. Company is firing me just like that. When they find out — before we are getting Yokohama — maybe they signal the Chief Officer to lock me up. I don't know. But maybe. But," and his round swarthy face shone and changed expression, "a million dollars I like. I like very much. I am sailor. Very bloody good. Yes. But also businessman I am. Business very good Captain. Good for people — good for world," he concluded with satisfaction and filled de Vries' glass again. "Here, Captain, drink. To good agreement. OK. I think you make very good business — for you. You get ship bunkered. I get sack. Yes, I get million dollars — but no more ship to sail. And I have many people in Greece. My family — my wife's family. Everybody come to good old Phrixos for money. My name Phrixos — not Midas," he said sadly. And then he thought of the Ionian Island where he lived, and of the simple folk who were his kin. And a lord-of-the-manor like look came into his small and darting eyes. He stood up and shook hands with de Vries.

"OK, Captain. You signal your tug he can alter course. Alright, we go on bridge. Then we can come back and have good eat." de Vries was silent. The afternoon's work had left him downcast and uncomfortable. If he'd been in Phrixos' place he would have refused.

The 'Lies Beatrix' slowly healed over to port as she and her massive charge swung round. The tow's E.T.A. 'Navis Pacifica' was 36 hours. de Vries spoke to Tresilian in prearranged code on the 'Oil Constellation's' R/T after which all three ships agreed to keep radio silence until they sighted each other for the rendez-vous. Later, as they fell to an enormous mixed grill, Phrixos pointed with his fork.

"One thing, Captain de Vries. You say your Principal, whoever he is, is putting my money in the Yokohama bank. What proof I can get? Because in Yokohama, I bugger off toute suite. No time for mistakes."

"Yes, I thought you would worry about that," de Vries said, "so we can do this. After the ship has refuelled, I'll come to Yokohama with you. I was going on the tug but for your security I'll stay aboard with you. Also, I'll probably have my Principal's son with me. He'll be staying with us in Osaka for a while. So you can keep us both aboard until you've checked that the dollars have been desposited for you."

"Yes. That is good. You live in Osaka, Captain?"

"Only until I've disposed of the maritime stuff in the Dutch pavilion," de Vries explained.

"I saw that Expo 67 in Montreal. That was good, yes. We were at the east end oil docks. But my ship then — she was much smaller than the 'Oil Constellation.' The Osaka Fair is good? Like Montreal?"

"Oh, yes. It seems to have gone very well. Captain Phrixos, what about Customs and Immigration for us in Yokohama? Will we be able to get ashore?"

"Only thing mattering is money, Captain. When I see that in bank, you get ashore very pronto. I worry about it. Not you."

Using a direction finder signal from 'Navis Pacifica' again, de Vries and the helijet whirled back to the old Liberty ship's after deck. Michael was delighted at the prospect of seeing Expo 70 and getting ashore once more. For some time the voyage had palled on the youngster who badly missed friends and age group. Although Tresilian tried to coax her to join de Vries at the same time, Julie was adamant in her determination to stay on board. Besides, she admitted to herself, there were other very good reasons why she didn't want to leave the ship.

"We've done a lot together already, Glyn. Let's finish it together," she said firmly.

"But it's so easy," he insisted "you can always fly down to Hong Kong, just before we leave. You'd enjoy a break in Osaka with your parents and Michael wouldn't you?" he suggested as persuasively as he could.

"No, and that's final."

"You win, and I love you for it. But I'll tell you this. When this little romp's all over, whatever happens, you and I, just the two of us, are going to have a vacation that no travel agent in the whole bloody world could dream up. Hell — just our luck. It would happen. See that lot?" he said and they looked out of the scuttle at a mounting sea and swell. The lame old ship fell and rolled into a trough.

They were caught inside the fringe of a cyclone. It had expelled the fog, but with its steady high gale force winds would bring on sudden rough and churning seas. Soon, the ship was rolling violently.

The weather worsened considerably and it took the 'Lies Beatrix' 12 hours longer than originally estimated to bring the super tanker to 'Navis Pacifica.' The re-fuelling operation would have to take place in heavy, near-typhoon seas.

On sighting each other the three ships broke radio silence and the air crackled on R/T with seamen's talk. Glyn asked his father-in-law to take charge.

"You do have enough fuel to steer her for a couple of hours, Glyn?"

"Yes, the Chief says three — maximum."

"Good, as long as it doesn't take us any longer to get the hose connected, we'll make it. She'd never lay alongside us in this weather. Got any really heavy fenders?"

"No, I'm afraid not, Captain. Just the normal berthing size."

"You'd better put them over anyway. Port side. Captain Phrixos, I'll want you to start pumping oil when you're about a mile off. I'll tell you when. Couple up hoses to maximum length and have them ready to starboard. Kees," and de Vries spoke to his former shipmate, Captain Kees de Jong, commanding the 'Lies Beatrix,' "keep her well to windward of us as she pumps oil. Then bring her up into the wind with just enough speed to hold her. When you've got her nicely, we'll get under way and come up on your starboard side. We can't get close enough in this sea to use the tanker's derrick as a hose suspension — so one of the helicopters'll hover between the ships and keep it up. Both pilots say they can do it. There's nothing we can do except believe them.

"Captain Tresilian has asked me to take temporary command for the re-fuelling — so I'll be giving helm and engine room orders to all ships from here. Don't leave your R/T's."

Slowly the giant tow came corkscrewing to within six lengths of the 'Navis Pacifica.' Using a vertical sextant angle for the distance off, de Vries gave the order.

"That's fine, Kees. Try and check her now. Go ahead Captain Phrixos — discharge, and put your pumps on full power."

In less than a minute, there were signs of a thousand U-Boat sinkings in the ships' area. Hundreds of tons of thick, gooey, black, slimy, bird and coastal resort killing crude oil threw up from below the mammoth tanker's heaving waterline. Like a zillion unseen octopi, the ugly fluid grabbed and partially tamed the storm whipped sea.

"How much you wanting me pump, Captain de Vries?" Phrixos asked in a voice carrying equal parts of exhilaration and terror.

"At least a thousand tons. I'll tell you when to stop. Don't worry, Captain," de Vries answered. To Tresilian he said. "Tell your Chief we'll be wanting to steer her in about ten minutes."

"Fine, Captain. The helijet's all set. The Bosun bent a special grappler on the man harness. With that added length he'll be able to get extra height too."

On the 'Navis Pacifica's' bridge they watched the oil spread. "That's enough Captain Phrixos. Stop your pumps. Kees, fall right down now. Come astern of us and then bring her into the wind," de Vries ordered. The tug pounded round steering the supertanker to leeward of the huge oil mass. With minimum power for steerage they would at least begin the transfusion in the relative calm of the fuel blanketed sea.

"Now, Glyn. Stand by main engines and helicopter," the Dutchman said as the tug pitched into the greasy reeking swell.

"Slow ahead then. Hard a-starboard. Let me know when she answers, Quartermaster."

"Aye, aye, sir. Answering now," the Belgian at the 'Navis Pacifica's' wheel shouted above the gale tearing through the open wheelhouse doors.

"Good. Ease your helm," de Vries shouted. "Midships. Steady now if you can. Very well. Now Quartermaster try and keep the tanker's funnel fine to port. About a point. That's it. That's good. Kees, can you slow any more and still hold her?" he asked the 'Lies Beatrix' on the R/T handset.

"Just a rev or two — but not much I'm afraid Jan," de Jong answered.

"O.K. Try to keep minimum possible way. Glyn, we'll put her on full for a minute or two." Glyn clanged the telegraph to maximum speed and 'Navis Pacifica's' stem drew level with the 'Oil Constellation's' stern.

"Send your helicopter away, Glyn. Half ahead, Third Mate. Slow ahead. That's nice Quartermaster. Keep her very steady if you can. Let me know at once if she won't answer. I'd rather part the hose now than collide with the big son-of-a-bitch." Captain de Vries, who didn't ordinarily use expletives, was swearing to ease the strain within himself. "Captain Phrixos stand by to make your hose grommets and bridle fast. Your people all set below for coupling at the filler pipe, Glyn?"

"Yes, Captain. Ready," Tresilian assured his father-in-law who, as he had done for years during nervous moments, eased the tension by rolling a cigarette out of his pipe tobacco pouch. de Vries brought the peace ship to within a hundred parallel bucking feet of the floating oil field. The helijet shrieked its way between the hulls.

"Now, hook on," de Vries snapped. "Glyn, tell the Chief to hold those revs exactly as they are. Kees, keep her like that for as long as you can. I'd say we're going through about 3 knots — and that'll do."

With a magnificent display of airmanship, the helijet, exposed to the gale between the ships, chopped down close to the super-tanker's deck and lowered the weighted harness line. The deck crew slung on the two bridle chain hooks and the helicopter slowly took the strain; the chains and hoses thus formed an Isoseles triangle suspended by the blades above. 'Navis Pacifica's' Chief Officer ordered his men to haul in on the heaving line bent on to the hose end and soon the life giving tube was inboard and bolted onto the filling pipe.

"Connected up and ready sir," the German officer reported to Tresilian in the wheelhouse. Glyn nodded.

"Thank you Mr. Mate," de Vries acknowledged. "Right Captain Phrixos — start your pumps please."

Three hours later, with thousands of tons of fuel oil poured onto the furious sea and into the 'Navis Pacifica,' it was over. The peace ship's tanks were full to capacity, the helijet was stowed in its hangar below, and the tow, with Captain de Vries and Michael aboard the 'Oil Constellation' resumed course for Yokohama.

.   .   .   .

The Liberty ship picked up her southwesterly course and sailed into finer weather heading for the Formosa strait and Hong Kong. As the vessel entered the water stretch between Nationalist and Communist China, Glyn ordered the helijets off for Tronphone drops on either side.

Surveillance began again as U.S. and Chinese ships and aircraft watched her constantly. But she was not accosted as she dropped anchor in the beautiful harbour at Hong Kong on September 5, 1970. Tresilian spoke to the ship.

"Very soon we'll all be stepping ashore for the first time since we sailed from the British Isles in the spring. I doubt that anyone could put into words the appreciation I feel for everything you've all done. Perhaps the best way is to look at what has happened since we began Talk of the World.

"The Middle East is calmer and hundreds of thousands of Arab refugees are being welcomed and cared for by individual Israelis. It's true that there's no sign of actual treaties being signed by governments — but does that matter when people themselves have decided to put a stop to wanton slaughter?

"In Americus the fighting's nearly over — but that's a mixed blessing with so much U.S. human and material resource being deployed out here to the Asian theatre.

"In the United Nations the Secretary-General is enjoying an authority the office has rarely known before.

"I think we cannot reasonably expect or want further proof of the rightness of our dogma, that in this age every man, woman and child depends on every other human for survival.

"Throughout our voyage we've learned how desperately the

overwhelming majority of people want to understand and co-exist. You Talkers have cleared the way for that to be said. Nothing must stop us now. Nothing. We'll be here for about ten days to give you and the ship a chance to refresh and recover.

"As we're a few days late, we won't be able to have more than a day from the London Opera Company. They'll be joining us aboard to-morrow and we'll go out just beyond territorial limits so that they can perform on the after-deck. Draw whatever cash you need from the Chief Steward. There'll be a 24 hour launch service to and from the ship so come and go as you please. Have a good time," and he clicked off the PA microphone switch.

.   .   .   .

The principals, chorus and orchestra of the touring London Opera Company performed in shifts for 12 hours the following day as 'Navis Pacifica' slowly steamed off the coast between Hong Kong and Macao. As Dame Gwynneth had promised, the musical fare was wide, varied and very international.

Particularly evocative for Western listeners were La Golondrina sung by one of the Company's Irish born tenors and the 23rd psalm tune 'Crimond' performed in the style and manner of the Glasgow Orpheus Choir. There were selections indigenous to all the continents, grand Italian set pieces, Strauss, Gilbert and Sullivan, Offenbach, Faust, Handel and the Hallelujah Chorus, Verdi's Chorus of Hebrew Slaves, some Mozart, Lehar. A feast of brilliant sound for every known taste.

That night, with the ship back at her harbour anchorage, Julie and Glyn dined with Dame Gwynneth Rhondda-Llandaff at a famous Hong Kong restaurant. Glyn and Julie told Dame Gwynneth of their recent adventures running out of fuel and the dramatics of the re-fuelling operation. When they had ordered, Dame Gwynneth told them how pleased Yerbury was with the operation. "He thinks things have gone very well. And how exciting it's all sounded. Wherever we've been that's all people seem to be talking about. And I've really had to bite my tongue hard whenever I've felt the urge to show off and tell them I know all about it . . . What are your long range plans Glyn?"

"A bit indefinite at present, Dame Gwynneth. We did discuss with Julie's father the possibility of going to Osaka after the Korean work."

"But how, when, and where will the voyage end actually? 'Y' will probably want to know," Dame Gwynneth persisted.

"Well that'll depend on how we do in the Gulf of Tonkin and off Korea. It's impossible to say. Anything can happen. But if we can help to get things going — or I should say stopping — the way we did in the Middle East and Central America, I think our work'll have been done. The rest'll be up to the U.N. If the fighting slows and stops in both Vietnam and Korea, I can't see China's UN admission being far behind. The S.G. could wave a really big stick then. We'll see. And just play things day to day as we've done all along. You've heard Alan Digby on the air I suppose, Dame Gwynneth? I don't know what we'd have done without him. A real tower."

"Yes, of course. Many times. Such a nice speaking voice — unshared I fear by some of his countrymen. I hope that's not unkind because the Australians are such generous and lovable people — but I do wish they would round out their vowels. Julie, you must have been so proud of your father when you ran out of petrol or whatever it is you use. Driving all those ships so carefully. Such cleverness," the old lady beamed.

"I was proud, Dame Gwynneth. But I know that Glyn could have done it too. You should have seen him taking the ship through the Suez Canal on his own without a pilot! All those sunken ships to go around. But I know Daddy was thrilled to bits that Glyn asked him to take command when we refuelled. Also, the helicopter pilots were fantastic, hovering for three hours holding up the hose in that awful wind with very little space between the ships."

"Glyn, I have an idea," Dame Gwynneth said enthusiastically. "No, I'm being quite serious. When it's all over and you've had a good holiday, you must write a book about the entire experience. All the fascinating tidbits as well. Of course the only reason that people will believe it is because they'll have to. It has all happened — hasn't it?

"And then we'll have a libretto and score set to the story and we'll make a fine opera from it. Because you like the Latin, and with the proper permission, we'll call it 'Pacem in Terris.' What do you think about that?" and she looked expectantly at the couple. Julie of course, was thrilled at the possibility, intensely proud. Tresilian laughed kindly. "It's a very flattering idea, Dame Gwynneth. But frankly I couldn't write such an account. It'd have to be ghosted. I'm a talker remember, and I find composition hard work. Much too laborious for a lazy moron like me, I'm afraid."

"Now he wants us to contradict him Julie, but we won't, will we?"

After the meal, Dame Gwynneth looked at her watch. "My word, it's quite late and we have an early start at the airport. Thank you so much for the evening — be sure I'll give 'Y' all your news."

Dame Gwynneth left by taxi for her hotel and Julie and Glyn took a rickshaw back to the launch jetty.

.   .   .   .

Soong Lee walked aboard the Kowloon Ferry. She was alone and on her way to a restaurant she knew on Nathan Road. As the small passenger vessel swung round to make its way across the junk and sam-pan infested harbour, she felt a tap on her shoulder. She turned.

"Hello, Soong," one of the two stern faced orientals said in Chinese. "Don't move or say anything. We came all the way from Peking to meet you. Talking here is difficult so we will wait until we reach Kowloon."

She walked between them to the top story of a delapidated building near a dry dock. In the room were some wooden chairs and an oil cloth covered table.

"Sit down, Soong," the other man who had not spoken until now gestured to her. "Why have you not done your duty?" he asked quietly.

"I was told in New York to use my discretion." Gone now was the gentle warmth of the seductress.

"And when do you intend to be discreet?" his companion demanded.

"That depends. I take it you have orders?"

"Yes," one of them said and took a wallet from his coat. He handed her a photograph. "Do you recognize any of these people?" She glanced at the group and gave it back.

"You know very well I do."

"We have them Soong, — and a letter from your father. You might like to read it."

"Our dearest Soong," she read. "We are all staying for a little while with the Peoples' Security Forces of the Interior. I feel sure there must have been a misunderstanding about your loyalty to our country — and that you will do whatever duties are required of you for Mao and Peoples' China. We are all well and comfortable. And look forward to seeing you in Peking when your work is done." Her father had not signed the letter. She folded the paper and the agent put it in his pocket.

"What are the ship's next movements?" he snapped.

"Gulf of Tonkin, for what they call 'mopping up' operations off Vietnam. Then to the Gulf of Thailand to work off Cambodia and Bangkok. They think there's a lot of trouble brewing there and they'll try to catch it before it gets any bigger. Then to Korea for the big one."

"Very well, Soong. These are your orders. Remember your family would like you to obey them. They are simple to understand. The ship must be totally silenced by the time she reaches the 30th. parallel. That is — before she get's to the Yellow Sea. That is all Soong. You are free to go and enjoy Kowloon."

CHAPTER 10

'Navis Pacifica' rounded Hainan Island and entered the Gulf of Tonkin on September 27, 1970. Although the Asian fuse had by now moved from Vietnam to Korea as a result of an official, but fitful truce born in uncomfortable talks between Washington and Hanoi, the fighting was by no means over in South-East Asia. A series of almost 'personal' wars was being fought by fanatical forces on both sides. Peace was still far away, with the South Vietnamese now overtly led by General Trac, who had successfully kept the Viet Cong out of any settlement. Large numbers of American soldiers were still in the country, 'protecting' the South Vietnam regime against Hanoi which had been lying low, having agreed to the official truce more for reasons of exhaustion than anything else. Communists both north and south of the border were still insisting on unity of the whole of Vietnam. Tens of thousands of Viet Cong still flung themselves out of the swamp and jungle and sniped and bombed South Vietnamese who, together with 100,000 U.S. soldiers were joined by small groups of extremists from the United States revelling in occidental versions of Hari-Kari.

When they had cleared Hong Kong, Tresilian and Digby gave the Talkers a statement to read indicating the ship's intention to close into the mainland Chinese shore for Tronphone dropping in the vicinity of the Luichow Peninsula and Hainan Strait. Within minutes they received an official wave off from Peking on R/T. Although more bellicose, the declaration was much the same as the one from South Africa — any territorial violation by the 'Navis Pacifica' would be returned by an immediate Peoples' Coast Defence Forces attack on the ship. Digby was amused by the signal's allusion to 'this floating warehouse of western trickery.'

At a maximum northerly latitude of 22 degrees, just south of the Chinese border, Tresilian ordered the helijets away.

With every take off the ship broadcast the fact and reminders of their flying areas, altitudes, and non-combatant status.

After a week of nerve torturing but unharmed operations, 'Navis Pacifica' rounded Point Camau and steamed into the Gulf of Thailand. She would stay here, in the relatively untroubled waters at the centre and slowly circle-steam. From this position, the Talkers would talk as they'd never done before, and the helijets would Tronphone drop between Bangkok and Chanthaburi. The undeclared peoples' war in Thailand had broken out late in 1969 and was now beginning to fan north and east to large areas of Laos and Cambodia.

Tronphone calls came in regularly from all parts of Vietnam and United States servicemen had also picked up a great many of the little communicators. The Plan at this time called for a concentration of dialogue between North and South Vietnamese; and repeated references to the Middle East and Americus. Once started, these exchanges rapidly turned into hysterical pro and anti-American tirades — with Viet Cong and South Vietnamese evidently having very little else to discuss. The depressing quarrels worsened when the ship arranged an 'official statement' Tronphone hook up between the U.S. C-in-C in Saigon, and a Viet Cong Colonel near the outskirts of Khe Sanh.

V.C. Officer: "The trouble with you Americans is that you don't understand our mystique. All we Vietnamese have an intense nationalism. Including the temporary traitors who are your lackeys in Saigon. You will never beat us because we have a limitless capacity for self-sacrifice. Even if you could destroy Hanoi, we'd go back to the jungles and fight again. And we'd win. And then we'd build a new Hanoi. Don't you people have any sense of history? Don't you realize the glorious guerilla tradition that we've had for centuries? You're not the only people who have tried to save us from ourselves. There were the conquering Monguls, the conquering Mings, and then the conquering French. Remember Dien Bien Phu? The only real difference between our fighting men and your Vietnamese is that you've taught them to want payment. But we kill you and all our enemies for very little or no money. We were not born free — but we are patriots and if our love of country means death we accept it — so that our children and their children may live at liberty even if we can't. As you know General, all war is murder anyway. But only you Westerners with your phony morality waste time with the hypocrisy of worrying about how the murder is done. You, above all, should know that we are not a faint people. None of the atrocities that we commit against you worries us at all. When one's hands are dirty with the work of destroying a great evil, one's soul and conscience are never more clean."

U.S. C-in-C: "I agreed unconditionally to join in on this broadcast in the first place because, in keeping with my country's policy, I will explore any avenue and any means that could help to bring a true peace with honour solution to the Asian war theatre. But as the world heard just a few seconds ago, such a settlement would seem as impossible now as it ever was. The 'Navis Pacifica' continually stresses 'international understanding through international dialogue.' And talk between peoples who understand understanding — rather than between governments who obviously don't. Now I am a soldier and have no wish to be drawn into vague philosophical arguments. But it would be foolish to deny the apparently secure cease fires that the ship's 'Talk of the World' broadcasts were able to generate in the Middle East and Americus. My joint Chiefs of Staff have issued no orders denying United States servicemen out here the choice of participating in the transmissions if they so choose. Can there be any serious hope of peace, however, when as we've just learned, one side is proud and even unctuous about the atrocities they wantonly commit on innocent human beings?"

The Viet Cong officer hit back.

V.C. Officer: "And I suppose napalm, gas, germ and anti-personnel pineapple bomb warfare are all fair play? I don't really care whether they are or not. We make no pretence at playing any rules-game. I just want the world to know that you play the same game too — but feign sportsmanship while you're doing it."

U.S. C-in-C: "Perhaps ordinary men and women everywhere will now realise how and why the prospects of peace out here seem so remote. In closing, I want to thank the ship's personnel for their co-operation and to reiterate my country's guarantee that a complete and lasting peace is our only target."

V.C. Officer: "We've been hearing that from the American

aggressors since they sent their 'Advisers' out here soon after we routed the French. We on our part have an unshakeable confidence that we'll drive every American out of our country."

"Oh, God Alan. What's the use?" Tresilian said and walked back to the bridge.

"I know," Digby commiserated; "pretty disheartening. Especially when you consider that those two lines are typical of about all we've heard for the last week since we've been here. Can't seem to make any head-way whatever we do," Alan finished morosely and looked at the sea ahead.

"I've been listening to us pretty carefully, Alan. There's something missing — we're not getting through. Perhaps we're milking the Middle East example too much. But about the only real impact we had was when that American nursing sister came on and described those North Vietnamese women and children in the base hospital." Tresilian paced the wing of the bridge twice; then turned and pointed at the Australian as he often did when a good idea came.

"Tell you what Alan. Let's get off the Middle East and Americus completely. Instead we'll get onto the brotherhood bit again — as we did off Suez — and call for individual and voluntary acts of fire pause. I know what. Quote that Viet Cong guy, 'All war is murder anyway.' Then follow that right up and say something like 'That's about the only real truth that's ever come out of this bloody mess. Right. All war is murder. Now, and give 'em hell as you do this bit, 'you there — Viet Cong, South Vietnamese, American Minute Man, Thai, Laotian, Cambodian — all of you — whether you're flying a plane load of bombs, or triggering a mortar, or sniping from a building or a tree — right now, just before you fire or drop — pause — think — and then stop. Do you really want to commit murder? Because we agree that's what it is. If you're hearing us at this very moment — don't pull that trigger — don't open that bomb bay.' That kind of thing. Let's see if we make any yards with it. Wait a minute. I don't think you'd better do it. It'll lose a bit in translation. Direct, I think. Brief them all in there will you?" He clapped Digby on the back. "Oh, and Alan, just before you go in — get them to hammer out the fact that so far — where we need results — we haven't had any. Ram home that all we've had on the air so far from both sides out here are the same tired old scraps — and that every one brings the outbreak that much nearer. Lay that on heavily. Let's scare the hell out of them. No one's got anything to lose."

The call for the individual cease fires was gradually taken up. The anti-murder and brotherhood appeals first got response in Thailand and spread slowly through Laos and Cambodia.

On 'Talk of the World' another American Nursing Sister spoke of unconfirmed reports that US pilots had started to jettison bombs over the Yellow Sea. Military spokesmen declined to comment. When 'Talk of the World' wasn't calling for individual cease fires, the broadcasts concentrated on appeals for refugee assistance.

"Does it matter who is right and who is wrong out here when friend and foe alike lack even a basic appreciation of humanity? When it is not enough that mothers and children in their arms are gashed and burned but must also get through the day without shelter from the wet? Listen again — does it matter who is right? Is not everyone wrong? And absolutely wrong?

"Unless we are all lunatics and madmen, surely we can share a pittance of food, some space even in a sewer tunnel, a piece of clothing. And if we can do that — can we not share the most precious thing of all — another human being's life?

"We urge you to ask yourselves these questions every minute of the day — and ask them unceasingly of others — especially those who may not yet have heard us. Turn up the volume of your transistor radios high: so that the sound of peace may be shared and brought to every heart . . ."

. . . .

The Plan gathered momentum. And four weeks later even the token courts martial, set up by the military in Saigon and Hanoi, no longer attempted to discipline soldiers and highranking officers who had fallen under its simple spell. The International Control Commission seized the chance, working closely with UNRRA. Between them, the agencies sprouted refugee and medical aid centers wherever the killing dissolved.

As the 'Navis Pacifica' cruised slowly on a twenty mile radius in the Gulf of Thailand, Tresilian and Digby kept 'Talk of the World' on the air around the clock. The gruelling six hours on, six hours off schedule strained the Talker's stamina and concentration. But even with bleary eyed fatigue showing through, their morale was high as they sustained a furious pour of words. The prize was on its way.

. . . .

Elsewhere, the recently popular Plan was losing the ratings battle. 'Navis Pacifica' had given them an overdose of 'peace.' Audiences switched to the other stations, or wanted their old programming back. Furthermore, the aura of danger surrounding 'Navis Pacifica' went out of 'Talk of the World.'

General Cosmetics' CRAK and other stations among the 300 of nearly 5000 in Canada and the U.S. alone, and on every continent now cursed the Plan for the near achievement of its purpose. Their shouts were louder now than when 'Talk of the World' first swamped them in the spring. As he prepared for yet another crisis, Burt Brewster held noisy court over noon tavern ale in downtown Montreal.

"Goddam that Tresilian," he bawled and signalled for beer. "I teach him everything he knows; then he screws up my frequency with all that ship crap, and then when we get every local and national sponsor on our air — what does he do? He screws it all up. That's what he does. We're losing thousands of the bastards now. They're tuning out in trainloads. No excitement. No oomph anymore. No Pope, no audience. Now tell me," and the tables fell silent. "What the hell have I done in my life that makes people like Tresilian keep coming at me. Eh? Well? Well, someone say something," and the Drom looked around him threateningly.

"Aw, quit griping, Burt," the waiter said as unloaded 12 foaming glasses of draught brew. Pocketing the change he winked at the Drom's companions, saying. "Now, what's more important than peace Burt?"

"My goddam ratings. That's what," and Brewster downed his first glass of the day.

. . . .

By the end of October, the Plan's peace epidemic had spread to massive numbers of combatants in South-East Asia. And by the middle of November bloodshed had been reduced to neglible bursts between fanatics who were still shooting each other.

In both North and South Vietnam, life for inhabitants and

servicemen took on an unknown normalcy. The impossible dream — that people singly, could be persuaded to refuse war — had come true. Both populations picked themselves up and out of the ravage. They returned to villages and quietly tilled the rice fields and worked again on bamboo and teak, coal and tin, and rubber and tea.

During these weeks the world quietened down. It was a silence of uncertainty in the great power capitals. At the Secretary-General's suggestion the General Assembly had been adjourned indefinitely. Talk now, he reasoned, could undo all the good that talk had done.

Korea was a different matter. The battle burned on. And as had happened after the 'Navis Pacifica's' peace work off Americus, several more U.S. divisions were released for war duty at home and in Korea. Tresilian, naive as always befitting his broadcaster-idealist role, had hoped that by now, the Plan's effect would have been felt in Korea.

"No, Glyn," Alan said. "It just doesn't work like that. If it did we could have packed up after the Middle East. But even though they can hear every word of what's been accomplished, unless and until people actually get involved themselves with those Tronphones, you haven't got a chance. By the way, do we have enough left, do you think?" Digby asked.

"Tronphones? Just enough I'd say. God it'll be good to get to Japan. I think we've all just about had enough," Tresilian said wearily as he rang for full ahead and put 'Navis Pacifica' on a course for the Yellow Sea.

"Glyn, what about giving 'em a rest for a day or so?"

"The Talkers you mean? Yes, you bet. We'll go off the air for 48 hours and then come back with just six a day until we get there. That'll be in about 11 days. Oh, thank you sweetheart," and he took a cup of tea from the tray Julie had brought up. He had long since given up banning her from the bridge.

"Glyn dear," she said. "I heard on the overseas news just now that the race rioting's become worse in the U.S. and the U.K. over the last few days and they said something about the long hot winter. Unemployment could go up by leaps and bounds and they're even calling certain parts of California, Georgia and Texas 'potential economic disaster areas'. He said something like 'peace in much of Asia could bring terrible hardship to large parts of the U.S. and U.K.' I think he said that too much of the economy had become rooted in defence psychosis — or words like that anyway," she concluded.

"Unfortunately," Glyn muttered, "that shouldn't surprise anyone at all. Get a fix, Second Mate. No, Sir Timothy was quite right. War's very good for business. The big problem is that the two've become one and the same thing more or less. Sure there'll be difficulties — but at least there'll be life. The world'll just have to re-tool. God knows the technology's there. All we need now is the will . . ." Tresilian, Julie and Digby went down to the dayroom and listened to more news broadcasts on shortwave.

From New York there was a financial commentary dealing with the possibility of a stock market crash 'if the present pace of peace' continued. Mercifully, the man seemed to have a sense of humour. But he made the point that a change-over from the tautly geared U.S. military industrial complex to a slow-re-alignment for non-war markets would prove too much for the system and millions of workers would be unemployed. He called for preparatory action by the government now — before 'the unbridled outbreak of peace.' If nothing was done immediately, he cautioned, the situation would become a 'political nightmare' for the President.

"Ah well," Digby said, "Churchill was right again, it seems. Governments certainly don't like peace interfering with their political objectives, do they?"

.   .   .   .

In the Soviet Union, the Plan had created 'disturbing signs of independence', according to a Mokba analysis. Power had been snatched in great chunks from the Supreme Soviet and Commissars. But while the newly born thought freedoms were given open airings, especially by Sinyafsky's contemporaries, the regime and the idea seemed safe enough. More than once, since 'Navis Pacifica's' Tronphones got into the USSR via Finland and eastern Europe, the Kremlin had pressed its Peace and Friend-ship Pact ally in Washington for direct action. A condition of the Pact called for mutual agreement between the Powers on offensive measures. Under it there could be no unilateral aggres-sion. Every time the Kremlin had called for an end to the ship, the White House had vetoed the attack, but in the face of inten-sive pressures from the Chiefs of Staff.

By the time 'Navis Pacifica' had passed Phanrang, the President's life was becoming unbearable. Pentagon opposition to the peace ship was based on a 'realistic evaluation of 'Navis Pacifica's compromising work in the Far East theatre.' With fighting all but eliminated in South East Asia as commanders and combat troops laid down their arms, Trac, Tuong and other regime heads were demanding U.S. action, convinced that the Plan had all along been conceived and reared by 'defeatist elements' in the U.S. led by Dr. Gunter.

At home, the President braced himself for battle on a closer front. While the Chief Executive had taken personal command of the White — Black Civil war, exercising his rank as Commander-in-Chief, he found open public hostility on all sides directed against the Administration. Putting its tremendous public relations resources to work, the Pentagon — dubbed the 'Khaki White House' by the still hostile liberal press — seized this initiative and carried most of white America with it, persuading the people that inefficient command of military forces by the President had escalated, not contained or stopped, the livid racial war. Powerful elements at the Pentagon were talking 'rational takeover to avoid racial war at home and retreat from our responsibilities abroad.'

In Europe and elsewhere there was little editorial sympathy. Commentators singled out a prediction made by Dr. Martin Luther King Jr. a few days before his assassination. The non-violent Civil Right's leader had said then that the United States would become a Fascist state by 1970 if Congress did not do more for the poor. He said that such a regime would 'suppress' negroes and riots — but at the time he did not elaborate on the form that the suppression would take. He spoke those words at Washington's National Cathedral in a sermon to an overflow crowd of 4,000 — five times the normal Sunday turnout. A bullet in the head killed him a few nights later, and riots, arson and looting broke out almost immediately. Curfewed cities were put under martial law as thousands of troops and national guardsmen moved in.

Acknowledged by millions as a prophet of his time, King's prophecy was now coming true and a right-wing takeover was fast incubating in the Pentagon.

The U.S. economy, firmly embedded in the military-industrial complex, would continue to flourish only with the nation solidly behind the Administration as it fought the Second Korean War. It was a vicious circle. As the boys came back from Vietnam and Americus, they simply added to the racial explosion. A reduction in war orders was already creating unemployment in several regions. Together the two factors were the formula for a national blood-bath. The irony: peace abroad meant war at home.

At the White House the Council of Economic Advisers was clear on one point: if the Asian conflict was de-escalated or stopped, the gradual cutback in military orders would shatter the American industrial motor. Torn between war abroad, and a peace at home which would pit the far left against the far right, the President, propped up by amphetamine and advisers, met and conferred with the National Security Council for days on end.

Finally, they agreed on all points of their plan. Korea was the locking pin and with this concensus on strategy, the Administration would be able to solve the looming economic recession and prevent the Khaki White House military coup at the same time. The President liked the artifice in general, although the ultimate portion of it relating to the 'Navis Pacifica' bothered him greatly. He'd been a founding member of the Civil Liberties Union.

"Thank you, Gentlemen," the President said. "Perhaps now Dr. King's prophesy will turn out to be wrong after all."

A short time later, thePresident finished a Hot-Line conversation with the leader of America's Peace and Friendship pact ally country in the Kremlin. The problem of the 'Navis Pacifica' called for a joint solution.

.   .   .   .

The world waited for 'Navis Pacifica' and her Tronphones to reach Korea. While the ship was on passage the kind of lull that made Brewster and others so unhappy set in on Talk of the World. Thinking back to the ratings battles, Tresilian arranged a hook-up with Dr. Gunter solely for listeners the world over to get free medical advice on urinogenital problems. He hoped things would soon liven up.

A quarter of an hour after the President's talk with Moscow, Sir Timothy Wooffenden was called out of a boardroom conference. "I'm very sorry, Sir Timothy," his secretary said nervously, "but we have an overseas call from Washington on the line. They say it's extremely urgent."

The shipbuilder spoke on the telephone for less than a minute. He was requested to take the first available flight to New York where he would be met by and confer with 'two gentlemen from the Administration.' That was all.

Ten hours later he stepped from the naval helicopter that had landed him on the Pentagon grounds. His flight companions from Kennedy airport had introduced themselves as Ray Brown and Don Newton from the 'Administration.' All they would say in the high flying helicopter was that the visit was pertinent to the naval nuclear work that Wooffendens were doing for the United States.

Once in the Pentagon building, Wooffenden soon realised that Messrs. Brown and Newton, or whatever their real names were, enjoyed sufficiently high rank and importance to be waved and saluted on past all security checks. At the end of a corridor, Brown turned a small key in a floor recess and the facing wall lifted. They went into a self contained suite and sat down at an oval conference desk. The wall closed and Newton began.

"It's not really important Sir Timothy, but we might as well tell you that we're members of the Central Intelligence Agency. About a month ago the Agency formed a very special branch. Ray here, and I were appointed to head it up. Let's get to business. Ray?" and he passed to his colleague.

"Are we right in assuming Sir Timothy, that our naval defence contracts are very important to you?" Brown asked.

"To us personally you mean? The yard? Yes? No, you're wrong in making that assumption. Candidly — they're vital to us. We haven't worked on any mercantile tonnage for about two years now," he said and felt uneasy. The guess he'd made half a day earlier looked like being sound.

"But that's not quite right, Sir Timothy is it?" Newton asked kindly. "You were converting the 'Navis Pacifica' up until March this year."

"Yes — that's true. But we didn't regard her as being er, mercantile," he finished lamely.

"Perhaps not Sir Timothy," Brown spoke again, "and of course we realize that you were probably committed to certain understandable obligations in the circumstances. We're also aware that the arrangement was a straight-forward transaction between you and Glyn Tresilian. Now, Sir Timothy, we'd like your assistance. Before asking you for help, can you predict what would happen if our defence work with you was cancelled?"

"Very easily. Our side of the Mersey would become an economic disaster area within days. It would take us a very long time to regain the merchant business our competitors picked up when we retooled and rebuilt for your requirements. I can neither conceal nor deny that." Sir Timothy took and lit a cigar from the box on the table.

"And much, if not precisely the same, applies to us," Brown took up the theme. "We are civil servants, Sir Timothy, not moralists or policy makers. The ground rule of all our training is obeying orders. Therefore we must ask you, even though you have no financial stake of your own in the 'Navis Pacifica,' to bring whatever influence you can to bear on your former son-in-law. Persuade him to cease his broadcast operations immediately and return with the vessel to your yards in Birkenhead. We will see that the ship receives all the necessary fuel and supplies for the voyage.

"Thank you Joe," Brown said to an orderly who brought in a coffee tray after Newton had pressed a button on the desk. There was silence until the uniformed man left.

"It'll be very simple, Sir Timothy," Newton said as he stirred the sugar in his cup. "After coffee we'll take you next door where we have a scrambled R/T connection to the ship all set up and ready. Take your time."

Ten minutes later, as 'Navis Pacifica' broke the 15th northerly parallel of latitude in the South China Sea, Wooffenden spoke to Glyn from the sound-proofed Pentagon room. He was alone with a speaker-phone set in a glass enclosed booth.

"Hello, Glyn hello. Although we've been hearing your voice so often, it's grand to be talking to you personally again. As you know, I'm in Washington. Delighted to get another card from Michael. He seems to be enjoying himself in Osaka. How is Julie?"

"Very well thank you, Sir Timothy. I must say your call's a surprise. What can I do for you?"

"A great deal Glyn. I hope. Look I implore you to trust my

judgment and sincerity in connection with what I'm about to ask of you. For reasons you'll understand, I can't go into detailed explanation.

"I'm doing this in co-operation with my American principals and for the sake of relieving and preventing hardship that could reach millions of families all over the world — but especially in the United States and Europe. I congratulate you Glyn, on the magnificent success of your scheme. Nobody and nothing can ever take that away from you. You ánd your exceptionally skill-ed linguists have brought cease-fires to the Middle East, Central America, and it seems as if you've succeeded in South Asia. But, as with everything there has to be a price. And the cost in this case is unbearable. The blame for a whole world situation becomes irrelevant when a global depression sets in. And there's no point in trying to disguise the fact that industry, running at the speed of war or the threat of war, has kept economies going in prosperity since the late forties. No, please don't interrupt until I've finished. As I was about to say — if you cut down the speed of production machinery too fast you . . ."

"Now, look Sir Timothy," Tresilian broke in angrily, his nerves on edge. "Don't talk to me as if I were a bloody juvenile. Yes, I do insist on interrupting you. I happen to have learned the elementary facts you're trying to teach me a long time ago. It's not our fault that economies have depended on war nerves so that they could thrive.

"We've just tried to eliminate the core of the neurosis. And we don't give a damn how much unemployment or lost profits there are as a result. That's too bad. If people like you had any real faith in the human race to begin with, you might have just predicted that people basically dislike killing and getting killed. With a bit of vision, you might even have been in some state of preparedness. But oh, no. You'd rather scoff and be cynical wouldn't you?" He knew his control was going and shook with fury as he gripped the handset. He went on:

"No, don't say a bloody word. If you as much as open your mouth I'll hit this switch and cut you off. Now look. Although we're not worried, as you are, about balance sheets, we're genuinely upset about so much mass unemployment. Of course there'll be hardship and hunger if we succeed. But goddam it, Sir Timothy, we've been shouting about this every day on Talk of the World.

"We've said that as fighting stops, this would be bound to happen. But as usual, governments, the very governments that started the economic motors you like to talk about, can't get off their butts and think about changing fuel until it's too bloody late. Well now they'll damn well have to start working for their employers. Who knows? They might even like it. As far as we're concerned, we haven't finished our job. Not by a mile. The Korean thing's escalating to Vietnam proportions and we're getting there as fast as we can. Now — carry on."

"I see," Sir Timothy said coldly and was glad that Glyn couldn't see the clammy forehead sweat. "As I said just now, I'd hoped that we wouldn't be drawn into this kind of argument. You probably remember that we've touched the subject before. And now I must come to my request — you may already have guessed it?" the Baronet asked.

"Maybe. What is it?" Glyn enquired curtly.

"I ask you, on my own and on my American principals' behalf to stop broadcasting now and return to the Birkenhead yards. You'll receive fuel, supplies and protection for the passage home. And I will personally guarantee you the warmest of welcomes when you reach the Mersey."

"Sir Timothy," Tresilian said, all his rage gone, "do you recall that evening in your library after dinner when I asked you to back the Plan?"

"But of course, my dear Glyn," Wooffenden said, feeling a ray of hope. "With pleasure, that was when you brought Julie over to meet us, wasn't it?"

"Yes, Sir Timothy. And you very kindly listened and congratulated me on the originality of the scheme. You said that naturally you'd have to ponder the proposal and then present it to the Board. A few day later you told me that on behalf of the Board you had decided, with regret, to decline the invitation with thanks. But still you offered help and sent a letter of introduction to Mr. Barton Mills-Cragley. That was very decent of you Sir Timothy."

"Not at all, Glyn. Don't mention it. A simple thing like that. Very least I could do," Wooffenden said kindly and waited expectantly.

"The very least you could do, Sir Timothy. But at the time

I suppose you thought it was the most you could do?"

"Well, yes — perhaps. Why do you ask?"

"Oh, it doesn't matter. But I wonder if you remember the words I used at the end of my appeal to you? No?"

Sir Timothy wavered, mumbling, but not quite speaking. "Not exactly? Well then, I'll remind you," Glyn said, his voice rising to a new pitch. "I asked you to back the Plan in the name of humanity. And now, in the name of the same humanity, I'm telling you to go to hell."

.   .   .   .

Tresilian went into the studios ostensibly to check the latest weather reports on a cyclone system building up in the area. But his main purpose was to glance at Soong Lee's note pad in her booth. What a relief she'd be right now, he said to himself as he stepped in the small sound proof cubicle. Yes — by God, there it was. "The world orange harvest needs urgent treatment.'

He went down to Port 17 for'ard. His blood was already racing as he made sure he was alone in the alleyway. Then he tapped on her door. Half an hour with her in Shangri-La was just what he needed now, he decided. Suddenly he compared her to Lillistrata Kay. Of course he'd not had her, but he was damned sure that if Negretto's wife was a joyful euphonious bass fiddle, then Soong Lee had to be a fine air on a Corelli Stradivarius.

"Come in," she said softly and Glyn noticed a worried expression that he'd not seen on her face before. He sensed something wrong.

"What's the trouble Soong?"

"A lot. Sit down. I'll tell — no don't get undressed. It's very serious this time." She lit a cigarette. Tresilian's loin fires went out and the ash-tray rattled as he put it on her small dressing table.

"Listen to me carefully, Glyn. We've made love many times since that night in the South Atlantic. You're the first Caucasian I've ever had and I've loved every bit of it. I think once you got used to me — you enjoyed it too. I got what I wanted, you were able to keep your Plan going; you like making love to me; and your wife doesn't know. So everything went fine, didn't it?"

"That depends very much on what you mean."

"Well, I want to go on — but we've got to help each other."

As if undressing a doll, she daintily unzipped her slacks and took them off, followed by her sweater and bra. She sat on the bunk and tantalised him in her pale wine coloured silk panties, playing absent mindedly with the hardening nipples on her small, but adequate breasts. Her mind and body fought for possession of his soul.

"When do we get to the 30th parallel, Glyn?"

"In about three days — why?"

"You've got to stop transmitting by then — that's why."

"What? Oh, my God I thought we'd settled all that with my . . . " he raised his voice in exasperation.

"Don't shout. It's not what we've settled any more — it's what they want. They got hold of me in Hong Kong and they've got my parents, sister and two brothers in Peking. Just a minute — before you say anything. I'm afraid it's a business relationship all the way at the moment. While I can trust you as a lover, I can't when it comes to unpleasant dealings like this. I'll give you 48 hours to make up your mind. You shouldn't need any time at all really — because you're going to be off the air one way or the other by the time the ship gets to the parallel. And I'm not going to have my family killed. Understand? Now, take a very close look at me," standing up to kiss him slightly on the forehead, and, with his right hand in hers gently rubbing against her now hard bosum, she went on. "I want your whole body to help your good sense make this decison. That's all. You'd better go now."

He got up to go, but hesitated to step out into the alleyway just then. Soong had raised his blood pressure to an embarassing degree, despite his mind's attempted concentration on the life or death of the ship. Seeing his predicament Soong giggled, and in her best Western manner, underlined her threat.

He went back to the bridge, and sat down in the chartroom wishing with all his heart that he could release his feelings with tears. He got up quickly when he heard steps outside. It was Julie. He composed himself rapidly and was busily shuffling charts on the table when she came in.

"Sorry, Julie," he said hurriedly. "No time now, I'm afraid sweetheart. I'm scared of this weather coming up. We'll try and go round it."

Hopefully they'd miss the center by altering course, but

they'd be meeting enough of it to worry them. Already the sky was dark and the sea was welling up. He gave orders for all ventilators to be backed to the wind and told the Bosun to rig life lines fore and aft. He'd been in one of these beauties before and regretted that his lack of experience hadn't told him to take avoiding action sooner. He warned the ship's company on the PA about the approaching cyclone and told them to stow all moveable items away.

He stayed on the bridge most of the night and tried to clear his head. By morning the 'Navis Pacifica' was pitching and rolling violently in a confused, near mountainous sea churned by force 12 winds.

The Third Mate answered the bridge telephone. He called Tresilian into the wheelhouse.

"Chief Engineer on the phone, sir."

"Tresilian here Chief — what's the trouble? For God's sake don't tell me the tanks . . ."

"No, we didn't make that mistake again, Cap'n. It's the feed pump this time, I'm afraid. Same thing I always find on these ships. Bloody water-tube boilers. You can't beat those Scotch bastards if you want to sleep well. We'll have to stop her, Cap'n, otherwise we'll explode louder than an H-bomb. Sorry son, but there's nothing else for it."

"Any idea how long it'll take?"

"No, but we'll turn-to right away."

"OK, Chief. Do your best. Stop her, Third Mate."

"Stop her, sir," the officer of the watch answered and the engine-room reply clanged like a soprano Great Tom. Soon, the ship lost steerage way. Groaning, she reamed herself into the lurching deep swells and spume topped seas. The Third Mate and helmsman wrestled with the halliards of the triatic stay trying to send the Not Under Command balls aloft. The wind screamed through the ship.

Tresilian grabbed the PA microphone.

"Pay attention please. This is Tresilian speaking. We'll be stopped for a few hours while the engineers work on some auxiliary machinery. I'm sorry for the discomfort but without any power we can't heave the ship to and keep her reasonably steady. As I said before, make sure that everything's secure and hang to something as you walk. Don't come on deck unless you have to. We'll resume transmission as soon as we get under way again. Don't say anything on the air about our being stopped. If you think you're going to be sea-sick, I advise you to eat something first, however hard it seems. That's all."

Spoiled by the ship's stabilizers, many Talkers soon became ill with the 'Navis Pacifica's' unaccustomed lurches through arcs of eighty degrees. For the first time, Julie was seasick. Except for the on watch personnel, the ship paled with nausea and took to its bunk. The doctor and nursing sisters, themselves weakened by the incessant rolling, stoically issued pills and potions.

Just before four o'clock in the afternoon, the Pakistani surgeon heaved himself up to the bridge. Panting, sick, and nervous he said to Tresilian. "Captain, sorry to bother you. Soong Lee. They're nearly all seasick and when she came in just now I thought she was under the weather like the rest. As you can see I'm not all that well myself. She was in pain and so I examined her. It's the worst, I'm afraid. Appendix — and it's bad. Normally I'd operate at once — in her case it'll soon be peritonitis and . . ." the surgeon ran down hill to the port navigation light and emptied himself. Clutching the dodger, he slipped and climbed his way back to the wheelhouse.

"That's not so good, Doc. But appendicitis usually hits you that suddenly doesn't it?" Tresilian shouted over the dull roar of the sea.

"Yes, in most cases."

"How long could you postpone surgery?"

"I'd rather not delay it at all. It should be done immediately," the frail-looking Pakistani said anxiously.

"But obviously you couldn't do it with the ship rolling like this eh?"

"Well, if there's no other way of course I'll attempt it. She'll die in any case if it bursts."

Tresilian knew how engineers hate being asked how long emergency work at sea will take. "I'll try and get some news from the Chief. What's the longest possible time you can wait? The doctor shouted back. "Two hours. But even that's taking a chance."

"So if we can get under way," and Glyn looked at his watch, "before six o'clock, and steady her up, you'll be alright. Now if we can't, what odds do you give yourself?" The doctor looked for'ard at the transmitter mast oscillating like a giant metronome.

"We must be rolling through 40 degrees on either side Captain," he said and Glyn nodded after a glance at the clinometer on the compass binnacle. "I'd say the chances would be 50/50 that I could operate in these conditions without killing her."

"I'll go down and see the Chief. Better than the blower. You hang on up here — unless you want to get back to the girl?"

"No, she'll be safe for a minute or two. We've given her some stuff for the pain — but the vomiting doesn't help either."

Down below in the engine room there was a devilish sound of metal hammers on steel, hissing steam from the shut in triple expansion machinery and swearing in half a dozen tongues as tools and parts skated back and forth on the oily tank tops to port of the main engines where most of the auxiliaries were housed. Sweating in a singlet, the Chief Engineer led the operation on the crucial feed pump without which the boilers could not get water. The Chief looked up and saw Tresilian. Irritated, he grabbed his way along to the boiler-room door where Glyn was standing.

"Now, Cap'n, I'm surprised at you. I really am. I thought you were quite a bright young fella. This is my domain, not yours. And you know very nicely you shouldn't be down here. Has a bad effect on the men," he shouted.

"Yes, I know all that Chief. But it's serious. I wouldn't have bothered you otherwise. One of the Talkers, that Chinese girl, has acute appendicitis and the Doc wants to operate."

"Oh, I see. I'm sorry Cap'n. You mean that lovely little Pekingese lassie eh? And the Doc wants to know how long it'll be before you can steer her and keep her steady for his knife I suppose. Well as near as I can say — about two hours. We should be finished with the gland job in roughly an hour and a half, and then it'll take about half an hour to box her up. We'll get speed on her for you in about two hours."

"Thank you very much, Chief," Tresilian said and pulled himself back to the bridge. The Pakistani looked at him expectantly.

"You'd better go right ahead Doc. It could be four or six hours before they're ready. And even longer. It's a bit like your work. You never know when complications'll set in. And the more we bug them, the longer they'll take. They're a breed apart — marine engineers. Unfortunately we can't pump any oil over the side either with us being stopped like this. That might reduce the motion a little bit but not much. No, there's nothing else we can do. Do your best Doc — and good luck."

An hour later, Soong Lee died on the operating table in the small ship's hospital. Minutes after the Doctor had given him the news, Glyn was joined by the Chief Engineer on the bridge. He looked haggard.

"Aye, Cap'n we're in some trouble now. You'd better tell the Doc to have a go. If she's only got an hour or so, as you said. We've hit a big snag down there. And I can't see us being finished inside another five hours," the old Scot said gloomily.

"Don't worry, Chief. It's not your fault. But we thought it best to make an attempt anyway. The Doc tried, but I don't think there's a surgeon anywhere who could've done it in this motion."

"She's dead, Cap'n?"

"Yes, afraid so, Chief. A few minutes ago. We'll bury her tomorrow."

"You'll miss her badly I expect."

"Yes, indeed. She was a very good broadcaster, but luckily we have a good back up to handle the Mandarin. Right Chief. Thanks for letting me know. I'll wait to hear from you," Tresilian wound up the visit almost brusquely. Funny bastard the Chief thought to himself on the way down to the engine room again. Smart enough and a bit callous into the bargain. No one'd believe him, but he could have sworn that Tresilian seemed glad. Oh, well, that must be just his way of playing the tough, hard, Shipmaster role.

At noon the next day, Soong Lee's canvas wrapped body, weighted with old winch parts and draped with the West African Republic flag was eased over the midship rail. Headlong, it dropped without a splash into the China Sea. Glyn closed the prayer book from which he'd read the burial at sea service, put on his cap, and ran up the bridge ladder.

"Full away and resume course, Second Mate. And let's hope we don't have to stop her again for a while."

As Talk of the World picked up its beat once more, enquiries about Soong Lee came in on Tronphone and R/T. Her soothing, beautifully modulated voice had been replaced by the comparatively harsher tones of a male Mandarin speaker. The

Talkers were told to tell the truth. In Peking, the explanation was instantly construed as dirty work with official accusations read over Radio Peking.

CHAPTER 11

Just after the 'Navis Pacifica' had passed the Pescadores Islands off Formosa, Michael Tresilian boarded an evening train in Kyoto after a pleasant day of sightseeing on his own. He was tired and looked forward to the bath and meal he would have at the hotel in Osaka with his step-mother's parents. He settled at a window seat in the fast, crowded train. His nose still had not accustomed itself to the smell of human dung that enriches the paddy fields of Japan. He used a large filtering handkerchief as the effluvian wafted in.

Ten minutes after leaving Kyoto, he glanced up at two broadly smiling men standing in the aisle, directly in front of him.

"Excuse me, you're young Mr. Michael Tresilian?" the first one said in a thick sounding European accent, maintaining his smile all the while.

"Yes, that's me," the boy said and looked surprised.

"Good. My colleague and I were hoping you'd be on the train. We're with National Pavilion Services at Expo 70 in Osaka. We were in Kyoto on some business today and Captain de Vries of the Dutch Marine Exhibition asked us to intercept you. He said you'd be returning on the evening train. He and Mrs. de Vries were called away to Nagoya unexpectedly after you left this morning and they want you to meet them at the next station so that you can join them for the drive. We'll be there in about five minutes. The Captain said that Mrs. de Vries will bring some of your clothes and things with her."

"That's quite a surprise. I didn't know anything about them going to Nagoya. But that's fine. I'm trying to see as much as possible of the country now while we're still here. Gee, it's lucky you found me. Thanks a lot," he said happily.

"That's OK, Mike. It's what we're paid for — service," the other man, obviously American, replied pleasantly. "Oh, by the way, the de Vries' know all the train times and they said that if you don't see them right away, don't worry. Just wait — but don't leave the station. If they're delayed they'll call you through the Station Master. Have a good time."

Michael put on his raincoat and got off the train after it stopped at a small village. Several other people hurried out and the train rolled away. Soon, he was alone. There was no sign of life or the de Vries. He paced up and down. He'd seen his father walk back and forth interminably on the lee wing of 'Navis Pacifica's' bridge. The youngster wondered how he and Julie and the others on the ship were getting along. He was dying to get back to his friends in Montreal and spellbind them with his own accounts of everything that had happened.

Boy, could he ever get marks for English composition now. To say nothing of geography and spherical trig. He stopped and listened to the sound of a car approaching the tiny station yard. Good — that must be them. He supposed the Captain must have hired a vehicle for the trip to Nagoya. The black European automobile drew up and stopped. A Western looking driver was the only one in it. And then without warning he felt a light tap on his shoulder. Flanking him were the two men on the train. The boy became frightened.

"Alright, Mike. Don't get scared. Everything'll be fine," the American said gently. "Here's the car. Let's go."

"Hey, what's all this?" the boy asked, bravely trying to conceal very real fear. "I thought you said Captain de Vries . . ."

"Yes, never mind what we said," the other man exclaimed spitting his words out. "Just come with us and keep quiet."

The car set off at high speed in a northerly direction. The American sat with Michael in the back. "OK Mike, now we can relax," he said, and offered the youth a cigarette. Michael shook his head and stared out of the window.

In the front seat, the other man and driver were talking in a language which from some 'nyets' and 'das,' Michael knew to be Russian. The car's headlights came on and shone through the onrushing dark. The younger Tresilian fought to collect himself and keep calm. He remembered the stern advice his father had so often given him. 'Never panic, Michael. Never, never, never. However impossible things may seem. Because if you're going to solve a problem you can only do it by thinking. And when you panic, you can't think.'

He boosted himself a little by wondering what James Bond would do. And then he was sure that he'd wake up in a nightmare sweat. This just couldn't be happening for real. He cracked his knuckles and pinched a wrist, but nothing changed.

"Right, Mike," the American said and smiled like a benign Uncle. "I expect you're asking yourself what it's all about. We want you to be our guest for a few days at a great little place in the mountains. We'll be there in a couple of hours. You'll really enjoy yourself — and we'll take good care of you.

"All we ask is that you don't try to leave before we're ready to take you back to Osaka — and we wouldn't want you to say anything to anybody about your visit with us. This is very important to us Mike; so important that I'd better show you this — although I hate to do it," and the man took a revolver from his chest, showed it, and then replaced it in the holster. Michael's face went white — and he only just controlled the instant loosening of his bowels. The front seat talk went on incessantly. Half an hour later, the boy had recovered sufficiently to speak.

"Let's face it sir," he said to the American, and was agreeably surprised to hear no quaver in his voice. "This is a kidnap isn't it?"

"Now, I wouldn't want to use those nasty words. We'd rather you didn't say that again."

Captain and Mrs. de Vries in Osaka, looked at each other in their hotel room and then at their wrist watches. They'd expected Michael back before this.

"I think you should call soon, Jan," Julie's mother said worriedly. "He must have missed the train — I'm anxious."

"If he's not back by eleven, I'll phone. Don't worry. Maybe some girl got hold of him."

"No. Don't joke about it Jan," she continued in Dutch. "I'm disturbed. You can never . . ."

The telephone rang and her husband grabbed it. "Yes? Hello, de Vries here."

"Ah, good evening Captain," a well pitched Serbian voice said in English. "You were waiting for some news of your daughter's step-son, Michael Tresilian?"

"Not news," the Captain answered and tried to avoid his wife's eyes. "We've been expecting him back after a day in

Kyoto. Who are you?"

"That's not important Captain. But we have good news. The boy is perfectly safe and well — but he'll be staying with us for a few days. The change will do him good and we promise that he'll come to no harm. We can assure you of that because we're positive that you'll oblige us by not reporting his absence to anyone. If you decide otherwise, we cannot of course be responsible. We will let you know about his return. Goodnight, Captain — and thank you for your co-operation."

The receiver clicked at the other end, and the voice was gone. Twenty minutes later the hotel doctor left the suite. Mrs. de Vries was under heavy sedation.

The car with Michael in it pulled up at the entrance of a resort hotel half way up the side of a low mountain. He and his captors were met at the entrance by three kimono clad Japanese girls. All took off their shoes. There was no conversation until the women bowed Michael and the two men into a room overlooking the valley. The American took the smallest and most attractive of the trio and handed her to Michael.

"For you, Mike. She'll look after you. Here — you might need this," and he gave him a long type written sheet of paper. On it Michael saw things like 'Please bring supper' 'I want a bath' 'I want cigarettes' 'I want a massage' and other requests set out in English and Japanese. And then he was alone with the girl in the darkly polished room. He looked around and the only furniture pieces he saw were a low table and rocking chair.

"Oh, Mike. I forgot to mention it," and the American was back. "We really mean it when we say that we want you to enjoy this experience. It's something you'll never forget. So don't spoil it. OK?" and he was gone again.

The girl slid open a bamboo closet and shook out a loose gown. She motioned the boy to sit down and then gradually undressed him. She arranged the calf length robe around him and left the room with his clothes under her arm. When she came back she pointed to the bath item on the paper and led him by the hand through a wide hallway to a large tiled room with three sunken baths. She disappeared into a cubicle and emerged naked with soap, towels, and a small wooden washing bowl. She undid his garment, and placed it gently on a low marble bench.

Slipping into the perfectly heated four feet deep natural hot spring water she beckoned him to join her. Michael looked down and saw her lovely limbs as she floated in the bath. He remembered that Bond was in such a situation once. At 16½ this was the first time that he'd seen a nude woman in the flesh. His throat went dry and his temples thumped. His terror went as young, untried manhood took charge. He jumped down and moistened his mouth from the pool. She resisted and fought strongly and slithered out of his grasp. Nonplussed, he smiled and nodded as she sign-languaged a sleeping posture. She lathered him with soap at the side of the bath and looked with mock reproach as his parts responded to her touch.

They took a rinsing plunge and she dried him in the cubicle. Back in the room she sat him down in the low rocking chair and returned with a tray of sake and exotic smelling food. The warm rice wine whistled through his being like a firecracker. She sat at his feet and with chop-sticks, fed him, as a child, from the small dishes.

Later, with the tray cleared away, she doused the two small floor lamps to a glimmer and brought out a single roll of bedding from behind the sliding closet door. She arranged it in the middle, and put two small pillows at the head. And then with maddening slowness, laid her kimono on the chair.

Michael woke up in the forenoon. He opened his eyes and several seconds passed before the sun strewn room and valley view made sense. And then the night and the girl came back. He got up and walked to the window. He turned and saw her come in. She was fully dressed and fresh eyed. She bathed him again and gave her boy partner his first massage. Then, after a breakfast of honeyed bread and tea, she dressed him in a clean robe, and led the way to an office. She bowed and left.

"So, there you are Mike," the friendly American greeted him. "We thought you'd be tired so we let you sleep in. Your companion'll take you for a walk this afternoon, but first we'd like you to do a little job for us. Right?" and he nodded to the Russian speaking colleague. The man picked up the phone and spoke rapidly in Japanese. He put it back in its cradle. There was silence during the two minutes it took to ring. The American picked it up. "Yes? Good. No, right now," he said and the scrambled R/T contact with 'Navis Pacifica' was ready. "Mr. Tresilian? Fine. I hope we're sounding as clear as you are.

Listen — we have Michael with us. Yes, that's right, your son. No, no, they're in Osaka. He's staying as our guest for a few days. What? That's beside the point," and Michael heard the irritation in the man's voice. "We'll let you speak to him now and then we'll talk with you again. Here's Mike."

"Hello, hello, Michael? What's going on?"

"Sorry, Dad. I don't know. I was coming back in the train from Kyoto last night and these men conned me into getting off before Osaka because they said Julie's parents were going to meet me there and drive . . ."

"Bloody luck. Never mind the rest. Can they hear what you're saying now?" Tresilian asked his son quietly.

"Sure. They're standing right here."

"Michael, you've been kidnapped. Now just keep calm. Remember what I've always tried to tell you. Have you any idea where you are?"

"Not really, Dad. But it was a fairly long drive from where I left the train. One of the men said that the de Vries know that I'm with them. But they don't know where of course."

"I see. They want money, I suppose. Don't worry — we'll take care of it. And then we'll have you back aboard with us very soon. Don't do anything foolish — just play along with them. Keep your head and chin up. Let me speak to that guy," his father said belligerently. "Now, whoever you are," he continued as the American came back on the line and the girl took Michael away, "let's get it over quickly. How much? Where? How?"

"If you're talking about money, Mr. Tresilian, your questions are out of order. You don't know our business, but believe me we'd like to get it done quickly. As you just heard for yourself, the boy is safe and well with us. He'll continue that way if you'll co-operate. Your son will be unharmed and will rejoin your wife's parents in Osaka immediately on the condition — and only on condition," the American emphasized — "that you stop all broadcast transmission from the 'Navis Pacifica' and return, as previously requested, to the U.K.

"As you've also been advised before," the mid-west voice bore on, "we confirm that all the necessary re-fuelling and supply and escort arrangements will be made. Have you understood my words, Mr. Tresilian?" There was a long pause. Glyn thought quickly and decided not to answer. The American spoke again.

"Whether you acknowledge your understanding of our message or not is immaterial, Mr. Tresilian. You heard it. We shall expect total silence from you within twelve hours from now. This period should give you ample time for reflection. When you go off the air, stop your engines and do nothing further until we find you . . . We shall not, within the next twelve hours, be communicating with you again, Mr. Tresilian. Please regard this as our only notice." The R/T line went dead. Tresilian went into the day-room and asked Julie to make some tea.

"But we had tea, dear. Only a few minutes ago."

"Oh, did we?" He laughed a shade too loudly. "After this voyage, I think I'll end up as a tannicolic or something. Right now I must be looking like a tea-pot. OK honey, never mind. I want to go round the ship for a little while. Won't be long. Let Alan know if he comes looking for me will you?" On his way forward to the foc'sle head, he stopped and chatted briefly with some of the off-shift Talkers who were on deck reading or monitoring their colleagues' work on 'Talk of the World.'

He leaned right over the ship's eyes, as he had done so often as a cadet lookoutman in his youth, and stared at the white and deep blue foam-wash below. He was glad to see some porpoises gambolling towards the ship. They were always fun. Soon they were rolling and frolicking in 'Navis Pacifica's' broad bow wave. Glyn watched them for many minutes as they swam just fast enough to let the heavy frothing waterfall scrape their gleaming bellies and backs free of maggots and lice. Then he walked aft to the docking bridge and watched the boiling screw-thrashed water drop astern.

He looked up at the clear sky and thought about his life. Ever since India, he'd been a robust believer in a deity and now he wished with all his heart that Julie's unquestioning personal faith would come to him. As he thought about the Plan and what would happen to it, he closed his eyes and prayed that he would be forgiven and that the Supreme Being that he could not name, would find in His wisdom and mercy, the way to take care of it.

.   .   .   .

Twenty four hours after the R/T ultimatum, the U.S. and USSR ambassadors to Poland were recalled urgently by their capitals. They both left Warsaw within the hour. In Washington and Moscow, the high level briefings were conducted with nearly fictional hypersecrecy. The diplomats underwent elaborate disguises stopping just short of plastic surgery. Two days later, ambassadors Gordon and Rudamov met with President Harold Negretto in Wafrilla. The Soviet envoy began the conference.

"Mr. Chairman, we understand that the 'Navis Pacifica' will be within range to-morrow for her helicopters to drop those Tronphone things on the Korean coast. The Peace and Friendship pact countries are now determined to prevent it. I think you will agree that our two Powers have shown unprecedented restraint in our attitude to this piracy. But the time has come to end it. The world is in a very confused and dangerous state. There is a chance of grave economic instability everywhere. Ambassador Gordon please," and he looked at the middle-aged crew cut American at his side. Negretto fidgeted with a bejewelled ivory paper knife as the American followed up.

"We all admit Mr. President that we didn't expect the vessel to go this far — and we certainly didn't anticipate anything like the disturbances it's caused. In official and government circles around the globe and especially in our capitals there was, until recently, a very strong reluctance to believe the impact that the illicit broadcasting was achieving. Personally I always felt that kind of eye shade to be wrong.

"In North America, we've had this sort of open line or people participation radio programming for years in local centers. And citizens have fought and won many a battle with City Hall. Now Mr. President," he noted hastily, "I'm talking about legally licensed and permitted operations — not piracy. I think that our unwillingness to take the ship's radio work seriously was due to the universally held belief that nowadays the only truly powerful communications force is in and through the visual medium of satellite television. I think that . . ."

"All that is very interesting Mr. Gordon," Rudamov came in impatiently, "but I think a more fitting place for your discourse might be at a Marshall McLuhan symposium." The Muscovite cleared his throat and smiled at his American associate. The West African Republic dictator looked at both men with an expression suggesting that he, Harold Negretto, would take immediate steps to ensure that no such local programming would take place in his country for the benefit of people who might be rash enough to want to fight the Presidential Palace. The wretched 'Navis Pacifica's' 'Talk of the World' had been bad enough for a day after it started. But the Palace order soon went out and in the weeks that followed, there were more than a few corpses hanging by their necks in public places around the W.A.R. Negretto's vigilance was such that for purposes of public safety, hundreds of thousands of his citizens took his advice and handed in their transistor radios to local authorities.

"Now, Mr. Chairman," Rudamov continued, "I don't have to remind you that our two countries are in a strong position to bargain with you. We are putting to you only a very simple request," he paused for several seconds. Negretto looked between them. "We want you to void the 'Navis Pacifica's' registration. And we want you to do it immediately."

"How?" the dictator asked.

"Very easily," Gordon said helpfully. "First call the ship on R/T and tell them. That conversation will be tape recorded in Washington and Moscow. Then you will sign a written declaration to the same effect which Mr. Rudamov and I will witness. Forgetting all about its contravention of I.T.U. rules and regulations, the ship, without registration becomes stateless — and therefore unlawful — whatever its mission."

"Please don't misunderstand me, gentlemen," Negretto said pleasantly, "but I've also been following the ship's progress. I'll concede that had I not been deceived at the time, she would not have received a W.A.R. registration and flag. Frankly, I am surprised that action of this sort was not taken before — but of course Mr. Gordon has more or less told us the reason." Negretto paused for a long puff on the cigar he was smoking. "Alright, so I speak to this, er, Tresilian, by radio-telephone and tell him that he is no longer registered in my country. He sounds more and more to me like a desperado — do you really think he'll turn round and go back where he came from?"

"Mr. President, we have reason to hope that he will. Let us begin." And Rudamov pointed to the telephone table behind Negretto's desk.

The following day, after Negretto's R/T statement to Tresilian on the 'Navis Pacifica,' the helijets took off and made
their first Korean Tronphone drops. As the ship neared territorial
waters in the vicinities of Inchon and Haeju, the pilots loaded,
flew, unloaded, returned and flew again non-stop for 36 hours.
They shuttled until there were no more Tronphones left.

On special martial orders from Peking and the P & FP
countries, issued within minutes of each other, commanders were
instructed to forbid all personnel, military and civilian, to touch
a Tronphone or listen to Talk of the World. Both sides stated
emphatically that immediate execution would follow disobedience. For nearly five days, the ship's broadcasts consisted of
Tronphone conversations with people from Scandinavia, all parts
of Europe, the Mediterranean and Middle East countries, India,
South and Central America, and South-East Asia. There were
even a few in South Africa and Rhodesia who tuned in smug-
gled Tronphones and heard the beeeeep cue to speak.

It was a long wait in the studios of 'Navis Pacifica' for the
combatants in Korea to respond on the Tronphones. But no
sound came from them. Instead, people in other countries took
the chance, and urged on by their governments, damned the ship
for perpetrating a possibly all enveloping depression. A European Finance Minister declaimed the warning on his nation's
television:

"Now perhaps people everywhere will realise that there are
worse things than stable governments in free countries — in
spite of the poison spread about by this floating bandit. Unemployment, misery and hardship will have the world by the throat.
The time for patience has passed."

On the sixth day, since the meeting in Wafrillia, Negretto
spoke to Tresilian by R/T for the 10th time. His wife, Lillistrata
Kay, was in the office and listened in with the ambassadors.

"Look, Tresilian, I implore you. If you've already gone mad
it's too late. But if you haven't — listen, listen, listen. For God's
sake listen man. You're destroying the world. People all over
will starve and die. Foreign aid from everywhere's being cut
off. There's cholera to the north of us and bubonic plague in
India. Food, medication and drug supplies will dwindle away to
nothing in these countries. Every stock market will crash. How

humanitarian can you possibly be, when having been the cause of all this inhumanity, you won't help to stop it?" He looked at the ambassadors — they nodded vigorously. After a long wait, Tresilian replied.

"Mr. President, as I think I've already told you many times in the last few days, 'Navis Pacifica,' since your cancellation, is a stateless ship. As your flag and registration were the only things we had in common before, I can't, now, see what we have to talk about." He cut off the connection. The diplomats shrugged and left the room.

"Harold," Lillistrata Kay said and came over to her husband, "I really don't know what to say. You know I've never tried to interfere directly in your politics. What will they try and make you do now?"

"I don't know. Let's not worry about it. Big party again tonight?"

"What? Oh, yes. Some cocoa people, you'll be pleased to hear. You know, I liked that man Tresilian. How awful it would be if anything happens to him or that ship . . . you won't let it — will you darling?"

"That's not for your pretty little cultured head to worry about my dear. Come — let us bath and change."

.   .   .   .

On the seventh day, after the first Korean Tronphone drop, it came. The voice of a North Korean soldier in the perimeter force surrounding the southern base at Seoul. In the beleaguered city, American and South Korean forces tensed and waited for the key offensive to break. Their Communist Chinese and North Korean enemies had been consolidating in the area for weeks. A war correspondent had called the coming battle 'The last foothill on the slopes of Armageddon.'

The North Korean blubbered incoherently as the Talker tried to hear and translate his words. His voice rose to a scream and the world heard the shot that stopped it. And then, wave after wave of Asian and American voices flooded Talk of the World. Many on both sides were caught at it, and shot.

But, as had happened elsewhere, the Plan took root and climbed the levels of command. After three days, very few executions were carried out as combatants spoke to each other and responded to the ship's appeals to pause at the trigger and

— 405 —

the bomb release. With the new drama of events, millions returned to their Talk of the World stations. The world listened and waited. The CRAKs were once more breaking ratings records.

It was a repeat of Vietnam. With widespread disobedience in the battle regions, effective discipline was difficult to maintain. Constantly, Talk of the World urged soldiers to keep calm and to disobey no orders other than the one to kill. To commanders went appeals not to give that order. The tension came off the mainspring in the second Korean war.

.　　.　　.　　.　　.　　.　　.　　.

A week before, ambassadors Gordon and Rudamov had left Wafrillia and returned separately to their embassies in Warsaw. Negretto had signed the necessary authorisation. In Norfolk, Virginia, the senior W.A.R. officer comanding his country's tiny naval detachment under United States training, put the Republic's one and only submarine crew on a military supersonic jet for the naval base at Sasebo, southern Japan. A day later they embarked in the nuclear submarine assigned on special loan to the West African Republic. The black submariners were thoroughly familiar with the 'Cheshire' class of undersea warship. They had been training aboard an exact replica in Norfolk; all been built and engined at the Wooffenden yards in Birkenhead.

The W.A.R. manned submarine sailed out of Sasebo harbour and submerged on reaching open water. Once past Quelpart Island, her commanding officer opened the tightly waxed envelope containing Negretto's orders. He read them and took a set of direction finder bearings in the radio-room. He went to the chart-table and brought the underwater vessel round to starboard on a north-westerly course.

Now, 40 hours later, he ordered the submarine to periscope depth off Sinuiju. He swung the prism column until he saw the white rust streaked hull of the old Liberty ship slowly steaming off the coast. He closed into a mile — then half a mile. And called for a quick submerge.

"Stop engines. Trim her off at that. Stand by to fire cannisters. Thirty degrees elevation. Green forty. In 10 seconds. Steady. Fire."

From below the waves, six oblong containers shot out of

the sea and broke out parachutes five hundred feet above the 'Navis Pacifica's' aerials. Julie, in a dressing gown, put her early morning tea on the dodger outside the day-room and looked up.

"Glyn," she shouted to Tresilian on the bridge. "Look, look up. What on earth's happening?"

"Get inside, dear — quick. Lie down," he shouted.

In the wheelhouse, the chief officer and helmsman flattened themselves on the deck. Moments later, four of the cylinders landed. There were no explosions. Clouds of blue dust rose in the air and swirled around the ship. In less than five seconds every man and woman on the 'Navis Pacifica' had been rendered painlessly unconscious. The ship began a drunken circle in the sea. The submarine's periscope cleared the surface.

"Stand by torpedo tubes. Up scope," the Cheshire's commander ordered. He manoeuvered the craft into firing position. "Stop engines. Planes and helm steady. Steady. Fire one." Seconds later at his periscope, he saw the 'Navis Pacifica' explode amidships. "Good. Now we'll put one for'ard. Steady, steady. Fire two. She's supposed to go down fast. Stand by to put one in the stern of her. Steady — right. Fire three. Excellent. Down scope and take her down to 50 feet. Pilot — guide us home to the Republic. I think we're a two sub navy now."

.   .   .   .

All around the earth that day, people turned on and fiddled with their radio sets. There was neither sound nor news of their Talk of the World. They phoned and asked and listened and waited.

In Toronto, in mid-December, it was cold. With the Christmas of 1970 only two weeks away, there were the sights and sounds of the holiday.

Gaston Yerbury's chauffeur switched on the car radio for the 8 am news as he drove his master to the downtown office building.

'Here are the headlines. The rumoured news about the 'Navis Pacifica' can now be confirmed. Moments ago a bulletin was issued by the United States Commander-in-Chief, Manila, stating that the ship sank yesterday with her entire crew off the North Korean-Chinese coast. There were no survivors. Neither is there news of the cause of the sinking. Meanwhile around the world, radio stations report that . . .'

Yerbury switched off the set from the back seat control. He looked out of the car window as they stopped at an intersection. Men were working on the cold steel skeleton of a big new construction. He watched for a few seconds and then turned away as the blinding light of their welding torches stung and hurt his eyes.

THE END